WHIPPED

AN ARTHUR
BEAUCHAMP NOVEL

THE ARTHUR BEAUCHAMP NOVELS

Trial of Passion
April Fool
Kill All the Judges
Snow Job
I'll See You in My Dreams
Sing a Worried Song
Whipped

ALSO BY WILLIAM DEVERELL

Fiction
Needles
High Crimes
Mecca
The Dance of Shiva
Platinum Blues
Mindfield
Kill All the Lawyers
Street Legal: The Betrayal
Slander
The Laughing Falcon
Mind Games

Non-fiction
A Life on Trial

WHIPPED

by William Deverell

To Amy, Rachel, Will, Sophie, and David.

PART ONE

VERY BAD BOY, VERY BAD DAY

"God help me! I was bad! Forgive me!" A *thwack*, as whip met bottom.

The bottom in question glowed pinkly at Lou Sabatino from the screen of a two-point-eight-gigahertz Toshiba Satellite laptop.

"I was a bad boy, very bad!" *Thwack!* "Please, Mother, I beg you! On my knees!" Which he was, in fact. On his elbows too, his wrists tied with thongs.

Lou figured it couldn't hurt that much, despite the pain freak's petitions for leniency. The voice was familiar. Someone he knew. Someone important? Whoever it was, he was on a gaudy Oriental carpet, his plump rear raised, his head down, out of view. In the background was a wall of rough-hewn logs, a blazing fireplace, a window overlooking an iced-over lake and looming hills clad with the skeletal trees of a boreal forest. The Laurentians, maybe.

The flogger was Svetlana Glinka, a professional dominatrix, whose elegant bared tits bobbed with every stroke. Other than those, her main adornment was something that looked like a leather corset. The real Svetlana, well clothed except for the apparent lack of underwear, was standing beside Lou, enjoying her little movie, exulting in the prospect of . . . What? Sweet revenge?

She had recorded this session with a hidden webcam, and was showing Lou her little docudrama in her therapy clinic, as she called it, in a ground-floor triplex in Montreal's Centre-Sud. Lou had the misfortune to live in the apartment just above hers.

He asked, "How long does this last?"

"I think maybe seventy seconds." Russian accent, a throaty voice that oozed sex. She made Lou nervous, and he drew away from her a little. "Watch this. He likes this specially."

The Svetlana on the screen was greasing a king-size dildo.

"No, not that, Mother, I beg you!"

She piggybacked onto her victim, riding him, penetrating him with the dildo as he crawled on his knees and trussed hands, screaming his repentance while trying to toss her like a rodeo bull.

§

This episode had come toward the end of what was definitely not the finest day in the once unremarkable life of ace reporter Lou Sabatino. He'd spent most of the day, as usual, in the frigid climate of the Sabatino household. "I've had it with this hole!" Celeste had yelled at him. "*C'est un trou, un dump!*" This after the kids had back-packed off to school.

Celeste's complaints were many and justified. The nineteenth-century triplex on Rue de la Visitation lacked the comforts of their former home in Côte-des-Neiges. It offered a covered, open balcony, but was cramped, worn, mouse-ridden, drafty, accessed only by an exterior staircase, a spiralling, wrought-iron, ice-slicked death trap. To top it off, sleep-disturbing thumps and howls regularly emanated from the poorly muffled ground-floor apartment. The top floor had remained empty ever since its tenant was busted a month ago in a drug sweep.

Lou escaped for a couple of hours into his computer room, then returned for lunch to more of the same. "I'm not going to be cooped up in this shithole for the rest of my life!" Celeste, a work-at-home couturière, had been threatening to pack up and ship out, take the kids to the crap mining town up north where her parents lived. Or out west. She had a sister in Calgary.

"We've got no choice," he whimpered. "My hands are tied." Which, he later recognized, put him in league with the flake in the video.

"You twerp! You've got the backbone of *un ver de terre*." A worm.

Once again, Lou proved he wasn't man enough to withstand her vivid detailing of his lack of manliness by fleeing into the relative comfort of a cold, drizzly mid-May morning, wishing he'd taken more than a scarf and a sweater. For most of his time in the house of horrors, he'd ventured out only at night, choosing ill-lit streets for the only exercise he was getting.

His fear was that he'd be recognized by one of his Quartier Centre-Sud neighbours or, worse, a Mafia hit man. There were assassins afoot. Lou's face had been in the papers, on the tube, the internet. He always wore dark clip-ons over his glasses, even on murky days like this, to hide his myopic, mournful grey eyes.

Lost for somewhere to go, he meandered down toward the Gay Village, then west on busy St. Catherine, stopping occasionally at storefronts, his breath clouding the plate glass behind which leggy women sold lingerie or jewellery. Fodder for his masturbatory fantasies. Ultimately he found himself at a Métro stop, wondering if he dared make another quiet visit to the Canadian Press bureau.

On paid leave from the wire service, Lou spent most of his time these days online or fiddling with his computers. He was a nerd. A horny nerd, since Celeste cut him off a couple of months ago. An out-of-shape nerd: fifteen excess pounds on his five-nine frame. Only forty-one, and he already had a comb-over bald spot. In compensation, he'd grown a moustache and full russet beard that hid his weak chin. All part of his new identity. He was now Robert O'Brien, computer analyst, and he had the papers to prove it.

Lou's fears were not delusions.

Three months ago, he had filed a four-instalment exposé of how deeply the Mafia had entrenched itself into the Montreal waterfront, buying off local politicians and public servants, some in Ottawa, at Transport Canada. He'd worked on this series for five months, a welcome long break from the rewrite desk. When the first instalment got play in every daily serviced by CP, there was champagne in the bureau chief's office, there was back-slapping. Waterfrontgate!

He'd got a lot of quiet help from his sister's husband's uncle, Nick Giusti, a former lawyer for the mob. Despite Nick's cunning, two of his Mafioso clients had been sent up for gunning down an informant, prompting the *compagnia* to withdraw their fat retainer, and he was pretty disgruntled.

Nick had an unsavoury reputation as a fixer, a washer of ill-gotten gains, but you take your sources where you find them. Jules "the Monk" Moncrief and his pals would fit him with cement shoes if they ever figured out he was Lou's Deep Throat.

Nick had been the source of voluminous court records, bank statements, notes, ledgers, hard copies of paper exhibits from a dozen trials. He would not be suspected as the source because most of the material was on public record, but without his help the research would have taken a year. As it was, Lou had to painstakingly assemble the jigsaw puzzle of waterfront connections. He'd got no cooperation from the cops — they'd gruffly refused to talk to him.

After the third instalment went nationwide, someone fired a fusillade of bullets at Lou from a passing car, outside his home in Côte-des-Neiges.

§

Lou's near-death experience, on a frigid ten-below evening in the midst of an unrelenting snowfall, had happened in mid-February. He was wheeling the big green recycle bin to the curb in front of his semi-detached. He'd had a few whiskys, celebrating his national scoop — heads were ducking, the Prime Minister was "concerned," the Montreal Port Authority was scrambling, refusing comment. The series was perfectly timed, with Parliament in session and the Opposition pelting a Conservative government that had squeaked to a minority victory on an anti-graft platform.

Fortunately for the slightly tiddly ace reporter, he slipped on the icy walkway, and the bin went down and so did Lou, just as a black sedan cruised by, just before a burst of automatic fire went over his head and took out the snowman behind him.

When the police came, he was still holed up in the bathroom, throwing up. He gave a garbled, frantic account, Celeste a more coherent one — she had seen everything from an upstairs window. Amazingly cool, this unyielding, practical woman. The police posted a guard that night, adding to the posse of media outside.

The next day, Superintendent Malraux came by and stayed for a few hours, talking about motive, about the famously ruthless Montreal Mafia. He was pissed off that Lou declined to reveal his sources, and on parting handed him a subpoena: he could either tell all to Malraux now, or tell it to the judge under threat of contempt of court and jail time. Lou apologized; he was bound by ethics, by the promises made to his informants.

What Lou hadn't realized was that his headline coup had almost blown a police task force's long and arduous investigation into corruption on the docks. Charges were filed hurriedly, and over the next few days thirteen men, francophone, anglophone, several of Italian extraction, were apprehended. Among them was the *capo*, Monk Moncrief. Many prime suspects eluded arrest.

Lou was put under a vague and unappealing form of witness protection: the supposedly safe house in an ungentrified quarter of

Centre-Sud, south of Sherbrooke. They'd offered a hideaway in a quiet village but Celeste had refused to move from Montreal, away from her customers — a decision she not only regretted now, but somehow blamed on Lou. So, for Lou, it was a life of hiding, lurking, and enduring her hostile emanations. For the kids, it meant a new school, which they claimed to hate. Meanwhile the whole family had to endure grunts and slaps until three in the morning from the apartment below.

Why had the authorities settled them above a dominatrix's so-called therapy clinic? Was it some hideous kind of joke? The only perk was that Witness Protection paid the rent for this dump. But it was hard to explain to little Lisa and littler Logan what those muffled screams were all about. They couldn't be persuaded the building wasn't haunted.

§

And now the last gruelling three months had culminated in this one exponentially shitty spring day, the mid-morning of which found Lou sitting in the back of a subway car, fearfully listening to two men talking animatedly in Italian.

He peeked over his copy of *Le Journal*. Surely they were too modish for the Mafia, too sharply dressed. Almost everyone else was staring at phones and tablets — except for the big oaf in the ski jacket. He was reaching into a pocket! His hand emerged with an iPhone.

Lou got off at Place-d'Armes and, wet from the rain, glasses fogged, scarf over his nose, worked his way down to the ponderous old landmark that housed the national wire service to which he'd devoted the last twenty years of his life. Hired on at twenty-one, right out of Carleton with a journalism degree, he'd spent fifteen years in Ottawa then transferred to Montreal. He was the head rewrite guy now, doing political roundups and the occasional piece of real reporting.

Looking behind to make sure he wasn't being followed, Lou stepped inside the offices and almost onto the toes of Louise, the shy copy girl. She blinked at him nervously until he slipped off the scarf. He tried to come up with something flip or jolly — nice to bump into you — but could only grin lamely. She hurried by, as if frightened.

Eight staffers were in the newsroom, at their monitors and keyboards, all pretending to be too busy to notice him and thereby giving off ominous vibes.

Those premonitions were validated when Hugh Dexter, bureau chief and living proof of the Peter Principle, beckoned Lou into his office. After the usual commonplaces about the crappy weather and their respective states of crappy health, Dexter let him know how deeply CP valued his two decades of service, whereupon Lou sagged.

He listened dully to Dexter's prepared text, an obit, the kind that CP prepared pre-death for luminaries. Client newspapers across the country were on the rims. Belts had to be tightened. Were it up to Dexter, Lou would be kept on despite his long absences. Dexter had fought for him — after all, Lou had brilliantly exposed Waterfrontgate. No matter that the cops complained he jumped the gun a week before a planned mass arrest — that was journalism. Sorry, Lou, but the final decision had been made in Toronto.

Unfortunately, because of some nonsense in the union contract, Dexter was required to dismiss him for cause — his inability to work while under witness protection, with no end in sight. But that wouldn't be mentioned among the many positive comments contained in the two-page letter of recommendation in this envelope. Along with a cheque for thirty-two thousand simoleons. Four months' pay! That should allay his disappointment. And he'll cut another cheque for the same sum after six months. Regrettably, the extra emolument would likely be held back if he went to the union. Sign here.

Before leaving, Lou scooped up a few items from his desk, a 500-gig external drive with all his Waterfrontgate research — he would hide it somewhere — and a few other electronic externals, a Bluetooth adapter, a 128-gig memory stick, a wireless mouse, stuffing them in his pockets. As he moped his way out, no one said goodbye.

And thus, as of about two o'clock that cruel afternoon, the ace reporter became the former ace reporter.

§

He began a soggy walk home, but soon was seized with such desolation that he stopped at a tawdry tavern on The Main, and quaffed a pint, then another, wondering if anything worse could happen on this black day in May. He was dizzy, he'd forgotten to eat, and ordered poutine.

The beer and thick food warmed him long enough to make it back to his street, his triplex, and he wearily ascended the spiralling *escalier*, rehearsing how to explain to Celeste he'd been declared economically inactive. Maybe she would get off his back, feel his pain, regret her intemperate reproaches.

Fortunately, Lisa and Logan would be back from school by now, and Celeste rarely made scenes in front of them. Lisa, eight, and Logan, six, were the only truly good things that had ever happened to Lou. Other than Celeste, his love lingering despite everything, hers long fled.

The front door was locked. That was puzzling, and when he checked the street, he saw no sign of the family vehicle, Celeste's actually, a Dodge Caravan. He fumbled in his pocket litter for his key, and entered to an unfamiliar stillness.

Her scribbled note was on the dining table. It simply said, *We're outta here.*

The air in the apartment was stuffy, dense, choking, and after a while he had to escape to his balcony, where he removed his tear-smeared glasses and leaned on the heavy concrete railing, breathing hard, feeling like his lungs were collapsing, or maybe it was his heart exploding.

He was vaguely aware of the game of street hockey happening below, pre-adolescents with sticks and a tennis ball. They scrambled onto the sidewalks as a familiar car, a blue Mazda Miata, pulled up in front. The sexy, leggy downstairs tenant emerged from it, scowling and muttering to herself, apparently enduring her own bad day. Svetlana Glinka, the S&M *artiste*, back from one of her house calls. She did at least one overnight a week, always on Sundays, taking off mid-afternoon.

Lou had a nodding acquaintance with her from occasionally seeing her on her front stoop, having a smoke. Tall, blonde, blue-eyed, with a doll-like face that seemed all wrong for a professional sadist. Her body was well honed from all that hard whipping and spanking and whatever else that went on.

Svetlana paused at her gate and looked up at him. "You, the reporter, come."

Alarmed, Lou surfaced from his sea of gloom like a gasping swimmer. He gestured at her to be silent, holding a trembling finger to his lips. He nearly did a header coming down, the shinny players laughing as he stumbled against the iron railing, grabbing his glasses to keep them from sliding off his nose.

She held the door open, ushered him in to a vestibule. An inner door opened to a parlour, presumably the therapy clinic: soft lights, plush lounge chairs, carpeted walls, erotic art. A well-stocked bar. Svetlana took his jacket, hung it up with her coat, shimmied out of her leggings, told him to be comfortable. As if that was possible.

"How do you know I'm a reporter?"

"Seen you on the news, darlink."

He'd been a fool to have expected anonymity in this crowded metropolis. He felt unsteady and sank with a shuddering sigh into the first chair he could find, a recliner. Would he enjoy a drink? Yeah, a whisky would go down good. She poured him a bracer, two inches of Johnny Red, then pulled out a cigarette, thought about it, put it away. She seemed agitated.

"From four months ago, I am making this prick happy. Four months' loyal service! He wants a change, says I'm too old to be his mother. Too old! He wants some bunny-fucking teenage slut. I'm a professional, not a whore! A therapist! He'll never find another Svetlana!"

When Lou put his glasses on she came into stark relief. So did her nipples, beneath a tight silk top. Incalculably long legs. Kohl eyes, a full red mouth. She didn't seem so old she'd need to be replaced. Late thirties.

"Okay, so here is plan." She lit the cigarette after all, but cracked open the balcony door, blew the smoke outside. "You, famous reporter Lou Sabatino, have contacts in news business, magazine business. Like *People* or *Rolling Stone*. Big newspapers, maybe big tabloid."

Lou sipped at his whisky, stalling until she came to the point.

"You get nice cut, Lou. Twenty points. What saying you? How much they pay? Five hundred? Seven hundred?"

"Dollars?"

She laughed. "Funny man. Thousands, darlink. Only thing, can't use my name. I am informed source. Deep Throat."

"Svetlana, if this is a kind of sex scandal, nobody will touch it unless you go public. They'll want pictures, everything."

A pout, a frown, a rethink.

"Show me what you've got."

She brightened. "All live, on camera. Because I not trusting this rat at first in case he's too kinky."

He struggled to his feet as she directed his gaze to a tiny GoPro camera hidden between folds of velvet curtain, the little round eye of its lens barely showing. "With new clients, I take it on calls, in case of hanky-panky." From dicks with anger problems, Lou presumed. "This was our first date, early January."

He followed her beyond the curtain, past a cot with leather straps affixed to it, past shelves with dildos and belts and thongs and objects he didn't recognize and didn't want to, into a small office, where her Toshiba was open on a desk, the video on pause, the client's bum raised, the riding whip suspended on a downward stroke. Svetlana clicked play. The date stamp: January 6.

"I was a bad boy!" *Thwack!*

"I teaching you, you bad boy, you piece of shit. You want harder?"

"No, Mother, I beg you!"

Thwack!

Half a minute of this and then they were playing horsey, Svetlana with her prod, the bad boy bucking, showing his face in partial silhouette, his voice and profile familiar, a prominent, someone he ought to know. He guessed she'd hidden the camera somewhere in that log cabin in the boreal woods. The postcard view from the window of frozen lake and snowy hills seemed surreal against the pornographic foreground.

Lou watched all this with anus-clenching dread, a tinge of nausea — he was wishing he hadn't had the poutine.

"Please, God, help me, make her stop!" the fat-assed fellow called, unavailingly, as he carried his mount out of view of the camera. A big voice, commanding, agonizingly familiar.

"That was back in January. No hanky-panky, so no danger, no more need for taking movies. Later on I learn he has troubles. I helped him through it, the back-stabbing shit."

"Through what?"

"His mother. Never mind. As an ethical therapist I can't repeat."

Still nothing on the screen but the background. Some guttural sounds, suspiciously like someone beating off. "Is there more to see?"

"Enjoy."

In a few seconds, the movie's male lead reappeared, shrugging into a purple turtleneck pullover, tightening the draw cord on his lounge pants, a full frontal view. Lou gasped as he walked off camera. The fat-assed masochist was the Honourable Emil Farquist, federal environment minister.

"This is ball-breaker, yes?" Svetlana said.

Lou's throat was dry, his voice croaking as he agreed, yes, this was dynamite, and explained again that she would have to put herself on the line. There'd be reporters, cameras, gawkers on the street. Maybe visits by the police. Lawyers. At any rate, no one in the media had the kind of money she was seeking.

She frowned. "Okay, maybe we write book. As told to Lou Sabatino. Half and half. But I keep all rights until." She closed the laptop with a firm click.

Lou asked for a glass of water, and when she went to fetch it, he dipped into his pocket and pulled out the memory stick he'd rescued from his desk and stuck it into a port in the Toshiba, lifted its lid. Enter Media Player. Open recent. Click on 'Last Played.' Control-C. Click on Drive E. Control -V.

The copying took fifteen tense seconds, but the USB drive was back in his pocket by the time she returned, not with water but sparkling wine, two glasses.

She sipped hers. "Well, Mr. Reporter?"

Emil Farquist. Lou knew him. He'd watched him in the House, at his press conferences, had even interviewed him. He was not one of the dummies that infested the Conservative Party. He was a much-published economist who ran a think tank in Alberta. He was also Chief Government Whip; the irony was breathtaking. "How bad do you want this very bad boy?"

"Very, very, very bad. Main thing is not money. Main thing is principle. Main thing is destroy him. But then we write book, yes?"

She took Lou's silence as assent and touched her glass to his with a confirmatory tinkle.

Her big blues went sad. "Is like love story, but unhappy ending, a woman wronged."

"A love story?" A jest, surely.

Another cigarette, a spume of smoke. "I told him it was the first time for Svetlana, to fall in love."

"You were in love with him?"

"Of course not. The prick!"

THE TRANSFORMATION MISSION

A banner outside the community hall demanded: "Wake up! Smell the Roses at the Spring Flower Show!" This being an annual event on the amiable island of Garibaldi, in the West Coast's Salish Sea. About a hundred locals were meandering about tables bedecked with blooms, inside the hall and out. The sun was in full bloom too on this warm May holiday weekend — it was Victoria Day; jackets had been doffed, collars undone, legs bared.

Arthur Ramsgate Beauchamp, QC, however, was in suit and tie, hair neatly combed, a new, well-tended moustache that he hoped in full flower would distract viewers from his overly robust nose. He believed in appropriate appearance for such lofty occasions — let them call him stuffy, but there were social rules, proprieties. Tucked in a breast pocket, adding a touch of flair, were his ribbons: two yellows, two reds, one first-place blue. That for his freesias.

Doc Dooley had won overall, as usual, but lost best arrangement to Ida Shewfelt's little elves cavorting through petals and sniffing at pollen sacs. She was standing at the winners' table, blushingly accepting raves from the event's honorary judge, Margaret Blake: certified agronomist, local Member of Parliament, Green Party leader, national icon. Also Arthur's wife — or, as she preferred, in the ponderous new language, his life companion.

"My goodness, Ida, this must have taken you a week. All these little elfin creatures. Can I take a picture of you with your lovely garland?"

Unstoppable Margaret Blake, forever campaigning. She was nearly two decades younger than Arthur, fit, slim, a feisty daughter of the counter-culture, and relatively, compared to Arthur, unsquare. With each passing year, she was blessed with a few more wrinkles and grey streaks in her hair, which made her all the more attractive, at least in Arthur's view, coloured by his helpless, abiding love.

On their first encounter, fifteen years ago, when he'd first put up stakes on Garibaldi, he'd wilted under the power of her silvery-grey eyes, their show of confidence and wit, and soon thereafter she accepted his fumbling proposal. She was widowed; he was recovering from a long, failed marriage. But several years later, Margaret won a federal byelection, and since then there'd been long separations, and they'd had to endure the clash of different worlds: laid-back Garibaldi versus the whirl of politics.

And finally — woe! — Margaret succumbed to a brief affair last year. Though she had ruefully confessed to it, Arthur's wounds had yet to scab over. He still bore the scars from his first, faithless marriage to Annabelle; from her uncounted lovers and his own forlorn, masochistic attachment to her.

Ida smiled blushingly for the camera. *Click.* "Did you really come all the way from Ottawa for this?"

"Gosh, I wouldn't miss it for the world." *Gosh. Goodness.* Margaret didn't talk like that at home, but Ida Shewfelt was a Pentecostal, a hard vote to win. The Conservatives, whose government was almost on the rims, would target the MP for Cowichan and the Islands, a bur in their sides, at a general election that might soon be called. She would be returning to Ottawa tomorrow to push for a non-confidence vote to precipitate it.

Arthur didn't enjoy campaigns. He found politics banal, reeking of pomposity and hypocrisy. Which was not to demean Margaret, who shone brightly among the lesser lights of Parliament. She could play the game (*gosh, goodness*), but on the national stage she was fearlessly outspoken, loved by many, unpopular with climate-change deniers, Tory cabinet ministers, and other victims of her caustic tongue. As much as Arthur doted on her, he dreaded the prospect of being her mainstreeting, flesh-pressing sidekick.

He was healthy enough to survive the ordeal: a tall, lanky man, unstooped by age, still with a full head of hair, and fit from his daily walks and farming chores. His mind was still sharp, if increasingly forgetful. He was shy and awkward in the political milieu — though not so in the rough-and-tumble of criminal practice: a star defence lawyer does not wear kid gloves to a trial for murder.

Margaret broke away from Ida Shewfelt and her pollen-snorting elves to join Arthur. "Who's the blond bombshell?" she asked.

Arthur didn't pick up on her wordplay until he realized she was squinting at an attractive, fair-haired man who had just got out of a small green van. The van continued on to the parking area, while the bombshell paused, taking in the scene. Posed was more like it. But that was snide. Arthur had increasingly found himself yielding to the curmudgeon within. Something to do with aging. Or anguish.

"Jason Silverson, dear. I'm surprised you haven't met him." That came off badly, a jab about her many absences. He bemoaned the subtle chafing that had snuck into their relationship since her extra-marital liaison.

Silverson was shaking hands, breezily engaging with the locals, filming them with a video camera. Arthur had met him a few times at the general store and taken a profound dislike to him, though he wasn't sure why. There was something about Silverson's penetrating blue eyes, the perfect white dentals of his flashy smile. In his mid-forties, he was clean-shaven, thin-waisted, graceful, almost balletic. "He's the reigning guru at Starkers Cove. Has them all in his pocket."

Thirty brainwashed disciples, if Reverend Al Noggins was right. Garibaldi's Anglican minister had been to their communal farm at Starkers Cove: a zoo of various species of edible animals, an extensive fenced garden, an aura of faux holiness pervading all. An adults-only alleged experiment in human relations — the Personal Transformation Mission, they called it, as if it was some kind of therapeutic religious order. Locals called them the Transformers.

Jason Silverson, the Transformers' unfairly and undeservingly attractive guru, headed to the winners' table, sharing his charms with several women mooning around him, inspecting their tulips, smelling their roses, as they posed for his camera. According to Reverend Al, several islanders had been transformed and were spending their free hours at Starkers Cove.

"Some folks think he's the second coming of Christ," Arthur said. Margaret gave him a disapproving look. "Quite the politician," he added. Even that sounded snide.

Margaret continued to stare at Silverson, sizing him up. "Can you introduce me?"

She wouldn't have to wait for that; Silverson was working his way toward them, a shoulder squeeze here, a few words there, a wink and a smile. He aimed his camera at Arthur and Margaret before approaching with one hand extended. "What a pleasure. I was hoping I'd see you, Mr. Beauchamp." Bee-chem, pronounced correctly, the Anglicized version, not the French. "Wanted to tell you I've been enjoying your biography."

A Thirst for Justice: The Trials of Arthur Beauchamp. An embarrassing 450-page strip search authored by lawyer–writer Wentworth Chance. Arthur's notable courtroom triumphs were chronicled, but also his lapses, his debauches in the El Beau Room or Chez Forget, court hearings adjourned because he was too potted to carry on, his arrest outside a Gastown bar for being drunk and disorderly. His failed first marriage. His years of cuckoldom. His battle against alcoholism, finally won many hard years ago.

"Compelling story, Mr. Beauchamp. Your discovery of an authentic life path seems almost spiritual." With that oblique compliment, Arthur was quickly disposed of, and Silverson shone his bright blues on Margaret. "Ms. Blake, I'm at your feet."

She seemed taken aback by his intensity — he held her hand for twenty seconds, talking all the while in a mellifluous purr. He insisted she call him Jason. He was her truest follower, a passionate supporter of all things green. She must visit Starkers Cove — "your husband too" — to observe "our little experiment in healthy, cooperative living."

It was a showcase for a sustainable lifestyle. Their goal was to live off the land, be dependent solely on their own resources. "No mechanized shortcuts, no exhaust-spewing engines, just the authentic peace that reigned before man's destructive conquest of nature."

Arthur read this as authentic cow flop, propaganda well rehearsed. Reverend Al called him Silver Tongue.

Margaret punctuated his eco-friendly discourse with supportive adverbs: "Exactly." "Absolutely." Maybe she'd succumbed to his flattery. If she was angling for the votes of his thirty followers, that would be a waste of time — almost all of them were Americans.

Maybe Arthur was just enduring another spasm of jealousy. He was prone to this, but repressing it only downloaded it into his fretful dreams. He'd been forced to accept that his feelings for Margaret weren't fully requited. Her Ottawa affair had been discussed once, apologized for, never spoken of again. Relegated to the trash bin of history, he kept telling himself. Though that was far from true.

Dr. Lloyd Chalmers, professor, social psychologist, author, eco-activist: he was handsome, rugged, long-haired, as observed on the small screen — a TED lecture Margaret had played for him, about something called climate-change-denial neurosis.

Arthur's morose musings were interrupted by the arrival of a young man, Silverson's driver and aide-de-camp, introduced as Morgan Baumgarten. Heavily built, dark, a trim beard that failed to hide a scar running laterally under his chin — inflicted in lethal combat or by his own hand? His smile was nearly as bold as Silverson's, but there was no life in his eyes. They seemed unfocussed. In contrast, the message on his T-shirt was eerily upbeat: "Just Do It!"

As Arthur shook his hand, Baumgarten stared past his right ear into the unfathomable distance. He didn't have much to say, except, "They call me Morg."

Arthur too was reduced to the role of silent sidekick while his life companion engaged Silverson in a spirited to-and-fro about the proposed Coast Mountains Pipeline that Margaret had been fighting tooth and nail, convinced it would irreparably pollute the waters and tar the shores of Super Natural British Columbia. Arthur found himself annoyed that Silverson was so alive to the issue, so . . . simpatico with Margaret.

Clearly this fellow was a con man — Arthur knew many, had defended some of the best — but he was unsure what his profit motive might be. It was known that he'd come here with about two dozen disciples and had added several dreamy-eyed locals. Freddy Biggs, for instance, who was working his way through a midlife crisis, and Herman Schloss, whose actress wife, Mookie, had left him for Hollywood to do a couple of low-budget films.

Having failed to engage Morg in any meaningful dialogue, Arthur went to help Reverend Al Noggins and his wife Zoë, who were at the refreshment table packing up dishes and coffee mugs to be washed and returned to the recycle station.

"Saw you talking to Silver Tongue," Al said. "I hope you didn't buy his guff, old boy."

"He zeroed in on us. Margaret, mostly."

"That guy Morgan Baumgarten, Silverson's dogsbody, did you see his eyes? Thousand-mile stare. Empty sockets, reflecting the emptiness inside. Blind and speechless as baby rats, all of them. Jelly-brained followers of Swami Charisma over there." Al wasn't normally so cantankerous; that was Arthur's traditional preserve.

Silverson finally parted from Margaret and looked about for others to schmooze, choosing, like the good publicist he was, Nelson Forbish, the 150-kilogram editor of the weekly *Bleat*. Several women hovered not far away, nudging each other, ogling, whispering.

"He gave me a brochure." Al pulled it from a pocket. "'Join us at our Personal Transformation Mission Centre. Enjoy creative growth. Awaken to love. Soul attunement.' Attunement! Have they no shame?" The good priest had a liberal view of most beliefs, but not the airy-fairy.

He had bluntly asked Silverson about his background. "Told me he made a name as a Hollywood *auteur*, a producer–director of small-budget films. He wrote the scripts, did it all. He obviously still loves the camera; totes it around everywhere."

"His switch to guru suggests he didn't enjoy a dazzling film career."

"Told me he rejected the Hollywood lifestyle after undergoing a 'revelational experience,' sort of like finding God, except he gets to play the part of God. His followers are in purdah, protected from worldly concerns, no newspapers, magazines, radio — Silverson wants them to have only happy thoughts in their quest for universal love and connectedness." Al dropped his voice to a soft, ominous whisper. "He wants to inhabit our bodies." He grinned. "Maybe they just do a lot of drugs."

Rumours abounded: an underground lab for meth, LSD, ecstasy; nude-fests on the beach; partner-swapping. But Garibaldi had a long tradition of mischievous gossip.

Silverson and Forbish were still at close quarters — or what would be considered close if it weren't for the barrier of the reporter's Falstaffian paunch. Doubtless, Nelson was cadging an invitation to Starkers Cove and a hearty meal.

Silverson would soon learn it was almost an inviolable tradition to regularly feed Nelson — almost every home on Garibaldi had

had him over. He had the uncanny knack of knowing when a roast was in the oven of one of his subscribers.

Silverson moved on, prowling for new adherents, pausing to video several young women running a raffle table, a fundraiser for the women's ball team, the Nine Easy Pieces. They bunched around him, cats lapping up the milk of flattery. He got a playful shove from Felicity Jones and slipped his arm lightly around her waist.

"Under his spell already," Al said. "Won't be long before they're out there feeding slop to the pigs."

§

Arthur and Margaret were late getting home to Blunder Bay Farm. They had to stop at the Legion for a traditional Victoria Day observance, then for a longer visit to the common room of the elders' hostel, where a throng of descendants of Winnie Gillicuddy were celebrating her 110th birthday. "Or 109, I ain't sure, but it's up there." A trooper, she had knocked on doors for Margaret.

Tea was poured. Great-great-grandchildren were cooed over. A massive heat-emitting cake was produced, requiring volunteer lung power to help Winnie snuff the candles. In the process, Arthur singed his new moustache.

Somehow, he bore up under the ritual of departure, the ghastly kissing and hugging of these touchy-feely times. Arthur had been raised in the 1950s, when restraint was still in vogue.

Twilight was setting in as they drove off in Arthur's venerable Fargo pickup. Margaret was on a roll, tuning up for the House of Commons, lashing the cabinet. They were addicted to tar sands, that cancerous drug. They were too busy shining the boots of the resource multinationals to care about poverty, education, health. They had a scheme to Americanize Canada. A cabal of right-wing ministers was running Ottawa secretively, denying privacy to others, tapping phones, scanning emails, clamping down on whistle-blowers; 1984 had finally arrived.

Arthur managed a few intermittent phrases of encouragement, about battles not yet lost, but kept the hopelessness he felt to himself. This country, the world, was on a downward spiral; Margaret was fighting an ever-rising tide. It was easier, though more guilt-inducing, to focus on immediate concerns. For instance, he hoped the Woofers had remembered to water in his freshly planted beans and brassicas.

Woofers — Workers on Organic Farms — were mostly youngsters, travelling the world on the cheap, working half-days for board and room. Blunder Bay Farm was currently hosting two of them, just back from college in Japan: Yoki and Niko, competent, hardworking girls. ("Young women, please," Margaret would chide.)

Arthur's mental meandering was interrupted, confusingly, by Margaret, as they turned onto Potters Road, the home stretch. "They seem to be doing something interesting with that sustainability project."

Arthur looked at her. "Who?"

"Starkers Cove. The Personal Transformation Mission. I don't have time, but why not take up Jason's invitation?"

Jason. Her new pal.

"Wander down there and take a boo."

"A little soul attunement might do me good," said Arthur, a failed effort at sarcasm. If the Transformers ran workshops for the grumpy, he ought to sign up. "Al Noggins has already taken a boo, and came away satisfied that Silver Tongue collected a bunch of weak egos and is emptying their minds of the ability to think critically and refilling their tanks with happy thoughts."

"Oh, God, that's typical Al Noggins, feeling threatened by an intrusion on his fiefdom, as if it's some kind of competing church. He can't abide anything that's outside the ecclesiastical status quo. He's got you infected, dear. I mean, you guys have become a pair of cynical old goats. I am one with the Transformers. They're trying to make a statement about sustainability. Jason simply doesn't seem like your typical New Ager, and I thought he showed a very good mind. Discerning. Quite charismatic, really."

Charismatic! Arthur detested the word. What was usually meant was showy.

"And he donated two hundred dollars to the women's ball team."

His astute political wife was normally not so credulous. The blond bombshell had worked his magic on her today. And on others too. Before leaving the flower show, he and his underling had invited all comers to see their "digs," as Silverson put it. For starters, they left with several Easy Pieces.

Skirting by his sheep pasture, Arthur could make out the lights from Blunder Bay's two sturdy gingerbread houses. The larger one was home. The smaller, older one was where Niko and Yoki slept, ate, and played incessant computer games. It used to be Margaret's, but their two farms were now consolidated into forty waterfront acres.

There'd been nibbles enough at the birthday extravaganza, so they skipped dinner, took turns in the shower, prepped for bed. This would be his last night with Margaret for the unforeseeable future, and a last desperate chance to make up for his tepid efforts at love-making — there had been bouts of impotence. "Let's just cuddle," she would say, letting him off the hook. But even as they cuddled, he was tormented by thoughts of her similarly entwined with Lloyd Chalmers.

Three times, she'd said. Only three times. It was over. *Finito*. A fling, no more. She'd been in a weak state, overburdened. She'd just needed a reprieve, a moment or two with, as she put it, "somebody with a sunny outlook." An outlook sunnier than Arthur's, she meant.

THE CHIEF WHIP

The daily order of business droned on: routine proceedings and government bills. The House barely had a quorum, but Margaret Blake was there, at her front-row desk, polishing her shot at the environment minister, Emil Farquist. She had fled the turmoil of her staff room for the somnolence of the Commons to rework it. It was a rare day that she got a turn during Question Period, and she intended to aim her bullet at where the minister's heart would be if he had one.

The Coast Mountains Pipeline, that was the issue that vexed Farquist the most. He didn't have the numbers. A poorly funded consortium was behind the project, its directors chummy with the government, and it would be a rush job, cutting an ugly scar across forest and park land and causing predictable spills. The pipeline had recently been given the blessing of the National Energy Board, composed of Conservative puppets. But several Western Tories were opposed, apparently unwhippable, and if they abstained, the pipeline bill would fail.

Here he was now, her *bête noire*, Emil Farquist, wandering into the Chamber, stopping to confer with several of his backbench vassals. As Government Whip, he was the shepherd to his flock, summoning them for crucial votes, assigning them slots for questions and speeches. This hatchet man for the Prime Minister was former head of a supposed think tank, the Bow River Institute. He was was nearly fifty years old, still unmarried, robust, quick-witted, conniving, on TV a lot.

A right-wing economist as environment minister!

To top it off, Farquist was a quasi-denier, a member of the jury-is-still-out school. If climate change is real, he'd said, let's regard it not as a crisis but a challenge. Free enterprise will find a way.

He was also often the go-to guy when Winthrop Fowler — Win, as the cold, soulless, secrecy-obsessed PM preferred to be called — was away from the House, as he would be today. Win was in Washington, selling out more bits of Canada, breaking bread with the nutbars in Congress.

Margaret returned to her task, altered a few words, but remained uncertain how to best frame her question. She was not good at staying on script. Maybe she should just play it by ear. Over-prepared challenges from party leaders lacked zip, intensity.

She was bothered by an unease that had stayed with her after last evening's board meeting of the Climate Action Network, where she'd sat across a table from Lloyd Chalmers. Had she known he was on the board, she would have found an excuse not to show up. She'd barely been able to look at him, found herself repelled by his crinkly, knowing grin. But he'd played along with her pretence that they were . . . what? Casual friends, nodding acquaintances? Ottawa was a cauldron of gossip but somehow, miraculously, no one seemed to know they'd had a fling, as she preferred to call it. No one but her husband.

Why, oh, why, had she told Arthur about it? What had got into her? Some kind of ghastly, guilt-induced purging. Fed by her belief that a marriage with secrets might not survive.

Only three times, she'd told him, as if that would make him feel better. Actually, there'd been five.

And Arthur was so hurt. She feared his love had died a little.

Margaret had no easy explanation for her misbehaviour. Yes, Arthur was better at cuddling than consummation — and there were the long separations, the loneliness, a physical yearning that in the end she couldn't suppress. Add to that a mild resentment that his distaste for politics, and for Ottawa, meant he was rarely at her side when the going got rough. But also she'd felt a little smothered by him, all his worrying and fussing and, lately, the cynicism, the crankiness. But she still loved him; she shouldn't have to convince herself of that.

That love hadn't happened instantly — the death of her first husband in his prime had still been fresh when Arthur first intimated his feelings, and she had gently put him off. But he was attractive, as older men can be, with his craggy, handsome face, his lanky frame. However, it was not just that, and not his celebrity as a lawyer, that finally impelled her toward him, but his humanity, his kindness, civility — and his awkwardness, his realness. She still warmed at the memory of the night he pronounced his love, so clumsily, with his ragged bouquet of garden flowers.

Then she'd betrayed him by sleeping with Lloyd Chalmers. She'd been disgusted with herself when, as the meeting broke up last evening, Chalmers took her hand in both of his. Her left hand, with the wedding ring. The ring she'd slipped off, sleazily, before their trysts.

Members were sifting in now, a few cabinet ministers, Tory backbenchers, the Official Opposition New Democrats, the two dozen Liberals who'd survived the last election, and the handful of Bloc Québécois separatists.

Her own rump group of Green MPs were taking their places behind her. Just three of them, including the whip-smart Indigenous-rights lawyer Jennie Withers, who remained a loyal friend and colleague even while many in the party were rooting for a leadership review. *Of course, we all love Margaret. But her sass, her confrontational style — isn't that holding us back just a little?*

Yes, she was confrontational. A couple of thin-skinned ministers had threatened defamation suits; Margaret had had to bow to legal advice and apologize to them publicly. Pundits liked to claim she lacked the give-and-take that greased the machinery of politics. The Conservative strategy was to portray her as anti-growth, anti-industry, against jobs, a downsizer. But she *was* anti-growth, damn it. There was precious little room to grow on this shrinking, resource-depleted planet. Sustain did not mean grow. The far right had co-opted the word but not the philosophy of sustainability, corrupting it into a flabby oxymoron: sustainable growth.

Wally Hognut, retired grain dealer, Member for Gopher Springs, but more popularly known as Member for Monsanto, rose from his seat. He was proud to introduce twelve members of a 4-H club who had helped a widow bring in her Roundup-ready soybean harvest.

Next up was the Member for Bay d'Espoir, seeking recognition for a foolhardy fellow who'd miraculously survived a plunge into the Cabot Strait while flying an ultralight from Newfoundland to Nova Scotia.

The Member for Trout River sought to introduce a constituent who'd won a Rhodes scholarship, but forgot her name. There was an embarrassing interlude while he scrambled through his notes.

Margaret's mind returned to Arthur. She should phone him tonight. Their parting a week ago had been incomplete, unsatisfactory, with long stretches of silence on the way to the ferry, then the ritual exchange of affection.

Seats were quickly filling for Question Period. There were a hundred and fifty on the government side, five more than the opposition across the aisle. Another non-confidence motion was expected next week. Would the Liberals, afraid of being wiped off the electoral map, wimp out again, and make sure six or seven of them were absent for the vote? Their previous administration, desperate, mired in corruption, had gambled on a snap vote in the last election, and got punished by losing 131 seats.

The NDP leader rose: Charlie Moss, with his moss-like beard and constant frown, a quick-tempered brawler, a dogged debater, but a seeker of the middle way, a reluctant socialist, touchy about that label, which the Conservatives enjoyed tagging him with as if it was an insult.

"A question for the Transport Minister. Given this government's oft-stated pledge to end the corruption that infested the previous administration, when will it come clean on the Montreal Mafia's infiltration of the marine division of Transport Canada?"

The minister stood. "May I remind the Honourable Leader of the Opposition that the matter is in the hands of police authorities. As a lawyer, my learned socialist friend must know it is grossly improper to comment on a case that is going to trial."

The usual escape hatch. "Hear, hear," came the Tory chorus.

The port scandal — Waterfrontgate, the media called it — involved a grab-bag of small-time politicians in Greater Montreal, but had spread virus-like to mid-level federal brass. All were out on bail, along with prominent underworld figures.

Margaret stood as the Speaker recognized the Member for Cowichan and the Islands. "Question for the Honourable Minister of the Environment. Given that the proposed Coast Mountains Pipeline would indelibly scar some of the most majestic wilderness on Planet Earth, with a hundred percent statistical likelihood of spills of toxic bitumen, will this government finally find the courage to withdraw its enabling legislation and stop playing lickspittle to the multinational profiteers whose exploitation of Alberta's tar sands has become a blot on this nation's once-proud international reputation?"

It may have been the longest rhetorical question in Parliamentary history, but she'd got it out — though found herself panting like a greyhound at the finish line.

Emil Farquist rose with a look of weary resignation. "That the honourable member's no-growth platform has been rejected by the vast majority of Canadians is reflected in the paucity of support her party earns in the polls. Canadians know that this government will continue to be dedicated to protection of the environment, while at the same time promoting responsible development to ensure the economic well-being of all."

Applause, table-thumping.

Margaret wasn't finished. "Supplemental, Mr. Speaker. How can the minister, who is a covert climate-change denier and has spent his entire career in bed with big oil and has never demonstrated the slightest interest in nature — how does he dare talk about protecting the environment when he's taken a sledgehammer to every bit of environmental protection that this country once enjoyed?"

Applause from the Opposition side, catcalls from across the way.

"Mr. Speaker, the Green leader's last breathless speech yielded at least four blatant falsehoods, among them an accusation that I am without feeling for nature. I should like her to know that during the annual Easter bird count in Jasper National Park, I identified twenty-three species of over-wintering and early spring arrivals."

There were howls of delight from his cheering squad, and laughter even from Margaret's side of the house.

§

The Commons Foyer, a lofty arcade of elaborately moulded arches and columns, was where the press routinely jostled, moiled, and grubbed as they corralled the newsmakers exiting the chamber. They were waiting for Margaret, like a wolf pack, and she was quickly engulfed in a cluster of cameras and sound-bite-ready microphones. She was still seething, praying she could control her temper. She had been bettered in that sharp exchange, a wounded bird knocked out of the sky.

Was she shocked, they demanded to know, to learn Farquist was a birder?

"Annual Easter bird count? Come on, you guys, he's a master of the staged photo-op. He wouldn't know a bird from a bat without some flunky whispering in his ear. I'll give you a list of bird species that Emil Farquist isn't able to count because they're endangered, like the burrowing owl and mountain plover, or extirpated, like the greater sage grouse. Species that have survived hundreds of thousands of years are now on their way to being as dead as the dodo, which is the deserved fate of this government, and will be if the Liberals show some balls this week."

Margaret became aware only then that Farquist was within earshot, several feet away, awaiting his turn with a big, boyish, patronizing smile. She took a deep breath, carried on, firing more ammunition, excoriating him for defiling prime farmland by giving tax breaks to a massive program of natural-gas fracking. She lost it a bit at the end, her voice breaking.

Cameras quickly swung toward Farquist, who was already mocking her "hysterical" tone, her ignorance of the relatively benign effect of fracking on the environment.

Margaret walked off, but then turned back. "Frack you!" She couldn't help it.

§

She isolated herself in her private office at the Green Party headquarters, numbly munching Chinese takeout until the six p.m. television news finished. She just couldn't watch it and dreaded hearing the reviews from her staff. She fought an urge to call Arthur for consolation. It was too early; he would be doing afternoon chores.

Eventually she went back to the war room, where the big wall TV was flickering. Her indispensable aide, Pierette Litvak, a petite, perky, multi-tasking dynamo, clicked it off with a remote. Jennie Withers was on the couch beside her. A lawyer, a land-claims negotiator, an honorary chief of the entire Cree Nation, Jennie was the Green's deputy leader and a catch for the party. She'd won a close four-way race in Ontario's far north. Not yet forty, slim as a runway model, and bronze of skin, she was striking in her long black braids.

"Such a pompous ass," she said, referring, Margaret hoped, to Farquist.

"You were brilliant," Pierette said.

"I was awful."

"I thought you got your point across," said Jennie.

Faint praise. "Did they run the bit about the Liberals not daring to show their balls?"

Pierette nodded. "Chantal Hébert said she couldn't imagine anyone wanting to see them."

"I suppose they caught my voice breaking. Hysterical female. That's how they're going to come after me."

"Well, Margaret," Jennie said, then hesitated. "Telling him to frack himself comes kind of close to the line. He was on the tube, blaring away at you, calling you a slanderous loose cannon."

"Oh, come on, Jennie. It was just a sound bite."

Jennie looked at her sharply, though her tone was soft. "Margaret, maybe you should try a new approach."

"Like what?"

"Cooler."

Pierette came to the rescue, bounding to her feet. "It's seven o'clock, sweetie. You have the thing at the National Gallery tonight."

Jennie got up to leave, and Margaret offered her a hug, warmly reciprocated, then fled into her office with her BlackBerry and speed-dialled Blunder Bay. She tended to call Arthur not when she was up but down — it must depress him. It rang three times, four times.

Maybe this wasn't a good time to call. She was still feeling the discomfort of having encountered Lloyd Chalmers last night. She must not mention that. Her fling hadn't been discussed since her teary confession. Arthur hadn't wanted to hear more.

Seven rings, and Arthur picked up, out of breath, but full of good cheer. He'd raced in from his planting and weeding, guessing it was she. The potatoes were in, a bed of lettuce begun. A glorious sunny day. No mink visits. The two new baby goats were over their wobbles and already bounding like a pair of jumping jacks.

"Please don't ask how my day was."

He didn't, and she told him anyway, a long dirge met with clucking, tut-tutting and other soothing sounds, a jest or two, and flattery twinned with a dig at the flatulent and overbearing toad who'd brought her to such despair. He narrated, with a Scottish burr, Tommy Douglas's favourite quote from Burns: "I will lay me down and bleed awhile, and then I'll rise and fight again." The medicine worked well. She laughed at herself.

Mischievously, she asked. "Seen any more of Jason Silverson?"

"Yes, indeed. Daily I sit at the master's feet, ingesting his pearls of wisdom."

"You bullshitter. You're about the most non-spiritual person I know. What are you afraid of — that you're going to be liberated from your false values?"

"They have served me just fine."

"Seriously, I'd like to know how it's working out at the Cove. I'm curious."

She was. Curious about what held that operation together, what glue. Garibaldi's Earth Seed Commune, a '70s back-to-the-land venture which she'd joined as a teenager, had disintegrated in quarrels and petty jealousies. Most communers left the island; she stayed on, a pioneer organic farmer.

She promised to call him if the government fell next week. He seemed less than thrilled at the prospect of a campaign. Poor Arthur. So shy in public but so relaxed and engaging when he was on stage, in the courtroom. Or so she'd been told — she hadn't met that other Arthur Beauchamp, never found the time to attend any of the several trials that kept interrupting his so-called retirement.

They exchanged vows of affection, Margaret's more spirited than usual, prompted maybe by Lloyd Chalmers's subtle come-on after that meeting.

A LADY HAS TO MAKE A LIVING

At midday, a lovely day — a warm spring sun in a cloudless sky, robins singing merrily in the trees — Lou Sabatino was trudging home to his haunted triplex, exasperated, in despair, scuffling along by the old residences of upper Visitation Street. In hoodie and dark glasses, he'd made it all the way from midtown without being assassinated. That was the only good news.

Lou felt like he'd just come out of a quadruple bypass after his encounter with the witness protection *administrateur*, a mindless, paper-pushing, closet separatist. He spoke English fluently, but expected Lou to pitch his case in his less-than-perfect French. At the end, after forty minutes, Lou had come away with dink.

He'd begged this cheeser to open up his heart — he was going slowly *dérangé* in the unsafe house, his wife hated it so much she'd left him, taking his two kids. He was desolate, alone, scared . . .

The bureaucrat had shed not a single tear. No, *monsieur*, you chose to take a place in the city.

But only so Celeste could be close to her customers. And now she was gone. Surely they could find them a comfortable rural place, a little bungalow, a cabin, a shack, a trailer home . . .

Nothing is available, sir. *Comme on fait son lit, on se couche.* Lou had made his bed. He must lie on it.

They call this witness protection? More like witness pretension. He had been abandoned by his family and by his government. And his employer. That shit Dexter, with his fancy King's College journalism degree, had never worked in the trenches like Lou, who rose from the ranks.

A greeting from a front porch: *"Bonjour, Monsieur. Une belle température, finalement."*

Lou kept it down to a simple *d'accord.* He was anxious to avoid even friendly contact with his neighbours, every one of whom seemed to be outside, on stoop or stairs, enjoying the sun after days of rain.

If Svetlana Glinka — *you, the reporter, come* — recognized him so easily, despite the beard, moustache, and dark glasses, wouldn't other locals? They read the *Journal de Montréal,* watched the TV news. It was on YouTube! Lou in his former front yard, trembling, waxen, re-enacting for investigators how he fell flat on his ass beside his overturned recycle bin. The zoom lenses outside the ribbon barrier had caught it all.

If that video of the bad, bad boy of Parliament got released, the press would again swarm around Lou, in greater numbers, like wasps. That's what he should have told that cookie cutter. Their so-called safe house in Centre-Sud could end up with its own Facebook page, half a million likes.

The memory stick was burning a hole in Lou's pocket. He carried it everywhere, reluctant to make copies. Copies get copied. Or stolen. He'd played the video once to make sure it was glitch-less, but didn't load it onto any of his computers, knowing government eavesdroppers were capable of wirelessly sucking everything from his hard drives into their massive electronic gullets.

He had no clear idea what to do with this blistering hot potato, this ball-breaker, as Svetlana called it. Anyway, the next step was up to her. He hadn't had a chance to sit down with her since that first meeting because she'd been away a lot and had stopped receiving clients downstairs.

He felt some guilt about poaching her video, but not much — she seemed flighty, changeable. He had explained his situation to her, that he was going by the name of Robert O'Brien, and she had promised discretion — but what reliance could he put on that?

Svetlana's Miata was in its usual place in front of their triplex, and she was on a bench on her terrace, in a sundress, blonde and bare-legged, painting her toenails.

She looked up as he passed. "Mr. O'Brien, come. Big change of plan."

That didn't sound good, but at least she remembered his pseud-onym. He could sense eyes on him from nearby houses as he reversed himself and went up her walk.

She picked up her grooming tools and led him into her salon. According to Wikipedia, BDSM was the current approved initialism for the art she practised: bondage-dominance-sadism-masochism. A growth industry — you just had to look at the string of classifieds in the tabloids. He'd not found Svetlana's among them; presumably she was too high-toned to advertise in such plebby outlets and gave her unlisted phone number only to a select clientele of the haute bourgeoisie.

She showed none of the prickliness of their first encounter as she chatted about the fine weather: "At last, sunshine. When normal, here is worse than Moscow." Again, she poured him a whisky, not Johnny Red, but Black. A clothing box from an exclusive shop, Unicorn Boutique, sat under the shelf bearing the straps and shackles. Nestled in her cleavage was what looked like a very expensive jewelled pen-dant dangling from a silver necklace.

"Am thanking from the heart your good advice, Lou. Too much exposing myself with that video. Forget you ever saw, okay?"

Lou stammered something about the tell-all book they were going to write.

"Maybe not so much profit. Not good for business. Police all over, like you say. Lawyers. A lady has to make living."

Clearly, she had given up plans for long-term profit, opting for immediate gain. She'd been in Ottawa, making discreet approaches, maybe with Farquist directly. *Half a million, darlink.*

§

On Svetlana bidding him adieu, Lou made his way up the spiral stairs, gathering up the dailies tossed there, the *Gazette* and the *Globe* and the *Post*. Once a newsman, always a newsman, still a junkie for the printed word, the rustle of paper.

He put them aside for now, got some coffee going, went into his computer room, and laid his memory stick — precious now, invaluable — beside the juiced-up desktop he'd built, cut the power to his modem and router, and began the laborious process of encrypting a file for "Jan15.mpeg," a complex code involving a thirteen-digit password that he carefully transcribed onto a slip of paper which, once memorized, he would eat. Then the Farquist skin-flick backup vanished into the cloud.

He removed the USB drive, stared at it. Does he keep it, does he trash it? He was stuck in a revolving door, going in circles, gripped by indecision. Does he go public with it and risk being whacked by those Mafia goombahs? Does he sit on it and continue with this witness unprotection joke? Or does should he do the brave thing? The right thing? He was a journalist, damn it — he'd scooped the juiciest political scandal of the decade.

Hugh Dexter would come crawling on his knees for such an exclusive, begging forgiveness, offering reinstatement. The fatuous ass had always been jealous of Lou. The only scoop he'd ever got was in a waffle cone.

On the other hand, could Lou be accused of seeking petty revenge? Farquist had diced him up pretty bad at a press briefing a couple of years ago. Lou had dared to challenge him about his frequent first-class flying at taxpayers' expense. The minister had called his remarks inane and irresponsible. A *Hill Times* writer later overheard the minister referring to Lou as a "vacuous twerp."

He stuck the drive back in his pocket, finished his coffee, opened a beer, and slid the remains of yesterday's Polish-sausage pizza into the microwave. Lou missed Celeste's fine cooking. Missed her, period. He loved her, couldn't help it. As the weak love the strong. He even missed the scoldings, their own B&D sessions. But mostly he missed Lisa and Logan. A week had passed and there'd been no attempt to contact him. Nothing on the answering machine. Nothing in his inbox. Her iPhone not receiving.

When he called her parents, her dad answered gruffly. "That you again, Lou?"

"Simon, hello, *bonjour.* Yeah, it's me. Just wondering —"

"For the umpteenth and last time, Lou, *elle n'est pas ici.*"

"If she was there, you wouldn't tell me."

"That's right, but she ain't here."

Here was a house just outside Rouyn-Noranda, way up in Quebec's northwest, on Lac Osisko, notable only because it was dead, poisoned by copper tailings. Simon Brault was a supervisor in the copper mines, a tough guy, unsympathetic.

Janine, her mom, came on the extension. "Oh, Lou, we're just heartbroken. Maybe you have to give her and the kids a little room to think things over."

Her and the kids? When were Lisa and Logan asked for their views? "Janine, please, I have a right to see my own children!"

This conversation, as had the many preceding it, ended nowhere. Janine was as tender-hearted as Simon was hostile, but clearly both were aiding and abetting in Celeste's kidnapping of defenceless children. Lou ended the call stammering in frustration.

He took his pizza and beer out to his balcony, opened the *Gazette,* scanned it for political news. The NDP's vote of non-confidence was set for next week while, asserted a metaphor-challenged pundit, weak-kneed Liberals were being strong-armed to support it. A photo popped out at him from an inside page: Emil Farquist facing off with Margaret Blake, the Green Leader, in a scrum in the Commons Foyer. A jocular head: "Battle of the Birders."

Her "frack you" actually had him smiling.

§

Lou snapped open the double locks and the chain, set the alarm system's ten-second timer, and slipped out the front door. It was mid-morning, another sunny day as May dwindled to a close. He blinked, stuck on his dark clip-ons, made his way down the spiral staircase, glancing at Svetlana Glinka's doorway. He wondered if he should talk to her again, tell her the jig was up, add bribery to Emil Farquist's sins, blackmail to hers.

It threatened to be another low-energy day. He was pallid, flabby with lack of exercise. He hadn't been outside much, except for food, booze, girl-gazing in Parc Lafontaine, a few trips to the pay phone by the pharmacy a block away — his cell was too risky, too easy to trace. He'd made those calls to set a private time to talk to the Green Party leader's chief of staff. He'd got to know Pierette Litvak pretty well two campaigns ago when he'd been on the Green bus, joining in her singalongs, sharing laughs and anecdotes and conspiracy theories. He trusted her but didn't relate as well to Margaret Blake, who lacked discretion, he thought.

In his philosophy of living, Lou had never risen above a personal existentialism — the anguish of just surviving, of getting by — and had never quite got into the eco-consciousness thing that was *au courant*. He could tell a bird from a bat and a robin from a crow and knew that seagulls shat white, but that was about it. Wilderness was something for people to get lost in. On the other hand, the tedious act of recycling had saved his life, so, okay, protect the environment.

Those issues aside, he was a Margaret Blake fan. He liked her vitality, her plain talk, her lack of bullshit, even her occasional careless eruption in anger. During his time at the Ottawa bureau, he'd watched her in the House. Yes, he could have taken the video to the main opposition party, the NDP, and let them train their big guns on Farquist, but Blake had earned the prize by standing up to that twisted blunderbuss. The government whip. Who'd called Lou a vacuous twerp.

LOVE ALL THINGS

Arthur waited until a heavy shower ended, then shouldered his empty backpack and set out for his daily health walk: the two miles to the general store. Today's list: chutney, lemons, eye hooks, an oven light, and traps for the rats that were seeking a beachhead at Blunder Bay.

His farm was at the dead end of Potters Road, and he could have taken that longer, drier route to Centre Road, across Breadloaf Hill to Hopeless Bay, but he chose the tougher trail along the rocky beach, then up the headland, forgetting, until he came upon it, that he had to work his way across a wet patch thick with nettles.

He was wearing hiking shorts, and it suited his persistently grumpy mood that the nettles lashed his legs — deservedly, he felt; penance for past sins. The stinging let up as he climbed the hill under tall firs still dripping from the rain shower, like tears. He couldn't avoid getting wet, and that too fed his mood.

The sun pried a path between the clouds as he emerged onto moss-thick bluffs ornamented with swirls of Garry oak and arbutus. He was rewarded with a sweeping view of the Salish Sea, the snow-peaked Olympics, and, across a wide channel, Ponsonby Island,

Garibaldi's wilder cousin. A bald eagle soared past him at eye level, regal and serene. The sun was sucking up mists from the sea.

He felt slightly annoyed that what had promised to be a dull and sombre day had turned so bright and warm and lovely, defying his resolve to remain in a sulk. And the weather continued to improve as he continued on up Breadloaf Hill, with its own rolling views of farm and orchard, grazing sheep and cattle.

The sun banished the last of the clouds as his path finally took him to Centre Road, and on to the island's funky six-shop downtown core and scatter of homes on small lots. Daffodils glowed from beside the driveways, between apple and pear trees dripping with rain and blossoms. Song sparrows trilled. Violet-green swallows darted over Evergreen Pond. Under these conditions, it was an act of valour to keep his grumpiness intact, but he was a determined fellow.

A number of factors fuelled his dour mood: Margaret's jitters as the clouds of war hung over Ottawa, her public spat with the environment minister, his own malaise as he looked dismally toward an election campaign.

And his partner's little affair still gnawed at him, especially when he awoke from one of his nightmares. Their current leitmotif: Arthur as a silent witness, usually at a window, as Margaret was vigorously seduced by a ruggedly built, long-haired bastard named Lloyd Chalmers.

But those dreams lied. He was married, and happily for the most part, despite the long partings; despite the starkly different worlds he and Margaret occupied; despite her episode with that reptilian psychologist, now rued, repented, forgotten. She had been fatigued, lonely, hadn't seen past Chalmers's undoubtedly bloated ego — Arthur accepted all of that. She was human. Humans can be frail.

Also bugging the old grouch was the Personal Transformation Mission, with its spreading tentacles. More islanders had fallen under the sway of the charismatic Jason Silverson. At least three of the Nine Easy Pieces were encamped at Starkers Cove. As were several others from the island's hippie community: soul-seekers, faddists, middle-aged New Agers.

None of these folks had much in their purses, so Arthur couldn't figure out how Silverson was scheming to fleece them. Instead, he was spending heavily: providing tents, building temporary barracks and cabins. So maybe his motive was not profit, but, as Reverend Al surmised, to feed a hunger for power over others' minds.

To Al, it was the invasion of the body snatchers. He was particularly peeved that Silverson had snatched several of his parishioners. The Chamberlains. Henrietta Wilks. The lesbian couple known as Wholeness and Wellness, not sisters but nearly indistinguishable, who ran the health food store.

That store was just across the road from Arthur now, among the little cluster of shops, and Wellness — or maybe it was Wholeness — was sunning herself outside with a mug of, presumably, herbal tea. "Just Do It!" exclaimed her T-shirt. A meaningless command, maybe a catchphrase. She called, "Love all things, Arthur."

He was uncertain how to obey such a broad command. "I will. I do."

"Oh, good. Here's your reward." She met him on the road, a crushing hug. Reward enough, but she also pressed on him a bag with two oatmeal cookies. "Sugar-free, gluten-free."

"How kind of you." He took a bite. It tasted of chalk. "Very delicious indeed."

He tucked the cookies in his pack for later. They might be more palatable paired with sugared tea.

§

Occupying the sturdy bench outside the general store was Nelson Forbish, editor of the *Bleat*. He was feeding, with a spoon, directly from a family pack of Frosted Flakes.

"Late breakfast," he explained. "Worked all night, had to catch up on my accounts. Your subscription is due."

"I'll mail a cheque."

"I was thinking I could maybe drop over and pick it up. Maybe some evening when you're not too busy."

The message was not well coded. Arthur would have to put a turkey on, or steaks.

Among a scattering of customers in the store were Tabatha Jones, Taba to her friends, and her daughter, Felicity, talking earnestly by the baked goods. Last seen, Felicity had been climbing into Jason Silverson's van, along with the entire infield of the Nine Easy Pieces.

Arthur overheard her: "You'll love them, Mom, honest, they're so spiritual."

"I'll take a pass," said Taba, with an edge of exasperation.

Arthur wandered about, collecting his sundries, pausing at the rack of magazines and paperbacks, its bottom shelf offering "Canadiana" and "Garibaldiana." Among the latter were a dozen thin books signed by Cudworth Brown, the local bawdy poet, and a few copies of *Garibaldi Potpourri*, an anthology by the island's Literary Collective. Beside those stood the store's last three copies of *A Thirst for Justice: The Trials of Arthur Beauchamp*. A thick volume, the cover of which had likely scared off many prospective buyers: squint-eyed Arthur with his eagle's beak in profile.

Apparently it hadn't deterred Jason Silverson. *Discovery of an authentic life path. Almost spiritual.* His overwrought guru-speak. It dismayed Arthur that the fellow knew all about his blemished past: his history of drunken revels, his stumbling failures with the opposite sex, his punishing first marriage to an indefatigably faithless partner.

His shopping done, Arthur stopped at the Canada Post counter, where Abraham Makepeace, store owner and postmaster, a gaunt man of funereal mien, was anticipating Arthur's arrival by shuffling through the mail from the Blunder Bay box.

"Most of this is for Margaret. Bunch of flyers you don't want."

He tossed those into a waste bin. "Your *New Yorker*, which I can tell you none of the cartoons make sense this week. This here's a postcard for one of your Woofers, pretty hard to read, it's mostly in Japanese except the smiley face. This big envelope is from the Trial Lawyers' Association of the USA, I think it's some kind of speakers' kit."

"Yes, thank you. I'm addressing their conference in Seattle."

"I know." He held a letter to the light. "And here's an invite from the Transformers, an opportunity to find awareness." He leaned forward as Arthur tore open the envelope. "I heard a theory they're extraterrestrials, and we've been invaded by the mind invaders. It's just like that movie I saw. Where they suck out your brains. Except these ones have a website."

It was right at the top of the page: personaltransformation mission.org. The letter began "Dear friend," but "friend" was crossed out and replaced by "Arthur" in longhand. It was an invitation to islanders to drop in to Starkers Cove to sample the new wares on offer, among them: yoga, "bodywork," and something called "phys-ioemotional release therapy." All conducted by qualified trainers newly arrived from California for "affordable fees."

Of even less interest to Arthur was a "not-to-be-missed opportu-nity" to learn awareness from "the great and universally loved Baba Sri Rameesh," who would be the Mission's guest for a few weeks in June. Arthur had enough awareness to see this as a con. There was no mention of a fee to enjoy the company of this fakir, but donations would be welcomed. Surely Silverson could not expect to make big bucks from these services, not from the small community of Garibaldi Islanders. What was his game?

Arthur stepped outside, observed that Nelson Forbish had risen from his bench and was talking with a pair of spandexed middle-aged cyclists toting camping equipment. Forbish had a map and, after giving them directions to Starkers Cove, began interviewing them. Fans of the universally loved Baba Sri Rameesh? Expensive bicycles, battery powered.

Arthur carried on to the Brig, the island pub. During his visits to Hopeless Bay, it was his custom to enjoy a tea break, weather permitting, on the tavern's outdoor patio, a wooden deck cantilevered over a narrow inlet off the bay. From Arthur's waterfront table, he could look below at waves surging and receding over the barnacles and the floridly coloured starfish.

A muffin, a hot mug of good black tea, a pretty view, Apollo riding high in the sky, all conspired to temper his sour mood. But he saw an opportunity to rekindle it.

At a pair of joined tables, half a dozen local scamps were quaffing pitchers of beer and ignoring the no-smoking sign as two men in RCMP harness appeared at the open doorway of the bar: Constable Irwin Dugald, a humourless hulk with a perpetual frown, and his volunteer Auxiliary, Kurt Zoller, who, when he wasn't playing policeman, operated a water taxi business.

Life hadn't been quite as relaxed since Dugald took up residence here a month ago for a two-year tour of duty on Garibaldi and nearby less-populated islands. He'd arrived here, as they all did, full of earnest intentions and imbued with a sense of duty. But he would learn, as they all did, that to survive Garibaldi, he'd have to adjust to its quirks and to mellow.

Zoller, a slight, wiry fellow, stiff in posture and manner, looked about hawkishly, sniffing the air, pulling out his notepad. "I'm taking names. Cud Brown is obviously holding a lit cigarette behind his back. Gomer Goulet was observed hawking a gob over the railing, so I also got him under the Health Act. Also, he appears to be in an illegal state of inebriation."

Ernie Priposki scowled. "Hey, instead of hassling innocent civilians, why ain't you guys out busting them Transformers at Starkers Cove? They're preaching immoralism, free love."

"Yeah, that's got to stop," said Gomer, without irony.

"You have evidence?" Dugald looked from face to face. Winks and knowing smiles hid the likelihood that all they'd heard was scuttlebutt.

Dugald left them to the mercies of Zoller, and joined Arthur's table. He leaned close. "You don't mind my asking, Mr. Beauchamp, what do you make of these Transformers? Only been beyond their gate once, I've got no reason to go back. They have all their permits. I've heard some rumours about drugs and sex, but that wasn't my basic impression."

"I know less than you do, Constable."

Dugald glanced into the bar, where Felicity and her mother were sharing a drink. "I can't investigate that fellow Silverson for consensual acts. Especially with certain ladies of this island, if you know what I mean." Dugald had obviously heard of Felicity's reputation as the easiest of the Nine Pieces and seen her fawning over the blond bombshell. Her T-shirt, a size too small, was fittingly captioned: "Just Do It!"

"Maybe he does want to inhabit their bodies," Arthur said, repeating Reverend Al's feeble joke.

"Well, no one's filed a complaint about that." Dugald was not a man of infinite jest.

"Might I suggest you send an undercover operator in." This time Arthur was only half joking, but Dugald was looking at Kurt Zoller, musing.

THEMES OF SEX AND VIOLENCE

Margaret Blake was slouched over her desk in the Greens' HQ staff room, growing angrier as she waded through the various bills that the PMO was offering as election sop — lower taxes, subsidies, development grants. The most blatant was a mushy act to "Strengthen Canadian Families" that offered a small tax rebate; the most hideous offered more incentives for petroleum exploration.

The Tories anticipated an election, expected the Liberals finally to side with the Evil Empire of the Left. The Greens were as ready as they could be, given their scant resources, but still short of candidates for the last dozen ridings. The poorly paid staff and volunteers that composed the campaign committee were working triple overtime on election prep.

Pierette entered, talking on her BlackBerry, giving her a wide-eyed look. "Let me put you on hold." Margaret sat up. "Lou Sabatino. You remember him."

A CP staffer. He'd been in the Press Gallery several years ago. He'd covered her first national campaign, and was now with their Montreal bureau. A gentle soul, sort of nondescript.

"He has something he wants you to see. Amend that. He has

something you'll want to see. He wouldn't tell me. You know he wrote that series on the Montreal harbour scandal."

"Yes, of course." She assumed he was doing the rounds with his contact list, seeking comment from party leaders on a breaking story. Had he dug up more good dirt on Waterfrontgate?

A little more conversation, then Pierette put him on hold again. "Can you go to Montreal? He doesn't like to travel. I think he's a little paranoid. Justifiably, I guess."

Margaret had always suspected Sabatino was slightly neurotic. Needy, socially awkward, he seemed obsessed with his electronic gizmos. But he'd pulled off a mighty scoop and barely escaped an attempt on his life by those whose crimes he'd exposed.

Pierette, on her BlackBerry: "Lou, is this super important?" A pause. "Hold again, Lou."

To Margaret: "Apparently one of the participants at a certain annual Easter bird count is himself a *rara avis*. No names mentioned. But I'm assuming it's you-know-who."

That caused Margaret to jerk upright. She didn't have to look at her calendar, but did so anyway. This was Thursday. On the weekend, at Montreal's Palais des congrès, the World Wildlife Fund was sponsoring an international conference on habitat preservation. Margaret had agreed to be on a panel.

"I'll be at the St. James through Sunday. Set up a time."

§

The gentle rocking of VIA Rail usually encouraged Margaret to drift off, especially when escaping Ottawa for a weekend. But with eyes closed, legs stretched out on the facing seat, she was merely pretending to sleep, her mind too busy with pre-election clutter and with the busy agenda for the WWF conference. For which she and her team — Pierette and Jennie Withers — would be late arrivals this Saturday morning.

Pierette was plugged into a podcast. Jennie had slipped away to another car to confer with some First Nations friends also en route to the conference. Subtly campaigning for herself as leader, of course. Good luck to her, with her "cooler" approach. So quick-witted, unbitchy. She'd be a fine leader. More cautious than Margaret, not prone to jumping into political mud puddles.

Margaret had agreed to a secret tête-à-tête with Lou Sabatino, planned for tonight, in some dark corner of a bookstore-cum-café near the McGill campus. He'd called again last evening, coins clacking and pinging from a pay phone, his voice trembling. He'd balked at joining her at the Convention Centre or her nearby hotel, the St. James, in Old Montreal. "They may be listening. We can't be seen. Clandestine is the word."

Should she go masked? It all seemed a little silly. But if this cloak and dagger was about that *rara avis*, Emil Farquist, clandestine *was* the word. She was tingling to know what this was about. Interestingly, Sabatino was no longer on staff at Canadian Press. A source at the bureau told Pierette that Lou had been let go recently. No address, no phone, no contact information. The witness protection program was mentioned.

The weekend threatened a complication. Lloyd Chalmers would be at the conference as a WWF panellist and the Sunday breakfast speaker. "Tearing Down the Walls of Climate Change Denial," something like that. He'd emailed her. "It would be lovely to rub elbows if your hectic weekend sked permits a free moment. Maybe a quick drink? The St. James, as usual."

That arrived several days ago. He was clearly interested in rubbing more than elbows. Knowing he'd booked into the St. James, she ought to have switched hotels. But she wasn't going to run from him like a scared rabbit. Margaret had deleted the message. Deleted it again, from her trash.

And of course whenever Lloyd got into her head, so did her life partner, his frowning image prompting another wretched guilt attack. Arthur would feel horribly threatened were he to find out she was registered in the same hotel as her ex-lover. Maybe he did know, because for the first time in recent memory he hadn't made his customary Friday evening call. She should have rung him, but waited too long, and then it was midnight, and Arthur might have decided on an early night, and . . . well, it was too early on the West Coast to call him now.

Margaret opened her eyes to see Pierette removing her earbuds, staring at her. "Honey, I know you're not sleeping. About Lou Sabatino?"

"Everything."

The coffee cart came by. Margaret roused herself, asked for it black. Pierette waited until the server moved along, then spoke softly: "Professor Lloyd Chalmers?"

Margaret almost choked on her café noir. She wasn't sure if Pierette knew or was just making a good guess. "Lloyd . . ." Then abruptly, defensively: "Nothing's happening there."

"Excuse me." Pierette looked away, offended.

The awkward silence was broken by Jennie introducing a delegate from the Idle No More caucus, who eagerly shook hands with the Green leader then shyly retreated. Jennie perched herself across from Margaret, took a file from her briefcase, and they began divvying up the issues to be debated at their Sunday panel, a Q and A. She and Pierette would be Margaret's wingers. The other two Green MPs would also be at the table, all of them miked.

Pierette had agreed, though with reservations, not to say anything to Jennie about Margaret's meeting with Sabatino. A veteran land-claims negotiator, she was overly cautious, would get all hawkeyed and legal on her. *Don't go alone, you must always bring a witness. It could be a trap, setting you up for a zillion-dollar defamation action.*

Such a worrywart.

§

Margaret attended a couple of data-rich scientific panels, avoided the plenaries, and kept clear of the buffet lunch sponsored by the provincial government. This minimized the chance of rubbing elbows with Dr. Chalmers. She spotted him once, ushering well-endowed woman into a meeting room, holding the door, flashing that smile, and she hated the little shiver she felt.

But finally, at about five o'clock, there was no escape. She had popped into a little reception for a few honorary WWF patrons and was on her way to the cash bar when the scandalously attractive psychologist stepped into her path with a glass of Chablis in either hand.

"You won't be offended if I offer you this?"

"Offended?" She stared at the glass, finally accepted it.

"I thought you might not want to encounter me," he said.

"Oh, your email. Sorry, Lloyd, I should have responded." She sensed people watching. Lloyd narrowed the gap, too close.

"I was sure I'd committed some terrible faux pas," he said.

"We both did. Does this conversation have to be about us? Right now . . . in public?"

"Margaret, guilt is a futile, unnecessary, and terrible burden. You feel so much lighter when you drop it. So much freer. We made each other happy. No one suspects. Not remotely. What about later, at the hotel tonight, just to talk, to clarify our concerns and feelings? We're both on the same floor."

"Sorry, Lloyd. That's not happening. It's over." She finished her wine, offered him her empty glass: a kind of symbolic gesture. He frowned, then accepted it.

"It all ended very suddenly, Margaret."

She had to stop this. She wasn't auditioning for the role of bashful maiden. Stand up, get tough, *carpe diem.* "I have a late meeting and you're chairing a panel, I believe. What is it about? Climate-change denial?"

He sighed, as if in surrender. "The question I'll be posing is whether denial is a neurosis or a form of insanity, the sickness of our times. Blinkers worn by the unmindful."

"Nuts or not, Lloyd, they're scary as shit and they want to kill all life on earth."

She took a deep breath and hairpinned through the reception, a few minutes of meet-and-greet before heading off to her hotel to cool out, to steady herself for the evening. Her last view of Lloyd was of him extending a wine glass to the 34E-cup delegate he was courting, apparently as a backup.

§

By half past eight, the weather had turned ghoulish, dark clouds blotting the dying light of evening, a storm approaching. Margaret was wrapped in a hooded rain jacket as she stepped inside the bookstore and made her way into the adjoining café. Only a few customers, with their books and smartphones. Comfortable chairs. Muted lighting. The tang of fresh brew, gurgle of frothing milk.

She ordered a soy latte and looked about. Lou Sabatino was sitting at a table in the shadows, his back to the wall, and nursing what looked like a hot chocolate. He slipped off a pair of dark clip-on glasses, glanced at her, then quickly down at an open laptop.

She fetched her latte, sat beside him, and slipped off her hood.

"Thank you for coming, Ms. Blake." In the years since Lou had been a regular on her campaign tours, he'd added a beard and a few inches under his belt and some lines on his puffy-eyed but not unpleasant face. He looked shy, sad, with his unkempt hair and aura of loneliness.

"It's been a while, Lou. How are you?"

She shouldn't have asked. There flowed from him a mournful cataloguing of his many sorrows. Deserted by wife and kids. Imprisoned in a cockroach-infested hovel. Under subpoena for a court case that might not go to trial for years. Mobsters gunning for him. He'd been screwed over by witness protection and callously fired by his long-time employer. The final outrage, after nearly twenty minutes of this: getting the runaround from a corrupt, self-serving dominatrix.

"A what?"

"Svetlana Glinka. Lives below me. You're about to see her in action. Warning, the images you are about to see . . . well, you'll see." He handed her in a set of headphones.

Margaret scooched closer to him as he tapped his keyboard. The screen went dark for a moment, then opened to reveal a cozy winter scene, a log home, a fire blazing in a grate, a snowscape out the window, a frozen lake. But exponentially more fascinating was the action in the foreground: an upraised, thickly cheeked, obviously male pair of buttocks being slapped with a quirt by a blonde siren wearing nothing more than . . . what could that be? A chastity belt?

"I teaching you, you bad boy, you piece of shit. You want harder?"

"No, I beg you! God help me! I was bad! Forgive me!"

Margaret recognized that voice. She watched, gaping, breath-less, her latte forgotten, as Ms. Glinka rode her victim out of view, then a long pause; then the Hon. Emil Farquist, Privy Councillor, Government Whip, Minister of the Environment to Her Majesty's national government, entered the frame, pulling on his clothes with a blissful expression, then went off camera again.

Lou turned the computer off, palmed a memory stick. Margaret rose shakily, went to the counter, and ordered a triple shot espresso.

§

Wired on caffeine, reverberating with shock, of the sort she imag-ined a bomb victim might feel, Margaret gave up her quest for a taxi, couldn't locate the nearest Métro, and walked the stormy streets of Montreal toward the old town, hood up, sheltering in doorways or under canopies while squalls came and went.

She stopped at a *dépanneur* on Bleury to buy some wine, and there she thumbed a text to herself on her BlackBerry. The highlights: the secret copying of the video, the conspiratorial chats between Lou and Svetlana Glinka, a woman wronged — until apparently bought off. She paused again in a bus shelter to call Blunder Bay. Seven-fifteen there, but Arthur didn't pick up. She had to shout over the wind and thunder: "I have something crazy wild for you, darling. Make sure you're sitting when you call."

She had spent another half hour with Lou after viewing the lurid video for a second time, but then the coffee shop closed and he insisted on calling it an evening. He gave her his cell number, but for emergencies only. It was basically: don't call me, I'll call you.

She was grateful and flattered that Lou hadn't shared this explosive material with anyone else. He trusted her above all others. She had earned this by her stout challenges to the perv, standing up to him in that dust-up in the Commons Foyer, by being an honest politician, a straight shooter.

Yeah, Jennie, cooler doesn't always pay off. Still, she worried that Jennie had been right about bringing a witness. Someone to back her up in case some Mafia goombah took Lou for a walk. An ugly thought, quickly dismissed.

Lou had balked at making her a copy of the video until they agreed on a plan of action, so now she would have to sit down with staff and develop a strategy. If Lou liked the plan, and it wouldn't put him in peril, Margaret Blake would earn an exclusive user's licence.

What could have driven Farquist to this? *Please, Mother, I beg you!* What was that, some bent form of mother guilt? His mother had committed suicide when he was eighteen — that was widely known, but rarely talked about.

She tried to turn off the prissy little voice that kept whispering about ethics. Fairness. Nobility of mind. How could a self-respecting political leader stoop so low as to make profit from it? Why should Farquist's private life, however bizarre his erotic fancies, compromise the public role entrusted to him by the electorate? Would she come out of this feeling like (or, horrors, being seen as) a spiteful witch? Yet if Farquist had bribed the dominatrix, that *was* a crime that merited exposure.

Without intending to, in the throes of her dilemmas, she carried on not to her hotel but to the Palais des congrès, a block nearer, and found herself standing dumbly among the throng of wildlife conventioneers wandering about the booths and book tables, or leaving receptions. The evening's main events were just finishing.

And there, coming down an escalator from one of the meeting rooms, was Lloyd Chalmers, several chattering fans following, mostly women, the buxom blonde apparently discarded. Several of them were carrying a copy of his recent work, *Climate Change Denial: The New Neurosis*, to be signed.

His panel had obviously been well received, and run late. She tried to shrink, to somehow disappear; she didn't want an encounter with him, and hurried to the nearest exit, phone to her ear.

"Sock it to me," said Arthur, in an oddly merry voice.

"Okay, give me a minute to get my head organized. I am two minutes away from my hotel . . . Did I tell you I'd be in Montreal at the Wildlife conference? Anyway, the weather's brutal here." As if to underscore that observation, there was a loud thunderclap.

"Then I shall ring you back."

"No! Just . . . just talk to me."

"My goodness. Are you feeling okay, darling?"

"Never better. I love dodging lightning bolts. No, I'm fine, really. Just need to share a delightful tidbit. How's your weather?"

"Sublime. The heavens are ablaze, the evening thrushes are competing with a chorus of pond frogs. I am on the veranda, witnessing a majestic sunset — a nine point five at least. The sun is just about to sneak behind that lovely old arbutus on the point — your favourite tree."

"Don't be cruel, Arthur."

"Now, as Apollo's fiery fingers reach beneath Flora's swirling skirts, he hurls his golden shafts across the gentle fields of Blunder Bay." Then came a burst of Latin poetry, lyrically translated: "'Come trip it, Fauns, and Dryad maids withal, 'tis of your bounties I sing.'" The master curmudgeon was in a rare ebullient mood.

The St. James Hotel, a grand stone-faced monarch, loomed from the gloom, its warm lights beckoning, as Arthur poured forth like the rain. "'Come, Minerva, thou virgin goddess of magic. Come gods and goddesses all, whose love guards our fields . . .' Atrociously garbled, I'm afraid, I used to have it down. Virgil's hymn to the rustic gods."

"Why are you so happy?"

"Well, the sunset, hearing your voice, and . . . to tell the truth, I'm not sure. I'm not finding it as much fun being the island grouch."

"Heavens be praised."

"Tell me about the crazy wild thing. I'm sitting."

Margaret kept the phone to her ear, hurrying past the doorman. "Okay, Lou Sabatino. He's the reporter who did that Montreal waterfront exposé? Put a hold on that, I'm almost in an elevator." She was joined by two couples, and put Arthur on hold.

On exiting on the fifth floor, she had a brief blank moment, then finally remembered her room number. *We're both on the same floor . . .* She sped down the corridor. "Anyway, I just met with Lou this evening. Wait, I'm having trouble with the key card." She finally pushed the door open, put the phone on speaker, and set it down and plugged it in, its battery low.

"What are you doing now?"

"I'm undressing, Arthur." Teasingly: "I am taking everything off."

"An image that eclipses even the glories of my sunset."

Margaret was pleased with this vastly improved version of her husband. She began a long, spirited discourse as she peeled, everything wet, her panties sticking to her. She opened a Malbec she'd bought earlier, poured a glass, and picked up her BlackBerry again.

Arthur listened in silence to her recitation of the Sabatino exposé, apparently struck dumb, though she'd expected him to burst into laughter. By the time she finished he was his old sober self, and commenced a meticulous cross-examination, requiring her to retell every word spoken, pertinent or not. Margaret, aching for a hot shower, guzzled the wine.

"When was this video made?"

"It's date-stamped January sixth. That was a Sunday."

"Let me understand. This Svetlana person claims she was betrayed by Farquist? She was too old to be his *mother*?"

"I know it sounds a little . . ."

"Preposterous is the word I think we're looking for. 'I helped him through it.' She also said that?"

"To Lou, yes. Her so-called therapy sessions, she meant, I suppose."

"Helped him through what?"

"According to Lou, she was about to confide something about Farquist and his mother, but then she decided that would be breaking professional confidence. Fill in the blanks. His dad walked out on his mom when he was eight. She committed suicide when he was eighteen. Barbiturates or something. You don't have to be Sigmund Freud."

A long pause. Margaret could almost hear him thinking. Then: "Can you be sure this wasn't a Farquist look-alike?"

"Impossible. He'd have had to be a sound-alike too. Nor does he have an identical twin."

"Does he own a log home somewhere up in the Laurentians? Or maybe the Gatineau Hills?"

"I'm sure going to find out."

Another pause. "Dare I ask, darling, have you been drinking?"

She felt insulted by that, but admitted to just having poured a second glass of the Malbec. "Otherwise, Arthur, I've been dead cold sober all day."

After a wordless few seconds — she suspected Arthur was carefully preparing his next remark — he said, "I hope you won't do anything precipitous, darling, because if you don't mind my saying —"

"I do mind your saying." She quickly apologized for her sharp tone. "I'm not blind to the ethical considerations, Arthur. I won't get involved in mindless mudslinging. If hiring a prostitute to whip his fat ass isn't enough to disqualify him from his sworn task of destroying the environment, well, bribery definitely is. If we can prove it. I'll want your advice, of course, and I'm sharing this quietly only with Pierette and Jennie. She's a very good lawyer, as you know."

"Fair enough, but Jennie is a land-claims lawyer. I can recommend one or two good Ottawa defamation lawyers who might acquaint you with, ah, certain risks."

"Oh, please, darling. I'm married to a man thrice voted by his peers to be the nation's top counsel, so forget —"

Her room phone rang from the nearby desk.

"Sorry, Arthur, can we talk about this more tomorrow? I'm exhausted and desperate for a shower. Is everything okay out there? How are the Woofers? Never mind. Tomorrow, before evening. Love you."

She disconnected, but the phone on the desk continued to ring. She stared at it.

UNTESTED FAITHS

"I love you too," Arthur said into his dead receiver, wondering at that abrupt ending. Another phone had been sounding in the background — maybe she was expecting an important call. He wiggled in his hammock, trying to get comfortable again, to regain the strange serenity he'd been enjoying.

It wasn't easy to assimilate all Margaret had told him — the *rara* (but prominent) *avis*, his ritual scourgings, the secretly copied video, the apparent buying off of a double-dealing dominatrix. The sordidness of it all. The serious implications. The rights and wrongs of exposing a cabinet minister as a practitioner of peculiar sexual practices. If it wasn't all just some weird joke.

Arthur was eternally fretting over Margaret's political missteps — she was, to put it gently, somewhat accident-prone, so it concerned him that she'd closed her ears to his distress signals.

It was all too imponderable to ponder right now. The curious psyche of Emil Farquist had to be put aside, grappled with in the morning with brain cells quickened by a mug of strong coffee.

He tried to regain the pleasant state of mind that had unaccountably settled over him in recent days. A fine sunset was being wasted

— still at least an eight point four: a scatter of clouds pilfering the afterglow, rose-petal pink turning a blander mauve. Musical accompaniment: the mellifluous song of a Swainson's thrush.

Arthur was amazed by his swift turnaround from old grouch to a state verging on Pollyannaism. A transformation — dare he actually use that word? *Just do it. Love all things.* He'd got too close to them, he'd been infected by their fairy dust. He tried to laugh at this terrible notion.

He sat up, packed his Peterson bent with his favourite mix, a mellow burley. He had taken up a pipe on quitting alcohol, and it helped to quell that old, crueller addiction. Which was nagging at him now, eroding his serene mood.

Margaret was the source of this discomfort. Her loathing for Farquist. Her access to a weapon that could either drive the Minister ignobly from politics or explode in her face. Her proneness to let fly, to throw caution to the wind, to . . . just do it.

§

Arthur had been attending Sunday service regularly of late, to bolster the crowd — out of duty more to Reverend Al than God. Today, as always, he'd taken care to dress appropriately: black oxfords, dark suit, white shirt, muted blue tie. Locals, many of whom didn't own suits, thought him a curiosity in such attire, or at best a tourist attraction, especially when he was at the wheel of his fender-bent, dirt-streaked 1969 Fargo pickup.

He was a little late, the Fargo's loose muffler wheezing as he chugged around the final bend to Mary's Landing, a tiny community snuggled into a mist-thick nook with a public dock, a pebble beach, and a low-tide islet commandeered by nesting Canada geese. Its central feature was St. Mary's Anglican, which squatted on a gentle rise, the Salish Sea to the east, the parking area to the west, and the island's cemetery beyond it, hidden from view by big-leaf maples and weeping willows.

Arthur stepped inside, taking a back pew and noting that Al was already sermonizing but was off his game, riled and loud. Oblivious to the imperative to love thy neighbour, he was firing another bombardment against the occupiers of Starkers Cove, decrying their "brightly tinselled offerings of untested faiths" and scorning "followers of the fast-food road to enlightenment."

Arthur picked up the sound of desperation. He counted barely twenty-five in the congregation, where on a normal Sunday there might be forty. Regulars like the Jespersons, and Brad and Barb from the gas station, had been seduced away, spending their weekends, and often evenings, receiving the communion of fast-food enlightenment. But, oddly, a woman Arthur recognized as a Transformer was also in the back row, a video camera on her lap.

Al's florid rhetoric was causing discomfort, and many parishioners were staring out the windows at a gentler place, the placid waters off Mary's Landing. Even Al's ever-supportive wife, Zoë, looked ill at ease at her upright piano.

Arthur found himself distracted by riding whips and a bad boy's buttocks, a volcanic scandal waiting to erupt, his impulsive partner unable to resist leaking this juicy scoop. He wondered if he ought to jump on a plane to Ottawa. He redoubled his effort to put it out of mind, at least until Margaret's promised call.

Occasionally he sneaked rueful looks out the window at his Fargo with its ailing muffler. He dreaded the thought of leaving it with Bob Stonewell, self-proclaimed master mechanic. "Your off-road vehicle," Stoney merrily called it. Because it was off the road at least four months of the year, in his repair shop.

Al finally switched themes from the scary and airy-fairy to the tried and true, the venerable Christian teachings. But he'd lost his audience, was aware of that, and was running out of steam. He finally gave up, and he and Zoë led the congregation in "Peace, Perfect Peace, in This Dark World of Sin."

Arthur stayed back with Al and Zoë as the congregation dispersed. He'd thought about telling Al about the Government Whip and the dominatrix, asking for his take on it. But speaking to anyone about the matter, even a dear friend, would be incautious.

Al was sullen, muttering about his muddled sermon and low turnout, proclaiming an intention to go home and get stinking drunk. Zoë reprimanded him, saying there would be none of that, put her arm around him, and led him to their car.

§

Arthur ascended Sproules' Hill on Centre Road, the Fargo's muffler roaring, warning him of its impending death. He had lost the contentment he'd felt a few hours ago; the familiar grumpiness had reclaimed him.

Did he dare render the Fargo to Stoney's mercies and risk losing possession for the summer? Should he instead sneak it off the island to a Speedy Muffler? He wouldn't be able to face Stoney if he did. Somehow, Arthur had found himself in thrall to his long-time, lackadaisical mechanic. Garibaldians had a strict tradition, almost a religion, of loyalty to one another, however perverse its effects.

At the valley bottom, he found himself slowing by a driveway with a cluster of signs on a post. "Stonewell Pre-Owned Auto Sales," "Rob's Towing and Taxi," "Loco Motion Car and Truck Rentals" — unlicensed businesses all. Plus a couple of Stoney's legitimate trades: vehicle and small engine repairs and "Island Landscraping."

Arthur pulled over on seeing Stoney up by his lopsided wooden garage, waving as he climbed behind the wheel of one of his working vehicles. His stubby little cohort, a fellow stoner known locally as Dog, also jumped in.

They pulled over beside him, and Stoney leaned out the window. A scrawny fellow with long, unkempt hair, a roll-your-own between his lips. The smell of cannabis. "Just the man I needed to see, Queen's Counsel Arthur Beauchamp, fighter for the little man. They're trying to deny my free enterprise rights — it's the first creeping step to communism."

Stoney passed to Arthur a grime-stained letter from the strict new constable, Irwin Dugald, warning Mr. Robert Stonewell to shutter his several illegal businesses.

It wasn't the first time Stoney had been put through this. With every new cop, he received a flurry of summonses and fought each one in court, sapping the energies of the law enforcers, who would finally, wearily, turn a blind eye to the operations of Loco Motion Auto Rentals and its allied unlimited companies.

Arthur reminded Stoney of his courtroom prowess: no lawyer could do better. But Stoney shrugged that off, passed his joint to Dog. "In return for your services, Padrone, I'm gonna replace that piece of rust you call a muffler, disbursements only."

Arthur was unmoved. "It must have slipped your mind, though I have repeated it countless times — I am officially, irreversibly, and for all eternity retired from the practice of law. I shall pay the going rate."

"Guess I'm on my own once again," Stoney said sourly. "Okay, counsellor, I'll put the muffler near the top of my list because I got no hard feelings about you leaving me stranded. Meanwhile I got a emergency to fix up an used tractor the Transformers bought."

A tractor. So much for Silverson's boast: no mechanized short-cuts, no exhaust-spewing engines.

Stoney retrieved the joint, took a last toke, and squished the remains. "Them pod people don't even know how to tighten a nut on a bolt. Could lead to bigger things, they're spending loot like water. Transformation Mission, that's a front, eh. It's a pharmacy. Some kind of love drug, MDA, ecstasy."

"No way," Dog said.

Stoney looked shocked. "No way what?"

"I been there. They believe in loving all things." A major effort for the laconic squat.

Stoney's mouth hung open. "They got to you." To Arthur, annoyed. "Now I gotta deprogram him."

§

At home, Arthur changed into jeans and a work shirt, made himself a sandwich. He rarely used his fancy new smartphone, Margaret's gift, finding it too complicated, so regularly checked messages on the house line. Today brought an offer for a quick and easy loan and an opportunity to earn millions of dollars working at home. Margaret hadn't called yet, as promised. She was still at the WWF conference. Maybe in her hotel room huddled with advisors, in deep debate over Farquist, their sleeping bomb. But was she not on some kind of panel today?

He idled by the desktop computer awhile, finally turning it on. He had some rudimentary skills with search engines, and managed to find a link to the agenda of the WWF conference.

He scrolled down to the Sunday afternoon agenda. An interactive session this afternoon, the Green leader and her cohorts fielding questions. Other political parties had also been given platforms, but none would feel as comfortable as Margaret with this crowd.

Arthur felt a niggling discomfort. A name had flashed by during the scrolling, a name he hadn't wanted to see. Dr. Lloyd Chalmers, "Climate Change Denial: A Mental Disorder?"

Margaret was staying at the St. James. Arthur couldn't bear to learn that Chalmers was also booked in there, so he didn't check. He felt a little queasy.

BAD NIGHT, WORSE DAY

Margaret was frantically trying not to feel frantic. Had Pierette not called her half an hour ago, arousing her at mid-morning, she would be ridiculously late. She jumped from the shower, dried off, attacked her hair with dryer and brush, then dove into the outfit she'd set aside last night.

She'd been awake until the wee hours, wired on espresso, her head buzzing with images of the Chief Government Whip and his dominatrix, wrestling with the moral dilemma of sweet vengeance versus fair-mindedness to a man who'd known unhappiness in early life. But surely forgiveness ends at bribery . . .

Somehow, she'd polished off the bottle of Malbec before finally falling into a tossing sleep.

Arthur had unsettled her as well during last evening's tense pho- nathon, first with his unaccountably mirthful mood, then quizzing her like she was a reluctant witness. Add to that his blithe assumption that she was prone to reckless acts.

And then the room phone ringing and ringing. And half an hour later ringing again. Thank God he never came to the door — he was just down the hall.

Earrings, necklace, a touch of colour on those pallid lips, and she grabbed her coat and shot out of her room, hung over, unready, feeling beastly. She was beyond grateful that Jennie Withers would be beside her, backed up by their two other MPs. But it was the heiress apparent who would get the starring role — Jennie would relish that. Pierette would be there too, to help with the tough questions.

It was a Q and A, so they had to be ready for anything. At least they'd be playing before a home crowd. The other opposition parties had already done similar events, but the governing Conservatives, anticipating catcalls and walkouts, had declined the WWF's invitation, with some blather about the event offering undue prominence to "extremist" views.

She had not looked out her draped window, so found herself blinking as she stepped outside into warm sunshine, mists rising from puddles. A pleasant turn in the weather seemed a good omen.

Pierette was waiting anxiously outside the conference room, its doors open, the room filling. "Honey, you look like you just stumbled out of a clothes dryer." She took her aside, found a comb, and attacked a few askew wisps. "For God's sake, what have you been up to? Your meeting with Sabatino — was it a disaster?"

"Anything but."

They were interrupted by two young autograph seekers. Margaret tried to be bright and bouncy as she engaged these eager supporters. They admired her for telling it like it was. They wanted to campaign for the Greens. Margaret told them they could *run* for the Greens. There were still holes to fill among the 338 ridings, they might enjoy the experience.

Pierette led her inside, where the podium table stood empty, with six chairs. There was Jennie Withers at the coffee bar, exchanging pleasantries with her two fellow MPs . . . and with Dr. Lloyd Chalmers. Him laughing, bestowing on Jennie that boyish grin that claimed, "I'm harmless."

Margaret hurried toward the front, up a few steps, and plunked herself down at the end of the long table. Pierette slid into the chair beside hers, leaning in, asking how Margaret's meeting had gone.

"Wow," Margaret said.

"Wow?"

"Emil Farquist. The sanctimonious prick, he's into S and M." She got what she wanted, a totally stunned look, mouth agape.

Pierette struggled for words, finally recovered: "S and M. I got it. It's a metaphor. As in Sour and Malicious, right?"

"Wrong. As in 'Spank me, Mother, I've been a bad boy.' Weekends with a Russian dominatrix. Svetlana something. Farquist likes giving her pony rides while she swats his ass with a riding whip."

"Freak out!"

That was loud, and was heard by Jennie as she strode toward them. "Hey, you guys, be careful."

Margaret hadn't paid heed to the nearby table microphone, and was startled to see a small LED light glowing green on it. Green. Jennie flicked a switch, and the light faded.

Margaret felt her guts heave. She glanced behind her, at the simultaneous translation booth. A young woman and an older man, neither in headphones, just chatting. Wireless headphones were also available to conference-goers, but she saw no one using them. No stricken looks coming her way. Just smiles.

Then she spotted a blonde, curly-haired imp rise from the press table, quickly gather up her phone, notes, and bag, and slip from the room. A pair of headphones remained, hooked on the back of her chair. Margaret had duelled with the imp many times: Christie Montieth, a political blogger and columnist for the *Ottawa Sun*. No friend of the Greens. She exchanged a glance with Pierette, who'd also seen Montieth leave. Probably a bathroom break. Early for that. A quick cigarette?

Jennie was hovering with a puzzled frown. "You guys look like kids caught stealing from the candy shop."

"I had a bad night," Margaret said. "You're going to have to save my ass in here, Jen."

Jennie nodded — she couldn't have missed seeing Margaret's red and tired eyes. "I'll do my best."

The moderator had joined them, and was urging them to take their places mid-table. Margaret could not avoid the encouraging gaze of Lloyd Chalmers, front row centre. She returned a tired smile. She was going to get through this if it killed her.

Christie Montieth returned to her seat just as the session began. No expression. Must have been a smoke break after all.

§

It was warm outside, the late afternoon sun beaming down on the three women sitting at a cloth-covered table on the patio of a small restaurant below Vieux-Port. Lebanese. Lamb on skewers. Pickled veggies. Flatbread. Pierette and Jennie were drinking wine, but Margaret was sticking to tea.

She had checked out of the James, reserved a room near the airport. She would catch an early morning flight to Ottawa, in time for the day's sitting.

Jennie had quickly been brought into their confidence in a few whispered words at the end of their Q and A: "Farquist. It's explosive." Margaret had withheld the details until they were safely in the privacy of the great outdoors. Even their hotel rooms felt unsafe — Margaret worried they may have been bugged. She was growing more paranoid by the minute, ever since doing that near backflip when she noticed the glowing green light.

The session had gone well enough, Margaret summoning the strength for a ten-minute opening and a five-minute closing, leaving Jennie and the other MPs to slug it out. Tar sands, wetlands, the Coast Mountains Pipeline, dying fisheries — so many issues, so little time, no cheap fixes. They were corralled for a long while afterwards, people seeking answers, hope. Margaret straining so hard to smile she thought her face might crack.

The Lebanese restaurant was by a waterfront park and looked over the island city's great river, the St. Lawrence, high with runoff swirling under the Concorde Bridge. A tug was maneuvering a freighter upriver, toward the industrial docks, where corruption had flourished. Waterfrontgate.

Jennie had a mild cigarette habit, but chain-smoked while listening to Margaret's account of her encounter with Lou Sabatino and his purloined video. She had been appropriately shocked, at one point coughing out smoke.

Good old Pierette — she'd tried to cop a plea to the flopola with the hot mike, but Margaret insisted on owning the blame. She had expected a few chilly comments from Jennie, but her response was reasonably forgiving, though regretful. "We'll know from the morning press." Working up a bright smile. It could not have been lost on Jennie that Margaret's gaffe could mean her leadership was in peril, maybe her seat.

Pierette had learned, to their great relief, that the sessions were not being taped. But they were concerned that Christie Montieth may not have run off to pee or for a cigarette when she so suddenly left with her phone. Was it to call her editor? Had she recorded Margaret's words? Was that possible, from headphones? Yes, with a phone wedged between ear and earpiece.

Author of the blog *View from the Hill*, the five-foot-tall Goldilocks also wrote a weekly column in the *Ottawa Sun*, a daily tabloid that viewed the Greens as anti-growth ideologues. The paper would not hesitate to publish a scoop like this.

Jennie lectured them about defences to defamation suits. Only one offered victory: the truth — clear proof that the plaintiff was indeed a bad, bad boy. The only other recourse would be a quick apology that might mitigate damages.

Margaret was shocked. "Apologize? I would jump off a bridge first."

"Then get that fucking tape."

Don't call me, I'll call you. But when would that be? Margaret had Lou's cell number, for emergencies. This *was* an emergency, and she found herself probing in her bag for her BlackBerry.

"Can't we hang fire until the morning?" Pierette said. "If the story doesn't break, then it was just a close call." Sounding too brave. "Did anyone see Christie with headphones on? No. Did anyone see her madly scribbling?"

Jennie said, "I was too busy being chatted up by Lloyd Chalmers." Margaret wondered if she had guessed about the fling. Probably. Pierette certainly knew.

Lloyd had embarrassed Margaret by vigorously applauding all the points she'd scored. He'd lobbed a couple of easy questions to Jennie about the role of First Nations in preserving habitat. After the session broke up, he gave her his card. Margaret got ignored. Good.

Their decision was to do nothing before tomorrow. When Lou Sabatino learned that the Farquist bomb had ignited, surely he would immediately contact Margaret. There could be no question that he would make the tape available. He respected Margaret, the honest politician, the straight shooter. He would not want to see her sued for millions.

Meantime, Pierette would seek confirmation that Farquist owned a log chalet somewhere in the mountains and make discreet inquiries about Svetlana Glinka.

They huddled over espressos, sharing conjectures about the secret life of Emil Farquist. *No, not that, Mother, I beg you!* Clearly, he'd been emotionally damaged by his mother's suicide. She was twenty-two when she gave birth to her only child. Quite pretty, in the old photos they had seen. A grade-school teacher in Calgary.

Jennie lit another cigarette. "Betty and Kavindar — should they be in the know?" The other two Green MPs.

"Betty ..." Margaret hesitated. "I don't want to be unkind, but ..."

"She has a big mouth." Jennie smiled. "Right. Let's keep it to the tightest possible circle for now." She grasped Margaret's hand. "What's done is done. Stop obsessing about it."

Margaret proposed they tell one other person: her husband, that rock of support. Jennie had no problem with that; she adored Arthur.

But Margaret, it turned out, couldn't do it. When she phoned Arthur that evening, she didn't mention the live microphone, or how Montieth had scrammed out of there. She was afraid it would upset him. His wife, being reckless again.

BANGLES AND BEADS

It was Arthur's recurring dream: being immobile, bound — often with rope, tonight with thongs — helplessly watching his faithless former wife rutting with some faceless, nameless lover. But on this Monday morning, on awakening, he remembered a twist at the end: Annabelle had been wielding a strap, the kind once used by the private school headmaster on dreamers like Arthur, and he was the receiver, not the observer. "Hurt me, please," he'd said. So polite.

Such dreams, in their early kink-free form, had been less frequent since his marriage to Margaret, but occasionally ill-repressed memories sneaked back. Triggered by irksome happenings like a seducer's name popping out at him from a WWF web page. A minister caught on camera *en flagrante*, or *en* flograte.

Arthur couldn't help feeling a vague empathy with Emil Farquist. Annabelle's whippings had been a less dramatic but more painful form of the art, directed at the heart not the rump. Her glaringly open affairs over their twenty-five years of marriage had been emotionally crippling, until she finally abandoned him for a flouncy Wagnerian maestro. Margaret was a far cry from her. Just one little fling. Apologized for.

She had sounded weary on the phone last night. The world on her shoulders. As to Farquist, no precipitous action would be taken. Pierette would make discreet background inquiries. Lou Sabatino would be prevailed upon to give them a copy of the tape, on the assurance his name would not be mentioned. Arthur would be consulted all the way.

The rest of their conversation had been desultory. Had she held her audience spellbound at her session? Not exactly, but it went all right. He hoped she'd found time to enjoy Montreal despite her busy weekend. Not so, she said. She'd slept poorly and needed to catch up.

He said he loved her and let her go. Lloyd Chalmers was not mentioned.

He lay in bed awhile, trying to switch gears, wondering how he'd so quickly lost that placid, floating state that had carried him through most of the weekend. It seemed delusory now, a mirage. What had caused it? The gluten-free cookies — had Wholeness and Wellness impregnated them with some kind of love-all-things potion? That was ridiculous.

Back to reality. Get more seeds, a second planting of peas was due. Buy more netting, the robins were in the strawberries. Fill that goat-cheese order for the Legion benefit. Drop by the food bank with new-laid eggs.

§

He set out on foot to the general store for his gardening supplies. He was leery of taking the Fargo, with its bad muffler and the threat of being hauled over by unforgiving Constable Dugald.

As he neared the Hopeless Bay turnoff, Nelson Forbish came chugging behind him, his ATV piled high with bundled copies of the latest *Bleat*. He pulled over, tossed Arthur his copy. "If no news is

good news, then all I got is good news. I'm late for the post office."
He sped on to Hopeless Bay, looking harried.

Arthur glanced through the little tabloid as he descended the winding road to the shoreline. Featured in the "Who's Who on Garibaldi" column were the two fully geared cyclists Forbish interviewed last week. Joanne and Henry, he called them, not having got their last names. One a nutritionist, the other an osteopath. "This daunting duo cycled all the way from Los Angeles, driven by a fervent desire to meet Baba Sri Rameesh." Joanne hoped to "complete unfinished parental issues," and Henry wanted to "cleanse away his layers of negative patterns."

The "What's Comin' Up" column: "Stay attuned, the next issue will give the inside scoop on the Transformation Mission, your Intrepid Reporter having enjoyed the hospitality of Mr. Jason Silverson (a truly mouth-watering pork roast — they're not vegan!) and being offered a 'no-holds-barred' tour this week of the inner workings of their intriguing experiment in alternate lifestyles."

Arthur could hear Silverson dictating those phrases, slowly, over canapés, so Forbish could take down all the adjectives. The guru, anxious about rumours of drugs and debauchery, would be assured of a complimentary review by serving another hearty meal as part of the tour package.

Arthur arrived at the store to find Forbish behind the post office counter — Makepeace had deputized him to distribute *Bleat*s to the boxes while he attended to customers. Arthur was second in line, behind Taba Jones, the potter, whose coffee mugs adorned the shelves of Blunder Bay. An attractive redhead, sharp of mind, blunt of tongue. Cropped hair and a potter's strong hands. Despairing mother of Felicity, whom Silverson was transforming.

Forbish was whining: it wasn't fair, this wasn't his job.

"I don't have time to post your so-called newspapers." Makepeace was shrill. "You got junk mail rates, so don't complain." Makepeace held a slim envelope up to the light, before handing it to Taba. "Money order for five hundred from some gallery in Seattle."

"Thank you. Let's broadcast it to the world." She quickly checked her copy of the *Bleat*, flourished it at Forbish, bent over his labours. "Why isn't my letter to the editor in here?"

"About the Transformers? I could have been sued and bankrupted. 'They're not from this planet' is one phrase I remember."

"You sell-out. Wined and dined. A VIP invitation."

Arthur chimed in: "Yes, Nelson, it looks like you and Jason have become quite the loving couple."

Nelson rose and turned to face them. "Contrary to false rumour, I think we got to give them the benefit of the doubt. They want to be accepted, they're having an open house in a few weeks and they actually ordered a half-page invitation to all comers to see for themselves about their vision for a sustainable and loving future."

"They're *not* from this planet," Taba snapped. She was clearly in a temper about Felicity.

With great effort, Forbish heaved himself up to full height, defiant. "A lot of what Jason says makes sense, we got our values all screwed up, we're mortgaging our future on frivolous things. I'm going to do an op-ed to correct the erroneous gossip, people should give them more respect."

"Your brains have been sucked out, sweetie. I'm not looking at Nelson Forbish, I'm looking at a zombie." Taba grabbed the rest of her mail and marched off.

Makepeace couldn't reach around Forbish to get at the Blunder Bay mailbox, so Arthur leaned across the counter and snaffled his letters and magazines, thus pre-empting the postmaster's traditional examining of Arthur's mail. It seemed a fetish, this fondling of other people's correspondence. Doubtless, the lonely bachelor got little mail of his own.

Makepeace began to moan about Arthur's effrontery, his flouting of Canada Post regulations, but was cut off by a woman's loud call from outside, the parking area: "Just do it!"

"Just *do* it," another woman chirruped. Laughter.

Arthur paused on his way to the gardening section to look out the store's big plate window. A VW van, the kind one used to see in the sixties: peace symbols, slogans in praise of love. To Arthur, the homage to summers of love seemed manufactured. The van had disgorged two women of indeterminate age: dark glasses, shaggy hair, peasant dresses.

Arthur carried on, found some netting, then picked through the racks of seed envelopes. He arrived at checkout bearing a few groceries as well and watched the two women wander about, admiring the century-old store. One was working a video camera.

"Funky!"

"It's so retro."

"And the locals!" Hushed but not enough.

"Hey, ask this old-timer."

Arthur was heading for the Brig when they converged on him. Bangles, beads, possibly cosmetic surgery, a suspect plumpness of lips.

"Go back up the hill," he said, "take the first right and the third left."

In the parking lot, he spied Kurt Zoller's orange Hummer parked behind the VW van. He was out of uniform, jotting down its licence number, a California plate. A few minutes later, as the retro-hippies drove off, he bounded up to the Brig's sunny patio, where Arthur was sipping his midday tea.

"I followed those hippie ladies from the ferry." He leaned in close, conspiratorial. "My mission: bust them."

"The hippie ladies?"

"The Transformers. My information is very hush-hush. Say no more." That vow was quickly abandoned. "We have reason to suspect certain salacious practices are being practised, lewd sex, hot tub orgies. A credible informant says they use a mind–altering herbal remedy called gupa. Your ears only."

Gupa. Maybe that's what they'd fed the editor of the *Bleat*. Maybe that's what was in those oatmeal cookies. Arthur chuckled. What nonsense.

He didn't invite Zoller to sit but felt compelled to ask how he planned to bust the Transformation Mission.

"I have my ways."

"Yeah, you nail those creeps." Taba Jones, behind Kurt, caused him to jump. "Don't screw up this time." She was holding a glass of something fizzy. Arthur rose and pulled out a chair for her.

Zoller showed annoyance. "This is top secret."

"Yeah, you told me," said Taba. As Zoller retreated down the staircase, she said, "Did he tell you about the gupa?"

"And the orgies." They watched Zoller drive off. "I think he plans a surprise raid on the hot tub."

"Felicity claims that's bullshit, the orgies bit. There's normal healthy sex but they call it sharing. I think I'm going to throw up."

Felicity had reached adult age, but Taba just couldn't give up trying to correct her wayward ways. Arthur suspected she harboured the guilt of a single mother. After Felicity's father ran off, she'd remained uncoupled, dissatisfied with Garibaldi's inferior selection of male suitors.

She was well put together, but her most commendable feature, at least to Arthur, was her ample bosom, a bounty not on offer from his life companion, or from his willowy ex. Arthur suspected this minor obsession of his had to do with having been poorly breastfed.

Forbish was now outside, his nose in a bag of Cheezies as he helped direct a familiar green Ford Econoline van into a tight parking spot. Morg was driving. Silverson was the first to climb out, and he slid open the side door to liberate four women: Felicity Jones and three of her baseball mates, all in "Just Do It!" T-shirts. They looked stoned, staring blankly at a heap of boxes waiting outside the store — groceries and sundries they'd presumably ordered in advance. Maybe they were waiting for a truck or delivery van to mysteriously appear.

"Zombie invasion," said Taba. She called down to her daughter and waved, somehow managing to smile through gritted teeth.

Arthur waved too, but earned only Morg's empty stare: unearthly, trance-like.

Forbish said something that earned him a friendly punch from Silverson and a cuddle from one of the girls. The scribe seemed a short step from joining their infatuated ranks.

Arthur worried that if he got too close to them he'd catch it too, some kind of contagion spread by touch or by gupa on the breath. He warned himself not to succumb again to feeling near-bliss. He must stay on top of himself. Maintain his healthy cynicism.

§

Hefting his heavy pack, Arthur emboldened himself for the trek home, but was met in the parking area by Taba. Heroically, he declined her offer of a ride — Blunder Bay was miles out of her way — but she stayed him, a hand on his arm. Silverson was approaching.

"Don't leave me alone with him. I might kick him in the nuts."

Silverson came close, favouring Arthur with his mint-scented breath and sparkling teeth.

"It would be an immense pleasure, Arthur, if you'd let me show you around our homely little scene. This afternoon. Along with your lovely companion." His eyes lingered for a moment on her bust. "It's Taba, isn't it? I don't believe we've formally met."

She avoided his extended hand by foraging in her bag for her keys. The guru casually turned and aimed his video camera at the Easy Pieces as they struggled to squeeze boxes into the back of the Ford van, then on Felicity as she approached.

Clipping his camera to his belt, Silverson turned back to Taba.

"You must be very proud of your daughter. So beautiful, so open to experience." A slightly mocking tone, though still that blinding smile. "But do come." A glance at Taba's pickup. A disarming grin. "Save us an extra trip."

The real reason for the invitation: half a dozen boxes of food, tools, and other miscellany remained by the van, which was stuffed, hardly room for passengers.

Felicity grabbed her mother's arm. "Come on, Mom, join us, they do a divine herbal tea. It's a really radical scene." She already wore the Starkers mask, the enduring smile. "Just do it, Mom."

Taba looked at Arthur. "What the hell."

Arthur shrugged. He had time to kill and was curious to see their radical scene.

WHO WE ARE IS WHO WE ARE

It remained a sunny, shirtsleeve afternoon as Arthur joined Taba Jones in her rattletrap pickup for her promised ride home by way of Starkers Cove. The day would have been even more agreeable were it not for the twitchiness Arthur felt, prompted by a concern — ridiculous, of course, but felt nonetheless — of being infected, transformed. Ensnared in an enduring state of happiness.

"You'll be my excuse not to stay," Taba said. "They spook me. That ogre Morg with his stupid, staring eyes. The hot guru with his gushy, fake smarm. Be honest, Arthur, don't these cheesers make your skin crawl?"

It would be unmanly to admit to such dread. "I merely regard them as bizarre and pretentious." And, he might have added, spurred by mischievous intent. Surely the Transformation Mission was an elaborate cover for a scam. The bilking of well-to-do Californians had emerged as a motive. Those middle-aged hippie pretenders — they obviously came from money.

Potatoes, oranges, and soup cans skidded from their bags and rolled about in the bed of the pickup as Taba turned onto the humpy, curling Lower Mount Norbert Road. Arthur had difficulty keeping his eyes off her breasts, as they bounced in tandem with the clanking old Chev.

The hot guru, the ogre, and Felicity and her pals were ahead in the van, and it was kicking up dust, so Taba let it gain distance.

"Felicity isn't saying, but I know Silverson is fucking her." Mimicking him: "'So *open* to experience.' She'd better not end up having another abortion."

They were descending now and had a view of the Salish Sea and in the foreground the placid waters of Starkers Cove and its small sandy beach.

On a bench of rock overlooking the cove were a lodge and a dozen guest houses, built for Starkers Cove's earlier incarnation as a nudist resort — a risky, ill-financed operation that went broke. Silverson and his group snapped it up several months ago on a bankruptcy sale. According to Postmaster Makepeace — the source of all local knowledge — it had recently been put in the name of the Personal Transformation Mission Society, newly registered.

The whole area was surrounded by a tall fence of stacked split cedars backed by chicken wire. An enormous pile of fresh manure sat outside a sturdy wooden gate, and when Arthur got a whiff of it, he understood why it had been deposited far from any living quarters.

The Ford van pulled up to the gate, and Silverson sprang out, swung it open, and focussed his camera on Taba's pickup as it moved forward. Arthur took in the roughly painted sign above the gate: "When you realize there is nowhere to go, you have arrived."

Taba idled until Silverson closed the gate. He bent to Arthur's window, swept an arm about. "Our *sangha*, our oasis from the chattering world."

His upper body was profiled by a golden aura, and Arthur felt his flesh crawl. Two possibilities came to mind: one, he was hallucinating; two, Silverson truly was Christ returned. Then he realized his host had placed himself in front of the lowering sun, its rays framing him.

The stench of the compost followed them until the pickup

reached a tin-roofed barn and a newly finished building that had the look of a dormitory. Carpenters stilled their hammers and saws to smile and wave. Arthur recognized the man on wheelbarrow detail: Garibaldi's eternally depressed school janitor. He looked serene, improbably content.

A housing crisis had been temporarily met with several tents and translucent structures of industrial plastic sheeting. The latest arrivals, the two women in the hippie van, were pitching their own tent. Happy workers in the fields, fencing, digging, planting. Chickens and rabbits free-ranging all over the place, amid a smorgasbord of other livestock: Jersey cows, llamas, guinea hens, and emus. The Farm Fantastic.

"Who designed this zoo?" Taba said. "Someone obsessed with the *Whole Earth Catalog*?"

The sturdy log-built lodge offered rooms for lodgers on two floors, all with views of the cove. Tossing grass seed about its grounds was yet another Garibaldi recruit, a retired teacher. She waved them down and approached Arthur's window with a Madonna smile.

"I hope you'll find what you're seeking here, Arthur. You won't find it unless you turn off your head. It's easy. Just do it, Arthur." Henrietta Wilks, before she fell under the sway, had been a reasonably normal person, a buyer of Blunder Bay's eggs and goat cheese, but she'd had a crackup after a relationship went sour.

"Ah, yes, thank you, Henrietta. Thank you, indeed." He leaned away from her — it could be catching; he could end up spending the rest of his days collecting emu eggs and planting kumquats at Starkers Cove. Doing so happily. Loving all things.

Felicity was by the van, and she directed her mother to back up to the lodge's wide, timbered door. Already parked near the door was the orange Hummer of Kurt Zoller, who was in uniform, talking with Silverson and Morg. Obviously Zoller had sped here from the pub to gather evidence of lewd sex practices, and Silverson had arrived to find him snooping.

"Maybe, Arthur, you can help him with advice," Silverson said, "about how to find his way out of here." And abruptly he joined Morg in unloading supplies from the van and the truck.

Despite feeling co-opted into donating legal services, Arthur drew Zoller aside. "This is not a good time, Kurt. Nor the right tactic. Jason thinks you're being unfriendly."

"I only asked if I could check around and see everything's according to code, and he and Morg took up umbrage."

"You don't have a search warrant and you don't have probable cause. Therefore you're trespassing."

Flustered by a show of incompetence now obvious even to him, Zoller altered tack. "That plastic sheeting is so transparent you can see everything they're doing. I seen a lady taking off a brassiere. Are you going to say indecent exposure isn't a crime neither? And group sex?"

"Kurt, no one here is filing any criminal complaints."

Arthur had difficulty seeing these cultists as Dionysian revellers — certainly not the locals, like Henrietta and the school janitor. Nor most of the American recruits, old and new, who seemed too bourgeois beneath the façade of hippiness to have had much experience with scandalous behaviour. Most of Silverson's original group, the thirty he'd brought across the border, seemed well into middle age: long-haired, paunchy men; women in ragged cutoffs or peasant dresses; long strands of beads; peace symbols; a pretence of youth; a blatant evocation of a decade Arthur had somehow missed.

Absent from this assemblage were children of any age. Presumably persons under the age of consent were either not encouraged or not allowed.

Silverson squeezed Arthur's shoulder, conspiratorially. "Is the problem resolved, then? I'm delighted to have met you, Constable." He thrust out a hand; Zoller took it numbly. "Thank you for caring."

Zoller mumbled some words of parting and retreated to his Hummer.

"What a bring-down," Morg said softly, but Zoller heard and turned quickly to glare at him.

Fifteen minutes into Silverson's guided tour, Arthur had seen nothing to confirm rumours of love-drug labs and open-air orgies. But he did see an epic display of rural naiveté. The planting of vegetable seeds late in the growing season. The fence-free gardens overrun with fowl and bunny rabbits. An emu had broken into the seed packets, and no one seemed disturbed that a cow was trampling over a newly seeded lawn.

One could hardly go back to the land if one had never been there, and clearly most of these Americans had never been closer to a farm than the local flower shop. Arthur felt sorry for them, for their ineptitude — yet, amazingly, they were the happy ones, while he was still wired into the world's hubbub and racket, its bother and pain. Arthur had never transcended the competitive life of the courts, the cold, hard logic of the law; therefore he was impregnable — or so he thought before last weekend's onset of calm, pleasant peace. It was worrying that the skeptic within had so easily been lulled.

The grounds could have been a set for a costume musical — might these joyous workers suddenly burst into song? He wondered if they'd truly found inner peace, or were victims of some kind of hypnotic delusion. He wondered if they were drugged. A ludicrous image came of Silverson performing frontal lobotomies in the spa.

Or maybe it *was* all a cover for something patently salacious. Happening right now behind the lodge, in the heated pool and hot tub where Silverson was leading him. The group-groping bacchanal that Kurt Zoller was so hungry to witness.

The several women in the water wore bathing suits. They smiled and waved. Arthur smiled and waved. He was rewarded with views of nothing more risqué than dripping armpit fluff. "It's the women's time," Silverson said. "They have the pool until dinner."

So far, Silverson hadn't treated Arthur like a senile senior or tried to evangelize him. But he was full of mundane bonhomie, bouncing about from one unspiritual topic to another: films, politics, sports. He'd once had a drinking problem. He'd suffered a cruel divorce. He knew Arthur's pain. They were one.

Silverson invited him to share a bench overlooking the cove, his "favourite retreat for morning meditation." Arthur joined him, perching a few feet away, out of range of his minty breath.

Silverson looked pensively at the lapping waves. "There's a sadness to every sunset, however lovely, but the dawn renews hope, renews our faith to be who we are." He mused. "Who we are is who we are. That is essential to our philosophy, the philosophy of Baba Sri Rameesh. We cannot lose who we are, no matter what we experience. A simple truth." He seemed for a moment to be lost in his own easy-listening formulations, then snapped out of it. "I'm boring you. I can't blame you for seeming . . . maybe doubtful is the word, Arthur? Cynical? Or maybe just distracted by concerns. You have more on your mind than the sun's rising and setting."

Arthur resisted the inference that he was caught up in personal concerns that dwarfed the earth's movement about the sun. There was not the remotest hope — one obviously embraced by Silver Tongue — that Arthur would give voice to any disquiet he felt. Over his long-distance wife, for instance, and her risky effort to bring down Emil Farquist. Over Lloyd Chalmers.

He'd managed to suppress all such unease during this cluttered Monday. But now it was back. He endured a few moments of agitation as he fought a freakish temptation to open up to this supposed spiritual healer, to seek solace, find fixes for his angst.

"Is there anything you'd like to ask?"

This was how they got you, sympathetic listening followed by futile nostrums, bargain-basement philosophies.

He looked hard into Silverson's glacier-blue eyes. "Tell me about your journey here, Jason."

"Actual or metaphysical?"

Arthur permitted himself a smile. "I'm interested in how someone becomes a guru."

"Live in the moment not in the mind. Erase the past." Silverson laughed. "Not so easily done under cross-examination."

But he showed few qualms about disclosing his unerased past. A Los Angeleno, born into the movie world, his father a documentary producer. Studied film at UCLA, wrote a few scripts that still embarrassed him, finally found his niche in the horror genre. "I became a schlock jock, ultimately attaining a state beyond embarrassment." He'd made good money, then lost most of it in the collapse a decade ago and simultaneously endured a "cosmic, transcendental awakening."

He'd gathered "friends," as he called them, not disciples, and brought them here. "Some well off, some not so. We ask each to contribute what he or she can. Rich and poor, we pool what we have. An enlightened communism."

Arthur was becoming impatient. He wanted him to drop the mask, reveal he was a fraud, instead of sounding so reasonable, so high-minded. Nor did he want to hear he was some kind of licensed guru, that he'd taken formal training in New Age therapies, but it turned out he had. After his awakening, he'd studied at the Esalen Institute, becoming certified in "humanistic hypnotherapy." He later ran a group-counselling program for people in emotional and spiritual crises. He spent a year in India, where Baba Sri Rameesh added a spiritual element to his new outlook. "Great and universally loved," said a pamphlet Arthur had seen. "Known to all simply as the Baba."

Arthur supposed he was telling the truth about these things — not the whole truth, just information easily verified. There would be time to reflect further on his apparent skill at hypnotherapy, but that detail had already buttressed Arthur's cynical estimates of the man. He could see how many might not resist the pull of his radiant eyes. At the count of ten you will awake. You will be free.

"I feel a bit of a chill," Silverson said. "What do you say we go back to the lodge and warm up with a mug of gupa?" He laughed. "That's what they jokingly call it around here. Specialty of the house, fruit toddy with a few organic spices and herbs, including a pinch of echinacea. You'll be begging for seconds."

Arthur blanched.

The tour ended in the lodge, in what Silverson called his business office: a wide counter, a desk behind it, a few comfortable chairs, the room clean, orderly, uninhabited — unless one counted the vacant presence of Morgan Baumgarten. Silverson indicated the door, and Morg silently sidled out into the lodge's common room.

The office hosted the commune's only phone, only radio, only computer. A fax machine. A mini-television. Even a security camera, with a blinking green light. This was the control centre, Arthur assumed, remembering Reverend Al's unkind assessment: "His followers are in purdah, protected from worldly concerns."

Silverson observed him studying the electronics. "These devices are civilization's enemies, sources of fret and despair. We believe the composed mind needs protection from them."

Arthur supposed Silverson had risen to the level where he could no longer be corrupted by the six-o'clock news.

His host excused himself for a moment, leaving the door open. Posted on the counter was a daily schedule: body movement therapy, bioenergetics, dreamwork. A rack of pamphlets from human potential schools. One was from Esalen for a course in advanced hypnosis. "We are committed," it read, "to integrating spiritual consciousness and global awareness into the psychotherapeutic community."

Silverson returned bearing a tray with some muffins and two mugs of gupa, an awful-looking purplish liquid, spices swimming in it. The happiness drug, it softened up his victims.

When Silverson insisted on clicking mugs, Arthur sought to avoid a display of impoliteness and pretended to take a sip, then returned the mug to the tray, remarking on how hot it was. He was almost certain those oatmeal cookies from Wholeness — or Wellness — had been gupafied.

Silverson took a healthy swallow, looking hard at Arthur over the brim of his mug, as if daring him to just do it, to prove he wasn't a cowardly old fogey. Arthur had no intention of drinking this concoction, let alone to beg for more, even if he must offend his host. He would explain he was allergic to echinacea.

The gupa problem was resolved when a matronly woman stormed into the office, knocking over the tray, spilling Arthur's mug. "I love you," she cried, making a beeline for her guru. "You are my reason for being." To Arthur's startled ears it sounded like a pop lyric.

"Morgan! A little help here!" Silverson vaulted the counter, found temporary refuge behind his desk. Morg rushed in, pried her off the counter, twisting her arm in a half-nelson. She continued vigorously to express her devotion to Silverson as she was wrestled from the room.

Arthur took a few moments to do a reality check. Her distant cry: "I love you!"

"That was Martha. She has . . . issues." Silverson no longer seemed on charisma overload, and was breathing heavily. "She'll be fine. She was in the ecstasy of the moment. Normally, it doesn't . . . Well, sometimes things happen." He failed to make eye contact this time, focussing instead on the purple stain on Arthur's pants, crotch to knee.

§

Arthur waited in Taba's pickup as she exchanged hugs with Felicity. His detour to this fantasy land had lasted too long — his pants were soaked with gupa, the sun had long set, and Niko and Yoki had invited him to dinner. He still couldn't get a fix on what was going on here but was sure there was hidden mischief, likely involving Silverson's pursuit of . . . what? Money? Sex?

Taba agreed. "That prick set this up so he can get his rocks off ten times a day."

As they drove off, the peasants were descending from the fields. There was the cycling L.A. osteopath, cleansing layers of negative patterns by watering the kale. And his nutritionist partner working out her unfinished parental issues by shooing robins from the strawberries.

Again, there came over Arthur, unexpectedly, that odd pleasant feeling that had captured him on the weekend. It continued to build into something approaching gaiety, and he struggled to fight it. Had he inhaled gupa from the mug? Had it seeped through his skin?

He couldn't overcome his merriment and was suddenly giggling, then laughing, unable to stop.

"What's so fucking funny, Arthur?"

"The look on Silverson's face, when she . . ." He sputtered, mimicking. "'I love you! You are my reason for being!'"

It wasn't the gupa. He was merely in the ecstasy of the moment.

THE DRONE AND THE SCRUM

An expectant calm had settled on the House, the calm that comes with high tension. Margaret doodled stick figures, hanging men. Other members fiddled and messaged and tweeted.

No one was paying much attention to the backbenchers enjoying their brief moments in front of the C-SPAN cameras. One of them introduced a mother of thirteen who'd won a fertility award from a pro-life group. From the Conservative backbench came loud applause and huzzahs for that splendid contribution to world over-population.

It was Thursday of an epically hectic week, and Margaret had resigned herself to an enduring state of frazzle. It was her default condition anyway, ever since entering politics, but it had been driven to new heights by the disappearance of Lou Sabatino. Compounded by her inability to do much about it should she find herself in full campaign mode.

With the non-confidence vote the first item of business, the chamber was filling quickly, party whips ensuring seats were filled with bottoms. But the twenty-four Liberal chairs were empty — the caucus was still in a heated divide over whether to force an election and risk their own annihilation. Shouts had been heard from their caucus room.

An old moose from the far backwoods of the government side introduced a group of wriggling fifth-graders who'd earned a trip to Ottawa. A reward for some exemplary deed — Margaret wasn't plugged into the interpreters and didn't get it all. Her French was barely passable. Jennie Withers, beside her, was fluent in both official languages and a couple of Algonquian dialects. But with an election in the offing, the deputy leader, to give her credit, had reined in her supporters, the nervous Nellies keen to toss their impetuous leader.

"What's your bet?" Jennie said.

"The Drone knows he'll lose his seat in an election. He'll chicken out." They called him the Drone — Xavier Martineau, the Liberal leader — because he droned on, had trouble ending his sentences.

Jennie disagreed. "I think his troops are revolting."

"The mice. They *are* revolting."

Jennie laughed. They were getting along fine, now that Margaret had made a soft landing over that appalling clanger with the hot mike. Four days now since her breathless tittle-tattle to Pierette. Nothing in the media about the Chief Whip playing horsey with a dominatrix. Nothing in Christie Montieth's weekly column in the *Ottawa Sun* or on her blog, aside from some caustic crap about Margaret's limp efforts at the WWF convention, how she'd wisely yielded the stage to her smart, attractive rival Jennie Withers. But nothing that might cause Emil Farquist to suspect he'd nearly been spectacularly outed.

There he was, front row, hands clasped across his broad belly, wearing an even broader smile. And why wouldn't he smile? Were his government to go down, a leadership convention would soon follow. Humourless, charisma-challenged Win Fowler wasn't exactly the most popular jock in the Conservative locker room, and Farquist was widely regarded as the deserving and rightful heir. The Tory backbenchers were beholden to him, as Government Whip. Margaret shuddered at the prospect. Prime Minister Farquist, of the well-paddled bottom, a fascist fetishist running the country.

Pierette had sleuthed out that he did own a small chalet, on Lac Vert in the Gatineau Hills — an hour's drive north of Ottawa. Bought two years ago, according to the Quebec land register. Four acres, a mortgage on it. Loyal, resourceful, indispensible Pierette had taken the week off, playing detective, and was now in Montreal in a last-ditch effort to track down Sabatino. Margaret feared he'd had a change of heart; not a lot of backbone there.

He had not returned calls to his emergency number. He seemed not to have been at home all yesterday — Pierette saw neither him nor Svetlana Glinka while staking out their triplex from a rented car.

Pierette knew the neighborhood. A Montrealer, franco mom, *anglais* dad, she had lived not far from Centre-Sud. Still, being bilingual with local roots hadn't helped her with Witness Protection. She'd talked to a sneering bureaucrat and got a quick, impolite brushoff.

Margaret had finally got up enough pluck to tell Arthur about her gaffe with the hot mike, though she desperately tried to minimize it: a peccadillo, without consequence. There'd been a bit of worry that Christie Montieth had been plugged in, but if so she would have been all over the front page; instead, her write-up was a typical put-down of Montieth's least favourite politician.

Arthur had listened to this silently, though she could almost hear him boiling. As to Pierette's sleuthing, he firmly urged discretion. Lou Sabatino attracted bad company, he was being targeted by the Mafia. Margaret and Pierette would be risking lives if they openly pursued him — his life, maybe theirs. Lou's enemies wouldn't care who got in the line of fire.

He'd reminded her there'd been another gangland murder last weekend in Montreal. Margaret had read the headlines: Nick Giusti, a former mob lawyer with a reputation for sleaze, had been gunned down outside his home in Laval, a fusillade from a passing SUV. He'd been returning from church.

Arthur had been relentless. Without Sabatino, without the tape, any mention of Farquist's bizarre fancies could backfire with ruinous results. She had been lucky to escape blowback from the indignities she'd so blithely shared with Pierette last weekend — that should be a flashing red light.

Margaret smarted at the reproof, but gritted her teeth and promised to restrain herself.

Suddenly, after scolding her, Arthur had undergone a weird transformation, another attack of over-the-top ebullience. He sounded high — Arthur? High? — as he amused her with the latest local sagas: Nelson Forbish's conversion to the Transformers, Zoller's mission to punish them for their sins, the saga of Arthur's excursion to Starkers Cove — the funny farm, he called it, agricultural anarchy — the spilled gupa, and Martha's lustful attempt to mug the blond bombshell.

"Gupa? Did you drink it?" She didn't let him answer, couldn't stop laughing. She liked this version of Arthur Beauchamp. His scathing critique of the chaos at Starkers Cove had shattered her benign view of Jason Silverson's bold experiment. It was all so comical and a relief from the daily strain of politics.

She'd been thinking a lot about her island lately. Not just the crazy stuff, like the Transformers, but its simple, homespun pleasures, its laid-back routines, its silliness, its lack of pretension, of urban slickness. The moist, salty air and the gentle breezes from the sea. She had started to ask herself: what the fuck am I doing here?

Xavier Martineau, the Drone, finally led his caucus in. Some looked defeated, some defiant, others dismayed — consensus had not been reached. Though Margaret was onside with the non-confidence vote, she was torn by the prospect of an election, of launching a campaign with loose ends hanging: Sabatino, the X-rated video.

The Liberals' entry disrupted Question Period, and the NDP leader muffed his lines. Something about the Coast Mountains consortium being too cozy with the government.

The Prime Minister was equally distracted, studying the Liberals for some kind of signal, and he hadn't quite grasped the question. "Once again, Mr. Speaker, my honourable friend demonstrates his penchant for wallowing in negativism. He very well knows my answer to his question."

"What is it?" someone shouted.

"What's the question?" someone else called.

"Order," said the Speaker. "Recognize the member for Dorval."

Xavier Martineau rose wearily, and received permission to make a brief statement.

"Thank you, Mr. Speaker. While vigorously rejecting the slurs cast by the Honourable Leader of the Opposition — I need not recite them, but 'panicking chickens' might be the most egregious — I seek to assure this House that our caucus has sought to assess the Canadian public's appetite for a summer election, with the season's many pleasant distractions and the consequent inconveniences vacation-goers would be subjected to, and so . . ."

The die was cast. Boos and catcalls from the opposition side.

"And so we have asked the voters, we have asked our supporters to canvass for the general view, and it seems there is insufficient appetite for a midsummer election . . ."

He carried on awhile, the world's longest sentence, but his words were drowned in hoots and boos from the Opposition side, while government members looked on grinning or yelling, "Call the vote!"

When it ultimately came — "Resolved that the government has lost the confidence of the House" — several Liberals of stouter heart voted for the affirmative, but the remainder abstained, and the nays won handily.

§

Margaret arrived in the Foyer late, expecting to see the Prime Minister holding the fort, but Win Fowler was a no-show and Emil

Farquist, surrounded by a platoon of press, was subbing for him. The Opposition leader was waiting in the wings to reply. There was a pecking order to these media scrums, and the Green leader was always the last pecker, usually sharing her sound bites with ragtag remnants of the press.

At least she had time to arm herself, to respond to Farquist's hokum. So she sidled behind him to hear better. He spotted her and scowled, but didn't break rhythm as he heaped scorn on the Opposition for trying to force an untimely election. Threatening to disrupt hard-earned holidays. Stalling the government's program for growth, lower taxes, and environmental protection. With that, a glance behind, a shot, a challenge.

It seemed an open invitation, and Margaret, despite — or because of — her frazzled state, couldn't help but grab the moment. Flouting the proprieties, she twisted under cameras and microphones and got close enough to smell his musky cologne.

"Well, that demonstrates the government's total lack of respect for democracy, doesn't it?" Farquist tried to interrupt but Margaret talked above his scattershot of complaint. "What's more fundamental to our way of life than the exercise of the people's right to choose who will represent them? That's so typical of the Fowler government, demeaning the right to vote — we should be *celebrating* elections."

She made a quick exit and several reporters followed her, deserting Farquist. She sensed she'd really got his goat this time, thrown him off his game. He would try to make light of it, tossing off some snarky put-down. *Canadians will want to consider whether rudeness is a quality they seek in a party leader.*

Had she been reckless in invading his scrum? Jennie Withers, standing near the West Door, apparently didn't think so. A smile. The current Green leader still had game.

And now she had her own mini-scrum, grown to a dozen, lobbing friendly questions. Yes, of course, she was disappointed in the spineless Liberals. The Greens were ready, had almost a full slate. The government had won a mere reprieve and would certainly fall in the fall.

Her cloud of gloom, exhaustion, and confusion had lifted. She felt energized.

§

But that didn't last. The entire day, the entire frenetic week caught up to her at Green HQ halfway through the afternoon, and she had to steal off to her inner office, needing its peace and solitude. She stretched out on a couch, fighting the urge to sleep, fiddling with her phone. She finally dialled Blunder Bay, thinking Arthur would be much relieved at having escaped a summer of main-streeting.

She caught him at home, in the kitchen finishing lunch. "No election. I guess you've heard. I hope that makes your day."

"Nonsense. You know how I love going door to door, invading the space of total strangers. Your sneak attack on Farquist was on the national news. I hope you're not tempting fate, darling."

She bristled. "I'm not going to lay off him just because ... Never mind. Anyway, I've got breathing space now."

"Margaret, I hope you aren't playing with the thought of tripping off to Montreal to join Pierette."

"Of course not," she said sharply. "That would be foolish and risky." But she yearned to do just that.

§

She slept like a dead woman that night, rose late to a sunny and excruciatingly pleasant day, and took a bracing hike to the Hill. She'd given her staff the Friday off, so her parliamentary office was ghostly quiet. She got coffee going and sat down at her desktop to review an array of iPhone photos from Pierette of tree-lined Rue de la Visitation, its row of venerable triplexes, their sinuous outdoor staircases, relics of old Montreal; Lou Sabatino's second-floor flat, its covered balcony and shuttered windows.

Below it was Svetlana Glinka's therapy clinic, though there was nothing to advertise it as such. A small, tiled terrace; a wrought-iron bench; wide, curtained windows. No sign of her Miata, which, according to Sabatino, was usually parked out front.

Margaret wouldn't be surprised if Glinka was in Cannes or a Greek villa, spending Farquist's hush money. Unless he was on the take, he had no great wealth, so he must be hurting. Had he retained another professional paddler to satisfy his obsession? A younger model?

He wants a change, says I'm too old to be his mother. Farquist's real mother became a single mom when her husband left her for another woman. Their son was eight years old. Ten years later, she committed suicide. Maybe there was tragedy enough here to turn a man into a fetishist.

As for Lou, he might be anywhere. Targeted by the Mafia, newly fired, separated from wife and children, bitter about that, bitter about his situation, his life. Had he given up? She pictured him hanging lifeless from a chandelier. Or sprawled on the carpet, a bullet in his brain.

With a mug of hot coffee at hand, she called Pierette, who picked up right away — she was still in her rented compact, stationed across from the triplex. "You got the pix?"

"Yep."

"More coming. Hey, sweetie, I'm worried this place is being watched. I saw a couple of goony-looking guys in a big black SUV prowling by yesterday, looking things over."

The Mafia? Had they traced him there? "Did you get a photo? The licence plate?"

"No, I was across the street chatting up a couple of old boys hanging outside the adjoining triplex. I didn't see the driver. One passenger, both male. Probably nothing."

"So what did the old boys have to say?"

"They figured Svetlana was a high-priced *pute*. They dug her, she gave the neighbourhood some tone. Lou was an utter nonentity, they hardly knew him, didn't know he was gone."

"Any chance he forgot to lock up?"

"Door won't budge, knob doesn't turn. There's a huge pile of newspapers sitting there, four days' worth, *Globe*, *Gazette*, *Post*, *Journal de Montréal*. Nothing from Monday, so that must be when he vanished."

"Could you see inside?"

"Just a glimpse through a gap in the shutters. All I could see was a clump of clothes, it looked like, maybe for the wash."

Had he run off suddenly with chores undone? Another dark thought: had he been disappeared? Likely not, if that was indeed the Mafia doing a drive-by, still hoping to target him.

"Whoops, hang on. Car coming."

Pierette went silent for several seconds, then, in a hushed voice: "Miata, its top down, just stopped and double-parked. It's Svetlana. I'm scooching down. I'll call back."

Margaret waited tensely. Minutes passed before Pierette rang. "Okay, she's outta here, all clear. I'm shooting you some video. Hang on while I check flights out of Dorval."

Svetlana was on the lam? Two videos soon arrived. The first showed Svetlana Glinka removing her dark glasses as she climbed from the driver's seat. Legs almost freakishly long, like a high-jumper. Blonde, if that was her real hair, blue eyes, cherry lips, a face like a Kewpie doll. Dressed for travel in skinny jeans and a multi-pocketed blazer. Knee-high boots, alligator or something.

Now she was hurrying to her building, carrying a flight bag, now opening the door to her flat, stepping inside. The second video showed her reappearing, pulling a wheeled suitcase that must have been waiting for her inside the door. She locked up, loaded the suitcase into the trunk, and took off.

Pierette sounded breathless. "I don't think she saw me. My guess is that she's on her way to the airport. I'm making a run for Dorval right now. Over and out."

Again, Margaret found herself dredging up dismal scenarios: Lou had vanished Monday, the day after the open-mike blooper. Had Christie Montieth, who had sprinted from the salon with her iPhone, held on to her exclusive to track down sources? She could easily have zeroed in on Glinka, prompting Glinka's sudden departure.

Maybe Christie had got a lead on Sabatino, tried to contact him. Had the nervous fellow, knowing the story was about to break, fled from the coming storm?

§

Fretful, impatient, yielding to an itch to be more than a passive bystander, Margaret sped off that afternoon in her Honda Civic hybrid over the Macdonald-Cartier Bridge to the Quebec side, for a rendezvous in the Gatineau Hills with her intrepid aide.

Pierette had confirmed that Glinka had flown out from Dorval — she'd spotted her in short-term parking at the open trunk of her Miata. A heavy-set man and a tall, fit-looking woman, in their thirties, seemed to be helping with her luggage — or searching it, because Pierette watched them close her suitcase from some distance away. No photos, her phone had died.

The mystery woman then drove off in the Miata. Her partner took Glinka's suitcase and led her to the terminal. By the time Pierette caught up to them, she was already being waved into security. Presumably first class, given the brief elapsed time. Her escort then returned to the short-term lot, drove off in a white van.

Margaret supposed that the two confederates had been hired by Emil Farquist to facilitate her quick getaway. Her presence in Canada posed a grave danger to him if a nosy reporter — Christie

Montieth, for instance — were to ask her questions. Emil had to be anxious — masked well, not on display at the scrum on Thursday.

The highway wove among forested hills and scattered farms and cozy villages, scenes that took Margaret back home to a gentler life that beckoned more urgently with the passing days. A wise woman was whispering: give up, get healthy, enjoy life, it's not too late. Jennie would be anointed acting leader; someone with more energy could run in Cowichan and the Islands.

North of Gatineau Park, farms gave way to forests of beech and birch and sugar maple in their fresh green dresses. It was a gorgeous day, but Margaret was too depressed to enjoy it. The spiriting away of Glinka seriously dimmed any chance of proving Farquist had bought her silence. With the world crowding in on her — the election, Farquist, Sabatino and Glinka's disappearences — Margaret was becoming like her husband, or at least one of his personas: pessimistic, morose.

Pierette was waiting, as promised, in her rented compact outside a café in the village of Kazabazua. Margaret parked and got in beside her.

"Not too pleased about this," Pierette said. "The leader of a national party can't be seen poking around anywhere near Lac Vert."

"Hey, it's just a couple of pals taking a scenic drive on a sunny afternoon. Don't be such a grouse." This was met with silent disapproval. "You've been a total wizard, Pierette. My hero. I love you."

That earned just a weary look and raised unforgiving eyes as she stuck a sun hat on Margaret's head, dark glasses on her nose.

Pierette turned onto a secondary road that wound east into hills thickly forested with spruce and aspen, birch and tamarack. Sunbathed lakes. Occasional cottages, but most of them hidden.

After about fifteen kilometres, they pulled in to a roadside lookout with a panorama of undulating forest on mountains scarred with ski runs. The large lake in the foreground was rimmed by forest and hill and was still as glass, ruffled only by a whisper of wind near the far shore.

"Lac Vert," said Pierette. A narrow driveway a hundred metres up the road was marked by a sign at a wonky angle. "*Privé*. Private." It led, Pierette had learned, to three waterfront chalets, none visible from here, the owners a retired judge, a computer engineer, and Farquist.

"I'm sorry, you're staying put. Pretend you're a tourist." Pierette tucked a camera into her day pack and hustled up the road and down the driveway. Margaret itched to follow her, but obeyed orders, lowered her seat-back, ready to duck should a car approach. Only two did, each slowing to catch the view, then carrying on.

She finally began to relax, to fall under the sway of this fair June day. Songbirds were in full throat, warblers flitting among the branches, and below her was a lush view of forest and lake. Ducks foraging among the reeds, a pair of loons diving for their lunch.

Pierette reappeared at the end of the driveway after what seemed an eternity but was probably only twenty minutes. She paused at the privacy sign, took a photo of it, ducked as a car drove by, then hurried to the car.

"Didn't see a soul, thank God." She handed Margaret her camera, its viewer on, then started the engine and drove farther up the road. "The one on the screen is taken from below his chalet window. Seem familiar?"

"Yes." The image of the still lake and hills beyond jibed with the wintry glimpses Margaret had seen on the video: the iced-over lake and skeletal trees rising beyond it, the grove of white birch.

She scrolled through the other pictures: a snug, attractive log structure with a deck overlooking a lake. No interiors, all the windows draped. A one-vehicle carport. A more expansive view across Lac Vert offered a glimpse of a neighbour's small boathouse, a dock, and a small cabin cruiser.

They continued their climb, hair-pinning to a summit where they could see the lake distantly. Lac Vert, so pretty but its name tarnished by the irony that the very non-*vert* minister of the environment claimed a piece of it.

As they made a similarly sinuous journey down, toward the highway that would take them to Ottawa, Pierette remained watchful and silent, occasionally commanding Margaret to keep her head low. Margaret worried that she might be losing her respect, losing her to Jennie Withers, who didn't indulge in spontaneous spying expeditions. She thought of confessing her notion to retire. But was she too hooked on politics? Her addiction.

UNSAFE HOUSE

Lou was running low on Cheerios and corn flakes. The last of his milk had gone sour in the fridge. He had half a Polish sausage in there, two rubbery carrots, and a sprouting potato. He would sell his left nut for a deluxe double-patty with fries and a chocolate shake.

It was Friday. For five days he'd been hiding in his stale-smelling flat, its doors double-locked, no lights, no sound, newspapers piling up outside. He rarely stirred from his computer room, a windowless box, except to sleep, shit, and peek furtively out the front window between a gap in the shutters.

Rue de la Visitation was rightly named. It had been like rush hour at Central Station for those five days. The traffic included several of Svetlana's clients who had appointments. Lou had heard her outside apologizing to one guy for not phoning to cancel. Other pain-seekers gave up when she didn't come to the door. She was away a lot.

Late afternoon on Tuesday, he heard rummaging noises in her suite, then spied a small unmarked white van parked out front. An hour later, he peeked through the shutters again and saw a man and woman, young, hip-looking, piling cardboard boxes into the van, then driving off. What was that about? No sign of Svetlana or her Miata.

And then there was Christie Montieth. Twice Lou had spied her out there. Peppery little Christie, journalist, opinionated blogger, digger — he knew her from shared press briefings. Both times, she had parked her Mini Cooper and knocked loudly on the locked door to Svetlana's flat, shouting, "I only need to talk to you for a few minutes." Both times, she'd been met with silence and retreated to her car.

What the hell was she up to? Had she somehow got a whiff of scandal? A leak about a certain high minister of state? Whatever, it unnerved him.

Infinitely more alarming was the black Lincoln SUV he'd seen driving slowly past. Four times, twice yesterday. He assumed they were hoping to catch him arriving or leaving home. That was their preferred tactic of attrition. The same theme, the same piece of work that got his kids' snowman beheaded in his former front yard. And last Sunday, a similar drill in Laval, probably the same goombahs in the SUV, riddling Nick Giusti as he was returning home from ten a.m. mass at Holy Rosary.

That event was lavishly reported on, all over the Internet, though no one seemed to give a shit about some crooked mouthpiece getting whacked. No one but Lou. It's why Lou had been holed up in this hole for five days, freaking out and starving. Nick Giusti, his uncle-in-law, his informant for Waterfrontgate. Somehow his ex-clients found out — or just guessed — that he'd ratted on them. And now that they'd also figured out where Lou lived, his life wasn't worth a popcorn fart.

There was no point in calling the police for help, especially not Superintendent Malraux, who was pissed at Lou for scuttling their planned bust and refusing to name sources. He would only refer him back to Witless Protection and its smarmy bureaucrat. This had to be the unsafest safe house on the planet. The entire Green Party must know where he lived.

Lou had panicked this afternoon on hearing someone coming up the staircase, shuffling about, finally clanging back down, at which point he found the balls to look out to see Pierette Litvak returning to a waiting car. To top off this dramatic interlude, Svetlana had popped by just then to grab a suitcase. It looked like she was about to do a Houdini.

Sorry, Ms. Blake, I wish I could have been of more help in exposing that bad, bad boy. Have a good trip, Svetlana. Live large in Mexico or Greece or wherever you're going. Robert O'Brien is hitting the road too.

Once again, he added up his resources. Celeste had cleaned out the joint account, but the severance pay, thirty-two K, was in his chequing account, untouched, accessible online. A similar amount due again in six months, if his boss didn't welsh. He'd paid his internet fees six months in advance, was still below his Amex limit, and he had half a grand in his wallet, enough for essentials, including the bus to Rouyn-Noranda.

He'd already loaded up a suitcase and a pack. After dark, he'd creep down the back fire escape.

He dumped the last of his Cheerios into a bowl and ate them dry.

§

Two days later, Sunday, Lou was in a stuffy, forty-buck hotel room in the gut end of Rouyn-Noranda. This hardrock mining town was looking a little scruffy, maybe copper prices were down, but it was living up to its reputation for weekend barroom brawls. The rumpus last night in the tavern below had been punctuated with shouted obscenities — "*Viande à chien! Maudite marde!*" — and when it spilled onto the street, the cops broke it up, hauling off the instigators.

None of which was conducive to sleep, despite his exhausting journey here: all day Saturday on a bus that stopped at every jerk-water filling station on the long, lonely highway north, finally pulling in at midnight. Now it was after ten as he dragged himself off a lumpy mattress, the street outside his window looking empty, dead, hungover. A bright, harsh sun.

Hunger was gnawing at him — he'd hardly eaten yesterday — and he felt grimy. He braved the shower, whose lukewarm water smelled of leached minerals, probably cancer-causing. A shampoo, a shave, a swipe of Mennen, a clean shirt and jeans. The tweed cap that Celeste had bought for him because it was so cute, back in the days when she loved him.

He powered up his phone, checked it for missed texts and calls. Nothing recent, just a couple of saved ones, urgent pleas from Margaret Blake and Pierette Litvak. Lou felt bad about not going through with the deal, but they'd get over it, life goes on. Lou's life, in particular. Hard to swim in cement shoes.

He thought of calling Celeste, wondering if she might accidentally pick up this time. *Hi, honey, I'm here in Rouyn-Noranda.* It was twenty minutes by foot to her folks' big lakeside split-level, where he and Celeste had taken family holidays. Where she was surely hiding out with the kids.

Better to catch her off guard. Maybe find Lisa and Logan romping on the front lawn, playing with their grandparents' puppy, Gruffy. They would run into his arms, a joyous, huggy reunion. Celeste, witnessing this adorable scene, would melt, and run tearfully into his arms.

§

But his fantasy of finding the kids in the front yard was not fulfilled. He'd convinced himself that Celeste's Ford Caravan would be there, but there was no sign of it. He found a path to the lakeshore, hoping to find Lisa and Logan there, maybe skipping stones, but his reconnaissance revealed only one life form: Gruffy, no longer a playful puppy but a brute, who raced toward him, barking loudly, summoning his equally bad-tempered owner, Simon, out onto his back deck.

By which time Lou was standing hip-deep in the water, fending off Gruffy, splashing him, calling, "Good dog, good dog." Then "*bon chien*," in case he wasn't as bilingual as his owners.

Simon called Gruffy off and put him on a leash while Lou limped red-faced and soaked onto the stony beach. Janine appeared too, holding a dishcloth, looking puzzled. A petite and pleasant woman married to a bear.

"She ain't here," Simon called. "You want me to write that in blood on my forehead? She ain't coming back, you twerp. Get a life. Go back to your safe house."

"Simon! Manners!" Janine threatened to slap him with the dishcloth. "Oh, Lou, you poor creature. You come in and we'll get you dried off and into a change of clothes."

Lou slogged forlornly up to the deck, fishing out his wet wallet, shaking drops from his iPhone. He didn't try to make friends with Gruffy, who was stiff-tailed, looking confused: why hadn't his master given orders to kill?

"I'll bet you haven't eaten," said Janine.

"Not much," Lou said woefully.

Simon groaned. "Yeah, stalking is hard work, I guess. Fires up the appetite."

Lou mumbled, "Can't stalk a missing family, Simon." He kicked off his shoes. A towel appeared. "She just blithely kidnapped those kids. *My* kids." Flaring a little. "I could get a court order. She's with her sister, isn't she?" Lucille, in Calgary, she'd married a consulting engineer, geophysics or something.

"Just give her some time, Lou," Janine said. "I'm sure everything will be all right. We'll throw those in the dryer." She passed him a robe, turned away as he stripped.

Simon wouldn't let up. "We're going to entertain a guy who's got an X on his forehead? Wasn't it your brother-in-law got bumped off by the mob? A scumbag lawyer — you got an upstanding family. The Mafia better not know you're here, Lou."

"Robert. Robert O'Brien. I even have a passport."

On his way to the bathroom he overheard Simon in French, saying, "Now you know why I never gave my blessing. She was too far ahead of him in the brain department."

"Now, dear, be nice."

§

By early afternoon, Lou was on the town's western outskirts, bound for Ontario and beyond. The next bus west wasn't till the evening. He had his thumb out.

He figured if he could make it to Sudbury, he could catch the train. Though that would cost him the best part of what he had left in his wallet. He'd have to scrimp until he found a Laurentian branch so he could access his severance pay.

Three more cars and a pickup passed. None slowed.

Calgary, that's where Celeste had to be hiding out. He'd read it from Janine's face, Simon's silence. A well-to-do neighbourhood called Upper Mount Royal, unless her sister's family had moved.

Two more vehicles. One driver at least waved apologetically.

For the sixth time in the last six days, he went online on his phone — undamaged by the waters of Lac Osisko — seeking comfort from the thirty-two K in his chequing account.

He frowned. Something was phenomenally wrong. The balance was zero. He logged out, logged back in. Still zero! Surely an error, a banking error, a computer error. Panicking, he scrolled through recent transactions. One stood out: yesterday, a $32,000 electronic transfer to one Charles Bandolino, a name unknown to Lou, from the Laurentian Bank, Montreal, Lou's branch. His password had been hacked. They couldn't rub him out so they'd robbed him blind.

He lay down on a patch of grass and wept.

HORNY IN SEATTLE

The American Trial Lawyers' Association had offered Arthur Beauchamp, as its wind-up dinner speaker, three nights in Seattle's grand old Olympic hotel, and on this Thursday mid-June evening he was feeling fairly full of himself, having earned a standing ovation for his treasury of courtroom anecdotes. He'd spent the next hour signing copies of *A Thirst for Justice*.

And now he was lounging deep in his suite's jet bath, massaging a kink in his neck, his legs splayed, bubbles rising between them, tickling his balls.

He was enduring one of his infrequent visits from Pan. The stirring in his groin had been induced by an enticing appellate counsel from Austin and her invitation to see her to her room. He'd got that far, then panicked, retreating with a mumbled excuse about catching an early flight.

Which was not true. He would be having breakfast with another of the conference's guest speakers, Francisco Sierra, the acclaimed private investigator, now retired in Victoria. Arthur had worked with him on a few trials, and they'd developed an easy friendship.

Helping body and soul to relax was the lack of unsettling news from Ottawa. Two and a half weeks had passed since Margaret's breathless, gossipy faux pas, and there'd been not a whisper from Christie Montieth. Seventeen days was a long time in the world of media. Crisis over. Probably.

Parliament was well into summer recess, but Margaret wouldn't be coming home until the end of the month. She was campaigning in the East, shoring up support, raising funds for an expected fall election. He ached to have her by him, close, touching.

Arthur felt guilty about saddling his two Woofers with managing the farm for most of a week. But he'd needed a holiday from laid-back Garibaldi with its Transformers and flaky Californians and twitchy cops and his faithless mechanic, Robert Stonewell.

He never ought to have left the Fargo with him. That was three weeks ago. Stoney had spent those weeks busily dragging his feet over a simple muffler job while answering multiple handyman demands from Starkers Cove. While Arthur went about by foot or tractor. Stoney had promised the truck would be waiting for him at the ferry landing tomorrow. Fat chance.

So, Arthur felt relieved to get away to civilization in this culture-conscious metropolis by the sail-speckled waters of Puget Sound. He had taken in a chamber concert, a competent production of *All's Well*, and had visited museums and galleries.

He was ashamed that he'd entertained a brief fantasy of a rollick with the slightly tiddly appellate counsel from Austin. That simply wasn't like Arthur. He had an allergy to adultery.

He suspected, shamefully, that performance anxiety had also been behind his panicked withdrawal. During his rare spells of horniness, he was rarely guaranteed a stiff erection.

Yet now, in the soapy froth of his Jacuzzi, here was his cock proudly standing at attention. What a waste.

§

Arthur met Francisco Sierra at the hotel's front entrance, where they shook hands — hugging might be the Latin way but it was not Sierra's way. Raised by upper-class Costa Ricans, he was reserved in manner and impeccably dressed in suit and tie whatever the occasion. Short and portly and balding, he easily melded into an urban crowd.

Until he retired, Frank Sierra had maintained an office in Vancouver, but they hadn't connected for a few years. Nor had they been able to spend much time together at the conference, so they caught up on each other's recent doings while strolling to a restaurant a few blocks away, a faux-1950s diner festooned with photos of old Seattle.

In a booth, over coffees, Arthur gave him a detailed rundown of the Farquist saga, concluding with an account of Margaret's futile attempt to track down Sabatino. "He has utterly disappeared. With or without what may be the only extant copy of the video."

Their omelettes arrived. Sierra studied a 1920s photo of the Pike Place market for several moments, before returning Arthur's imploring gaze. "You are telling me this for a reason, my friend. It is not to titillate me, though I must say the matter is singularly bizarre. But the answer, with heartfelt regrets, is no. I am too occupied growing roses in the garden of a cozy bungalow near Beacon Hill Park, where I regularly walk my beagle, Bolivar." The hint of a Spanish accent added a charming timbre to his perfect diction.

"Frank, it's a private eye's wet dream."

Sierra seemed shocked. He had the prudishness of English gentry.

Arthur pressed on. "A missing video and a missing reporter, possibly dead. Scandalous behaviour in the highest councils of our land. A dominatrix bribed to be silent."

"I am especially enjoying the sunny blooms of my miniature polyanthas, which seem born to our West Coast climate. Let us eat. I am famished." He tucked into his omelette.

"And I can throw in a damsel in distress. My wife."

Sierra had been a guest at Blunder Bay and knew Margaret well. "But it appears she is not distressed. She remains unscathed, *gracias a Dios*."

Arthur nibbled his meal, depressed that this astute investigator was not seeing this case as the crowning event of his career.

"How grows *your* garden, Arthur?"

"Much neglected."

"Perhaps because you are too often drawn away from it. Each year since your purported retirement — when was that? a decade ago? — you have defended some dastardly villain. You do not know how to retire. I do."

"Matters got in the way, Frank. But you'll be fascinated to know that I was re-invigorated every time I walked into a courtroom. There was a feeling of being fully alive again. At our age, with our wisdom and experience, our skills are at their apogee. What a shame not to use them."

"I recommend the Puhl Agency. Sam Puhl. Top notch. They're in Ottawa, and know their territory."

"All disbursements would be covered. Airfare, hotels, a car. A reasonable daily fee. My office has a slush fund for such adventures." Scandal leading to the fall of the Conservatives would be much appreciated by Tragger, Inglis, a Liberal firm. Old Bullingham, the skinty senior partner, might have a word to say about this one, though.

Sierra dabbed his lips with his napkin. "A little weak on the mushrooms, that omelette."

Arthur pulled out his wallet.

"No, I must insist." Sierra's wallet was out too, a credit card already plucked from it.

"It was I who invited you for breakfast."

Sierra signalled the waiter with his card. "Come, come, Arthur. This is negligible recompense for the enjoyment of your company. I'm sorry to have disappointed you, but . . . alas."

Arthur let him pick up the bill. "I understand. A rose is a rose is a rose."

"Exactly."

§

There were pigs rooting in his garden and emus eating his beans and lettuce, and he could only watch: helpless, sluggish, voiceless, tangled in sheets and blankets. The neighbours watched too: ghosts, immobile, expressionless, waiting for their orders. Overcome with loneliness, Arthur reached out to Margaret, but she too was without substance, another ghost, lost to him.

Prompted by the need to pee, Arthur awakened to sunshine streaming through his bedroom window. His visit to Starkers Cove had stayed with him, so the dream seemed self-explanatory. Except for the part about Margaret — he missed her, that's all it was saying. He wanted her. Physically. He was still, uncharacteristically, in heat.

It was Saturday, and he had just returned from Seattle. He'd been shocked, on walking off the ferry, to find his Fargo waiting for him. The keys were in an ashtray along with a roach clip and some loose pot. A peek under the chassis revealed a new muffler. He could only assume Stoney had had a crisis of conscience.

He disentangled himself from the sheets and looked out to make sure there were no pigs or emus in his garden. The only encroachers were thistles and creeping buttercups, and horsetails in the strawberries. No sign of Niko and Yoki, who had promised to help weed that garden. There, parked out front, was his Fargo. He was not imagining it. He had actually driven it here yesterday.

He checked his bedside clock. Nearly ten! A rare long sleep. He had a misty recall of being invited to a major event tomorrow, Sunday, June 23. A function he wasn't looking forward to, that he'd intended to shun. Yes, an open house at Starkers Cove. A chance to meet and commune with the great Baba Sri Rameesh. Music. Fun, frolic, free food and refreshments. Their famous gupa.

Arthur would be tending his garden all Sunday. Enjoying real peace. Not the artificial kind that the dreaded happiness drug delivers. He wondered if gupa was the key to Silverson's control over innocent minds. Reverend Al, though, had claimed to have tried it without effect — it was all in the mind. Al preferred to believe that Silverson, with his certificate in "humanistic hypnotherapy," was utilizing some form of post-hypnotic suggestion on his adherents.

Arthur took a luxurious sit-down pee — *this* was happiness — and was pulling up his pyjama bottoms when he heard an engine, tires crunching on gravel. From the window, he saw the Transformers' Econoline van rolling down the driveway to the Woofer house. Niko and Yoki came out the front door, carrying buckets of what looked like cleaning supplies.

This smacked of a kidnapping, the girls enticed in some unearthly way into a state of mindlessness. Still in pyjamas, Arthur found his slippers, scrambled downstairs, and raced outside to see the two Woofers being ushered into the van by Morg Baumgarten and a starry-eyed woman acolyte armed with one of the Transformers' ubiquitous video cameras.

Waving, hollering, he clambered over a snake fence to the Woofers' yard, losing a slipper in his haste.

He gasped: "What . . . what's all this, where are you going?"

"Help cleaning dining hall," Yoki said with a bright smile, pointing to the buckets. "Open house tomorrow. Meet the Baba. Everyone come. You come. No problem."

"We very happy give help," said Niko. "Also serve refresherments . . . drinks at open house."

Arthur suspected his very happy helpful Woofers had already been into the gupa. He'd been gone four days, and already Silverson had sucked them into his maw.

Morg, with his distant stare: "It's a long way for them to walk, Mr. Beauchamp."

"Just a second here," Arthur said. "How many times have you girls been to Starkers Cove?"

"Three," Yoki said. "Always do chores first."

"We every time hitchhike," said Niko. "Very easy. Everyone happy."

"No problem," said Yoki, her favourite phrase for practically everything. "Come back by five o'clock, weed garden."

"I'll bring these ladies back, Mr. Beauchamp." Morg looked as zombie-ish as ever when he smiled.

The young women appeared embarrassed, averting their eyes from the foolish old man standing there in his pyjamas. Well, he wasn't their father. They were of age. They'd come to North America to explore Western culture. Let them.

"Please, you come tomorrow, Arthur," Niko said.

"I doubt I will."

"Just do it," Yoki called, as the van drove off. "No problem."

Arthur went looking for his slipper.

§

After dressing and arming himself with coffee, he checked Margaret's schedule, a computer printout on his desk by the phone. June 22: Antigonish, Nova Scotia. A speech at a social this evening. It would be mid-afternoon there. She would be hitting the bricks with her candidate. He dialled her cell.

"Hang on a sec," she said, then addressed someone else, sharply. "No, Mr. Wiggins, I *do* believe evolution should be taught in the schools. It was nice meeting you."

The sound of a door closing. "Asshole," Margaret muttered.

"Exactly why I would rather eat razor blades than go door to door."

"He believes God made everything, especially himself, in God's image. That's Teresa laughing. She's on the school board." She called, "I thought you knew this neighbourhood."

Arthur apologized for interrupting her campaign and told her about the crisis, the transforming of their two young charges. "I've got to rescue them."

Margaret laughed it off. "Cool. They're having fun. I'd like to meet Baba Sri Rameesh myself."

"Please don't joke. I can't return them to their Hokkaido parents as zombies. The international Woofer program would come under attack. I have to snatch those innocents away before they get immersed."

"Darling, you sound very harried. Have you not been feeling well?"

Arthur hadn't yet related his suspicions of having been drugged into states of euphoria. He was embarrassed by those events, by how she might see them as evidence of creeping senescence.

"I am sharp enough of mind to know that Silverson is up to no good. Fleecing well-to-do Californians, that's my bet."

"Yes, and while that is going on, the environment ministry is gagging its scientists. Farquist just had two of them fired for whistle-blowing. And the fix is in on the Coast Mountains Pipeline, I think they're planning to bypass Parliament."

Arthur got it. The Transformation Mission was a trivial pursuit.

"Still no blowback?" Code for repercussions from the hot-mike episode.

"Nothing. Did you talk to Frank Sierra?"

"He declined, I'm afraid. Prefers to grow roses."

"Too bad. Back to work. Love you."

SUCH SIGHTS AS YOUTHFUL POETS DREAM

Arthur had washed the Fargo that afternoon, proud of it, proud to have the oldest working truck on the island, and was pleased to see eyes turn as he slid it into a slot in front of the general store.

He'd planned a major supply run, but on entering the store was dismayed to find its shelves and bins almost empty. No bread, no oranges, barely any juice. Presumably the Transformers had looted the store for their party tomorrow. Fine. He could do without his regular morning toast and juice. He had a flourishing garden, a bounty of eggs and goat cheese.

He found better luck in the hardware section, the screws and hinges he needed for a broken gate. He carried on to the checkout, where he bought a newspaper, and to the mail counter, where Nelson Forbish was trying to mollify steely-faced Abraham Makepeace.

"I wasn't in a good mood last week, because you rode me pretty hard. I have struggled with that and achieved calm and forgiveness. I respect you, Abraham. I love you, as I love all living beings."

Makepeace ignored him, went to the Blunder Bay box, crammed with a week's mail, and began the slow process of sorting it.

"Postcard from Deborah." Arthur's daughter in Australia. "Looks like she's getting along with that new husband of hers. They're on holiday . . . I can't make it out . . . Papua something."

Forbish was standing his ground, leaving Arthur little counter space. "I ask you to search your heart, Abraham, and heal the bitterness. Please don't cut off my mailing privileges. Tell him, Arthur, explain that's against the law."

"So is libel." Makepeace passed Arthur last week's *Bleat*, with a front-page spread about the Transformation Mission and a back-page ad for their open house, promising "peace and oneness and coming together," along with "free eats, free drinks, and fried minds." The *fried* was one of Forbish's typically grievous typos. Freed minds?

Arthur turned to the "Who's Who on Garibaldi" column. The final item counselled the island's postmaster to "start thinking seriously about retirement given the recent snippy attitude he has shown yours truly and many others."

"I'm printing a correction for this week," Forbish said, "along with a profile saying our postmaster has served relentlessly for two decades. And a photo." He brandished a camera.

Makepeace turned his back to him and showed the camera his scrawny rear end. That freed up Arthur's mound of mail, which he scooped up and stuck in his pack. Next stop would be the Brig for his afternoon tea. He took the elevated walkway, pausing to enjoy the ocean view, checking out the scene on the patio.

Cudworth Brown was passing pints to a tableful of cronies, grateful disciples today because he was buying. One of Canada's lesser-known poets, the muscular one-time ironworker subsisted mostly on grants and readings and hand-selling his three slim published works. Arthur assumed they'd found a niche market with their recurrent themes of carnality and bodily functions, because Cud had been offered an advance for his fourth. It must have come in.

Cudworth was half pickled, going on loudly about the open

house. "Free eats, free drinks, and bet your ass there'll be free drugs. That dude Jason will naturally want to dip into his jar of Upper Shelf and chop a few lines to share with his literary and artistic colleagues."

"Free drugs, man," said Honk Gilmore, a retired marijuana broker.

"Fried minds," yelled the wild-haired sculptor, Hamish McCoy, to raucous laughter.

"Free love, baby." Cud chased a shot of whisky with a beer. "Not just of the spiritual variety. We expect better than that from the king stud at Starkers Cove."

Arthur heard a note of sarcasm, or maybe envy. Cud was known to have bedded a multitude of local women and likely resented being relegated to second stud behind the blond bombshell.

"Speaking of scoring some free love," said Honk, "how about those three hipster chicks from Pasadena that dropped in here last night? Drove off the ferry in a top-down Mercedes Cabriolet that's got to price out at eighty K all in."

"Youthful adventurers with rich daddies," said Cud. "Seekers of light and truth who will find it totally awesome to invite a famous poet into their tent. Gonna be hard to protect my virginity." He raised his glass. "To peace and oneness, baby, and coming together."

Arthur skirted around them, to the bar, where Taba Jones was sitting, in shorts and well-filled T-shirt. The flame-haired potter had been spending a lot of time in the pub since Felicity took up with the Transformers. She was chatting with Emily LeMay. A closed conversation, Arthur felt, womanly things or gossip. He sat at a table with a view of the parking area and the dock and opened his newspaper, yesterday's *Globe*.

The front page was depressing, Zika virus everywhere, the Middle East at constant war, another oil spill in Hecate Strait. Arthur fled to the staid inside pages, the political coverage. The main story: an uproar over Farquist's firing of scientists critical of the Coast Mountains Pipeline. Margaret earned a paragraph, calling him a "tinpot dictator kowtowing to his corporate masters."

Lower down, another mention of Margaret, under the head, "Star Candidate Runs for Greens," quoting Margaret as being ecstatic about her catch: Dr. Lloyd Chalmers, who would be seeking the seat of Halifax East, in his city of birth.

Margaret had introduced the "well-known psychologist and author" at a rally there. On Thursday, two nights ago. Arthur didn't recall her mentioning that during their conversation earlier today. This had become a pattern, the not-mentioning of encounters with Chalmers.

As Emily approached with his tea, he folded the paper quickly to the crossword puzzle, as if hiding embarrassment or shame. He decided on shame. Cuckolded once again, the central theme of his life. Alternatively, another kind of shame could be his lot: unwarranted suspicion, jealousy falsely held. He hunched over the puzzle.

"Mind if I join you?" Taba had already done so, startling him as she sat down. She saluted him with her four o'clock regular, a gin and tonic, a refill. "You look woebegone, Arthur. Raccoon get into your garden?"

She offered a welcome distraction from thoughts of the Green leader's ecstasy over her star candidate.

"I was pondering a nine-letter word for 'self-abuse.'"

"The word masturbation comes immediately to mind."

"Twelve letters."

"Try masochism."

"It fits." Albeit in an unnerving, ironic way. The conversation had taken on an earthy edge that had Arthur feeling awkward, fumbling for words. "I don't see your truck out there, Taba."

"I hitched, out of necessity." She indicated the several rolls of toilet paper protruding from her pack. "Or else I'd be wiping my ass with this week's *Bleat*. Did you read that sycophantic twaddle? About Forbish receiving all those 'powerful vibrations of love'? Praising their 'latter-day prophet'? They must have spiked his nacho chips with powdered gupa. You're not going to their circle jerk tomorrow?"

"I would rather jump naked and bleeding into a tank of piranhas. What happened to your old GM pickup?"

"Won't start. I think it had a heart attack."

"A perfect opportunity to return your generosity. My chariot is ready . . . Voila." He pointed down to the washed and shiny Fargo. "Delivered as promised, to my astonishment. I wonder if the Transformers got to Stoney."

"He's too good at shit-detecting to buy their goop. A scammer knows a scammer." She was still turned to the window. "Oh my God, there he is."

Gliding toward the parking area came the Mercedes Cabriolet, the top down, two of the Pasadena hipsters in the back, the third beside the driver, Robert Stonewell. As it nestled beside the Fargo, he passed a roach on a clip to his seatmate, a slender black woman with a burst of untamed hair and a very mini mini.

"Scammed himself right into their hearts with his homegrown Garibaldi gold," Taba said.

Her laughter was contagious and helped Arthur overcome his shock that Stoney had maneuvered himself into the driver's seat of this sleek, expensive machine. The car had been a powerful magnet, the pretty girls a bonus, and his prime bud had likely earned him the job of tour guide.

The two women in the back — a sultry East Asian in tight shorts and a leggy Caucasian stunner with orange hair and patched cut-offs — demonstrated their fitness by vaulting over the sides of the convertible. They paused awhile, their cameras on video, panning the bay, the dock, and the old store. Daughters of wealth for sure, unless they'd stolen that Mercedes.

"God, they make me feel so old and plain," said Taba.

"Nonsense. You are quite lovely." He gulped his tea, flustered, the compliment too bold.

"You need glasses."

He considered assuring her she also had a wisdom and maturity those kittens were decades from attaining. But again he couldn't get the words out.

"Emily told me they were here last night doing tequila shooters. Becky, Gelaine, and Xantha, with an X. Starlets, though you could mistake them for hookers. Anyway, Emily got out of them that they drove the convertible up here for Silverson. I guess he got tired of pretending he was just a laid-back average Joe with an Econoline van."

Arthur liked Taba's wit and cynicism. He enjoyed sharing their contempt for Silverson and speculating about his game. He'd needed a friend to banter with, a distraction from the green-eyed monster and his worries about Margaret's gossipy indescretion.

The two camera-toting starlets came into the bar from the store, placed an order with Emily, then headed toward the patio, pausing close enough for Arthur to hear the orange-haired woman say, "Those crackers look like leftovers from a horror-flick audition."

They were staring at Cud Brown's table. The men seemed struck dumb, gaping as the two women strolled past them and leaned over the sturdy railing, looking directly down to the frothing little inlet below, its orange and purple starfish clinging to the rocks. More aiming of cameras.

A glance outside revealed Stoney and his wild-haired friend strolling toward the dock, Stoney chattering nonstop on a cannabis high, she laughing, taking his arm.

Starlets. Presumably, Silverson still had connections in the film industry. These young women showed no signs of having yet succumbed to the thousand-mile stare. Indeed, they hardly seemed Transformer material. They would probably be a little less lively after their first taste of gupa.

"The good stuff," Emily whispered as she went past their table with a bottle of champagne in a bucket.

Cud was already pulling from his jacket pocket one of his poetry books, a well-used tool of seduction. He rose and moved toward the starlets' table. One of them, the orange-top, began to film his advance.

That put him off stride, and he paused to pull in his gut. Forced to depart from his game plan, he improvised, grinning in a loopy way at the camera and announcing in a booming voice: "Cudworth Brown, your friendly neighbourhood prize-winning poet, at your service, ladies." He bowed deeply, staggered, and almost went over the empty chair in front of him.

The starlets moved the champagne flutes to safety, on top of the railing. Xantha was the Chinese-American. He'd overheard the other called Becky.

"Sorry, gals, but you caught me celebrating. Just got a handsome advance from my publisher." Cud displayed his copy of his latest vulgarity, a collection called *Cunnilinguistics*, then produced a pen. "Got to warn you, these are for the mature mind. For the full erotic effect, I'd need to read them aloud — don't be shy about asking. Now how do you want me to sign this?"

"With your dick," said Xantha.

§

Taba's two gin-and-tonics had made her a bit unsteady, and she took Arthur's arm as they descended to his truck. On reaching level ground, she tugged that arm around her waist, and pulled him into a hug, her elegant breasts pressed to his ribs.

Arthur found his pulse quickening, and felt embarrassed and guilty. The embrace was far too pleasurable, fraught with risk. He hoped she wasn't coming on to him — he wouldn't know how to handle that.

He looked up to the patio to see Becky filming them, and Taba noticed too and quickly pulled away. On the other side of the patio, staring gloomily into space, was Cud Brown, back with his cronies — who had been ribbing him when Arthur was paying his bill and, despite her protest, Taba's.

She was also looking at Cud. "Such a cliché, the poet as obscene drunk. Contrary to local legend, he's the world's worst lover."

Arthur didn't care to speculate on how she knew that. Becky's camera was now on Stoney and the black woman, Gelaine, who was pulling on leggings by the open trunk of the Mercedes. Stoney seemed torn between ogling her and her car. She in turn was admiring the Fargo.

"Yo, Canuck, I love your truck," she said, after peering into the cab. "Authentically cool."

Stoney didn't miss a beat. "All scrubbed up and ready for you, gorgeous."

"Wait," Taba said, clinging to Arthur's arm, restraining him from racing to his truck's rescue. "They haven't seen us." She led Arthur to a bench behind Makepeace's delivery truck, out of view but within earshot.

He didn't want to spoil Taba's fun, but wasn't able to relax until he fished into a pocket and found the Fargo's ignition key, which he displayed to her triumphantly. It usually stayed with the truck but Arthur had removed it. Here was a rare opportunity to enjoy Stoney's misfortune.

Stoney had been rhapsodizing about the pickup, the most prized of his many vintage vehicles, and now was holding open the passenger door. "Front seat of an old bone-shaker like this is the only way to see the real Garibaldi. I know all the secret coves, I got stash beaches, stash lakes, waterfalls. I got one special place only God and Bob Stonewell's ever been to. Half an hour there and back."

"Well, let's fucking go." Gelaine shouted up to her friends. "I'll be back in half."

Stoney gave her a hand up, then went to the driver's side. Arthur fought his Pavlovian response to rescue the Fargo, tightened his grip on his key. Stoney got behind the wheel, then softly voiced what sounded like a profanity.

Arthur expected to see him scrambling around for a hidden key and was shocked to hear a familiar sound, usually pleasant to his ears: the rich rumble of the Fargo starting up. Either Stoney had a spare key or it had taken him ten seconds to hot-wire the ignition. By the time Arthur launched himself from the bench, the Fargo had backed out and moved onto the road.

From the patio, Becky filmed the Fargo as it accelerated away, then turned her camera on Arthur as he ran onto the road, shouting and waving, then ceasing his useless pursuit, out of breath.

§

Arthur had his own stash of hideaways, and the one to which he was escorting Taba was on East Point Ridge above Hopeless Bay, a stiff twenty-minute climb — they'd left their packs at the store — which paid off with views of meadow, forest, and rocky shores; the green islets and sparkling sea beyond; and, Arthur hoped, of Stoney driving the purloined Fargo. The path was little more than a deer trail, and he'd had to assist Taba over fallen logs and a root mass.

Throughout the climb, Taba politely endured Arthur's complaints about Stoney and his rustling of the truck. She merely chuckled over it, urging him to relax: it wasn't the end of the world, he'd be back, *carpe diem*.

The climb brought them at last to a mossy knoll with a full-compass view, but no sign of the Fargo.

"Stunning," said Taba. "Thank you." She startled him by rising on her toes to plant a quick, soft kiss on his lips, then spread her arms to the horizon, the distant Olympic Mountains, her cropped hair flaming even redder in the sun. "I have arrived," she shouted. Her announcement echoed back. "I am nowhere!" No-where, no-where, the hills replied.

"How does one arrive nowhere?"

She turned to him. "Because when you realize there is nowhere to go, you have arrived. Though you're still nowhere."

She was mocking the slogan above the Transformers' gate. Arthur had to laugh.

"So, do you come here a lot?" she asked.

"As often as I can."

"Always alone?"

"'In solitude, where we are least alone.' Byron. Sorry, yes, quite alone."

"Until now."

"Yes." Arthur wasn't sure what the rules were here, alone on a hilltop with this saucy single mom. He hoped matters would not go too far. But he could still feel the softness of her lips from that quick kiss, and felt confused, conflicted.

They settled on a carpet of moss under a giant arbutus with its reddish papery bark, its trunk and branches snaking skyward above them, a complex, colourful canopy.

"This is softer than my mattress," Taba said, lying back.

There was a strong essence of invitation wafting from her, red hair splayed on the moss, legs slightly parted, arms behind her neck.

He dismissed the carnal urge this prompted. He was having a testosterone issue, that was all. He was still suffering the spell of horniness prompted by the tiddly Austin litigator. He was a married man. He believed in his vows, even if someone else didn't. Fortifying his resolve was the spectre of performance anxiety, always hovering, chiding him. You can't get it up, Arthur. Don't even try.

Quite right. Taba will be only a friend, a willing ear, a confidante. A female buddy with whom he could share misgivings about the Transformers. Maybe about his life companion and her star candidate. But that would be too confessional, too self-pitying.

The silence was uncomfortable, so, lacking anything original, he offered Lowell's hoary rhetorical question: "'What is so rare as a day in June?'"

Taba moved to a sunnier spot, several feet away, and sat, her back to him. "How does the rest of that go?" She pulled her T-shirt over her head, undid her bra, and lay on her back again.

He tried. "'Then, if ever, come perfect days . . .'" The rest was a blank. Hypnotized by those two bared mounds, he could only fumble for words. "I forget. I can do better." He struggled to untie his tongue before racing through a line from a favourite Keats sonnet. "'To one who has been long in city pent, 'tis very sweet to look into the fair and open face of heaven.'"

"What else have you got?"

Arthur had never forgotten the lines that moved him as a student of the classics, and he couldn't resist showing off. He recited Milton's "L'Allegro": *Such sights as youthful poets dream, on summer eves by haunted stream.*

He got through it with only a few mental typos, and by the end of it had given up pretending not to see her, pretending not to feel aroused. "Not bad. I wrote a paper on it when I was nineteen."

"Not *bad*?" She was looking at him raptly.

A distant engine hum. Arthur stood up and saw the Fargo below, on its return journey.

"Come here, Arthur."

"That's my truck."

"Come down here with me."

He took a hesitant step toward her, and she sat up and took his hand and pulled him down, easing him onto his back.

"In case you think my interest is only platonic, it's not." She rolled on top of him and kissed him with open mouth and tongue. He answered, and felt a rush of unalloyed pleasure as his hands found her breasts, her engorged nipples. He was shocked and thrilled to feel an erection building, a message she was receiving, her body answering.

When she sat up, his hands rose with her, continuing to heft her breasts while hers unsnapped his belt and reached under his shorts and found his thick, engorged cock.

Clothing was cast aside, boots, socks, and underwear. All shyness was dismissed, all resolve forgotten, and quickly he was on top and entering her with deep, hungry thrusts. He was amazed and proud that he so quickly found completion, and his exultant shout echoed off the hills.

PENNILESS IN PORCUPINE PLAIN

The hitchhiking had been beyond crappy, especially across the sparseness of Northern Ontario, all rock and lake and forest extending to infinity, and Lou had to resort to long, slow hops by bus, staying in cheap motels in scraggy, scrubby, nothing-happening towns on the old Trans-Canada highway, his wallet getting ever thinner.

It took him almost two weeks to get to Winnipeg, and by then his Amex was over the limit and he was down to flophouses and the Sally Ann. In Regina, he was rousted by the cops after trying to nap under a tree in Wascana Park.

Meanwhile, he was still battling his bank, long-distance on his phone, which was quickly running out of minutes, to recover the thirty-two grand stolen by the Mafia imposter Charles Bandolino. Somehow that shithole had hacked his password, password hints, and debit card number. The bank was looking into it. There were papers to be filled out. Affidavits. Please provide a mailing address. No, sir, it can't be done online.

On the first day of summer, he landed in a burg called Porcupine Plain, somewhere, he guessed, in the hilly southwest of Saskatchewan, beyond the endless flatlands that his Greyhound buses had crawled across.

This is where his money ran out. This is where he was totally broke except for $16.55, less the cost of the all-day bacon and eggs that the Quill Café had just fried up for him.

Porcupine Plain was in a valley formed by a meandering creek and surrounded by grain fields spread beneath green hills where cattle grazed. Aside from its pastoral setting, the town had earned the right to be called plain, a main street called Main Street with a dozen storefronts, a paint-peeling two-storey hotel and tavern, a post office, a two-pump garage, a lumberyard, a credit union. A couple of church steeples. A curling rink. The dominant structure a grain elevator.

The Quill seemed the place to be, at least for lunch. All booths were taken, just a few stools available. A real old-fashioned diner, not one of those faux ones in the city, full of grizzled men in suspenders and tractor caps, with a fair number of middle-aged women, likely farmers themselves. Dust on their boots. Lingering over coffee, joking and gossiping, like he'd imagined they did in small towns instead of staring hypnotically at iPhones. Occasionally they looked him over, a nondescript little man with a big suitcase.

He was wishing he'd packed a tent. He had no idea where he was going to sleep tonight, maybe in a cattle pen.

He ate slowly, dipping toast into yolk, relishing each mouthful, his last square meal before he had to resort to the local soup kitchen, if there was one. There were only three jobs up on the community bulletin board outside the bus stop: a skilled mechanic, a licensed pilot for crop-dusting, and an assistant to the local veterinarian.

He wiped his plate clean with the last of his toast and waited for the bill, nursing his coffee, his third refill, eavesdropping on the two men in the booth behind him.

"The screen goes all wonky. And the colours ain't right."

"I heard if you turn it off and on again it resets."

"I tried that twenty times."

"You sure you ain't got a battery issue?"

"Battery's charged, according to the manual. See this here green light?"

"Did you do anything, Oscar?" A woman's voice. "Like spill beer on it when you got plastered the other night?"

"I got three years out of it. Planned obsolescence, that's how them computer companies earn their billions."

Lou looked over his shoulder at the back of the bald head of a man in a rumpled suit. Across from him, staring at an open laptop, a Dell Inspiron, was a guy in a John Deere cap who had to be Oscar, and his cherub-faced wife.

"Let me have a look at it." Lou went into his bag and brought out his repair kit.

§

In the half hour it took to run tests, open up the guts of the laptop, and fiddle away with tiny tweezers and a small soldering iron, Lou had gathered a crowd. Oscar and his wife and his bald friend — who turned out to be the mayor — leaned over him in frowning fascination. A dozen others milled about the counter space that had been cleared for him near an outlet for the soldering iron.

He checked the screen to ensure all colours were true before closing up, saying, "I think that's done it." There was a cheer.

"I got a desktop where the monitor keeps going blank," someone said.

"I can't get mine to boot up half the time," said another.

§

"It's taken us to Arizona a couple of times," said Oscar. "I'll hook up the power and water."

"I'd want to give everything a good dusting, Mr. O'Brien," said Dolores, his wife. They owned an eight-hundred-acre spread down Porcupine Creek, along with a big house, barn, chickens, horses, and this fully equipped house trailer.

"Please don't go to a lot of trouble," Lou said. He looked gratefully about. "Looks like a palace to me."

"The kids use it when they come," Dolores said, "but they pretty well flew the nest. We got two empty bedrooms as well, if you prefer."

"This is just grand."

"Dinner will be ready in an hour. Give you a chance to settle in. Oscar, throw some steaks on the barbie."

"You like to start with a brew?" Oscar said. "I'll put some cold Pils in the cooler."

After they left, Lou unpacked, then stepped outside to take a deep breath of air perfumed by wolf willow and watch the lowering sun paint the hills golden.

NO ONE NEEDS TO KNOW

"I sentence you to life!" cried the judge. A Greek chorus in the jury box called out, "And a hundred lashes!"

Arthur started awake as the rising sun cleared the trees and glared at him through his bedroom window. In the dream that aroused him so rudely from his troubled sleep, he'd been found guilty of adultery in the first degree, adultery planned and deliberate, aggravated by the sin of pride in having achieved chest-thumping virility. The verdict was fair because he *was* guilty. His punishment was the lash of self-flagellation.

He shrugged off the dream and let his mind spin back to the rutting, mindless glory of yesterday's tryst with Taba Jones. Fuelled by too much Milton, Taba had been more the seducer than the seduced. But Arthur had been the eager pushover, aroused, abandoning reserve. Forget the Fargo. Forget Margaret.

He'd done the inconceivable, but with what he suspected, in the mind-clearing brightness of a new day, was a disgraceful motive. Had getting even with Margaret been as much a driving force as lust? A response to the repulsive images he'd endured of Lloyd Chalmers entering her. How sad was that?

He could barely remember the aftermath, its embarrassment and awkwardness, averting his eyes from naked Taba as they fumbled for their clothes, their hurried descent from East Point Ridge. The Fargo was waiting for him; Stoney wasn't. He drove Taba home.

"It was a one-off," she'd said, kissing him goodnight at her doorstep. "No one needs to know."

Arthur had had the good grace to thank her for being so warm and generous and desirable. Both knew why there would be no sequels. Both knew where Arthur's deepest affections lay.

No one needs to know. Certainly not Margaret. Ever.

He should have showered last night; his body smelled of the day's excesses. He hadn't eaten dinner either. His stomach was empty and his bladder full. Before bed, still quivering, he'd made a strong herbal tea to settle his nerves.

He looked out the window and wondered why Niko and Yoki weren't tossing feed to the chickens and stealing their eggs. They were nowhere to be seen. Could they still be at Starkers Cove? He ran downstairs to the phone to check his messages.

Niko: "We having sleepover. No problem." Then Yoki: "Very happy, working hard. Baba Sri Rameesh, he really cool."

Al Noggins would be putting his final touches on his Sunday sermon right about now. St. Mary's would be Arthur's first stop. Al would be enlisted as the deprogrammer.

Arthur showered then gathered up his clothes from yesterday, ruefully observing the semen dribbles on his Stanfields, and was on his way to the washer when the phone rang. He grabbed the hallway portable and carried on.

"Hi," said Margaret. "Finally."

Arthur cleared his clogged throat. "Did you call earlier?"

"Yeah. Where were you yesterday?"

Arthur gulped back the impulse to blurt the truth. His free hand was having trouble releasing his underwear into the top-loader, a kind of paralysis.

"When are you going to remember you have a cellphone? Oh, never mind. Arthur, there's been a palace revolt in the Liberal caucus. The Drone was overthrown. He's resigned. Their caucus picked Marcus Yates as interim leader. Fresh, young, gorgeous, hip, athletic, outdoorsy — but a former prominent pothead, if he isn't still one. Risky choice, but there you go."

"My goodness." That was all Arthur could manage.

"Anyway, they've agreed to join in bringing down the government. That came after the PM withdrew the Coast Mountains bill. They're approving it by cabinet order. October election."

Arthur's stained briefs finally fell into the washing machine, followed by socks, shirt, and moss-stained pants. He took a breath. "And, uh, how are you feeling about that?"

"Well, good. Obviously. Get this country back on track. Okay, I'm in Fredericton now, heading back to Ottawa for a strategy session. I have a couple of pit stops up north on my way back home for the Canada Day weekend. I'll have to attend a few events, but I won't force you to . . . I, um . . ." Her voice trailed off, then returned with an intensity that frightened him. "There's something I need to talk to you about, Arthur." A silence. "Are you still there?"

"Sorry, I'm just . . . I'm starting a wash."

"Arthur, you may have heard that Lloyd Chalmers is running for us. I spoke at his nomination in Halifax on Thursday. It's been in the papers. I didn't mention it to you, and I feel shitty about that. It's just that . . . how do I say it? You get so hurt when his name comes up, and I've caused you so much pain over what happened . . . I'm babbling."

Arthur listened numbly.

"Nothing has happened between us since then. I've actually been avoiding him, but . . . well, there was the requisite hug in front of the cameras. He's quite the womanizer, really, I honestly don't know why I ever . . . He's turned his attention to Jennie Withers, anyway. They were spotted at a table for two at Le Gourmand. I wouldn't be surprised if they're making out . . . Stop me. Say something."

"I love you," he said weakly.

"I love you too, darling. I do."

§

Only fifteen parishioners had shown up today, average age on the cusp of seventy, and the service was brief. Reverend Al continued to rail outside the church. He was convinced that God was losing the battle for souls on Garibaldi Island. The cult was eating away at the island like cancer. Freeing Arthur's brainwashed Woofers from Silver Tongue's spell would be like wrestling with the devil.

But Al agreed to take on the task, and they were on their way to the open house at Starkers Cove, in their Sunday suits in the Fargo — which, at one point, drifted onto the shoulder, causing Al to cut short his list of grievances. "Do you want me to drive? You seem in some kind of altered state, old boy."

"I'm fine. Distracted." Here was Arthur with his closest friend, his confidant, a man of the cloth, and he could not confess his sin: a shameful act of infidelity prompted by false suspicion, compounded by an inflated sense of achievement. He would be all the more ignoble were he to mention Taba's name. He resolved to bury the matter.

A light drizzle had begun, and he focussed on the road, driving so slowly that a convoy of Garibaldians was backing up behind him. He pulled into the lookout above Starkers Cove to let them pass. Below, scores of cars and trucks were already parked outside the gate.

"That looks like Morg down there," Al said. "Appointed by his master to direct traffic. A simple task for a simple mind."

"Let's see what he says about his promise to bring the girls back."

They carried on, waiting their turn near the former manure pile — its stink still pervaded the area — while Morg waved drivers onto a newly mown field. Dog, the Transformers' eager early convert, was bustling about as assistant parking attendant. It was still drizzling, the western sky grumbling. "Let there be rain," said Reverend Al, his hands together in prayer.

The column of vehicles stalled while a couple of volunteers chased two chickens and a duck that had slipped out the gate. Enjoying the acrobatics of fowl and pursuers, recording them on camera, were the two latter-day hippies who'd arrived in their flower-powered VW van.

Al glowered at the painted sign. "'When you realize there is nowhere to go, you have arrived.' What horseshit. That's when you should be rethinking the purpose of your journey."

"Remember, don't eat, don't drink. I still think I got high from that gupa spill."

Arthur had told him about being transported into that disturbing state of bliss. Al's response hadn't been satisfactory: "They're called mood swings, old boy."

Morg came to Arthur's window, his expression blank. "I have a special place for you, Mr. Beauchamp."

"I expect you have a special place for me too, Morg," Al said.

Morg ignored that, maybe confused, sensing a double entendre but not getting it. "Yoki and Niko wanted to stay, Mr. Beauchamp. They needed to meet the Baba." He called to Dog: "Put them over by the fence there."

He hurried off before Arthur could say a word. Al muttered, "They *needed* to meet the Baba? I want to see this fraud in action."

Dog led them to the VIP parking section, and Arthur pulled in beside the Mercedes Cabriolet, its top up, doors open, and Robert Stonewell inside wielding some rags and leather wax. A plastic bag on the dashboard held several beer caps, butts, roaches, and an empty cigarette pack. Gelaine, Stoney explained, had asked him to get it shipshape for Silverson.

Arthur pocketed the Fargo's new spare key, reluctantly handed over, though experience suggested that was a futile effort. "Ah, yes,

Gelaine." The black hipster with the mat of wild hair. "And how is that relationship working out?" An improbable one.

"I had to dump her. She told me she likes to do it with girls. That just turned me off."

Dog held Al's door for him, offered him some promotional material, and recited what seemed a scripted greeting: "Welcome to the Personal Transformation Mission. Buddha is love."

"Kindly expand on that great thought," said Al.

"I am Buddha. We are all Buddha."

"Who told you that?" Al asked.

"The Baba. He is Buddha too."

"Christ," said Al.

"Him too." Dog hustled off.

Stoney stood by expectantly, so Arthur brought out his wallet. "The muffler works splendidly. How much?"

"Eighty-five bucks for parts and I'll eat the labour."

"That seems unusually generous." Arthur offered a tip but Stoney, astoundingly, declined it.

"Everything isn't about money, Squire."

Maybe Stoney had been into the gupa. "Have you been talking with Silverson?"

"Yeah, this morning. Cool dude. Not what I thought. He has some deep thoughts."

Arthur was confounded: could he be witnessing the gradual conversion of Robert Stonewell? He asked if Stoney had seen Yoki and Niko.

"Yeah, Jason kind of took them under his wing."

Arthur didn't like that at all. He and Al walked briskly to the gate, following the bearers of the arrested chickens and duck. As it opened for them, a volunteer snagged a small, agile pig, thwarting its own brave efforts to escape. "The animals know," Al said. "They sense the evil."

More tents had sprung up around the lodge and cabins. Games

were underway in a nearby field: volleyball, bocce, Frisbee-tossing. The pock-pock-pock of table tennis. Massage tables had been set up under an awning. The new dormitory loomed, ugly, motel-like. Henrietta Wilks was hanging bunting over its main door, under a banner demanding that all who enter must bring love.

She bowed to them with palms together. "Namaste," she said. She was wearing a sari. Al went to Arthur's ear. "Hinduism, Buddhism, New Ageism, everything goes at Starkers Cove."

Arthur asked if she'd seen Niko and Yoki.

"I saw them with the Baba." She gestured to the beach, where a large marquee tent had been set up above the tide line. A scrawny Ghandi clone in a dhoti sat cross-legged before a sprawl of several dozen truth-seekers, kneeling, sitting, lying on blankets or sleeping bags.

"Reverend Al, don't look at me so sorrowfully," Henrietta said. "I know I've missed your last few services. I hope you understand." She cupped her hand to her ear. "You have to stay tuned. Sometimes Jason calls. Isn't that fun? Sometimes he calls from the forest. I thought it was the wind at first, but he says if you stay tuned you can hear his thoughts."

Hearing voices. More proof, said Al as they walked on, that Silverson had mastered post-hypnotic suggestion.

Jason kind of took them under his wing. What exactly did that mean? As they descended to the beach, they could make out that Baba Sri Rameesh was powered with a clip-on microphone, amplifier, and stereo speakers and was fielding questions from the audience.

"I am asked, how do we maintain a peaceful mind." Arthur was expecting a reedy voice but his was deep and sonorous. No accent to speak of. "The unspiritual mind is cluttered with frivolous thoughts, my friends. They come at all hours, all day, thousands of useless, repetitive thoughts. We can reduce that barrage, even end it, by meditating, by focusing on the moment." Murmurs of agreement.

"You can't deny, Al, that that makes good sense for some."

"Right. Empty the mind. Let them fill it up with tripe."

Al's inexhaustible cynicism was starting to get to Arthur. Yes, there was innocence here, but also warmth, smiles, comfort. That useful triteness, good vibes, came to mind. Arthur was feeling them.

They shooed away a goat and took cover from a sudden shower in the tent by a corner pole. Arthur had a good view of the fifty or so bodies splayed about but couldn't spot the girls. Maybe they were in the dining area, passing out refresherments. There was no crisis. They were safe.

"Baba Sri Rameesh." A woman's voice from somewhere. "What happens when we meditate?"

"True meditation has neither direction, goals, nor method. It is an awakening to our true nature, and it may happen for a moment, or it may happen for an hour or day or week, or it may happen permanently. Whichever way it occurs, it is perfectly okay. There are many paths, friends, but there is no true path. The great Maharishi taught us: 'Let what comes come; let what goes go. Find out what remains.' That is at the true heart of meditation."

Arthur found himself nodding. He was warming to this sage, such a kindly voice, such a free, undemanding philosophy.

"Here is a simple mantra to take with you on life's beautiful journey. 'Joy is wisdom, time an endless song.' Do you know who penned those lovely words?" The Baba looked about brightly. "Does anyone know?"

Arthur couldn't resist and called out, "William Butler Yeats."

"Excellent!" the Baba cried. "Yes, the gentleman in the back — you, my friend, are a scholar, a literary man. Yeats, indeed. A voice from the West that sounds of the East. And why is that? Because West and East, we are all one. Yes? Let us sing it!"

A chorus from the floor: "We are all one!" Arthur was about to add his voice, but held back, noticing Al's shocked and disapproving look.

"Let's get out of here." He tugged at Arthur, who resisted, held by the Baba's sonorous voice, but finally allowed himself to be pulled away. He was feeling a little light-headed, even disoriented, because the day had suddenly — miraculously, it seemed — turned fair, the greyness above dissolving, sunlight glinting on the placid bay.

"Good Lord," said Arthur, "have they cast the clouds aside?"

Al asked if he would like to sit for a minute. Arthur said they should continue their quest; he was fine.

"You're not. You've turned all gooey. Suddenly you're a celebrant of the Baba? Because he called you a literary scholar?"

"I found him quite poetic. Don't scoff, but I think I'm having another attack of calmness."

"I'm starting to wonder if you've developed some sort of mild bipolar disorder. You might want to have yourself looked at."

As they strolled back up toward the lodge, the Baba's voice followed them: "However you seek the beauty that is truth, the message seems always different. But it is also always the same."

"What crap."

"It's a conundrum. We are being asked to work through it."

"He probably gives the same scripted spiel at every stop on his worldwide tours. Get over it."

That was hard. Made more difficult, somehow, because a long arc of rainbow had appeared above the green hills of Garibaldi.

Arthur paused on the grassy ledge above the beach to marvel at the sight. He tried focussing on the moment, letting what comes come and what goes go, but was getting interference from Al, who was asking passers-by where they got their sandwiches and soft drinks.

Al nudged him ahead, and they arrived at the back of the lodge, where, under an overhang, was a long table arrayed with sandwiches, vegetable dips, fruits, and cheeses. Predictably, Nelson Forbish was there, loading up a plate. But no sign of Yoki and Niko. Felicity Jones and a couple of other Easy Pieces had taken over server duties, ladling out scoops of chili.

Felicity winked at Arthur, which made him uneasy. Al deserted him to graze at the table, deaf to Arthur's advice about gupa additives, leaving him to deal with Taba's daughter, who was suddenly beside him, grinning, poking him in the ribs. "What's this about you and Mom getting all torchy outside the Brig yesterday?"

That unexpected and overly generous hug, witnessed from the patio. Surely that's all Felicity knew. Taba would not have breached their pact of secrecy, even with her daughter. Would she? "Oh, that. A friendly embrace. I offered to drive her home."

"And did she invite you in?"

"Of course not. Put your imagination to rest, my dear." Felicity was just teasing, the scamp. But he felt his face redden. And all of a sudden the whole peccadillo came rushing back, desire under the arbutus tree. The good vibes evaporated like mist from the Salish Sea; time stopped being an endless song.

"Excuse me, Felicity, I . . . I'm looking for Niko and Yoki."

"Oh, I heard they're being prepared for transformation."

"Prepared?"

"Jason likes to personally initiate the new ones."

"What does that mean?"

"It's just silly, nothing to worry about." A smile, a shrug, and she returned to the chili pot.

Arthur called Al over. "This is becoming serious."

§

Arthur couldn't calculate how long he'd been sitting on this bench, staring out at the sea. Maybe minutes, maybe half an hour — the same bench, behind the lodge and heated pool, on which he'd sat with Silverson on his first visit. Al had deposited him here, ordering him to relax and get his head together while he searched for Silverson and the Woofers. Who were being prepared. *Jason likes to personally initiate the new ones.*

He was barely aware of Wellness and Wholeness when they came running from the lodge, calling out: "Come on, everyone, they're demonstrating yogic inner exploring." That caused a dispersal toward the grassy area by the tents, leaving Arthur alone with his own inner exploring. About infidelity, guilt, and forgiveness.

Al finally approached, studying him, a look of concern. "Feeling better? You look wrung out." He handed him a bottle of soda. Arthur was thirsty, but hesitated — the cap was off. "It's only Canada Dry, for Christ's sake. I opened it myself. Drink."

Arthur took a deep swig. "I'm okay. I was just missing Margaret." Somehow he must make it up to her. Not flowers, chocolates, or a starlit cruise. Something large, memorable.

"Shake the cobwebs. Kurt Zoller has a line on the girls. He just got back from snooping through the lodge."

Zoller was on a deck chair by the pool, in dark glasses and a T-shirt that proclaimed, "Everything has beauty." He seemed in no hurry to enforce any laws against the several women splashing about the pool topless. Californians. Uninhibited. A few others were in the hot tub, locals who had brought bathing suits.

Al slumped wearily into a recliner while Arthur knelt beside Zoller. "Al says you know where the girls are."

"Act normal, pretend you're looking at those half-naked ladies." A low, cautious tone. "I've pretty well infiltrated the scene here. I can talk their lingo, peace and love and all that. So they let me tour the lodge. All except one room — don't be obvious about it, but look up, top floor, the big windows with blue curtains."

A quick glance identified those windows.

"Anyway, the door was closed and I could hear girls' voices. Giggling. I interpreted some noises as relating to sex. I have reason to believe it's Jason Silverson's bedroom."

Arthur blanched. "What reason?"

"Mainly because Silverson's gorilla, that Baumgarten character, Morg . . . Reverend Al said he kidnapped your Woofers, eh?"

"Sort of."

"Well, he came out of a hallway bathroom and caught me at that door. Told me to get out of there or he'd jam it up my ass. He's always had it in for me."

Arthur's anxiety surged. Some dark sexual ritual was underway. *They're being prepared for transformation.*

"There he goes," Zoller said. They watched Morg hurry past the yoga demonstration, across the grounds, back to the parking area. Zoller jumped up. "Follow me."

Arthur and Al looked to each other for guidance, found none. There seemed no option but to follow him, and they did so at a distance. Zoller had obviously reconnoitred well because he entered the lodge by a back door, near the hot tub. Inside was a flight of fire stairs that led up to a long hallway, its living units variously named with flower-embossed signs: "Thoughtfulness." "Creativity." "Harmony." The undercover sleuth had removed his dark glasses and was pressing his ear to a door labelled "Radiance."

They approached warily to a point a few feet behind him. Arthur could hear female voices, high, spirited. "Oh, yeah!" one cried. "Yes! Yes!"

That didn't quite sound like either Niko or Yoki. Astonishingly, the door wasn't locked, and when Zoller sprung it open three nude bodies were exposed on a king bed, blankets and sheets askew. A woman with a crop of orange hair was supine, in the throes of orgasm, another with her face in her crotch: Gelaine, with her cloud of wild hair, bringing Becky to climax. Xantha was sitting against the headboard, filming their progress, and on spotting Zoller frozen in the doorway, shrieked, "Whack off, you cretinous pus bag!"

Arthur and Al had already bolted, but Zoller stood bug-eyed for several seconds before recovering use of his arms and legs, slamming shut the door, and racing after his confederates down the stairs.

§

After releasing Zoller from any further investigation, Arthur and Al spent a while recovering, speechless, watching a grizzled Transformers veteran lead a yoga class. Several of his students lost their balance and a few fell when Al finally gave way to sputtering laughter. Arthur joined in helplessly. Under the instructor's reproving gaze, they retreated, still cracking up.

The laughter broke Arthur out of his buzzy space. He put his marital guilt on hold, and refocused on the Woofer hunt. While Al looked elsewhere, Arthur went directly to Silverson's office, found it locked and uninhabited.

He hurried outside, past the massage centre, and braked when he heard a woman ask: "Hey, Jace, you want the full Rolf?"

Jace. Jason. There he was, prone and shirtless on a massage table. A hefty woman approached him, rolling up her sleeves.

"Just one of your good hard rubdowns, Molly," Silverson said. "Those girls gave me quite a workout." He welcomed Arthur's approach with a grand, sunny smile. "Here's the great man himself, how delightful that you found time to join us. It's turned into an splendid day, hasn't it? Just give me ten minutes with Molly and then she can have at you. Loosen up all those tight knots. Ow, ow, yes, right there."

"I'm trying to track down my two Woofers, Jason."

"Yoki and Niko? Lovely, lovely girls. Worked up quite a sweat with them. Very agile young ladies. I thought myself quite the whiz at the ping-pong table, but they took turns cleaning my clock. Ah, that's good, that's lovely, Molly."

Ping-pong. Arthur turned. There, just beyond the volleyball court, were the girls, playing doubles, agile indeed, smashing their opponents' balls with sweeping arcs of their paddles, having a whale of a time.

Arthur smiled with relief. "I was told you'd taken them under your wing."

"So to speak. They wanted to be initiated into our creative

growth program. I gave them the beginners' lesson. Life-path coun-selling. Preparing them, we call it."

Though he continued to smile, there was something mocking in those impenetrable blue eyes.

§

An hour later, close to goat-milking time, Arthur drove from Starkers Cove with Niko and Yoki. Al had got a ride home with a neighbour.

The girls were repentant, of course. "Sorry, so sorry. Work very extra hard. Do milking. No problem. Weed garden. Sorry."

They seemed reasonably together. No hundred-mile stares. But Arthur couldn't get past the niggling concern that their supposed initiation had involved a trespass upon them.

"Sorry, but I have to ask. Did Jason touch either of you?"

"Of course," said Niko. "I touch him too."

"What is meaning, touch?" Yoki asked. "Everyone touch."

"More than that. Intimately, I mean."

"Intim . . ." Yoki grappled with the word and failed. "What you mean, Arthur?"

"Like sex?" said Niko. "Is sex what you thinking? We are shock."

"Very shock," said Yoki.

"Sorry," said Arthur.

TWEETS

Pierette was staring glumly at her iPhone. "Houston, we have a catastrophe."

They were flailing, lost in space. Margaret had a vision of herself plummeting earthward in flames.

"Let us pray," said Jennie, an atheist. She was sharing a laptop with Margaret, scrolling through Twitter feeds.

It was Tuesday afternoon, June 24. They were in Margaret's home, a converted coach house in Rockcliffe Park, in a small study with wide windows that looked out over the Rideau River and the spires of Parliament Hill, now just vague shapes in the lashing rain. The river was swollen and grey and forbidding. A thunderstorm was happening. Metaphorically too.

They'd gathered here hurriedly after the most recent tweet showed up. The first one had appeared three days ago, on Saturday, but they had dismissed it as a typical slur from one of the Greens' many trolls. *Margaret "Loose Lips" Blake has blown it this time. Her slip is showing, her ship sinking.* Posted by @BDsmother, the Twitter handle of a sourpuss who made sure it got to the Green Party by adding its hashtag.

Margaret was troubled by the author's clever phrasing — it

seemed carefully crafted, polished. Also sinister was that BDsmother had joined Twitter only that very Saturday. One follower retweeted, maybe accidentally: @Big_Al_23, a fat, frowning biker, fan of a band called Shit in Your Face.

But BDsmother, in typical trolling fashion, was incognito: no photo, no profile, no link. B.D. Smother? B.D.'s mother?

Margaret had tried to laugh it off and almost succeeded until Pierette, after a squint-eyed study, deciphered the handle. BDSM — bondage-dominance-sadism-masochism. "BDSM fused to Mother, get it? As in, 'Spank me, Mother, I've been a bad boy.'" Words that, twenty days ago, Margaret had gleefully shared with Pierette and a live microphone.

Margaret had quickly got a headache. She'd finally convinced herself she was out of danger, but here was the almost unassailable truth that Christie Montieth, the right-wing bloghead, had heard all. She must be BDsmother.

Still, there was zero proof, and Margaret hadn't dared mention the tweet to Arthur during her rattled talk with him on Sunday. But then a second tweet, more explicit and volatile, showed up today. Also from BDsmother, also tagged #GreenPartyCanada. *Ongoing cat fight between Loose Lips and Enviro Minister has got down and dirty. Sour and malicious, Ms. Blake? Is that you?*

A twist on Pierette's live-mike jest about S and M: "Sour and malicious, right?"

Scores of retweets poured in. Mostly from anti-Greens and Conservative hacks with malice in their hearts. One of them had created the hashtag #SourAndMalicious.

Ongoing cat fight. Down and dirty. Margaret, Pierette, and Jennie agreed this was Christie Montieth's blog voice. Their worst fear was that the indelicate exchange at the WWF panel had not only been heard by her, but recorded on her iPhone.

"It's as if she wants us to know," Pierette said.

"The question is," said Jennie, "how far will she go with this?"

Pierette had a shrewd theory: "She's beating the bushes for reaction. She took it to her editor, and they brought in the lawyers and decided it was too hot to touch. They embargoed it until she could come up with something hard. We know she tried to hunt down Svetlana."

Jennie let out a whoop. "Gather around, ladies, here's a new one." They huddled close around the laptop, as if for safety. Another from BDsmother, under the SourAndMalicious tag: a response to the many who were clamouring for details, stalwarts such as Hardnosed Harry and Tax My Ass: *Stay tuned. Here's a clue: Sour and Malicious = S and M.*

Christie Montieth was building an audience. The tweets were coming fast. SandMLover: *Are you out? Want to get together?* PainMaker31: *First consultation free. Find your own level. Click here.* George Figelhof, a known Tory operative: *If the GP leader likes getting her ass whipped, she'll really enjoy the next election.* A knee-jerk assumption that Margaret was the whipee in an S&M relationship.

"Okay, let's think," Jennie said. "Christie's opened the floodgates, and now this alleged defamation is being spread to the entire known universe. She must be pretty dense not to know that a Twitter pseudonym won't save her from being sued for libel. She doesn't know about the video, right?"

"No way she could," Pierette said.

"So, who else knows? Besides Svetlana and Sabatino, wherever the fuck they are."

"Arthur," Margaret said. "Francisco Sierra." Who preferred to grow roses than get involved. They would never find a private investigator as competent, and she could be facing a huge defamation suit with no clear way to prove her innocence.

Margaret needed Arthur's counsel, desperately. She would brave the scolding. Again came that little insistent voice. Time to get out of politics, girl. Pass the baton to the photogenic Cree warrior. Return to husband and hearth. She picked up her BlackBerry, fiddled with it, unsure how to break the news to him.

"What's Margaret's schedule?" Jennie asked Pierette.

"The midnight sun tour. Yellowknife tomorrow, noon flight. Then Whitehorse, Fort Smith, then down to her riding by the long weekend."

"Maybe that gives us time to get a handle on this," said Jennie. "God knows how, though." Normally so cool, so efficient, Jennie seemed off balance. She went out for a smoke while Pierette made tea in the kitchen, allowing Margaret privacy. Arthur came on just as the message recorder was about to click in.

"Sorry, dear, I was watering the carrots. We're suffering through another lovely summer day." Trying to be jocular, sounding strained.

"Wish I could share your suffering. We have a typhoon. How are Yoki and Niko?"

"Safely back at the farm. False alarm, really, following an epic search."

"I can imagine."

"I doubt that you can."

"Okay, hold the details until I see you on Saturday. And I *really* need to see you, darling. I don't suppose you know how to tweet?"

"I hold to the view that tweeting is for the birds."

There was no point giving him lessons now. Margaret took a deep breath and gave him the whole rundown, tweet by tweet. Pierette's speculation regarding Montieth's delay. Her planned trip to the far north. Arthur, sombre now, asked for the odd clarification but was mostly silent.

"Hold on a sec," Margaret said, as Pierette hurried in from the kitchen, gaping at her iPhone. She stumbled blindly into and onto a stuffed chair, listening to her voice coming from that iPhone: "S and M. I got it. It's a metaphor. As in Sour and Malicious, right?"

Followed by an even more familiar voice: "Wrong. Spank me, Mother, I've been a bad boy. Weekends with a Russian dominatrix. Svetlana something. Farquist likes giving her pony rides while she swats his ass with a riding whip."

Then Pierette's exclamation: "Freak out!"

Jennie bustled inside, tamping out her cigarette, in time to hear her own voice: "Hey, you guys, be careful."

Then silence. Then Arthur's faint inquiries, from the BlackBerry that Margaret had dropped on her foot. "Darling? Are you there? Hello?"

Margaret picked up the phone and put it on speaker. "Wow. Shit's hit the fan, Arthur. Big time."

Scrolling through her laptop, Jennie located this latest, climactic, spectacularly alarming tweet from BDsmother. *Here's how Loose Lips lose elections. And maybe the family farm. #SourAndMalicious #GreenPartyCanada.* A link to a transcript of Margaret's live chat with Pierette and another to the recording just played. All of fifteen seconds, but for Margaret time stood still. She trembled at the thought of the havoc to come, reporters breathing hot in her face, demanding answers, a possible lawsuit.

She could hardly bear having it played again, but Arthur insisted on it. Then she said, "So, I think I'm going to need a lawyer."

"I shall find you the best specialist."

"I don't want any goddamn best specialist, Arthur. I want you."

A long silence. Margaret sensed he was agonizing over this, over his vow never to walk again into a courtroom, that he was seeking words to explain how unprofessional it would be to represent a spouse in such circumstances. Lawyers were expected to maintain distance from their clients, to shield themselves from emotions and the clouding of reason.

But suddenly he blurted: "Yes! Of course! No problem!" He sounded enthusiastic, even triumphant. How bizarre. "Are Pierette and Jennie both with you?"

They waited until Pierette brought a tea tray, which she put down beside Margaret's phone.

Arthur said, "I assume I have consent to represent all three of you." No one demurred. "Very well, I am instructing you, on pain of excommunication from this planet, not to discuss this matter with the press or anyone. You needn't be unpleasant with them, but your hands are tied." A moment of reflection, then he laughed. "Well, *that's* a rather unseemly metaphor, isn't it?"

"Our tongues are tied and our lips sealed," Pierette said, attempting to lighten the mood.

"Refer all inquiries to me as your lawyer. I'm including both of you, Pierette and Jennie, though you two may not be personally at risk."

"Got it," said Jennie. "We know too much."

"I can't comfortably make an afternoon flight, so I'll be on the overnight. That will give us a few hours in the morning before Margaret has to leave for Yellowknife. Margaret, please pack your bags right away, and then all three of you are to head out to an airport hotel before the mob descends and stay there until I arrive."

Margaret pointed out that an overnight would leave him exhausted, but her objection was overruled. He urged them to relax over a bottle of wine in their airport hotel room and leave their concerns with him. Everything would work out. At some future time, they would regale each other with tales about these hilarious events. Highly unlikely, Margaret thought, however reassuring.

"A personal note to you, Margaret."

She turned off the speaker, braced herself for the requisite stern advisory about her notorious tendency to shoot off her mouth. "Yes, dear?"

"I love you, Margaret. Truly. Deeply. And I . . . I will just leave you with Alexander Pope's eternal advice: 'To err is human; to forgive, divine.' *Omnia vincit amor.*"

She found that tender and warming, if not altogether clear. Tears came, and she looked out the window to hide them. The storm seemed to be letting up.

§

Margaret woke up disoriented. She was slightly hungover. In her pyjamas but in a strange bed. She heard a plane taking off and blinked away the haze of sleep. She was in a bedroom of an airport hotel suite.

She peeked at the bedside clock: almost eight — Arthur would have landed by now. Pierette would be at arrivals to meet him. To err is human, he'd said. What error had he meant? Her careless fling? Yet it almost felt *he* was seeking forgiveness for some transgression. *Omnia vincit amor.* Their love would heal all wounds?

Arthur the Obscure.

She twisted to her left, saw her door was open — maybe so Jennie could guard against her jumping out the window. She was at a desk, bent over her laptop. Two empty bottles of Cabernet on the counter.

They'd gone through those last night while morbidly watching the tweets roll in. There was advice on the proper way to do the pony ride. A link to an S&M consumer study of riding whips. An occasional semi-supportive message: *Wouldn't it be lovely if true?* Some crudities. *Svetlana was lucky that big-ass Farquist didn't mount her, she'd be flattened.*

Margaret was about to launch herself toward the bathroom, but heard Jennie on her phone, cooling someone out. "Hey, Charmer, chill, we've got it under control. Very important strategy session going on. Keep smiling. *Arrivederci.*"

"Charmer?"

"Chalmers. I gave him my personal number. Mistake."

"I'll say." Margaret was sure Jennie knew about their fling. She could picture Lloyd making a casual hint over too many drinks. *Frankly, she was coming on to me. I'd rather not say more.* Maybe he'd told his buddies too. *Keep it under your hat, but I scored with the Green leader.*

Margaret felt sticky — maybe from the mention of his name — and rushed to the shower. Lloyd Chalmers was the mistake, that was what she should tell Jennie. He was all about himself. A narcissist.

An obsessive user of women. She should warn Jennie about that —
though thankfully she seemed to be cooling on him.

After drying her hair and doing what she could with her wan,
white face, Margaret joined Jennie, snapping on her bra, pulling on
jeans, pausing to peruse the front page of the *Globe*. "Racy Political
Voice Clip Goes Viral" — a brief, carefully worded piece in which
this decorous daily avoided quoting from the clip, naming the parties, or elaborating on its raciness, other than referring to alleged
unusual sexual practices. The source of the clip, which had "lit up"
the internet, was not known. Voice analysis was underway. The publisher was studying legal options before "fleshing out" the story.

"Other mainstream media are being just as coy," Jennie said. "But
it's all over the internet, the blogosphere, Reddit. Don't even look
at Facebook."

Margaret put her shirt aside and tried to work on her hair. "How
do I look?"

"You always look good." Studying her. "Sexy. Do you want some
time alone with him?"

Margaret flushed. "Well, I . . . no. That will have to wait." An awkward response to a kind offer. Casting about for a quick change of
subject, she fumbled with words. "Jennie, I think we have to consider
. . . for the good of the party . . ."

"Ill-advised," said Jennie. Then added, "Right now." Even a hint
that Margaret might resign would be an admission of wrongdoing.
That matter, as with everything, must await Arthur's counsel.

As tense as she was glum, Margaret started at the sound of the door
opening, and there was Pierette ushering in Arthur and another man,
whom she could not immediately place. She was focussed on her husband, his rumpled suit and tired eyes, his grin on seeing her doing up
her shirt. They kissed, then held each other. Margaret did want to take
this man to bed, and was dismayed she couldn't. Not now.

Standing by, looking extremely awkward, in a contrastingly
unrumpled suit, was the small rotund man she now remembered as

a dinner guest at Blunder Bay: Francisco Sierra, the courtly private eye, who bowed before shaking her hand.

"But what about your roses, Frank?" she said.

"There will always be roses. I've left Bolivar with friends." His dog.

"You're the best news we've had all day. I'm so happy you've come."

"My pleasure, madam." He too had flown overnight, but showed no signs of wear or weariness.

There was little time for pleasantries. Sierra was introduced to Jennie, who brought him up to date on the media coverage while Pierette took orders for room service. For the next hour, Sierra meticulously questioned the three women, taking notes.

Afterwards, he sat back with a cup of after-breakfast tea, musing, polishing his glasses as if that would improve his view of the matter. Margaret settled beside Arthur on a couch, curling against him like a cat needing comfort. Jennie returned to her laptop.

"Speak, Oracle," said Arthur.

Sierra nodded and smiled. "Of particular interest, of course, are Mr. Sabatino and Ms. Glinka. She cannot be that difficult to locate, even in Europe. Forward and outgoing. Flashy may be the word. A vigorous spender of money. I shall likely have to go overseas."

"That will be looked after," Arthur said. Margaret wondered how he could be so confident that his office would bankroll these costs. But he'd assured her that Tragger, Inglis, with friends in the Opposition, would prosper from the government's embarrassment.

Sierra continued: "I find it difficult to believe there are no copies of the video. Even a relative novice to computing would know how to make duplicates. External drives, DVDs, the cloud. Ms. Glinka is no novice; she has shown herself capable of producing *cinema verité*. And Mr. Sabatino is a computer nerd, if I may use that commonplace. Surely, if only for self-protection, he would have hidden away a copy or two."

He turned to Margaret. "He told you he'd been undeservedly fired?"

"With some niggardly amount in compensation. I got the impression he has minimal resources. His wife cleared out their joint account."

"He talked to you about the sad state of his marriage. Let's run over that again."

She tried hard to remember. Sabatino had moaned and groaned about his dressmaker wife, Celeste, and their two children. A boy and a girl, young, grade school. Her calumnies, her threats to leave him, and, finally, running off with the kids. He'd mentioned her parents might be hiding them. Somewhere in northern Quebec.

Sierra probed until her well ran dry. It was nearing eleven, Pierette was jiggling her car keys, it was time to leave for the plane. Margaret was about to give Arthur one last hug when Jennie bolted from her computer and snatched up the TV remote. "Farquist. A live press briefing."

She found the public affairs channel, CPAC, and in a few minutes they were looking at the stage of the National Press Theatre. A few minutes of confusion as sound checks were made, flashing cameras, rustling sounds. Then Emil Farquist strode toward the rostrum, backed up by stern-faced staff. He waited stiffly while he was introduced by a subaltern, then took the microphone. Dark suit, blue tie, hair badly combed, a face like a clenched fist. He launched right into it, without notes.

"It has been brought to my attention that certain scurrilous and egregiously false remarks have been made about me by the leader of the Green Party. I would say *Honourable* leader of that party, but she is without honour. Her remarks, which I understand were taped under circumstances that remain unclear, are not worth repeating here, though they have apparently inundated the internet. Let me add that I have consulted experts in voice identification, and there is no question as to who the speaker was."

His voice was raw, maybe over-exercised by the profanities that must have flowed liberally the previous day and night. Margaret felt like a zombie watching this, stripped of feelings and emotion, standing still as a tree stump, her carry-on over her shoulder. She started when Arthur put his arm around her, then sagged as they listened.

"In less grievous circumstances I might allow some time for Ms. Blake to frame her apology, but I am instructed that no apology can undo the damage done by her irresponsible and callous comments. As I speak, lawyers in Calgary are filing a writ and statement of claim naming her as defendant in a suit for five million dollars plus forty-five million in aggravated and punitive damages. That is all I have to say. No questions."

But of course there was a clamour of questions. They went unanswered. Farquist's political aide took the mike to "respectfully" caution the press that an injunction was being sought to restrain further publication of the defamatory words, but he could barely be heard. Farquist made for the exit, tripped slightly over a power cord, flapped his arms out like a penguin to regain his balance, then disappeared.

Jennie turned the TV off, and there was silence until Sierra said, "Not very nimble of foot, is he?"

Maybe it was that comment, maybe the preposterous claim in damages, but Margaret released an unladylike snort of laughter.

"Very well," Sierra said, "we have our work cut out for us."

PART TWO

THE CLIPPINGS FILE

Ottawa Citizen, THURSDAY, JUNE 27

OTTAWA — A political earthquake is shaking the staid corridors of Parliament Hill over alleged incendiary comments by Green Party leader Margaret Blake about Environment Minister Emil Farquist, who has launched a slander action against her for $50 million.

The claim is for $5 million in general damages, $25 million in aggravated damages, and $20 million in punitive damages. If upheld, the award would be the largest by far in the history of Canadian defamation suits.

In announcing his court action on Wednesday — at a five-minute press conference in the National Press Theatre that set Parliamentary records for brevity — Farquist appeared visibly outraged, and was unsparing in his condemnation of Ms. Blake. He described her alleged remarks, caught on tape, as irresponsible, scurrilous, and egregiously false. He said experts had identified Blake's voice on that recording.

Although links to it have gone viral on social media, their

further publication has been restrained by a Canada-wide injunction granted Wednesday by Justice A.J. O'Donnell of the Alberta Court of Queen's Bench. A hearing to determine if the injunction will stand is set for this Friday in Calgary.

Justice O'Donnell has granted standing at the hearing to major media outlets.

Ms. Blake is on a pre-campaign swing through Canada's northern territories, and has not been available to the media. Green Party staff have referred inquiries to the law firm of Tragger, Inglis, Bullingham in Vancouver, which has indicated a statement will be forthcoming from senior trial counsel Arthur Beauchamp, QC, who is Ms. Blake's husband.

The injunction also bars reporting the specifics of the alleged defamatory comments contained in the complainant's five-page statement of claim. The *Ottawa Citizen* and Postmedia have announced they are joining other news agencies, publishers, and broadcast and visual media to oppose continuation of the injunction.

The controversial recording and the massive suit in damages loom darkly over the national political landscape, with the Liberal caucus under their untested new leader, Marcus Yates, planning to support an Opposition motion to bring down the minority Tory government early in the fall session, precipitating what may become one of this nation's wildest election campaigns.

§

CBC News, THURSDAY, JUNE 27, 4:05 P.M.

CALGARY — Lawyers for Green Party leader Margaret Blake arrived at the Calgary courthouse this afternoon to file a formal statement of defence to the slander action launched against her yesterday by Environment Minister Emil Farquist.

Copies of the document were not made available to the public or the media, pending a ruling expected tomorrow on whether a publication ban will be continued or stayed, but a spokesperson for Blake's defence team said the team plans to meet the accusation of slander head-on, and will seek to prove that references to Farquist made in a sensational voice recording are founded on fact.

"We believe in the fundamental fairness of Canada's justice system and shall defend this action with the weapons of truth," said noted trial lawyer Arthur Ramsgate Beauchamp upon his arrival this afternoon at the Calgary airport.

He said he did not blame Farquist for "seeking home-field advantage" by filing his suit in his own city, and complimented Calgary for being "modern and alive and renowned for its generous and fair-minded citizenry." He declined to discuss the case further, but when asked if he felt comfortable representing his wife, he joked that she had often found their marriage to be a trial.

Farquist will be bringing on board another of Canada's top litigators, George Cowper Jr., who is widely regarded as the go-to counsel for defamation actions. Cowper told the CBC he felt privileged to be asked to represent "such a forthright and well-respected political leader."

Presiding over the injunction hearing tomorrow will be Madam Justice Rachel Cohon-Plaskett, Chief Justice of the Alberta Queen's Bench and a former counsel of note herself.

Counsel for the CBC and other news media will be at the hearing to oppose the injunction.

§

The New York Times, FRIDAY, JUNE 28
BY Holly Lorenson

OTTAWA — Canada's reputation as a land of the bland and uneventful is in tatters this week following explosive allegations that a senior minister in the federal Conservative cabinet played sado-masochistic games with a Russian dominatrix.

Emil Farquist, the environment minister and parliamentary whip, has filed a $50 million slander suit against the leader of Canada's Green Party, Margaret Blake, over a voice clip in which Ms. Blake, apparently unaware she was being recorded, spoke excitedly to her parliamentary aide, Pierette Litvak.

Farquist, in a brief statement on Wednesday, did not mince words in describing Ms. Blake's comments as false, irresponsible, and callous. Only one day after his action was filed, counsel for Ms. Blake answered with a statement of defence conceding that she did make the impugned remarks and that they were true "in every word and particular."

According to Canadian lawyers, the $50 million claim is at least ten times higher than any previous judgment for defamation in Canada.

This is the conversation that has our northern neighbours all atwitter:

Ms. Blake: "Emil Farquist. The sanctimonious prick, he's into S and M."

Ms. Litvak: "S and M. I got it. It's a metaphor. As in Sour and Malicious, right?"

Ms. Blake: "Wrong. Spank me, Mother, I've been a bad boy. Weekends with a Russian dominatrix. Svetlana something. Farquist likes giving her pony rides while she swats his ass with a riding whip."

Ms. Litvak: "Freak out!"

A cautionary female voice then interrupted: "Hey, you guys, be careful."

It is not clear when or where this inflammatory exchange occurred, and the dominatrix referred to as Svetlana remains a mystery woman. Journalists have been scouring public records in an effort to locate her, but to little avail. A cursory internet search reveals several hundred Svetlanas in Ontario and Quebec alone.

It is hoped details will emerge during a hearing set for today in Calgary, where the slander suit was filed.

The hearing will determine whether the Canadian media — or the Canadian public — will be permanently banned from publishing or repeating that brief to-and-fro, an embargo that would raise eyebrows in the U.S., where First Amendment rights remain paramount.

There is a history of fierce friction between Ms. Blake and Mr. Farquist, whom she has dubbed the "Minister of Environmental Destruction" because of his lukewarm approach to climate change and his support for the continued exploitation of Alberta's controversial oil sands.

Meanwhile, the minority Conservative government is expected to fall when Parliament resumes in September, with four opposition parties aligned to vote no-confidence in the government, a move bound to precipitate a heated election campaign.

§

National Post, SATURDAY, JUNE 29
BY Ivor Johnson, columnist

CALGARY — The opening round in the punch-up between two combatants who are arguably the most colourful and volatile of a mostly monochromatic herd of MPs took place on Friday in Room 1503 of the Calgary Courts Centre. The hearing lacked a little in suspense.

Right from the opening bell it was clear that this was no contest, when the referee, Chief Justice Rachel Cohon-Plaskett, began throwing her own knockout punches.

Details of the event and the voice clip that prompted Emil Farquist's $50 million slander claim against Margaret Blake appear elsewhere in this journal, but I had a ringside seat, close enough to see the sweat on the brows of counsel and to hear their muffled oaths.

Many leading lights of the bar were there, representing the *Post* and other news outlets, all eager to get their licks in, to storm the fortress of censorship. I had read their briefs: the right of the public to know, justice must not merely be done but seen, secret trials are a hallmark of totalitarian states. Strongly worded stuff, even stirring, but little of this was voiced.

Emil Farquist's smooth and erudite counsel, George Cowper Jr., was only ten minutes into his submission when Chief Justice Cohon-Plaskett asked, "Are you really serious, Mr. Cowper?"

He had little option but to say yes. To give him credit, he ducked and danced, showed impressive footwork. Should the injunction fail, he said, "a sterling reputation already sullied by a wild and unsubstantiated accusation would be exposed to an almost exponential barrage of repeated slurs."

Cohon-Plaskett referred him to an affidavit filed by the media group which estimated the alleged slurs had attracted 3.5 million hits to date on the internet. "If that's not exponential, I don't know what is," she said.

It went without saying (though she said it anyway) that the injunction was ineffective against people who post on the internet, and not lifting it would cause the mainstream media a massive disadvantage.

However, she added, with a glance at defending counsel A.R. Beauchamp, quashing the injunction may encourage unrestrained public debate about the alleged slander and expose Ms. Blake "to the prospect of substantially increased damages should she not ultimately prevail in court."

Counsel for the various news organizations — there were twelve of them, all primed for battle — looked disappointed when the judge said she didn't need to hear from them. She then asked Mr. Beauchamp if he had anything to add. He did not. He hadn't thrown a punch all day.

But this was only round one.

§

The Globe and Mail Op-Ed, TUESDAY, JULY 2
BY M.R. Mathews, QC, LLD.

OTTAWA — Lost amid the sensation and political turmoil of Farquist v. Blake, or what is known in some circles as the "Freak out!" case, is the more subtle interplay of the strategies likely to be employed by two opposing counsel of stellar reputation and contrasting backgrounds.

Representing the plaintiff is George Cowper Jr., QC, of Cowper Linquist, a Toronto boutique firm that specializes in defamation law, a field in which Mr. Cowper has won several notable victories, most recently in pursuing the claim of slander by Bishop Augustine O'Meara, involving allegations of pederasty, and defending muckraking author J.R. Haskett's bestseller, *Scum*.

Arthur Ramsgate Beauchamp, QC, of the national firm of Tragger, Inglis, Bullingham, is the husband of defendant

Margaret Blake, and has caused a stir among his colleagues by offending an unwritten rule of legal practice against acting for a close family member. Perhaps the top gun among Canadian criminal lawyers, Beauchamp has never taken on a defamation case, but he is a fierce defender and brilliant cross-examiner.

The venue of the lawsuit is also not without controversy, the plaintiff having chosen his hometown of Calgary, a move that many observers consider a too-obvious attempt to give him an edge but also raising the question of whether he lacked the confidence to sue in a more neutral territory.

The claim for $50 million seems extravagant if not exorbitant, a figure unsurpassed in the annals of Canadian defamation law. A $3 million jury award against an airline for firing a pilot falsely accused of drinking alcohol before a flight remains the largest on record, followed by a $1.6 million judgment in favour of a lawyer defamed by the Church of Scientology. Minister Farquist's massive claim is likely a rhetorical gesture, but an award in the millions may well be justified.

Mr. Beauchamp's gambit of responding to the plaintiff's writ and statement of claim with such unprecedented speed — one calendar day — was clearly intended as a bravura show of confidence. However the plea of justification, or truth, that is central to Mr. Beauchamp's pleadings may be enormously risky, exposing Ms. Blake to a judgment in damages that could bankrupt her and drive her from politics.

The safer route might have been to plead that her comments were made in jest, or that having been intended for the ears only of her parliamentary aide they were broadcast unintentionally and therefore protected under the defence of qualified privilege. That defence, however, is defeated when the words, as here, resound with apparent malice.

An option that might substantially moderate an award in

damages would be a quick and unreserved apology, but the doors to forgiveness have clearly been shut and barricaded.

It remains to be seen whether either party will seek a trial by jury as opposed to judge alone. I suspect the latter is the more likely choice. Chief Justice Rachel Cohon-Plaskett will preside in any event. While Mr. Farquist's legal team may be feeling bruised by her peremptory dismissal of the effort to restrain further publication of the alleged slander, they will be aware that she was not only a Conservative appointment but a candidate for that party, albeit a losing one, in a federal election nearly a decade ago.

Still, she is said to have been allied more closely with the party's progressive wing — the so-called Red Tories — than with its current hardline leadership. So Mr. Beauchamp may well opt for the relative safety of a bright, tough-minded, no-nonsense former defence counsel than risk a jury pulled from constituents of Mr. Farquist, who won his seat in a landslide.

There will be no rush to judgment. The trial is unlikely to take place for at least a year, but expect much sparring, in court and out, as the parties gird for a final showdown.

At the least, the trial and the anticipation around it will do much to divert Albertans from the moribund state of the province's economy.

§

Calgary Herald, FRIDAY, JULY 5

CALGARY — Nearly all proceeds from Emil Farquist's $50 million defamation suit against Green leader Margaret Blake will be donated to the Alberta Sick Children's Hospital Foundation, it was announced on Wednesday.

The promise was made by Jonas Hawkes, chief political aide to Environment Minister Farquist, at an impromptu press conference during the annual "Across the Border" ceremony honouring America's Independence Day at the Calgary Stampede grounds. He said "every cent" of the $45 million claim for aggravated and punitive damages would be earmarked for the hospital fund. The announcement was greeted with cheers.

Hawkes met with reporters following a flag-raising ceremony and the introduction of prominent politicians from Canada and the U.S., including Farquist, who received an ovation that was notably louder and more sustained than that bestowed on Alberta's popular new premier. Indeed, the entire event evolved into a tribute for the minister, who worked the crowd with back-slapping bonhomie. However, he refused to answer questions relating to the controversial slander action.

When asked, Hawkes denied any effort to sway a Calgary jury was intended. And he took issue with a suggestion that the idea of a charitable gift was prompted by criticism — particularly in legal circles — over the lavish claim for $50 million.

He took umbrage when asked whether Farquist's legal fees were being paid by the federal government, saying that any discussion about fees was "inappropriate."

Ms. Blake, who has returned to her home and her Vancouver Island constituency, was not available for comment, but her lawyer — and husband — Arthur Beauchamp, said, with apparent wryness, "Very generous of him."

§

Fit to Be Tied (Online Newsletter of the Canadian BDSM
   Society), MONDAY, JULY 8
BY the editor

Are we having fun yet? Your faithful editor certainly is, as all eyes in the BDSM community are riveted on the magnificent rumpus over the claims of fun and games engaged in (allegedly, of course) by political top dog Emil Farquist, who holds the delightful title of Chief Conservative Whip. (Or is he, as reputed whipee, the bottom dog?)

The controversy certainly has its upside, in terms of giving more public awareness and legitimacy to the playful, healthy, stress-relieving games our society was formed to defend.

But we are disappointed that lawyers for Margaret Blake (the Green Dominatrix, as we like to call her) haven't raised a defence that should have been staring at them in the face. Whether or not her lovely little tale was true (pony rides! Haven't we all loved them since we were toddlers?), is it defamatory?

That implies BDSM activities are shameful, when there is ample evidence that they have been powerfully therapeutic for many who have gone on to lead successful lives through channelling anger, guilt, and shame into a form of theatre. Sexual play with a frisson of danger, but never harm — a per-session accident rate of 2 percent.

As all readers of this newsletter know, BDSM is practised by thousands of respectable citizens. We count in our ranks bankers and accountants, business leaders, artists, professors. Many of us condemned by prejudice to remain closeted.

This was a historic opportunity for Ms. Blake, a missed chance to denounce bigotry and honour her commitment to cultural tolerance and diversity. Witnesses could have been called, expert psychologists, to say that Farquist was doing something sexually and psychologically healthy.

If the allegations against Mr. Farquist are true, it is sad that he is in denial. We hope that one day, when all the feathers have settled, he considers joining our society and becoming a robust campaigner for our goals.

B.J. Anon, Editor.

(P.S. On page two, there is a discussion about quirts and riding crops — their appropriate uses and recommended brands. On page three, the Tips'n' Techniques column features the Pony Ride.)

THE SIERRA FILE

Monday, July 8

Dear Arthur,

Lest you fear I have become incommunicado, or have
somehow disappeared, I am very much in this world,
though I confess to having avoided contact by telephone
or email, thus this couriered, typewritten report. One
worries about tapped lines, hostile ears and eyes; we dare
not assume our opponents are without resources. I am sure
you and Margaret will take appropriate caution.

Very well. Dates, times, places, and detailed observations
are precisely recorded in my notes, but you will prefer
an overview. Which I am writing in the front room of an
upper triplex that is barren but for a few furnishings,
including this table and chair, left behind by previous
tenants. They also abandoned this marvellous old Olivetti
portable — how I have missed the clatter of keys.

The flat has a pleasant outlook, upon old, well-
preserved Montreal — in particular this neighbourhood in

Centre-Sud, below Sherbrooke, with its lovely spiralling staircases.

Some of these buildings date from the late nineteenth century. The seemingly ingenious concept of saving living space by means of outdoor staircases seems to have been a factor in many accidents, and in the 1940s a law was passed prohibiting their further erection.

This I learned from the owner of a dozen duplexes and triplexes hereabout, who self-mockingly described himself as a "slum landlord." R.J. "Rocky" Rubinstein, a trial lawyer, owns the flat from which I can see across the street the triplex once occupied by our two desaparecidos, Mr. Sabatino and Ms. Glinka.

Mr. Rubinstein, who has remained lithe and wiry well into his late-middle years, seemed unable to sit during our long conversation in this flat, which he has generously offered to me for the time being — he is quite a fan of yours, Arthur. He talked effusively, jabbing or blocking an invisible opponent's punches with every uttered phrase. This disconcerting habit apparently stems from a youthful career as an amateur boxer.

He was surprised to learn that Robert O'Brien, whom he hadn't met — his six-month lease for the upper triplex had been signed and mailed — was Lou Sabatino, the reporter. Nor did he know Witness Protection was paying the rent, which arrived in his office at the end of each month as cash in an envelope.

The rent for July had been paid in this way, and Mr. Rubinstein learned only through me that his tenant's family have deserted him and that he has gone missing. Nor was he aware that Ms. Glinka has packed up and gone. Her July rent remains unpaid.

Happily, Mr. Rubinstein has little regard for Emil

Farquist, whom he believes is a closeted anti-Semite, and
he seems gleeful at the prospect of bringing him down.
He is, in a word, onside. He has assured me he will not
extend cooperation to investigators for the plaintiff or
assist the media — though, as you will presently learn,
the press has already zeroed in on her "therapy clinic."

Now to my observations. There have been reporters in
the neighbourhood, including Christie Montieth — who we
assume is BDsmother but who has been silent in print
(if that phrase makes sense) since posting the Freak Out
recording.

One would have thought that Ms. Montieth would be
lying low, given the risk she runs of being added to a
$50 million defamation suit. But this mop-haired pixie
has come by twice.

On Wednesday, July 3, in the late afternoon, she
arrived in a Mini Cooper, which she double-parked in
front of Ms. Glinka's apartment. She took a photo of its
exterior with her phone before entering the yard and
knocking on the door.

Her efforts to peer within were prevented by blinds
and curtains. She looked about, as if for assistance from
a neighbour, but none was about, and she drove off.

She returned yesterday, July 7, in a Sun Media van,
with a photographer, who took several photos from
different angles of her knocking at Ms. Glinka's door.

The arrival of the van attracted many residents to
their stairs and balconies, and Ms. Montieth interviewed
several, including the two octogenarians who live next
door and to whom Ms. Litvak spoke last month. With the
window open, I could tell Ms. Montieth was struggling
with their dialect-heavy French (as I do, when chatting
with them on my daily health walks).

Ms. Montieth did not venture up to Mr. Sabatino's flat, from which I surmise she remains unaware he was living there or has any connection with the case.

Not an hour passed after their departure when another van pulled up, and a man holding a writing pad and a woman with a camera got out. Toronto Star, said a card on top of the dashboard, as viewed through my binoculars.

The reporter knocked on a few neighbouring doors, earning audience from most. This gentleman did also hammer on Mr. Sabatino's door but to no avail, of course.

There have been other visitors to the neighbourhood. I observed a black Lincoln Navigator SUV (presumably the same vehicle seen by Ms. Litvak) drive by slowly on July 2, late afternoon, and again two days later in the evening. Two men occupied the front seat, though I was able to view only the driver: heavy-set, moustache, black hair, dark glasses.

This vehicle returned at twilight yesterday, and this time pulled to the curb. Same driver, but the person who alighted from the passenger side was a woman, fit, perhaps in her thirties, tall, dark hair, dark glasses. This, I assume, is the couple whom Ms. Litvak spotted at Dorval Airport's parking lot, aiding in Ms. Glinka's getaway. The woman quickly mounted the stairs to the Sabatino suite and tried the door, but did not knock. The pile of uncollected newspapers may have persuaded her that her quest was futile, and they drove off.

I have photographs, of course, relating to all these appearances. The licence number of the Navigator reveals the registered owner to be one Lucas Laframbois, with an address in Laval that appears to be that of a second-hand store and is doubtless as fictitious as his name.

I have also observed several gentlemen attempting to visit Ms. Glinka, one of them at least three times. Since I am not at my post at all times — due to my daily jaunts — I rely on my DropCam to review other comings and goings by clients seeking her services.

I am already on a chatting relationship with the three-time visitor, one Harvey Plouffe, and we have arranged to have coffee. I am hoping my facade as a devotee of BDSM will not be the cause of any personal awkwardness.

I extend my continuing good wishes to you and yours. I am available for your comments and further instructions by mail at the postal box number on the envelope.

Yours sincerely,
Francisco

THE CLIPPINGS FILE

Toronto Star, MONDAY, JULY 8
AN EXCLUSIVE BY Jack Feigel

MONTREAL — "Weekends with a Russian dominatrix. Svetlana something."

So spoke Green Party leader Margaret Blake on the
infamous Freak Out recording that has given rise to Emil
Farquist's $50 million slander suit against her.

Who is this alleged dominatrix with the Russian name?
Well, it turns out there's a woman who might fit the bill:
Svetlana Glinka, who has apparently been operating an S&M
"therapy clinic" on Rue de la Visitation in Montreal's old
section, east of downtown.

But she seems to have disappeared.

Her address, and her alleged business as a dominatrix, was
called in to the Star anonymously, by a man who claimed to
have received "her services."

Svetlana Glinka seems not to have been shy or reclusive

— if she was hiding she was hiding in plain view, openly entertaining a male clientele at her ground-floor triplex.

Neighbours whom I interviewed yesterday described her as tall, shapely, blonde and blue-eyed, and friendly and engaging. Most assumed she was a high-priced prostitute, though she apparently called her business a "therapy clinic."

It was also her home, and she lived there for about three years, according to long-time area resident François Godeau, who added that she drove a blue Miata sports car and usually spent weekends away.

She has not been seen for the last month. No one answered my knock. Curtains were drawn across her windows, back and front. Several flyers were on her front stoop, the oldest dated one was from June 9.

According to Montreal police, there has been no report of a missing person by her name, nor is her apparent disappearance being investigated.

The landlord of this triplex is a limited company owned by R.J. Rubinstein, a lawyer, who declined to speak on record, asserting that his tenants were entitled to privacy.

Spokespersons for Blake and Farquist have also declined comment.

§

Ottawa Sun, TUESDAY, JULY 9
AN EXCLUSIVE BY Christie Montieth

MONTREAL — Now it can be told. This is the story of how I recorded the startling and spicy accusations by Margaret Blake, which have now been heard around the world.

The date of her outburst: Sunday, June 2. The scene: the

World Wildlife Fund international conference at Montreal's Palais des congrès. The cast: Blake, her aide, Pierette Litvak, and Jennie Withers, MP, the rising star of her ragtag little party.

Just after lunch on the conference's final day, the cast gathered in a salon prior to selling their wares to an audience of eager buyers — eco-activists all.

Once Blake was seated at the podium table, Litvak joined her. The conversation that took place between them hardly needs repeating, but for anyone who's been lost in the jungle or the Arctic for the last ten days, it's reproduced verbatim in the sidebar.

Blake and Litvak were unaware they were talking into a hot mike. So was everyone else, even the simultaneous translators in their booth.

For no particular reason, I had my headphones on while texting on my iPhone. When I heard Blake exlaim "Wow," I set my phone to record and placed it under my right earpiece. I listened, thunderstruck.

Sadly, Withers soon spoiled the fun, with her "Hey, you guys, be careful." She switched the mike off.

Blake had been looking frazzled to start with, but as I hurried from the room to call my editor, I glanced back, and she was visibly distressed. After I returned she continued to seem distracted and fidgety for the presentation and basically let Withers and her other two MPs do the heavy lifting.

Now let me state an irrefutable fact: I did not leak this recording. I am not the BDsmother who put it all online in a series of tweets. I don't know who BDsmother is. No such person is on the news staff at Postmedia. All of us were sworn to silence.

Why have we held back on this scoop? Well, some on our editorial board expressed the concern that Blake's remarks might be an utterly tasteless jest, and the decision was made to hold the story while I investigated further. My assignment was to prove that this Svetlana existed.

And I did. I found a positive review of her services in a B&D forum. The reviewer, pen name ToyBoy, generously awarded four and a half stars to Svetlana Glinka. "Pricey but so delicious!" he gushed, obligingly providing a link to a Google map with Glinka's street number on Rue de la Visitation, south of Sherbrooke.

I made several visits there during the first week of June, futilely knocking on her door. I tried again two days ago, a last-gasp effort before we went to press with this exclusive story.

It appears that she has fled, escaping for now a terabyte-sized slander suit. (Perhaps Margaret Blake is wishing she'd joined her.)

Neighbours described the woman as almost Amazonian — tall, blonde, and well endowed, fluent in both official languages as well as Russian. No photographs of her have come to light.

According to a pair of old-timers who live next door, she regularly entertained male visitors, except on weekends. Many of them arrived at day's end, attired in business suits. They would usually arrive by taxi, though occasionally on foot.

Although Emil Farquist is one of the most recognizable figures on the political scene, none of the neighbours — all were shown his offical photograph — identified him as one of those visitors.

§

You have to feel sorry for Christie Montieth. The *Ottawa Sun*'s hatchet-wielding star columnist got her scoop scooped this week by the *Toronto Star*'s Jack Feigel.

Despite a month of relentless digging to track down a certain whip-wielding star of an infamous horse opera, Montieth's front-page spread in the *Sun* tabloids came as the journalistic letdown of the decade. A month's work, and beaten by one day.

Blame the powers-that-be at Postmedia. Frozen with fear at the prospect of facing a massive libel suit, they muzzled Christie until she got her facts checked and backgrounded. Doubtless they worried she was the infamous twitterer BDsmother — who, incidentally, has not been heard from since the recording went viral.

Christie vigorously denies being the leaker. But it's obvious that Margaret Blake's notorious gossip was bounced around the various *Sun* newsrooms like a badminton bird, and BDsmother could, for all we know, be some mischief-making cub reporter. That wouldn't free them from liability. Thus their imposed silence.

That's how you get scooped. Playing it safe.

§

Reuters Business Briefs, THURSDAY, JULY 11

CALGARY — Sibericon, the Russian energy consortium, has bought a 5 percent shareholding in Coast Mountains Pipelines Inc. for $900 million.

Owen Gilman, Coast Mountains's CEO, said the infusion

of capital puts his company on a solid footing to pursue construction of the multi-billion-dollar pipeline currently awaiting Canadian government approval.

The Russian investment, he said, is intended to satisfy the Canadian government's demand for a performance guarantee before signing off on the project. "All our ducks are now in a row," Gilman said. "We are ready to work with the Canadian government and the energy sector in helping grow our economy."

The project, which has stirred controversy in Canada, would connect Alberta's tar sands with a West Coast deepwater port at Prince Rupert, B.C.

§

Canadian Press, TUESDAY, JULY 16

CALGARY — Canada's preeminent conservative think tank has announced the resignation of Alfred J. Scower, its executive director.

In its press release, the Bow River Institute praised Scower, who has a doctorate in economics from Princeton, for his "unsurpassed leadership" during his five-year tenure, but said its board of directors was in disagreement with him on "some fundamental principles."

Those were not stated, but Scower has been quoted as questioning the merits of the Coast Mountains Pipeline project, which was formally approved on Monday by cabinet decree. Opposition parties have loudly condemned the government's decision to skirt a Parliamentary vote on the hotly contested pipeline issue.

A source at the institute told Canadian Press that Scower's lukewarm approach to oil sands development was scaring off the institute's major donors, the energy sector. "There was a feeling here he was turning a little green on us," he said.

Scower declined to comment other than to deny he resigned under pressure. He said he expects to return to his professorship at the University of Alberta.

Scower's immediate predecessor as executive director was federal environment minister Emil Farquist, who, after winning a seat in Parliament, announced he was cutting off all ties to the institute to avoid any suspicion of favouritism.

Bow River is a major recipient of government research grants.

THE SIERRA FILE

Thursday, July 25

Dear Arthur,

Mucho tiempo has passed since my last report, and I
have no excuse that wouldn't properly be answered by a
boot in the sternum. I have been travelling about Quebec,
but that's an insufficient answer. I had felt besieged by
the throngs of press and onlookers outside my barren
little flat. That's weak, too.

The truth is I have not until tonight been visited by
the muse of composition. But I have opened a bottle of
Provencal Rose (in honour of the neglected roses of my
garden) and have lit an Escepcion de Jose Gener, Havana-
rolled, and, with window open, am enjoying the heat of a
midsummer evening.

Rue de la Visitation has finally settled down, the
curious having found there's little to see. The street
is so named to honour the Virgin Mary's visit to her
pregnant cousin Elizabeth (Luke i. 39). In another sense,

a visitation connotes divine retribution, usually for one's sins, though occasionally God comes bearing favours.

And He visited me with one, as you'll learn.

But let me deal first with other matters. The passenger manifest for Ms. Glinka's flight on June 7 (I won't divulge how I came upon it) shows she flew non-stop to Paris with a connection to Nice. If it will not break the bank, I propose to travel there myself.

I have been to Mr. Farquist's retreat in the Gatineau Hills and have cautiously approached a few persons living or working nearby. None could recall seeing Ms. Glinka or her Miata. But theirs is a less-travelled road, and a car may easily slip down unnoticed to Lac Vert. I shall be returning to the area.

I have not seen the Lincoln Navigator wander by since its last brief visit, on July 7, when its passenger, who remains a mystery woman, tried to rouse the absent Mr. Sabatino.

The prints of my photographs of her and the driver are sharp and clear, despite being blown up. What is interesting (and becomes more interesting as you read on) is that detectives in the Surete's organized crime unit failed to identify them as known Mafia figures. One officer said they looked "vaguely familiar," but that was it.

Enter Harvey Plouffe. And here I gratefully pause to blow out a plume of fragrant smoke from my Escepcion. (I confess I became addicted when you sent me to Cuba: the Narvaez case — you remember that? — death by exploding cigar. I must have visited fifty cigar factories.)

M. Plouffe, the steady customer of Svetlana Glinka whom I mentioned in my last report, took me to lunch at an expensive restaurant in the Old City. He insisted on paying. He is of the moneyed class – an inheritance, I gathered. A plump, rose-cheeked fellow of almost unchecked amiability.

I had to confess to him that my interest in bondage-dominance was purely intellectual, but he was quite accepting of that – indeed intrigued that, as a private investigator, I was looking into Ms. Glinka's disappearance. He took no issue with my being bound by confidentiality as to my employer.

M. Plouffe is gay and he's well out of the closet. He is out, as well, as an aficionado of BDSM, and openly espouses it as therapy.

He too had enjoyed Ms. Glinka's strokes – the "delightfully erotic shiver that comes with anticipation of pain," as he vividly put it. He admitted to no clear understanding of his need for this, though he mentioned strict, religious parenting and "une montagne" of guilt.

He believed he was Ms. Glinka's favourite. They would chat "like old girlfriends" after sessions, and she shared something of her history. Born in Moscow, entered the sex trade as a teen, arrived in Montreal a decade ago in response to an internet marriage proposal. After getting her papers, she left her husband and went back to the work she knew: call girl, madam, finally graduating to her specialty of the last several years.

M. Plouffe had a regular weekly slot with her, Tuesdays at four in the afternoon, and would usually stroll there from his home in the Gay Village. But on Tuesday, June 4, he slowed his pace on seeing a small white van parked out front, and a man and woman carting heavy cardboard boxes from her home. They had a key to the door, and locked it, then loaded the van and drove off. There was no sign of Ms. Glinka or her car.

M. Plouffe had no idea who these two persons were
but recognized them from my photographs of July 7:
the moustachioed heavyweight behind the wheel of
the Lincoln Navigator, the tall brunette who tried
Mr. Sabatino's door. This is the same couple Ms. Litvak
observed at Dorval. Farquist's lawyers are using the
Puhl Detective Agency and I hope to confirm that the
couple in question work for it. Sam Puhl himself is
likely running the show. I worked with him a few years
ago on a corporate fraud matter. He must be doing well
to use a pricey Lincoln as his ghost car.

Back to June 4. After the couple drove off,
M. Plouffe called Ms. Glinka's unlisted number and left
a message. She never called back. ("I am bereft," he said.)

Her landlord, the estimable Rocky Rubinstein, has
subsequently confirmed that her suite is empty except
for furniture and some clothing. The tools of her trade
are gone. As is her phone, voice recorder, computer
equipment, and files. Clearly, the couple observed by
M. Plouffe were tasked to remove all records that might
connect the Hon. Emil Farquist to Ms. Glinka.

Doubtless, the terms of the deal to buy Ms. Glinka's
silence required her to spill all the beans, including
admitting to sharing the Farquist tape with Lou
Sabatino. And so Mr. Farquist's agents have been prowling
the neighbourhood in their big SUV looking for him. To
try to buy him off? To question him? to threaten him?
or worse?

If they do locate him, and if they learn he copied
the video, is it conceivable they would weigh solving
their Sabatino problem by tipping off the Mafia? I doubt
George Cowper Jr., QC, would go so far, but one of Mr.
Farquist's devoted minions might not be as scrupulous.

It is therefore ever more vital to locate the poor fellow. His wife, Celeste, might know his haunts, but she may be almost as hard to find. His parents are deceased, and he has just one sibling, an older sister, Antonia Colombo.

Her husband's uncle, Nick Giusti, has recently been done in by the Mafia, so when I talked to her she was nervous, though cooperative, and in much distress over her brother's disappearance. She was of little help, other than to connect me with Sabatino's wife's father, Simon Brault, a mining supervisor living in Rouyn-Noranda.

M. Brault had earlier, by phone, declined my request to visit, but relented when your office called with our scripted white lie — that I was investigating Mr. Sabatino's disappearance on behalf of his co-workers in the media.

M. Brault is francophone but perfectly bilingual, a brusque fellow and not fond of his son-in-law, who made an impromptu visit to his home on Sunday, June 9, while on a quest to locate his family.

That is the last time that Mr. Sabatino surfaced. M. Brault believes he's suicidal — at one point he apparently jumped into the lake outside their home. My notes read: "His funeral ain't going to attract any vast throngs."

I finally persuaded M. Brault to connect me with Celeste Sabatino who, it turns out, is living in Calgary with her sister, Lucille. He telephoned Celeste and explained to her my mission. I spoke to her briefly and won her permission to visit.

So far, Mr. Sabatino hasn't shown up there, which seems surprising, and adds to my foreboding about his prospects for survival. Mind you, no bodies have been found, and the Mafia usually does its work openly. But if they do dispatch him, our tasks become very difficult indeed.

For what it's worth, I have a jump on the opposition. It appears that neither M. Brault nor his daughter have been visited by any detectives from the Puhl agency, so it's unlikely they know the couple has split up.

Now I have wasted half that Escepcion — still burning but with a thick curl of ash — and allowed my wine to lose its chill.

Au revoir, my friend.
Francisco

THE SIERRA FILE

Tuesday, August 13

Dear Arthur,

I am sorry I missed you in Calgary, where you had a
chambers motion to speak to, but on winding up my tasks
there, I caught a flight back to Montreal.

Let me encapsulate my visit to Mrs. Celeste
Sabatino. She and her children are temporarily with
her sister, Lucille Wong, and her spouse, Langston Wong,
a geophysical engineer, in a ranch-style home in Upper
Mount Royal, a prosperous Calgary neighbourhood. Lisa,
eight, and Logan, six, were in school when I came by. The
Wongs are childless. Langston Wong was at work.

Though alerted by her father to expect me, Mrs.
Sabatino seemed wary of me until satisfied I was who I
am. Apparently some noxious fellow has been trying to
lure children from school playgrounds in Calgary — it's
been in the news.

Mrs. Sabatino's sister was a soothing presence during my interview, and helped Celeste open up. A fetching woman, Celeste, as blunt in speech as her dad, she has taken on part-time work as a designer for a downtown dress shop.

She hadn't been aware her spouse had been laid off. She confessed to being worried about him and feeling guilty about her manner of leaving him. "I just had to escape from that shitty, cold flat. Even the mice were shivering."

And she needed a break from Lou, who kept "dragging me down with his paranoia and gloomy vibes." He had been more of a husband to his computer than her.

She conceded that he wasn't at fault for his dire situation as a hunted man. Indeed, she had been proud of him for breaking the Waterfrontgate story.

And she ruefully admitted that her children missed him, for he'd been a loving, considerate father. "If only he wasn't such a . . ."

An incomplete sentence, but her lips seemed to frame the word "twerp."

She is shrewd, and at one point tested me with: "This [my investigation] wouldn't have something to do with that vile dominatrix living below us?"

Lucille commented: "Yes, isn't that so weird, it's all over the news."

Celeste said of Ms. Glinka: "I thought she was a poseur, une vache. The noise they made!"

I hedged by saying I was interested in Svetlana only insofar as she had also strangely disappeared, at about the same time as Lou.

Celeste: "I hope she didn't get him involved in something."

We let it go at that. Celeste promised to alert me if Lou made contact. I tried to assure her that the absence of any calamitous news about him showed he was alive and, hopefully, well.

My interview ended when Mrs. Sabatino apologized for having to run off to take her turn as a voluntary guard at her children's schoolyard. (Several children at various Calgary schools have been approached by this suspected pedophile, but none molested.)

The ambivalence that Celeste displayed about her husband hints there is hope for reconciliation. If only I could reunite them – that might persuade him to do the right thing by Margaret.

I spent the entire last week in Calgary, which, despite the downturn in the energy sector, was bustling, its inhabitants friendly and accommodating. But of course I felt the general anxiety about the schoolyard prowler.

The other topic on most lips is Farquist v. Blake, and while the minister is widely supported, there were doubters, one of whom provided an enlightening background on Mr. Farquist.

Before introducing him, let me say I have spent far too much time in fruitless research into the plaintiff's background. There is not much of value in the public record beyond the oft-repeated mention of his mother's tragic suicide – it appears in his surprisingly brief Wikipedia entry, which focuses on his degrees and accomplishments, his political history.

Work has been his mistress all his life, and he has never married, though he has had relationships with women. Perhaps the trauma of his broken-hearted mother's suicide deterred him from seeking a bride.

Assembling all the bits and pieces, I have this:

his father, the late Dr. Sandor Farquist, fled from
Communist Hungary during the revolt of 1957. His
original surname was Farkas but on adopting a new
country he adopted a new surname. He studied economics
in the States and Canada, taught it in Calgary, and was
a prominent polemicist of the Right.

Sandor Farquist remained a bachelor until 1969, when
he married Lee Watters, a grade school teacher – he was
44, she half his age. She took his name on marriage.
Emil was born in 1971, their only child. They divorced
eight years later. Sandor remarried; Lee did not. He died
of a stroke some time ago at 77.

Emil remained with his mother until she died at 40
of a barbiturate overdose. He was 18. Accounts describe
him as having braved this loss, but there are hints
he suffered severe depression. However, during the next
several years, he buckled down, emerging at 25 from the
University of Chicago with a Ph.D. in economics.

By the time he was 35, Farquist was chief economist
for Mobil Canada, and went on to the Bow River Institute,
rising through the ranks from Senior Staff Fellow to
Executive Director. He then turned to politics, and the
rest we know. Or think we know.

I expect, Arthur, you have read about Dr. Alfred J.
Scower's recent forced resignation as executive director
of the Bow River Institute. He is now regarded by former
conservative colleagues as a black sheep, or perhaps a
green one, because of his evolving views on conservation
and climate change.

Dr. Scower is soon off to Edmonton to teach a fall
semester, and when we met at his Calgary home, I found
it full of packing boxes. He is a big, ruddy, amiable
man in his late sixties, and quick of mind. My lame

explanation for wanting to see him was shredded before I could utter it.

"You're working for Margaret Blake, I suppose."

To have pretended otherwise would have been foolish, especially since Dr. Scower didn't try to conceal his delight in her public shaming of Farquist, whom he suspected of influencing the Institute's board to cashier him.

He holds some admiration for your wife but has little good to say about Farquist, under whom he worked for several years as a Senior Fellow.

He went on at length about our opponent's political sins and seemed particularly upset by what he called his "wheedling" to win cabinet approval of the Coast Mountains Pipeline.

That approval came only four days after a Russian consortium bought into Coast Mountains Pipeline Corporation. A mere 5 percent stake but worth close to a billion dollars.

My notes read: "Stinks to high heaven. Russians? Those thugs have got more petro resources than they know what to do with."

He was helpful with Mr. Farquist's personal history, though he regretted that much of it was anecdotal. "It was known that Emil regularly had a physical therapist come by his home [in Calgary]. Office gossip had him enjoying a little sex with it. Maybe it was something different."

I append several more quotes from our taped conversation:

"He never talked about his mother's death — or about her at all. It was as if he'd repressed it, buried it." But clearly hers was not a blissful marriage.

Lee Watters had just got her teaching certificate when she met Emil's father. "She was quite the beauty, and deeply in love with Sandor, but was apparently no intellectual spark plug." It appears Sandor became bored with her, and several years into his marriage began an affair with a fellow academic that led to the divorce. Emil had little contact with his father after that.

"The consensus was that Lee's broken heart never mended, but she waited until Emil was of age before ending it all."

We chatted awhile about how her death might have impacted Farquist in perverse ways. Dr. Scower didn't press me but obviously was curious about the source and details of Margaret's tale told out of school. I explained I had to seek your permission to divulge more.

I thank you for your note saying that you stopped by in Victoria to water and deadhead my roses. How grows your garden?

Stay well,
Francisco

THE CLIPPINGS FILE

Edmonton Journal, WEDNESDAY, SEPTEMBER 4

CALGARY —The trial of Emil Farquist's $50 million slander suit against Margaret Blake has been set to begin in six months, on Monday, March 4.

At a hearing Tuesday in the Alberta Queen's Bench, Chief Justice Rachel Cohon-Plaskett scheduled eight days for a trial that most observers believed would take at least a year to get underway.

Speaking to his application for an early trial date, George Cowper Jr., counsel for Environment Minister Farquist, said, "It's vital that my client's name be cleared as quickly as possible, given the massive and unseemly publicity this case has roused."

A.R. Beauchamp, counsel for Margaret Blake, the Green Party leader, agreed to the date but spoke against another application by the plaintiff for "further and better particulars of the statement of defence."

That document, he said, is "clear as a bell" and needed no

amplification. His client had admitted to speaking the words complained of and stood by them, he said.

Cowper argued that his client had the right to know the source of Blake's "salacious" comments and the circumstances surrounding them. Beauchamp contended it was not the purpose of court pleadings to recite evidence.

Chief Justice Cohon-Plaskett denied the motion, saying, "I agree with Mr. Beauchamp. There are other ways of seeking and testing the opponents' evidence." She advised counsel to arrange for early discovery, a procedure by which parties are examined under oath before an official court reporter.

§

Montreal Gazette, TUESDAY, SEPTEMBER 10

The sudden disappearance of three men accused of racketeering at the Port of Montreal has forced a postponement of the trial of the Waterfrontgate Seventeen, originally scheduled to begin next month.

A motion for a delay was granted Monday in Quebec Superior court after Crown Counsel J.R. Charlebois announced that the three men, alleged to be high-level Mafia figures, failed to sign in Saturday to Montreal police headquarters, as required each week by their conditions of bail.

A new date will be set at a hearing on September 29.

Warrants have been issued for Sergio Castellani, Mario Baptiste, and Jules "the Monk" Moncrief. Airports and U.S. border crossings are being monitored, said Superintendent A.R. Malraux of the Sûreté de Quebec. He expected, however, they had already left the country. Moncrief is known to have business interests in Colombia.

The remaining fourteen accused include two employees of Transport Canada, five elected municipal councillors, a business agent for the Longshoremen's Union, and six reputed mid-level Mafia figures.

§

Calgary Sun, FRIDAY, SEPTEMBER 13

Fear has gripped Calgary following the attempted abduction of an eight-year-old girl from a quiet north-end street.

The girl, whose name and address have not been released, was walking home after school on Thursday, when a man stopped his car and offered to drive her home. According to police, when she backed away he reached out the car's passenger door but was only able to grab her backpack as she ran into a neighbour's yard.

He abandoned the backpack and drove away.

He is described as of middle age, of medium height and build, either balding or with short hair, and wearing glasses. A neighbour who answered her door to the girl did not see him or his car, the make or colour of which the frightened girl could not remember.

Over the last three months, there have been three reports of children being approached by a suspected pedophile of similar description. Police have increased patrols near primary schools, aided by Street Watch, a volunteer parent organization that escorts children to their schools and watches over playgrounds.

Environment Minister Emil Farquist, who represents Calgary North-Centre, where the attempted abduction took place, told reporters he will seek unanimous consent in

Parliament, when it resumes next week, for the passage of an amendment to the Police Powers Bill allowing warrantless searches of suspected pedophiles.

In a press conference at his constituency office, he said combatting crime will be "a number one priority of this government" in the expected fall campaign, "especially crimes against our most vulnerable and cherished citizens, our children."

§

Island Tides, TUESDAY, SEPTEMBER 17

The Personal Transformation Mission, a New Age commune that has set down roots on Garibaldi Island, plans to sponsor a rally on behalf of local MP and Green Party leader Margaret Blake.

Jason Silverson, leader of the group popularly known as the Transformers, says the commune's several dozen adherents have expressed unanimous support for Blake's platform for a healthy, sustainable environment.

Though as a U.S. citizen he isn't qualified to vote, he said, "We are all in the same race — to save the planet from environmental catastrophe — an issue that transcends all borders."

The rally will be timed for early in the campaign, expected this fall.

Silverson's announcement was received with surprise by local Greens. Rev. Al Noggins, Blake's campaign manager on Garibaldi Island, declined to comment.

§

Global News, TUESDAY, SEPTEMBER 24
BULLETIN

With unexpected suddenness, Canadian Prime Minister Winthrop Fowler dismissed Parliament today, immediately after the reading of the Throne Speech. A federal election is set for Wednesday, October 30.

§

Huffington Post Canada, WEDNESDAY, SEPTEMBER 25
My Two Cents' Worth, BY Eugene Popoff

I call foul, Fowler. What a sham. But it was to be expected from the dirty tricksters that guide the fortunes of the Tory party.

I was in the Press Gallery and saw it all. No sooner had Governor General Bouvier finished his throne speech — a gift bag stuffed full of election candy — than PM Fowler dissolved Parliament, forcing what headlines are calling a snap election. A misnomer, given the government was about to fall on its kiester anyway.

The intended result was that Opposition parties were denied what has always been regarded as a solemn right to reply to the throne speech. Silence the Opposition! Another in an escalating series of assaults on what we once proudly called a democracy.

High-fives from smug-faced Tory backbenchers greeted Win Fowler's announcement, while Opposition MPs stormed out and railed into the microphones of the assembled news media.

I have rarely seen Charlie Moss in such fine form, almost spitting mad as he heaped venom on the tricksters while aides passed out copies of his Throne Speech Reply. Clearly Moss, who has led the NDP from third-party status to Official Opposition, expects to topple the Fowler regime and return Canada to the international prestige it once enjoyed.

Marcus Yates, the Liberals' hunky new leader, offered a cooler approach, with some levity directed at Fowler's rush to get out of the Chamber. "I guess he really had to go," he told a scrum of laughing (mostly female) reporters. Expect the Tories to launch a smear campaign against the thirty-nine-year-old former social worker, as they dig through their trove of old news photos showing him toking at pro-marijuana rallies.

It's tragic that a fair clump of Canadians have bought into the image of themselves that the Conservatives are selling: tough, no nonsense, get things done. Things like an enhanced police state and the destruction of the environment.

Latest polls have the Tories at their traditional 33 percent. Enough to form a government if the Opposition splits its vote. The NDP is at 31 percent, the Liberals at 20 — a number likely to deflate as diehard Grits flock to the NDP as the devil they know. The Bloc has 8 percent, all in Quebec, and the Green Party, astonishingly, is holding at 6 percent.

My guess is that will evaporate too. In which case I expect Margaret Blake to lose her already tenuous hold on the GP leadership. Anyway, she has other things on her mind these days.

This election will be about democracy, Moss said. But a failure by Liberals and Greens to rally around the NDP could mean they'll end up getting the government they deserve. Four more years of autocracy.

Eugene Popoff is research director
for the Canadian Labour Congress.

THE SIERRA FILE

Wednesday, October 9

Dear Arthur,

I have just returned to my empty flat on rue de la Visitation from a fortnight in the Gatineau hills, where I made forays from a comfortable little hostelry in a village delightfully called Kazabazua, near Lac Vert.

Kazabazua (called Kaz locally) is the Algonquin word for underground river, and one does in fact disappear for several metres before surfacing and passing under a pretty bridge near my inn.

Residents are bilingual and very friendly. Those I chatted with in the restaurant and tavern found me rather fun and charming, I believe. I was a retired gentleman seeking to buy a chalet for my family. My children and grandchildren were skiing enthusiasts, unlike me, a clumsy oaf.

For what it's worth, I now have one confirmed sighting of a blue Miata, this from a bartender who once owned a similar model. (As did I, I lied.) He recalled that about mid-morning one day last March or April it accelerated past his vehicle heading north on the Laurentian Highway, not far from Kaz. In his rear-view, he glimpsed a lone woman at the wheel. Une fumelle blonde.

Not very probative, I agree, but every bit counts. Of greater interest is that Emil Farquist has put his holiday home up for sale. Discreetly. No realtor's sign is posted at his entrance road, no advertising of any kind.

My cover turned out to be un coup d'eclat, giving me access to area realtors, a talkative lot from whom I learned that the scene of the crime, as it were, is being shown by a private broker in Ottawa.

Her name is Rhoda Plumb, who, my inquiries revealed, is also a Conservative fundraiser. I met her by appointment at her downtown brokerage office. She was wary, fearing perhaps I was some kind of spy or investigator. But she recognized the names of the Gatineau realtors who had tipped me off, and seemed comforted to learn I had prospered through the private gem trade. I said I was interested only in a cash deal and her ears perked up.

She was careful not to mention the name of the vendor, but gave me a brochure with the specs on his property, described as "a stunning, private lakeside chalet on four pristine acres."

Offered at $750,000. The owner was motivated.

Ms. Plumb advised that the property is encumbered with a $200,000 mortgage, and here I must admit to a horrendous lapse. I'd been aware of that mortgage — it's recorded on the Quebec Land Register — but only on gong back to it online did I realize it was taken out on May

25, just a few days before Svetlana Glinka, according to Mr. Sabatino, suddenly lost interest in destroying Farquist's political career. Telling, yes?

A few days later, Ms. Plumb picked me up at my inn and drove me to the chalet. I would love to say that I found various bondage implements lying about, but there was only furniture, nicely arranged for show. All personal possessions had been removed to storage. Photographs of the interior are being couriered by separate package.

I realize this doesn't get us very far, but I think we can assume that Mr. Farquist's legal fees are not being covered by the government, let alone whatever substantial sum was paid to Ms. Glinka.

Meantime, in my role as prospective neighbour, I made several fruitless attempts to connect with the other two property owners on this stretch of the lakeshore. They have not been out to the lake since summer. A groundskeeper serves the three properties but he seems to be avoiding my attempts at contact. I shall return.

As to Svetlana Glinka, I now have a lead, through various brain-deadening efforts on search engines, to a woman of that name who has recently opened a business on the French Riviera.

My flight leaves on Sunday.

Wish me well, as I wish the same for you.

Francisco

THE CLIPPINGS FILE

The Bleat, WEDNESDAY, OCTOBER 16
BY Nelson Forbish

Almost our entire island and much more turned out at Starkers Cove for the Thanksgiving fundraising barbecue for Margaret Blake. Counting about 60 boats anchored in the cove, I'd guesstimate at least 400 locals and visitors came by to meet and greet her and enjoy the Transformation Mission's homegrown chickens, ham, lamb, and veggies.

Margaret made a spirited talk asking voters not to believe in the polls and predicting that the Greens would surprise everyone on Monday. She accused the Conservative government of making an under-the-table deal to get Russian financing for the Coast Mountains Pipeline, saying it stinks. (See her Report from Ottawa, page 2.)

Margaret has just returned from the East on her cross-country "Train Campaign," and, with five days to go before the election, she will be swinging up through Vancouver Island with a final weekend rally in Victoria.

Several fellow journalists from the mainland were on island enjoying our traditional hospitality, and despite a few complaints of overcooking from a cynical few, especially the ones from Ontario, this reporter had no beefs and even rejoined the line for seconds.

I learned the feast almost decimated the Transformers' flocks and herds, and when asked about this, Spiritual Leader Jason Silverson said, "We believe in giving back. Whatever bounty we are blessed with, we share with all."

Music was provided by the Fensom Family Singers, backed up by the Garibaldi Highlanders. Guided tours helped acquaint off-islanders with the Transformers' program for sustainable, healthy living, and included a Q and A with the Eastern mystic Baba Sri Rameesh in his tent.

Your intrepid reporter dared approach His Grace after that session and got him to agree graciously to an interview and a profile. Expect a front-page exclusive in the next few weeks.

§

Maclean's, OCTOBER 28
BY Douglas Fellows

If recent polls are to be believed, the Tories' divide-and-conquer strategy is paying off.

As the opposition vote continues to splinter, it increasingly appears Win Fowler may enjoy the dubious comforts of 24 Sussex Street for another four years — with a majority, if the chips fall his way.

Though only 33 percent of decided voters back the Conservatives, they may be breaking out of the pack. Last week they squeaked two points ahead of the New Democrats, who, despite a lacklustre campaign, hold at 31. Still a virtual tie, given the margin of error, but Fowler's aggressive law-and-order theme song is being listened to in the too-close-to-call ridings.

The Tories' crusade to keep the socialist menace at bay, blasted relentlessly over the airwaves, also seems to be having an impact.

Marcus Yates, the personable Liberal leader, is surprising pollsters by holding his own, with a recent jump to 24 per-cent of committed voters — a figure buoyed by his growing female fandom. But the Tories are counting on siphoning from the Grits' once-robust pro-business element. The question is whether the Liberal left will stay with Yates or go over to the NDP, led by the more combative but less attractive Charlie Moss, with his stiff, unconvincing smile.

Pre-election talk of a Grand Coalition to defeat the Tories has softened to a whisper, and that suits Fowler just fine. His aim is to ensure there's an ample piece of pie for everyone on the left, especially the Greens — the PM is banking on its soft vote resisting the blandishments of the NDP. In the last leadership debate Fowler almost seemed to fawn over Margaret Blake, whose party is polling at only 5 percent, as is the Bloc Quebecois.

The Tories don't compete much with the Bloc, which will remain a presence in its Quebec bastions, but Green sup-port is spread across the country like a thin layer of cheese-topping, and they will be lucky to retain their four seats. They've been riding a one-trick pony: the oil sands, unproven allegations of hanky-panky relating to the Russian energy giant, Sibericon, and its investment in the Coast Mountains Pipeline.

Speaking of the Greens and their leader, let us not be blind to the issue that dares not speak its name: a certain $50 million slander action. It remains to be seen if the controversy, which has been muted during the campaign, will damage either combatant on election day. So far, Emil Farquist is riding high in Calgary, but Blake seems in for a fight on the unpredictable West Coast.

Despite the usual breast-beating, one detects the sweaty scent of pessimism in NDP campaign offices. You can almost hear Charlie Moss kicking himself for ducking the pleas, many from within his own ranks, for a united front against a government he disdains as autocratic and in thrall to that ever-handy bogeyman, big business.

Expect a leadership contest in the NDP should the Conservative strategy succeed.

§

Canadian Press, WEDNESDAY, OCTOBER 30

OTTAWA — Marcus Yates pulled off a stunning upset today as his Liberal Party rode a surge of support in the campaign's last days, winning the federal election with 169 seats, one short of a majority.

There was jubilation in Liberal campaign offices as early results showed the Conservative and NDP vote collapsing in Atlantic Canada, with all seats going Liberal. The trend continued through the evening, Liberals gaining 145 new MPs, with representation from all ten provinces. Late polls were reporting a near-record turnout, widely believed to be due to the appeal of the charismatic young prime-minister-in-waiting.

With three seats remaining too close to call, the Conservatives will become the Official Opposition with 114 Members. The New Democrats fell to 45 seats, the Bloc

Québécois took six, down from nine, and the Green Party retained its four ridings.

Prime Minister Winthrop Fowler, in his concession speech, told muted supporters he will step down as Tory leader.

Meanwhile, pundits and pollsters, nearly unanimous in predicting a narrow Conservative win, have been left scratching their heads.

THE SIERRA FILE

Thursday, October 31

Dear Arthur,

It seems I am wedded to this primeval typing machine, my wireless, unhackable Olivetti portable, for it has faithfully accompanied me to the French Riviera.

First off, let me offer congratulations to your intrepid wife for her solid and well-deserved victory in Cowichan and the Islands, and her party's handsome showing overall in bucking the tide that brought the new government to power.

I must say I sat riveted and sleepless as I watched the polls report online. If the recount in Halifax East turns out well for the Greens, there will be more reason to celebrate. Professor Chalmers is only fourteen votes behind — hardly insurmountable.

Meanwhile, I have been two weeks in a lovely ancient stone cottage that I can't believe has not been

immortalized by Paul Cezanne. It is in a village in
the hills above Nice, and rents by the week, though
not exorbitantly compared to the Riviera hotels. (I
have doubtless overspent in restaurants, and am feeling
embarrassed.)

But now to Svetlana Glinka.

It was astonishingly easy to find her, and just as
hard to get her to spill, if you'll forgive the argot.

She has opened up a small shop on Rue de la Loges,
in the old quarter. The sign on the door simply says
"Intime." A sex shop, its wares are displayed candidly
behind a lattice window: lace delicates, love juices, dildos.

I lurked outside awhile with camera and notebook,
watching Ms. Glinka assist a young couple. From what
I could make out she was stretching what seemed
a demonstration condom, displaying its strength and
elasticity to her two customers.

I entered after the couple left with their purchases.
Ms. Glinka looked at me pleasantly, welcomed me, and
offered to answer any questions.

I thought that was a good beginning, and I jumped
at the opportunity too eagerly, asking if she knew that
Lou Sabatino had disappeared.

That took her aback; her mouth opened but no sound
came out.

I explained I was an investigator — I gave her
my card — and that I'd been tasked to find Lou. His
disappearance, I said, may have had something to do with
the video recording she had shown him.

I was hoping for a quick admission that we could take
to court but made the classic error of ignoring sound
practice. I ought to have warmed her up, flattered her,

congratulated her on her new business, asked to be shown about, perhaps bought an aid to masturbation. But no.

Wordlessly, she advanced on me, and I braced myself for a physical attack. But she merely gripped my right elbow, turned me around, and propelled me toward the door.

I dared not resist this athletic woman, but urged her to hear me out, to help save the life of her good friend and former neighbour.

But in seconds, I was outside her door, which she locked. I was without a plan, and could only stand there, staring within, as she made a phone call.

Handily, there was a cafe directly across the street, and a sidewalk table was free. So I ordered a latte and pretended to read the Guardian while peeking over it.

When Svetlana showed up at her window, still on the phone, she observed me observing her. I was feeling very foolish. The best I could do was wait her out. During the next thirty minutes, a few customers tried her door, peered inside, then wandered off.

Then a tall, thin gentleman in a natty suit, with an old-fashioned cravat, alighted from a taxi directly in front of me and came to my table.

"Would you permit me to join you, sir?" he said — in English, for which I was thankful, my French being laboured. This was obviously Svetlana's emissary, and he seemed a decent sort, and I offered a chair beside me.

He was, as I had guessed, un homme de loi. He gave me his card: Emmanuel Lopez, avocat, of the firm of Guelle, Lopez. He thanked me for my card, but merely glanced at it — its contents had already been relayed to him.

"I am honoured," he said. "You are highly regarded.

I read several comments on Google praising you as
number one in Canada at your profession."

I assured him that was an exaggeration, but regaled
him with a few anecdotes, which he enjoyed. He in
turn told me some of his own background. He was from
Seville, though he took his law degree in Paris, and
does entertainment law.

I admitted to my Costa Rican roots, and we were
delighted to be able to switch to our mother tongue. His
seemed more loosened as we went along, though that may
be due to the excellent carafe of Merlot we shared.

I made no bones about why I was in Nice, and on
whose behalf, and put everything on the table, except
for Lou Sabatino having pirated the tape. M. Lopez had
followed the Great Canadian Scandal, of course, and found
it highly amusing. He reverted to French: "A peu près
francais."

I suggested that his client might not find it
amusing once the press descended, as it eventually would.
He shook his head sadly at that. She had no choice but
to be fuerte, he said, and still her tongue.

Of course M. Lopez was forbidden to relate any of
his conversations with his client. Instead, what he did,
as the Merlot flowed, was pose a "fictional" scenario.

It went like this: let us assume a certain woman
of the world, in return for financial favours, signed
a non-disclosure agreement, and she risks all, perhaps
her very life, if she whispers a word about a certain
politician.

Let us also assume that no copies exist of a certain
little film showing the politician taking his pleasure
in unorthodox ways. That is because our hypothetical
woman has rendered up her only copy of it, along with

all her computer equipment, external drives, webcams, recording devices, everything electronic, as well as address book, memo pad, notes, even the calendar on the wall and stickies on the fridge.

(And here, Arthur, I footnote my earlier reference to the couple who were armed with a key to Svetlana's therapy clinic and were seen carting this stuff off.)

Let us further assume (he went on) that this certain woman's luggage and purse and pockets were thoroughly searched before she was escorted to the airport's personal security screening area. And, oh, yes, let us also assume the needle of a polygraph machine did not waver when she denied having access to any copies of that video.

I asked M. Lopez whether, in his imaginary scenario, the woman mentioned to her inquisitors anything about a certain news reporter.

A shrug. "Let us presume she did," he said sadly.

I mused over this, dispirited. Doubtless, Farquist's team have been beating the bushes for Mr. Sabatino, hoping to silence him one way or another. They wouldn't know about Sabatino's pirated video, but would know he'd seen Glinka's original version, and presumably suspected he had related the contents to Margaret. Despite all their precautions, they may be worried that a copy is floating around somewhere. Lou would be at severe risk if they discover he'd copied the video.

M. Lopez told me politely but adamantly that he could not allow me to interview his client.

You will doubtless consider the option of subpoenaing Ms. Glinka, which you know better than I would be costly, difficult, and subject to the vagaries of French law. I fear she would be a dangerous witness in any event. I don't like to say this, Arthur, but much hinges on our finding Lou Sabatino. Everything.

These notes will go to you by Federal Express at a premium rate, so let us hope for their timely arrival. I am very sorry for this failure.

Your friend,
Francisco

PART THREE

EIGHT SECRETS TO A LASTING ORGASM

It was mid-November, and things were looking up. The second instalment of Lou's severance pay, thirty-two K, had landed in his account at the Laurentian Bank. Hugh Dexter had come through, and Lou was almost ready to forgive the downsizing desk-sitter for being a prick.

And odds were good for recouping the thirty-two big ones the Mafia had poached from his bank account. That was one of the reasons he went to Calgary — Laurentian had a branch there. Lou drove to Calgary — he now owned a car, your basic Chev Cavalier, standard trans. He'd bought it from an auto mechanic up in Maple Creek for one grand plus setting him up with a website. Lou hadn't yet registered the car in either of his names — he was leery of leaving a paper trail — so it was still in the name of Maple Creek Car and Truck Repairs Ltd.

The manager at the Calgary branch was a cool guy, and Lou opened up to him, showed proofs, documentation, printouts, the Waterfrontgate stories, the Mafia's attempt on him, his status as a protected witness.

The transfer order had originated in Montreal, but Lou could prove he had been visiting in-laws that day in Rouyn-Noranda. The manager promised their security people would investigate. He would be in touch. If it all worked out, Lou would likely get his money back.

The other reason he was in Calgary was the child molester. Still on the loose. Another little girl had been approached. Lou had family in Calgary.

He was buoyed on leaving the Laurentian bank, and found the mojo to drive over to the Upper Mount Royal area, GPSing his way to the address of Celeste's sister, Lucille. What people would call a better neighbourhood: sizable homes, mature trees, and broad, frozen lawns. Lou drove past Lucille's sprawling house on Hope Street and got a quick peek at a modern extension at the back, maybe an in-law suite for Celeste and the kids. He parked about five houses down.

The two-car garage looked to be full — Celeste's Dodge Caravan was parked outside. It was mid-afternoon, the kids at school: Logan, who had just turned seven, Lisa, whose ninth birthday was coming up. Lou hated himself for not being able to even send them a card. He ached to see them.

He didn't get too close, in case someone was at a window. Mafia dread restrained any impulse to go farther. It was risky enough telling the bank manager everything, his pseudonym, his status as a protected witness. He was worried about loose lips, his wannabe assassins zeroing in on Calgary, his family being targeted.

He drove off to the nearest public school, a few minutes away, found it in afternoon recess. A platoon of adults with Street Watch was hanging around and eyed him suspiciously as he drove slowly past. His heart leaped when he saw little Logan, bundled up, romping, sliding on a frozen puddle. And just a glimpse of Lisa yakking with girlfriends.

That shithole pedophile. Lou wasn't into extreme measures, but a little surgery to the nuts didn't seem too over the line. But he felt assured his kids were safe.

Lou then headed off to his Travelodge, where he spent the evening composing a letter to his family. He posted it the next morning before driving back to Saskatchewan. No return address.

§

The next day found him back at work, arraying his tools beside a desktop in the storefront office of Sally Rosewell, Porcupine Plain's combo realtor, insurance agent, and notary. He pressed the on switch. Nothing. An XPS desktop, 8000 series, only a few years old. The monitor seemed okay.

"It went on the fritz three days ago," Sally said. Early forties, pretty face, pretty stacked, pretty good-looking generally, not too heavy.

"I'm sorry, Sally. I was away. I got your text."

"Where did you go?"

"Just a little road trip to Alberta. Business. See some friends." All the external inputs were in place. He hoped it wasn't the processor.

"I like the way you trimmed that beard, Rob. Suavé."

He'd seen a barber while he was in Maple Creek. He felt he looked scholarly, less nerdish. He figured he was beyond recognition. Robert O'Brien, but they called him Rob.

He got under the desk, had a good look at Sally's ankles as he followed the power cord to its outlet, a surge protector. The plug was stiff but partly out. He jammed it in, and the computer booted up.

"Oh, shit," Sally said.

They laughed off her embarrassment. "You owe me a drink," he said.

"How about dinner? At my place?"

Lou was into doing that, and said so. He liked his chances, the way she was coming on. Her husband had run off to Moose Jaw last year, with the crop-duster's wife.

Lou hadn't been close to a woman for six months, but he saw all sorts of problems. The main problem was that he loved his wife.

"Hey, Rob, you still looking for a place to move to?"

"If something comes up." His benefactors' trailer was far out of town, and he had ended up doing a lot of his business in the Quill over coffee or, too often, beer. "Wouldn't be the Johnsons' place? Royce and Gertie are moving."

"Exactly what I had in mind."

A handsome brick house near the bottom end of Main Street. Royce was in his eighties, erratic ticker, murmurs. Lou had helped them do an internet search, found them a nice retirement community in Swift Current.

"I like that house." It could double as his office. Two storeys, a full acre, garden, well maintained. A big fireplace, warm shelter from the coming gales of winter. He shuddered at the memory of his spooky flat in Montreal.

"Ninety thou' is the asking. Fifteen down and they'll take a mortgage back to the right guy."

Tempting. But did he dare put his name on a property deed? Maybe just rent it long-term. He could certainly afford that. The computer-repair business had levelled off, but he'd gotten into an internet sideline that was working like hot buttered fuck. Selling Facebook-ready lists to websites, fuel for the hits that kept the ads flowing. TEN FAMOUS ACTORS YOU DIDN'T KNOW WERE ALCOHOLICS. EIGHT HOT TIPS TO WRITE GREAT FICTION. TEN BIZARRE SEX ACTS THAT WILL BLOW YOUR MIND. TWELVE HOLLYWOOD HOTTIES WHO HAD ABORTIONS. Most of those twelve were guesses, but Lou was betting that abortions were as common in Hollywood as apples in an orchard.

"Any dietary issues?" Sally said. "I can rustle up a sizzling pork roast."

"Sounds sumptuous."

"Tomorrow night?"

"I'll bring wine."

She gave him a big hug at the door. She smelled good.

§

Lou carried on to the Quill, returning greetings as he waded between the tables. Everyone was in a good mood, a lax time in November — the snow had held off, the granaries were full, cattle prices up. A lot of post-election analysis going on, folks suspicious of the new Liberal government — it was pretty Conservative around here.

You'd think Emil Farquist had enough going on, but he'd tossed his hat in for the Conservative leadership — even while his humongous suit against Margaret Blake headed for the courts. Lou was plagued by guilt over breaking his promise to her. But he felt handcuffed, impotent, with those Montreal mobsters bent on blipping him off. All of them were out on bail, their trial adjourned because Sergio Castellani, Mario Baptiste, and gang leader Jules "the Monk" Moncrief, who had given one-way tickets to several snitches, were on the loose.

Margaret Blake had the goods on Farquist, she was innocent — surely that would become obvious at the trial. Svetlana would be Witness One. Arthur Beauchamp would eviscerate her on the stand if she tried any bullshit.

Assuming she was alive. No one had been able to locate her. That was a concern that fuelled Lou's drive to survive.

On the bar, a laptop was waiting for him, an older Toshiba A215, a dinosaur. "Welcome back," said its owner, Harry Schumann, the mayor — or reeve, as they called it — a bald, rotund, cracker-barrel kind of guy. "You been gone three days, and the government of Porcupine Plain has come to a standstill."

"Still faster than normal, Harry," a patron called.

Lou sat down. "What's the problem?"

"Flickers on and off ever since I accidentally sat on it."

"You need a new computer."

"Ain't in the budget. As it is, we're a hundred and twenty-seven dollars in the hole." He looked around, lowered his voice. "You been a little derelict, Rob, in obtaining a business licence. I'm empowered to waive the fee."

Lou didn't want a business licence, didn't want his name on any public document.

The mayor handed him a pint. Lou took a gulp, and ran some tests, then began opening up the Toshiba.

"So where you been, Rob?"

"Calgary. I got relatives there." He had pictures stuck in his mind of Logan sliding on that frozen puddle, Lisa bantering with her new friends.

"Something the matter, pardner?" said Mayor Schumann. He'd seen Lou cover his face.

"Something in my eyes." Embarrassed, he accepted a Kleenex from the bartender.

The mayor watched gloomily as Lou laid his tools down and shook his head. "Say sayonara to this computer, Harry. I can save the hard drive. I'll fix you up with one of my spares."

He retreated to a lone table with his beer, ordered a cheeseburger, took out his iPad. TWELVE JESUS QUOTES YOUR MINISTER WILL NEVER READ. YOU'LL BE WIPING TEARS OF LAUGHTER AT THESE KITTEN VIDEOS. He would have to scour YouTube for those. EIGHT SECRETS TO A LASTING ORGASM.

DOUBT THOU THE STARS ARE FIRE

Arthur was spreading straw over the raised beds of his garden. He'd been a week on Garibaldi, a week of hard work with spade and fork and hoe. The last of the winter pears and apples were in. The hay was in. The root cellar was well stocked, and kale, potatoes, and carrots would continue to provide from the soil. Now, finally, the garden was almost tucked in.

It was Saturday, the tail end of a week of relative peace, getting back to the routines of Blunder Bay, renewing friendships with goats, geese, and sheep, battening the hatches against the mid-November chill. A brief deliverance from the grind of Farquist v. Blake, which had been taking an emotional toll.

He had undertaken Margaret's defence as a *beau geste*, driven by a volatile blend of love for her and guilt over his romp with Taba Jones. He had broken his pledge never to step again inside a courtroom and the unwritten rule against a lawyer acting for a loved one. He was consumed by anxiety about failing Margaret, torn up by that fear.

They had managed only a couple of weeks together in the summer, an uncomfortable time, with the stress of the lawsuit and a pending election. Margaret had been constantly on the phone, long distance.

She'd spent all but those two weeks campaigning and had remained back East since the election. She had won comfortably, but Emil Farquist's victory was the more impressive: Calgary's defamed hero.

Compounding Arthur's discomfort was the forever-looming figure of Dr. Lloyd Chalmers. Would Arthur never see the back of that man? His judicial recount was set for the day after tomorrow, Monday, in Halifax. He'd been five votes behind the Liberal candidate at the Official Count. Arthur assumed Margaret would be there, giving moral support — a victory for Chalmers would ensure the Greens the balance of power in the new Parliament.

But Arthur didn't know how he could survive four years of his wife caucusing with him.

He briefly considered imbibing a mug of gupa, in hope of finding again the transcendental peace that had brought him such strange and misty comfort in June — a notion he quickly rejected. It would be less risky to embrace the Baba's mantra — so he recited it aloud several times to his wheelbarrow. "Joy is wisdom, time an endless song."

It seemed to work. He remembered where he was, on a pleasant little farm overlooking the Salish Sea, in his cherished garden, on a brisk and sunny Saturday. To complete the scene, the two young Woofers were wending their way from the goat pen with filled milk pails — a bucolic landscape by Constable or Pissarro.

The girls seemed to be fully deprogrammed — Reverend Al had spent considerable time with them, enlightening them about the dangers of cults, and they'd not been enticed back to Starkers Cove.

But they were an exception to the growing, overpowering presence of the Transformers, whose aura had settled over the island like a warm, fuzzy blanket. Silverson had swollen his ranks by opening up Starkers Cove to children, and on weekends it seemed half the island passed under the Mission's gate, teased into empty-mindedness by its message: "When you realize there is nowhere to go, you have arrived."

Their latest recruit, according to bar talk, was Auxiliary Constable

Kurt Zoller, whose awakening to a hunger for self-realization seemed as likely as a sudden cessation in the earth's rotation.

Arthur's plans were to spend the rest of the weekend reading some poetry, playing some Bach, maybe doing a little fishing, gaining strength for another pre-trial skirmish in Calgary on Tuesday. George Cowper Jr., the very able counsel for the plaintiff, was applying to adjourn the trial for six months. Farquist was too busy running for the leadership of the Conservative Party to give sufficient heed to his slander suit: that was the bald truth of it.

Arthur was in a dilemma. His instinct was to oppose the adjournment. But the trial date was only a few months away, March 2, and he was not exactly armed to the teeth with proof. Svetlana Glinka had cashed in her chips and was out of the game; Lou Sabatino was still AWOL. Francisco Sierra had doggedly collected many useful bits and scraps, but hardly enough to tilt the scales.

Arthur and his diligent investigator could use that extra six months to build their case, track down Sabatino, alias Robert O'Brien. Who, as of two weeks ago, was still alive. In Calgary, from the postmark on a letter he'd sent to his family. That good news had been conveyed to Francisco Sierra by Celeste Sabatino. Also much alive were Sierra's chances of finding Sabatino, especially with the gift of half a year.

Without Lou to save the day, Cowper would make short work of Margaret in cross. "And where is this amateur video you claim to have watched in the dark recesses of a bookstore café? Why hasn't Mr. Sabatino come forward?"

Again, that welling of despair. This lawsuit had become more difficult than the toughest of his murders, cases in which he wasn't literally wed to his client. But Margaret hadn't wanted "any goddamn best specialist." She had wanted her life companion.

Guilt had triggered his response: "Yes! Of course! No problem!"

He paused to stretch his creaky back, thought of Baba Sri Rameesh again. "Let what comes come; let what goes go. Find out what remains."

But it was hard to let what goes go. What remains? An awkward, messy trial of Sisyphean difficulty.

He emptied his wheelbarrow of the last of the straw, decided to clear his head with a brisk hike to pick up his mail and a few sundries at the general store.

He did not get far before Reverend Al came by in his Honda Civic and insisted he get in beside him. "I was just on my way to see you. There are things to talk about, old boy. I'll have something to say at service tomorrow about the Transformers. I'd like you to be there — we're forming an action committee. There's no time to waste. They are truly about to own this island. They're not just colonizing minds, they're taking over the Trust."

The two-member Islands Trust was Garibaldi's governing body, serving under a government mandate to preserve the unique environment of the islands of the Salish Sea. Arthur hadn't been paying much heed to local politics, but had read in the *Bleat* that Garibaldi's two quarrelsome incumbents had quit in a huff, and two of Silver Tongue's favourites were running in a special election called for December. Ida Shewfelt, a Pentecostal Christian converted to the teachings of Baba Sri Rameesh. And, *horribile dictu*, Kurt Zoller.

"Kurt has gone completely under," Al said. "Hypnotized, hears Silverson's voice coming from the trees. Silver Tongue is about to become the dictator of all Garibaldi through his two anointed proxies. No one else is running, and nominations close Monday. Christ, the bishop's edict be damned, I may have to run myself. Ida Shewfelt! The queen of kitsch." Winner of best arrangement at the annual flower show, with her little elves dancing among the blooms.

They were descending now from the brow of what locals called Shewfelts' Hill, their framed, brightly painted two-storey down there, guarded by a fleet of garden gnomes on its neatly trimmed lawn. Forty days before Christmas and they already had their decorations up, Rudolph on the roof.

Al kept going on about the Transformers. "I still can't figure out their angle. Old Barry Peale wanted to make his will out to them, and they declined. Something corrupt has to be going on there. Porno movies? They've always got their cameras going. They just brought in a big van. No idea what's in it. Maybe a lab for crystal meth."

Arthur, however, was no longer persuaded that anything illegal was going on. Silverson was a trained hypnotherapist; he was surely motivated not by money but by ego. Exerting power over others' minds. It almost seemed an experiment.

Al continued to vent even as he dropped Arthur off at the store. "They're selling what's left of their livestock, by the way, in case you're interested in an emu or two. They're going vegetarian. What Silverson calls achieving another plane. Wish they'd leave on one. I guess you've got enough on your mind. How's Margaret?"

"I thought she might come by this weekend, but Parliament opens in nine days. Lots of things going on."

"That's right, Lloyd Chalmers, the judicial recount. Margaret will be fairly keyed up over that. Good friend of hers, isn't he? Brilliant chap, I recorded his TED Talk."

§

Arthur picked up a few things in the store and lined up at the mail counter behind Joanne and Henry, the Transformers featured in the *Bleat* who'd cycled all the way from L.A. to meet the Baba.

Abraham Makepeace was scanning a postcard intended for Joanne. "This here is from a talent agency wishing you happy Thanksgiving. You an actress?"

"I'm a nutritionist," Joanne said, rolling her eyes at her partner.

"I wouldn't have thought a nutritionist needed an agent. Maybe in L.A."

"He's a friend." Joanne gently pried the postcard and a couple of letters from Makepeace's grip while Henry filmed the exchange. Arthur couldn't figure out why, but the Transformers were constantly chronicling the nosy postmaster.

Joanne and Henry bowed to Arthur, each voicing a "Namaste." Unsure of protocol, Arthur bowed back. "Same to you."

They left him to deal with Makepeace, who was massaging a special delivery envelope. "Cardboard backing on both sides. Return address is a box number in Montreal. My best guess is it's about that libel charge against Margaret."

§

On his way back home, Arthur came upon Kurt Zoller on the side of the road, pounding in a stake bearing the stencilled sign: *Trust Zoller. Just do it.*

Arthur could see a pile of such signs in the back seat of the orange Hummer. The thought of the island's infamous obsessor becoming Island Trustee under Silverson's thumb was truly alarming. Reverend Al was right, the Transformers had to be stopped. But how? This was a democracy. Even the hypnotized had a right to vote.

Zoller watched him approach. He too now had glazed eyes, a distant stare. How quickly he'd fallen under Silverson's sway. He had them believing he was omnipresent, speaking to his subjects from the sky and the forest.

Zoller greeted him in a slow, mechanical way, then held him up for a while with a confusing ramble about his program for governing Garibaldi. As far as Arthur could make out, he wanted to prepare his subjects for the enlightenment that flowed through all life and was based on a universal energy. Arthur thanked him for that, and carried on home, clutching his envelope from Francisco Sierra.

§

After setting a fire, and with a mug of tea at hand, he settled into his favourite club chair and unfolded a notarized copy of Lou Sabatino's handwritten letter to his family. Clipped to it was a note from Frank, expressing the hope this got safely to him.

A copy of Lou's envelope was included, postmarked November 12 in Calgary. It bore no return address, nor did the letter, which was on lined pages torn from a steno notepad. His message to his family was pensive and thoughtfully expressed, wishing wife and children happy lives, promising to respect Celeste's wish that they remain apart.

The letter offered up some odd, tender touches. Poetic phrasing about a love kindled by absence and memories. A snippet from Hamlet's note to Ophelia: *Doubt thou the stars are fire, doubt truth to be a liar, but never doubt I love.* Lou had prepared a list: "Eight great ways to say I love you." Nothing here to suggest a death wish. Yet suicide was a worry. Lou's father-in-law had mentioned something about Lou making an attempt at it, jumping into a lake.

Particularly touching was Lou's recall of his shy, fumbling pursuit of Celeste years ago, how he'd first set eyes on her, at a Christmas party, how he'd been struck dumb by her grace and beauty, how he'd spent an hour rehearsing an opening line, then flubbed it, something banal about how her lovely dress reflected the colours of autumn, then being reminded it was winter.

There were other light anecdotal remembrances of Celeste and the kids. Regrets over his failures as husband, as father, as a human being. A thank-you to Celeste for protecting Lisa and Logan from the child-stalker haunting their city. Assurances that he was safe and well, "building a new life." He added: "Despite all, I am happier than I deserve to be."

But there was little more about himself or his whereabouts. Parsing the letter for clues, Arthur took note of two references. A comment about a Chinook wind. That suggested the western prairies, which were occasionally embraced by that warming wind from over the Rockies.

"I am beginning to realize that the city made me feel small," he wrote. That was the other clue — he had likely found some rural refuge.

LET WHAT COMES COME;
LET WHAT GOES GO.

Driving home from St. Mary's church in his pickup, Arthur instinctively ducked at a roar from overhead, then looked up to see one of Syd-Air's float planes descend toward the coast. A charter, not one of its regular runs. Maybe for the Baba, whose term, Arthur had heard, was up.

The day was crisp but sunny, warm for the third Sunday of November. He couldn't wait to get out of suit and tie into something casual for this do-nothing day. He'd dutifully attended Reverend Al's service, patiently listened to his depressing sermon, a call to arms against "phony spirituality exported from La-La Land." The tirade merely seemed to frighten the diminished congregation of the aging faithful.

Al had boldly announced his candidacy to run for Islands Trust, but no one answered his call to join him on the anti-Transformers ticket. Arthur expected Al would be beating the bushes all day to find someone, anyone, to team up with him before tomorrow's deadline. Arthur had hurried off after the service, fearing Al would approach him to run. A distasteful three-year commitment that no sane person would undertake, but Al was prepared to martyr himself.

On turning in to his driveway, Arthur was startled to see the float plane at his dock, Margaret alighting, smiling, waving. He almost drove into the snake fence as he swerved into the farmyard.

He bounded out, and they met on the grassy ridge above the beach and hugged wordlessly until the plane lifted off. "What a beautiful surprise," he said.

"Escaping from the zoo for a couple of days. I was missing the island, the farm. Missing you."

"And I you." Arthur was too flustered to say more. He was dazed, delighted, and puzzled. Why wasn't she in Halifax? Wasn't Lloyd Chalmers's recount tomorrow? She hadn't flown six hours here on a whim. He wanted to believe she was declaring her commitment to him, to their marriage.

But their time would be limited. "I hope you remembered that I'm due in Calgary tomorrow evening," he said.

"I know. We'll have a day and a night together."

He found himself nervous about the night, his carnal role as husband, as adulterer.

§

Arthur tidied up the house as best he could while Margaret showered and changed into outdoor wear. She needed to be outside, she'd said, "to breathe the clean Garibaldi air." A walkabout on a crisp fall day would help put cold, wet, gloomy Ottawa out of mind.

So after sitting down to chicken sandwiches and goat cheese as guests of Niko and Yoki, they went on a tour of the farm: the animal pens, the garden, the beach, Blunder Point, and her favourite spreading arbutus.

Arthur talked all the while, keeping to safe subjects, the local news: the Transformers' livestock sale, their political ambitions, and their cutout candidates. Silverson's power-tripping bothered

Margaret, who had welcomed his political support but was now finding him and his cohorts "a little too creepy for comfort."

She had read Lou's letter over lunch, but had little to say about it. She did not share Arthur's dilemma about the proposed six-month adjournment, was keen to get the trial on and over with.

She ordered him to bury the slander suit for the one day they had together and suggested a trek to the Brig for a drink — "I really need one." En route, she remained mostly silent, watching for sheep poop, holding his hand as he led her up the north pasture trail, the shortcut to Centre Road.

So far she'd made no mention of Chalmers or the recount, and Arthur felt she was holding back to avoid reopening wounds. But he too was being skittish about it, and felt silly, and finally said, "I expected you to have gone to Halifax."

She pulled him to a stop and looked squarely at him. "I thought about it. It didn't feel right. That's when I realized I wanted to be with you."

"Thank you, and I love you all the more for that. And I want you to believe that your . . ." A struggle for the right word. "That your episode with Lloyd Chalmers is forgiven and forgotten. One can't be haunted by sorrow and guilt."

He beat back an impulse to blurt out his own sin. "I know, Margaret, that tomorrow's recount is important to you, and I wish Dr. Chalmers well."

"It is a very big deal, Arthur. The Liberals will be begging at the door. They might be able to count on the NDP to support the wishy-washy stuff, but they're bruised and angry. So Yates will have to suck it up and go green to keep us onside. Goodbye Coast Mountains Pipeline. Never mind, enough of that."

Then, as they climbed the knoll above Hopeless Bay, she said: "I'm actually thinking of getting out, Arthur." She was gazing at the valley below, a nest of small farms, a soft mist rolling through the pastures toward the sun-sparkled bay with its funky dock and store and bar.

They remained there a while, Margaret confessing to her growing distaste for the political life — the nastiness, games, and energy-sapping tension. She had paid her political dues, had a worthy successor in Jennie Withers, and she longed for a return to her placid island.

Arthur encouraged her, of course, but both knew that a decision had to await the outcome of the defamation action. A loss, and the issue would become moot. Margaret's political career would be in the gutter.

§

Outside the bar and general store, the local guru's Mercedes convertible sat regally among a dozen beaters, one of them Reverend Al's old Civic — he would be enjoying his traditional post-service tot of rum, and maybe campaigning, pressing flesh. Parked across the road, causing Arthur a spasm of distress, was Taba's GM pickup.

Arthur stalled for time — he hoped Taba was just picking up some items from the store, a quick in-and-out. "Shall we wander down to the dock? Oh, there's Gomer's crab boat — maybe we can buy a couple of fat ones for dinner."

"Let's go up for a drink first. Al and Zoë are here."

He saw them at a window seat in the Brig — talking with . . . yes, the island's bold-breasted potter. Margaret forged ahead up the ramp to the patio, and Arthur hurried to catch up, proposing instead an outside table, in the fresh air.

"It's a bit nippy, dear. Come on, they'll be offended if we ignore them." Waving to the threesome by the window. "Oh, and there's Taba. I missed seeing her last summer."

"They seem to be in deep discussion, so maybe you'd like —"

"A drink."

She pulled him inside, past the three Pasadena hipsters, who were knocking back shooters while enjoying the ribald rhymes of the louche poet, Cudworth Brown, looking cool in a beret, on his enduring quest to make out. Xantha had been filming him, but swivelled to Arthur and Margaret, capturing his stiff smile and her wide one, practised, camera-ready.

Al and Zoë greeted Margaret with hugs as Arthur and Taba studiously avoided eye contact. Margaret took the one empty chair while Al dragged another over, depositing Arthur beside his seducer, too close to her. Their knees touched, and Arthur quickly withdrew his.

Al gestured at the starlets' table. "Cud is giving the Transformettes one more chance. He's determined to believe they're not lesbians."

"This is their farewell," Zoë added. "They're driving that pricey gas guzzler back to Hollywood."

Arthur found that odd. They'd brought it up for Silverson, who'd rarely driven it. Maybe he felt it reflected poorly on his image as a back-to-the-land conservationist.

"God has answered my prayers," Al said. "Taba is taking one for the team. She's agreed to run for Trust. We're filing our papers tomorrow."

"Good on you, Taba," said Margaret.

"I need to have my sanity tested," Taba said. "I already have nightmares of being strangled in red tape."

Al beamed. "We're hoping you'll both lend your names to our campaign."

Margaret clapped her hands. "We'd be honoured."

Al called to Emily LeMay at the bar: "Pop a cork, old girl, and a coffee for Arthur." Turning to him, he said, "I know you're busy fighting the good fight for your loving client, but if you could spare a little time to be Taba's Official Agent . . ."

"Well, I, um . . . I'm not sure."

"No work involved. Just help her through a few technicalities, sign her papers, merely a matter of holding her hand."

Words failed Arthur. He flushed.

"It's the least you can do, darling," said Margaret.

"It's done, then," Al said, then pulled the nomination papers from a satchel. "Sign here, old boy."

§

Arthur was in bed, reading then rereading the first few pages of a historical novel, retaining nothing, starting anew, distracted by his old enemy, performance anxiety. He and Margaret had been apart for three months; she had come all this way to be with him and deserved better than going to bed with a lifeless lump.

She was still downstairs on the phone, strategizing with Pierette: the recount in Halifax, the new Parliament about to go into session, a new cabinet, new challenges. The never-ending toils of a party leader. Maybe she would be too exhausted . . . But that deep and tender kiss before he went up to shower said otherwise. He sought peace, mindlessness. *Let what comes come; let what goes go.*

But the tension-laden afternoon in the Brig was still with him — they'd stayed for a painful two hours, Arthur somehow maintaining a pretence of normality and, after Taba slipped away, making an effort at bonhomie.

Abandoned early by the Hollywood sprites, Cud Brown had remained stuck to his chair, descending into a state of muttering intoxication by the time Arthur and Margaret left. There sat the hairy goat, alone, abandoned to his masturbatory fantasies, and here was Arthur, wimpily waiting in the connubial bed for the woman he loved.

What was the matter with him? It was ridiculous to feel so torn up by a careless, impulsive moment of desire. Margaret need never know. Get over it. *Vincit qui se vincit.* He conquers who conquers himself.

He was pretending to read as Margaret came in, but looked up as she greeted him, and smiled bravely. She examined him with her penetrating grey eyes. It was as if she saw through him, and she let him off the hook. "We're both under a strain. I just need you to hold me."

She looked quite lovely, really, her hair down, her slim, trim body casually revealed to him as she stripped. A peek at him, as if for reaction. Then strolling gracefully, nakedly, to the shower.

That vision stayed with him until she returned. As she slipped under the sheets, his book slid from his stomach onto the floor with a thud. He caressed the woman he loved, kissed her, passion welling. Her hand moved over his thigh, and felt the swelling there.

"Oh, my," she said.

GRAVE SECRETS FROM THE MORGUE

A Monday morning layover in Vancouver gave Arthur time to stop at his law office, a visit prompted by his concern that Roy Bullingham might be vexed by the mounting costs of AltaQB-889, that being the Alberta Queen's bench file more widely known as Farquist v. Blake.

Arthur was still glowing from the pleasures of last evening — he had risen to the occasion! — as he walked briskly into the BMO tower. Joining him in the high-speed elevator were several of Tragger, Inglis's crisply attired young lawyers, new faces to him, though he was clearly known to them — they were sneaking looks at the smiling old warrior in his old-fashioned suit. All but Arthur got off at the fortieth floor, where the working class strove — he carried on to the forty-third, where the senior partners reigned.

The most senior among seniors was Roy Bullingham, known as Bully, but only to intimates, the last surviving founder of the firm — Tragger and Inglis were long deceased. Bully, at ninety-three, was still as sharp as a stiletto, a skinflint who had built his firm from five lawyers to five hundred in Vancouver, Calgary, Ottawa, and Toronto, with satellites in Shanghai, London, and Washington.

Arthur exchanged greetings with long-time staff as he made his way to his commodious old office. Bully had never quite accepted the notion that Arthur had retired, and kept it clean, empty, and unaltered.

Arthur ruefully studied an expense sheet from his in-basket. Francisco Sierra's bill of disbursements for France came to $11,000 and change. That was on top of his fees, at three hundred an hour.

Arthur steeled himself, because Bullingham, whose antennae had somehow picked up his presence, had just strolled in. But the rake-thin ancient seemed unusually buoyant. Stabbing a bony finger at Sierra's bill, he said: "Drop in the bucket. One of the best investments we've ever made."

Arthur was confused, and Bully explained: file AltaQB-889 was bringing in business. Emil Farquist, an Ayn Rand devotee, was loathed by the new government, and hefty contracts were being switched to the firm from Conservative-leaning offices.

"You see, Beauchamp, that unreformed pothead, Yates, now has to curry favour with your Greens." This was his way of speaking to Arthur, like a tutor to a new boy. But he was right. Prime Minister Yates, who was no fool, desperately needed the Green votes in the House. He was buying their support by helping at second hand to fund Margaret's battle against Farquist.

Arthur was shocked to see Bully scrolling away on a sleek cell phone — he'd never seemed adept with such devices. "Two thirds counted, and your man is now only two votes behind."

Your man . . . He realized Bully meant Lloyd Chalmers, the Halifax recount. Good luck to him. The smooth womanizer had lost the more crucial battle.

"I read Mr. Sierra's reports," Bully said. "Hope you don't mind."

"Of course not." Nothing was kept from the senior partner.

"Is your case as weak as I suspect it to be?"

"It's shaky, Bully."

"What do you think they'll settle for?"

"We won't be settling."

§

At the airport, waiting for his Calgary flight to be called, Arthur's attention was drawn to the soundless TV mounted above him: CBC Newsworld, words and numbers rolling across the wide screen. A poll had either been miscounted or wrongly reported, and Lloyd Chalmers had won Halifax East with a thirteen-vote plurality. Footage of the esteemed professor, handsome, triumphant, greeting supporters.

§

The next morning, Tuesday, in Calgary, Arthur popped into Tragger, Inglis's branch office. He had conscripted its sharpest litigator to help guide him through the civil processes: fortyish, bookish, bright-eyed Nanisha Banerjee, well versed in the Rules of Court.

For Arthur, this was a strange world, the civil courts — he'd done a few personal injuries as a young barrister, but the rest, the thousand other trials, were criminal. Both specialties demanded endless prep, slow slogging, and quick thinking. Civil cases were more flexible, the rules more relaxed, the burden of proof was less, and counsel met few surprises — all secrets had to be bared, all documents, and plaintiff and defendant faced probing pre-trial examination.

So far, Farquist's lawyers had not agreed on a date for such discovery and were claiming solicitor-client privilege for all records except copies of the alleged, much-tweeted slanders. But the defence documents, including Sierra's reports, were similarly protected. The Glinka video had never been in Margaret's possession, and Arthur would resist until the last minute making it known that Sabatino had copied it. The plaintiff's legal team had to be assuming that Sabatino had merely described its contents to Margaret.

"Are we opposing or not?" Nanisha asked. The motion for the six-month delay, she meant.

"Let us test the waters."

"I have some law, Mr. Beauchamp, if you need it."

He glanced through her brief on contested adjournments. In summary, the court ought to use its discretion wisely. Meaning the judge must justify making a gut call.

It was time. They headed off to the gleaming modern Calgary Courts Centre, Canada's largest house of justice, seventy-three courtrooms in two towers separated by an even taller atrium, on busy Fifth Street. Farquist v. Blake had been allotted one of the roomiest of them, on the thirteenth floor, the lucky one, Arthur hoped.

§

Chief Justice Cohon-Plaskett was trying to wrap up a boring chambers issue — about a presumed trust, as far as Arthur could make out — and was goading counsel to finish their submissions.

Arthur had done a duet with Cohon-Plaskett many years ago, as co-counsel on a bookmaking conspiracy. Her quickness of mind had impressed him, her brisk, edgy demeanour complementing his cooler, folksier style. Short, stout, and pug-nosed, a tough little package. Right now, she was nagging a harried-looking lawyer. "Is this submission included in your memorandum of law?"

"Yes, Milady."

"Then why do you need to repeat it?"

Next up would be Farquist v. Blake. Arthur had a motion of his own, to set a peremptory date for discovery — the other side had been stalling.

Sharing the barristers' bench with Arthur and Nanisha, but several empty places down, were George Cowper Jr. and two attendants. Cowper, a tall, dignified septuagenarian with a sad, weary expression, must be uncomfortable, Arthur figured, with having to come cap in hand to ask for a delay of the trial.

Cohon-Plaskett reserved her ruling on the trust issue, and counsel packed their book bags and filed out as a clump of reporters pushed in. Her Ladyship waited for the rustling to stop, then asked Cowper why he wished to adjourn the trial.

"Unanticipated matters have caused extreme time pressure, Milady."

"That seems rather vague, Mr. Cowper."

His sad face creased into a smile. "Let me be plain. It has been widely reported that my client is seeking the leadership of the Conservative Party of Canada. The convention has been scheduled for late in March. It is surely too much to ask Mr. Farquist to proceed to trial under such pressing circumstances. Nothing will be lost if the trial goes over to the September sittings."

Measured, concise, and to the point, the way the no-frills judge liked it. As Cowper recited the salient points of Farquist's two-page affidavit, Arthur asked Nanisha to fish it out, and flipped to the last paragraph: Farquist's complaint that democracy would be ill served were he forced to lose focus on his leadership campaign. It seemed an overly blunt afterthought, maybe at Farquist's insistence.

He was no shoo-in for the leadership, but remained the favourite. So far, two others had announced, including Clara Gracey, the finance minister, a penny-pinching economist but liberal on social issues, and friendly with Margaret. Arthur would be willing to bet that the Chief Justice, a Red Tory, would find herself more comfortable in Gracey's camp than Farquist's.

"Mr. Cowper, it was only about ten weeks ago, on September 3, that you came before me, saying" — the Chief Justice checked a transcript — "saying it was vital that your client's name be cleared as quickly as possible. You sought an early trial date. Mr. Beauchamp consented. I was forced to do some difficult juggling to free up a court for early March."

"As I say, Milady, we were not anticipating the former prime minister's resignation and a leadership contest."

"Might you not have seen it as a reasonable possibility? And am

I to be accused, as seems implied in your client's affidavit, of acting undemocratically by declining to delay the trial?"

"I beg your Ladyship to believe no such imputation should be found."

Once again, the Chief Justice seemed to be doing Arthur's work. He hoped he wasn't being set up. Beware the overly supportive judge, giving counsel every break, then calmly throwing him under a truck at the end. Who then would accuse her of harbouring bias against the defendant?

"What's your position, Mr. Beauchamp?"

"I oppose. We are eager to go to trial. My learned friend sought an early date — may I quote him — due to the 'massive and unseemly publicity this case has roused.' Nothing has changed in that regard. The defendant equally has an interest in putting this matter to bed without further delay."

"You also have a motion to speak to, Mr. Beauchamp?"

"To require the defendant's timely attendance at examinations for discovery. Your Ladyship will recall, when setting the March 2 date, instructing counsel to arrange for early discovery. Our several efforts to bring the plaintiff to the table have been to no avail."

Cowper went to bat again, strove mightily, but went down swinging.

"The motion to delay the trial is denied," Cohon-Plaskett said. "Reasons for judgment reserved. Now let us agree on a discovery date."

They spent half an hour digging through calendars for free days. Cowper finally, candidly, conceded that Emil Farquist had booked a post-Christmas holiday in the Bahamas. He looked more lugubrious than usual as Cohon-Plaskett cancelled that holiday and set discoveries for Friday, December 27, and the following Monday and Tuesday, which would be New Year's Eve. Farquist would be examined first.

Watching the courtroom empty out, Arthur noticed a portly gentleman in a suit pause at the door: Francisco Sierra, an unexpected guest appearance. He acknowledged Arthur with a slight nod before he disappeared. Arthur packed his valise, apologized to Nanisha, and hurried out.

§

They met at a nearby coffee house, the Urban Bean, and settled down at a corner table with their roasts — light for Sierra, who seemed jolly; dark for Arthur, who worried that Frank was masking annoyance over having been denied an extra six months of sleuthing.

He obviously had news — Arthur could read it in his cherubic smile — but seemed in no hurry to divulge it, instead commending Arthur for his performance in court.

"I do not question your wisdom in pushing ahead with the trial, though like Minister Farquist I face extreme time pressure. Lou Sabatino, alias Robert O'Brien, remains an elusive figure. As a desperate effort, I have placed carefully worded ads, with my contact information, on select Kijiji and Craigslist websites."

"I admit to some bravado in pressing for a quick trial. A calculated gamble, Frank."

"Prompted, I assume, by the apparent disarray of the opposition."

"They're sweating. Farquist has a hotly contested campaign on his hands, and he doesn't know what we have up our sleeve."

Sierra sipped his coffee, mused. "Are you harbouring the hope that his leadership ambitions will trump his suit for damages, and that he will abandon it?"

"That might require more face-saving than Farquist is capable of. But we have to appear confident, and we do that by squeezing them. They are gambling that Lou won't show up; we are betting everything on him. Now tell me what you've got."

"I've been in the Calgary morgue, to wit, the records office."
Sierra tilted his cup again, dabbed his lips with a paper napkin, teasing
Arthur, making him wait. "Lee Farquist, née Watters, was with child
when she took her life."

He savoured Arthur's look of consternation for several beats,
then reached into his briefcase and passed over a copy of an autopsy
report by a Calgary pathologist, dated August, 1987.

There it was, a reference to the deceased carrying a foetus,
estimated at four to five months post-conception. Farquist's forty-
year-old mother, the deserted, troubled wife of his faithless father,
Sandor.

A light blinked on. "I was a bad boy, very bad! Please, Mother, I
beg you!" Svetlana Glinka's cryptic comment: "His mother. Never
mind. As an ethical therapist I can't repeat."

Arthur was stunned. "Emil was sleeping with his mother?"

If so, the veils had fallen from the riddle that was Emil Farquist,
a man buffeted since adolescence by deep, insurmountable forces, a
man who had sought to atone for the sin of incest through the masochistic agency of a riding whip.

LANDSLIDE LLOYD

Corks popped from organically grown Prosecco as Lloyd Chalmers was prodded to the front of a room packed with aides and volunteers. Margaret joined in the applause as he turned to face his celebrants with an apologetic shrug. That disarming grin on his craggy mug. Margaret sensed a mass swooning of straight women and gay men.

The conference room at party HQ in Ottawa was the locale for this tribute to the Atlantic provinces' first Green MP. Landslide Lloyd, they jokingly called him.

He riffed on that for a while, to laughter, then turned serious, emphatic, proclaiming his dedication to the program of his party: preserve Canada's precious natural heritage, move from a carbon-based economy, ungag the scientists, all the right things.

None of which allayed Margaret's niggle of doubt about Landslide Lloyd. One of her staff had spotted him Friday evening at Wilfrid's in the Château sharing canapés and cocktails with an attractive Liberal backbencher. Just wolfing about, Margaret hoped.

As she downed her Prosecco, another bottle appeared, hovered over her plastic flute, and poured.

It was just after noon on Saturday, November 23, two days before the opening of the new Parliament and two weeks after the outgoing administration, having shredded about a ton of documents, turned over the reins to the Liberals.

Though he was short of a majority by one vote, Marcus Yates had yet to ask Margaret for a sit-down. That was annoying, but the Greens held the trump card, and Margaret wasn't about to go crawling to him. Among the shiny new faces on the front bench would be a former marine biologist as environment minister. Other than protesting the previous government's muzzling of scientists, she had no history of activism.

Chalmers raised his glass, fixing his gaze on Margaret. "Let me add only this, that I shall continue gladly to serve as a loyal foot soldier under the command of Margaret Blake. Let us salute our gifted, tireless, lovely leader."

A scatter of cheers. Margaret grinned but felt uncomfortable. "Back at you, Lloyd," she said, holding high her own plastic flute. "To you, to your amazing campaign team, and to all the dedicated workers in this room." Hearty applause as she tilted the flute.

After mingling for a few minutes, she slipped into her office, needing time alone. She went to the window and studied the thick grey sky, the pelting rain, the splashing of tires on the busy street, oppressed Ottawans walking by, umbrellas braced against a sharp north wind. The soft, temperate clime of Garibaldi was calling again.

A man in a dark coat paused, glanced up, carried on. Tall, long-haired, unshaven — she'd seen him before, shadowing her. Presumably one of Farquist's minions.

The dreaded examinations for discovery were looming, less than six weeks away. Farquist's team didn't need a spook on her tail — the discoveries would reveal how weak her defence was. Transparency would be demanded, their case stripped naked. She had not a smidgen of proof to corroborate what she'd seen on the copied video.

An element of queasiness was now in play among the many repellent feelings Margaret held for Farquist. Arthur, ever cautious on the phone, had dispatched Frank Sierra to confide the shocking but plausible surmise of an incestuous relationship between Farquist and his mother. It was not demonstrably relevant, said Arthur, nor easily proved — unless Sierra dug up a witness to bedroom taboos being broken a few decades ago. A neighbour, a housekeeper, an unexpected visitor.

Everything would be so easy if Lou Sabatino somehow found the grit to do the right thing. The cowardly little bugger.

The door squeaked open, and Jennie Withers sidled in with a wine bottle and two glasses. "Interrupting?"

"Not at all. Lock the door, Jen."

She did, then poured. "The fawning was making me ill. Pinot okay? The bubbly ran out."

Margaret nodded. She was already high; one more drink wasn't going to do any damage. Jennie seemed a little tight too, her voice teasing. "He likes you better," she said.

Margaret's smile froze. "What does that mean?"

"Sorry. Don't mean to be flippant. I felt you should know. Lloyd told me about . . . This is awkward."

"About sleeping with me."

"Pillow talk. Charmer couldn't resist." Jennie rolled her eyes. "He said you were great in bed. I felt fucking insulted, not to mention appalled. The guy has a mouth disorder. That's when I decided to get out of his gravitational field. Sorry, honey, it was bugging me, I had to tell you." She gave Margaret a hug, and she returned it, and kissed her.

Jennie refilled their glasses. "You heard he's moved on to Francine Lafontaine?" The rookie Liberal. "He claims he can bring her over."

"He expects us to believe that? Damn his big mouth."

"Mine is shut."

"It's okay, Jen. I totally trust you."

She did not trust Chalmers, however, whose mouth was clearly not shut. His need to boast about his conquests could prove horribly awkward — while hiding behind their Twitter usernames, Farquist's troops would gleefully mock the adulterous Green leader. Though she had long regretted her confession to Arthur, she now realized she'd been wise to be honest, to cleanse her marriage of secrets that could poison it.

A tapping on the door. She opened it to Pierette. "Excuse. Marcus Yates just sent an emissary with a note. The PM wants an audience with you."

Margaret looked down at her empty glass of Pinot — she hadn't remembered finishing it. She was feeling very light-headed.

§

After two coffees and a liberal dose of Listerine, Margaret found herself in the horseshoe-shaped lobby of the Prime Minister's office in the Centre Block, trying not to wobble on her heels as Marcus Yates's personal secretary opened a door and ushered her in.

A commodious office, regally done in carved oak throughout, blinds open to an overlook of the West Annex and the Hill's frost-seared lawn, with its usual cluster of grumps with placards — anti-abortion diehards today, huddled under umbrellas. Dominating one wall was a portrait of Sir John A. Macdonald, Canada's first prime minister and arguably its most famous drunk. He gazed fondly upon his tipsy visitor, with the merest hint of a smile.

Yates rose from a capacious oak desk piled with files and binders and greeted her with outstretched hand. Graceful, trim, clean-cut, a boyish smile. Margaret couldn't shake off a more youthful rendition from the attack ads: Yates in a cannabis-leaf T-shirt at a pro-pot rally. But those ads had boomeranged on the Conservatives — they'd merely encouraged young voters to shake off their torpor and actually vote this time.

"Thank you for coming, Margaret." He pulled out a chair for her. "Can we get you anything? A coffee, a juice?"

"I'm fine, thanks." Just a little hammered.

Yates dismissed his secretary, settled into his padded leather desk chair. They began by exchanging complaints about the unending toil of political life. That segued briefly into mention of Farquist's slander suit, Yates expressing sympathy over the strain she must be under. "May the best woman win," he said.

She laughed, a little hoarsely.

He talked about the mess left behind by the outgoing administration, and the long task ahead to clean it up. The former social worker had a genial, confiding manner that nibbled away at one's defences. A clever fellow, and she reminded herself to be on guard. Commit to nothing, she told herself. Wait until sober second thought kicks in.

Finally he got to the point. "We assume you have a wish list."

She had rehearsed for this, and spoke slowly, fearful of slurring: "Let's start with our twelve-point election platform, and see if we can build on that."

He nodded, smiled. "Proportional rep, Senate reform, pulling the plug on the Extended Police Powers bill — a definite on that — repairing the Species at Risk Act, curtailing energy subsidies, tackling carbon pricing — we can go along with a lot of that. I think you'll be pleased with the Throne Speech. Much of it has to be done incrementally, of course."

Margaret didn't like that imprecise afterword, but this was sounding not too bad. If he was being honest. "I hope Dr. Lecourt has enough gumph to stand up to the Goliaths." Diane Lecourt, his environment minister. A political novice.

"She's a fast learner and a tough cookie."

"As a jester ... gesture of good faith, Marcus, let's start with Coast Mountains."

A pained look. "Look, I'm with you, but you see the problem — the pipeline is a done deal, signed and sealed. Our opinion from Legal is we can't renege without a massive suit in damages."

Margaret refused to believe that. "A deal done behind the backs of Parliament."

Yates merely shrugged. "We're looking for loopholes. Meantime, let's get our teams to prioritize other areas of shared concern. Oh, congratulations on your success in Halifax East. Bright guy, Chalmers. We approached him ourselves, you know."

"No, I didn't." Why hadn't Chalmers mentioned that?

"He spoke admiringly of you."

How admiringly? she wondered. *She's a passionate woman, Marcus, in more ways than one.*

§

Sobriety was kicking in by the time Margaret returned to her office, but so was a headache, and she washed down a couple of extra-strength ibuprofens with strong coffee before sitting with Pierette to work on sound bites for the Throne Speech scrums. But they kept returning to Margaret's one-on-one with Yates, debating how to keep pressing him on measures to re-green Canada.

"Keeping his feet to the fire," Pierette said. "Is that scrum-worthy?"

"Sounds too much like an enhanced interrogation technique."

"Keep them on their toes?"

"Too timid."

"Stick a broom up their ass? Oh, just wing it, do your awesome best."

Margaret rose to look out her window. There he was again, on the sidewalk, the tall spook with about ten days' growth of beard, holding a briefcase, pausing to talk on his phone. She nudged Pierette, who'd joined her at the window.

"That guy was right on my butt the other day on Sparks Street. I did the old duck-and-doodle into a shop, and he looked in as he walked by. A few minutes later, back on the street, there he was again."

The private eye, if that's what he was, tucked away his phone then glanced up at their window before carrying on.

"I know that face from somewhere," said Pierette. "Creepy. Maybe they're hoping to catch you with Sabatino."

"I wish." Maybe they'd heard about her and Charmer, were hoping to spot them making out by her office window.

Just as Margaret was about to call it a day and head for home — she was beat, hungry, had smelly armpits and a throbbing head — the receptionist came to the door. "A Mr. McGilroy is here. Insists you'll be interested in what he has to say. He's with CSIS."

Canadian Security Intelligence Service, the spy agency. Margaret shared a puzzled look with Pierette, took a deep breath, smoothed her hair, tucked in her blouse. "Okay, send him in, please."

The tall, bearded man who was ushered in was the same guy who had just been outside, Margaret's stalker. Late thirties, handsome in a dark and forbidding way, well built, probably a gym junkie, steely eyes taking in the full measure of the two agape women.

"Thank you for seeing me, Ms. Blake. I'm sorry for the lack of notice." His handshake was quick, firm, confident, and his manner of speech formal, almost toneless. "Ms. Litvak, you may not remember that we were in the same political science class at McGill."

"I do remember you. Parliamentary Democracy 200." A tentative smile, a nervous flutter of eyelashes.

He showed them his wallet of credentials and passed them each a card. Fitzgerald W. McGilroy, senior officer, CSIS.

"We used to call you Fitz," Pierette said.

"I still have to live with that."

Margaret offered coffee. He accepted, and Pierette went off to fetch it. Margaret seated him in an armchair and herself on her high-backed desk chair, her throne, the power position. She was on guard.

She distrusted CSIS, always nosing around front-line environmental and Indigenous groups.

"Mr. McGilroy, you have been doing a very poor job of following me."

"I apologize. I was merely keeping you in sight until I got approval to approach you. I now have that." Without hesitation, he took a ten-by-eight glossy from his briefcase and passed it to her. "Do you recognize this woman?"

A tall, blonde, blue-eyed Barbie doll in a pantsuit speaking to an attendant at what looked like an outdoor security gate. "Svetlana Glinka." She just blurted it out. Stupid.

"Have you met her?"

"No. Just a guess." She didn't care to admit she'd seen photos of her, taken by Pierette during her stakeout on rue de la Visitation.

"Good guess."

Pierette returned with a tray bearing mugs, milk, sugar. Margaret bought time by picking up hers and taking a mouthful right away. Black, to get her brain in gear. McGilroy stirred milk into his, waiting. Pierette studied the photo without expression.

Margaret took a deep breath. "Mr. McGilroy, as you obviously know, I am currently facing an extravagant claim for an alleged defamation. If this discussion is to go further, I need to set boundaries. I will not jeopardize my court case."

"I guarantee you that this conversation is in complete confidence."

"I'm prepared to hear you out, but I will not answer questions without legal advice, I'm sorry."

"Then I encourage you to get advice. Or even have Mr. Beauchamp present when we reconvene. But you will need some background."

He had obviously expected her to be close-mouthed — his quick opener with the photo had been a tactic to catch her off guard.

McGilroy sipped his coffee, studying her, then Pierette, as if for signs of their agreement. Or weakness. "Can we agree this is in total confidence?"

"Other than with my husb… my lawyer." Why was that always so awkward to say? "And Pierette. I have to insist that she stays."

"Of course she can stay." He unexpectedly beamed at Pierette, who blushed as she sank into a chair beside him. Had she had the hots for him in Parliamentary Democracy 200?

"The photo I gave you was taken in front of the Russian Embassy on Charlotte Street on April 24, this year." Margaret now recognized, in the background, the Russians' rambling stone fortress by the Rideau River. "Glinka had just got out of a taxi. Here she is entering the grounds." Another glossy, Svetlana from the back, being escorted into the building by a functionary.

"She remained inside for nearly ninety minutes." A third photo of her, departing, outside the gate, getting into a taxi. "We had no idea who she was. She could have been anyone, an émigré getting papers stamped. But a week later she showed up in more curious circumstances."

More photos. These were taken in a fast-food restaurant, maybe a McDonald's. Svetlana was sitting at a plastic-topped table, in a long, low-cut dress, beside a leering, bald man.

"Igor Novotnik. Ostensibly a trade officer. We've had eyes on him for some time." Another shot: Novotnik pulling a letter-size envelope from an inside pocket. A thick envelope.

"That was the last day of April. I had taken over the file, but still had no idea who she was or what services she was being paid for. My ears perked up when your voice clip went public. 'Weekends with a Russian dominatrix named Svetlana.'"

"Broadcast a billion times," Margaret said, getting a look from Pierette.

"Novotnik's paid informant fit Glinka's physicals: tall, blonde, blue-eyed, well endowed. I was certain she was the dominatrix. But by then she had fled the country."

A picture was forming for Margaret. A week after Novotnik paid her off, Sibericon opened negotiations to buy into Coast Mountains. Talks were completed in July. Cabinet gave it the green light in August. Margaret couldn't help herself. "So you suspect the Russians had a . . . let's call it a pipeline, into Coast Mountains."

He didn't confirm that, but said: "I am curious, Ms. Blake, to hear what you know of Svetlana Glinka's association with Emil Farquist."

Margaret raised her hands: a halt sign.

McGilroy packed away his photos. "I gather you'd like to reserve on that."

"Why come to me now, Mr. McGilroy? Why not months ago?"

"We hesitated to approach you, given the court action. But matters are now more difficult."

Glinka, he explained, in his monotonous way, had been under observation in France, but had pulled up stakes, sold her sex shop, and returned to the motherland. "Moscow, we believe."

"The heat was getting too hot."

"Meaning what, Ms. Blake?"

"When would you like to continue this, Mr. McGilroy?"

EXODUS

At tea time on Saturday afternoon Arthur was comfortably seated in his Vancouver club, the Confederation, flipping through *Maclean's* while stirring his Earl Grey and eavesdropping on a trio of codgers at the table behind him. Retired tycoons, all hard of hearing, he supposed, given their high decibels.

"Sorry, J.O., I disagree. Farquist is too risky. In fact, I just cut Clara a cheque."

"Clara Gracey, gentlemen, is a radical feminist. Liberal in sheep's clothing. Emil's a hard-hearted bastard, I give you that, but he's the man to take on those weepy-eyed Liberals."

A third voice. "I've always been able to work with Clara. She's the best finance minister since Don Fleming, and better looking. I'm hoping she whips Emil's ass."

"Give it to me, Clara, I've been a bad boy." Loud guffaws.

"Emil will get the last laugh, boys. That climate alarmist he's suing, Blake, she's about to get *her* ass whipped."

Arthur knew this loathsome threesome, though not well. Banking, timber, and real estate. And they knew him, though obviously hadn't observed him being led to his chair. The prediction by the Farquist booster soured Arthur's mood. He sipped his tea, played with his smartphone, on which the Woofers, with painstaking effort, had finally taught him a few basics.

Arthur had stayed a couple of nights in Alberta after the chambers hearing, debating strategies with Sierra, reviewing case law at the Tragger, Inglis branch, then went on to Edmonton for one night. He'd met with Alfred Scower there, a pleasant evening in a restaurant.

Dr. Scower hadn't tried to hide his shock or his glee over Arthur's surmise about the incestuous adolescence of his *bête noir*. He was eager to help bring Farquist down but lacked ammunition. He offered one remote possibility: Emil's mother, Lee, had regularly attended mass; her priest from the late 1980s might still be alive. Sierra would follow that up.

Arthur had been nearly a week away from Garibaldi and was aching to return. The Sunday morning ferry would take him there to begin another seven-day reprieve from the wearying monster of the coming trial. He was repelled by the prospect of Margaret being cross-examined in open court, probed and needled, portrayed as the queen of the careless remark. He dreaded seeing her embarrassed or, worse, flare up, losing her temper. The trial had to be avoided. Without Sabatino, without the video, Margaret would lose.

Somehow Arthur would have to pull off the biggest bluff since they broke the bank at Monte Carlo.

His thoughts were interrupted by an intrusive sound from somewhere near. A banal, repellent tune. It took Arthur a moment to realize it was coming from his phone. He finally answered it with a brusque hello.

"Hello, darling. I just had a very interesting visitor. Have I caught you at a bad time?"

§

The Sunday morning ferry to Garibaldi was famously slow, with three pit stops, and Arthur spent the time pacing the upper deck, bundled up against the November cold, determined to walk himself back into shape after dining out all week and otherwise sitting on his rear.

It hadn't yet rained, but the clouds were low and ominous. The grey sky melded on the horizon with the darker shade of the frothy, white-capped strait. The islands of the Salish Sea were still far away, formless green mounds. Occasionally cormorants and guillemots beat across the waves.

He hadn't been in touch with Garibaldi except for a mid-week call to Reverend Al, who reported that he had been busy campaigning with Taba. The anti-Transformer slate was losing ground: the *Bleat* had endorsed Shewfelt and Zoller. Arthur promised he would pitch in. He owed it to his pal, and to Taba, who had been so commendably discreet about their *liaison amoureuse*.

More central to his thoughts was Margaret's sudden, intriguing visit from a CSIS agent. Despite his fears about tapped phone connections, Arthur had recklessly and raptly listened to her account. Tromping up and down the deck, exercising his mind as well as his legs, Arthur struggled to collate the bits and pieces she'd gleaned from her briefing by McGilroy.

Assuming his information was reliable, Svetlana Glinka was not a spy but a businesswoman selling secrets. Emil Farquist had enjoyed her services over the course of five months. As he was showering away his exertions in his log chalet, had she seen, or even copied or photographed, some confidential memo on his desk blotter? Perhaps an alert that the PMO was about to bypass Parliament and approve the Coast Mountains Pipeline by cabinet order.

It was hard to believe that Farquist had gotten so close and loose with Glinka that he would confide government secrets. Maybe he had merely advised her to buy Coast Mountains stock, with a telling wink as he was pulling on his pants. Or maybe, the most delicious conjecture, he was using Svetlana as an agent to earn a rich payoff from Sibericon.

But that theory, lamentably, was most unlikely. Even Margaret refused to entertain it. According to Sierra, Farquist was financially strapped. The chalet was still up for sale. The owner, the realtor had said, was motivated.

It was also telling that in mid-May Farquist fired Glinka. Because he suspected she'd passed secrets to the Russians? Sabatino recalled she'd been furious — he'd thought it was pride, but perhaps it was because this lost connection meant the Russians' wallets would close. Vengefully, she'd shown Lou the video, talked of exposing him, writing a book. About a week later she'd been bribed into silence, possibly to the tune of $200,000, the proceeds of his mortgage on the Lac Vert property.

The comment by Arthur's ever-so-talkative wife had hit the mark: "The heat was getting too hot." Glinka had been under siege: visits from Farquist's lawyers, from Sierra; the press might not be far behind. Afraid she'd be summoned back for the trial — and forced to lie under oath and face a perjury charge — she'd found a bolthole in Russia, where she was extradition-free.

Arthur had given up on her anyway. The CSIS backgrounder was redolent with scandal, and though not central to the slander suit, it might be of some use. But Arthur didn't trust CSIS one iota, and was aghast that Margaret had had a cozy chit-chat with their man. What if his information was false, those photos doctored? What if they were trying to set her up, tempting her to test the defamation laws once again with this explosive new allegation?

Arthur had left a message with McGilroy's office saying he would be pleased to see him when he was next in Ottawa. He didn't add that he was prepared to listen but would be offering no quid pro quo. Not until, maybe, after the trial in March.

He had found himself exasperated with Margaret — she was too keen to pursue the Glinka–Farquist–Sibericon connection. In all his years at the bar, he had never had such a trying client. He'd instructed her not to talk to McGilroy any further — and that went double for Pierette, who'd been practically drooling over him. They were to be cautious on the phone, erase all saved messages, phone numbers.

After he had caught his breath, he apologized for his severe tone.

She'd responded stiffly. "Thank you for your advice, Counsellor."

§

Standing in the bow of the ferry as it grunted into the slip at Ferryboat Cove, he was relieved to see his truck — the Fargo-napper hadn't struck again; it was still on the steep side road where Arthur had parked it, pointing downhill, because of its lazy battery.

He retrieved his bag from the ferry van and joined the several cyclists and backpackers making their way over the ramp. Standing there, staring past him with a pained expression, was Henrietta Wilks, retired teacher and early convert to the Transformers. Her daughter, Melanie, was tugging at her arm.

"Come on, Mom, let's take you home."

"He's gone," Henrietta announced to Arthur. "But I can hear his voice. Can you hear it too?"

Melanie pulled her out of the way of the vehicles rolling off. Arthur asked if he could be of any help.

"She's been practically camped here, ever since Thursday."

"Where have they gone?" Henrietta asked Arthur, somehow assuming he would know.

He helped guide her to Melanie's car, in the pick-up lane. "Who's gone where?"

"Jason," Melanie said. "The Transformers. They've all gone."

It was almost noon. Reverend Al would be seeing off his parishioners after Sunday service. Arthur climbed into his Fargo. It started right up.

§

The parking area at St. Mary's Landing was emptying as Arthur pulled in. Al shook a last hand, waved a last goodbye, then strode toward the Fargo with a jaunty, crinkly-eyed look Arthur had not seen for half a year.

"Packed house, old boy. Quadrupled from last week. Eighty-seven larynxes joined in song: 'Ring the bells of heaven, there is joy today.' Yes, the flock has returned. Rueful, ashamed, forgiven. A dalliance with a false god. Come. Sit. Let us enjoy this splendid fall day."

It was cold, an occasional spit of rain, but Arthur could not deny him, and they took a bench on the bluff, above the little inlet with its shell beach, its resident geese and bossy, patrolling ravens.

"I have my island back," Al said. "There *is* a God. He *does* listen to my prayers."

"I met Henrietta Wilks. She's still hearing Silverson's voice."

"Mass hypnosis, old boy. The poor lady was extraordinarily susceptible."

Arthur packed his pipe and lit it, wondering if he too had briefly fallen under Silverson's sway: those gupa attacks, those strange episodes of tranquility. "Did the cultists just evaporate into the air?"

"Practically. They took the late ferry Thursday, in the dark. Jason and his space-case sidekick, Morg, all the Californian disciples and seekers, their bikes and VWs, plus that moving van they'd brought in. This had to have been planned some time ago, when they started dumping their pigs and chickens. They were giving machinery away too, toward the end. Gardening tools. Fridges, freezers, household appliances."

"All done without a goodbye?"

"Not even a parting namaste. Poof. Gone."

§

Reverend Al had wanted to continue their conversation at the Brig, over his customary Sunday tot, but Arthur first checked in at Blunder Bay. Niko and Yoki insisted on taking him around the grounds, a meet-and-greet with the goats and sheep and fowl. Eggs and cheese and a bumper crop from the walnut tree had sold out at the Saturday market, and hay was baled and in the barn. Both girls seemed indifferent to the flight of the Transformers, well free of their pull.

"Been there," said Niko. "Done that."

Arthur was perplexed by the Transformers' exodus, and by their unexpected generosity. Maybe they'd decided Garibaldi was small potatoes and were moving to more fertile ground. What had Silverson gained from Garibaldi but the hundred or so adherents he had abandoned? Except, possibly, a handsome profit should they sell or subdivide Starkers Cove, which they'd bought on the cheap. Al had done a title search — it remained in the name of the Personal Transformation Mission Society. Al still insisted they were scamming. He was set on finding out how. Al was a bulldog.

Arthur returned to the house to take stock and make a shopping list, then got back into the Fargo. Again, he was startled to hear the engine fire up.

§

He had time for a brief detour up Stoney's driveway, with its motley signs still proudly displaying his unlicensed businesses. It had taken a while, but Constable Dugald had finally surrendered to Stoney, to the island's grand tradition of breaking bylaws.

The Fargo ascended past rust-buckets in the weeds, alder trees growing from them, and pulled alongside Stoney's garage. Arthur found the master mechanic sitting with Dog, under a tarp, taking a beer break.

"And what brings you to my humble abode, good sir?"

"I felt I should express my astonishment and delight that my truck seems to be in proper working order."

"My pleasure. She is the proud possessor of a relatively new battery. Started right up."

Arthur wondered how many miles he'd put on it.

"Meet the latest addition to our fleet. We scored this baby off of the Transformers, a John Deere 7500." Stoney gestured toward a handsome green beast behind the garage.

"*We* scored this baby?" said Dog.

"Okay, Morg gave it to Dog for being such an absolute jockstrap. He put in some big hours for them."

"God bless them," said Dog, with a rare smile. Arthur wondered whether he was still under their spell or had gone back to being a good Christian. Either way, clearly there were rewards for getting transformed.

"As for the battery, please let me have your bill. And, if you don't mind, your spare key."

Stoney pretended to be confused, then dug into a pocket. "Oh, yeah . . ." He handed it over.

§

The Brig was busy with locals, chatting, caught up in the mystery of the Transformers' disappearance. Reverend Al and Taba were across the room at a table for two, looking merry. The mail counter was closed today, and Abraham Makepeace was performing a rare stint behind the bar.

"Call, raise, or fold." The loud voice of Cud Brown sailed across the room, from where half a dozen poker players were seated at two joined tables. Arthur observed a pot of money in the middle, tens and twenties.

"Make up your mind," Cud growled at Herman Schloss, a

retired insurance executive and a man of means but a recovering Transformer. He'd been easy prey for them, in a woebegone state since May, when his actress wife, Mookie, had returned to Hollywood and her B-movie career.

"You've got aces showing, Herman, they beat his jacks." This was Nelson Forbish, who was hovering like a hot-air balloon, kibitzing, his back to Arthur.

"Shut up, I'm concentrating." Schloss looked dazed, maybe because he was still not fully untransformed. Cud Brown and Emily LeMay, the off-duty bartender, were also at the table, sipping cocktails, a frothy purple potion. Three others were drinking beer: Honk Gilmore, Scotty Phillips, and a sixth player obscured by Nelson's bulk.

Forbish refused to let up. "Cud's bluffing, you can see it in his eyes."

Schloss growled, "Bugger off, Nelson."

Arthur ordered a pot of tea, and leaned toward Makepeace. "Abraham, surely you know this is illegal. Gambling in licensed premises."

"It's legal today." He went off to fetch the tea.

Schloss tossed some bills on the pile. "I'm calling you, pal." He turned up his down cards.

Forbish groaned. "Full house beats three aces. Nice try, Herman."

Schloss rose to slap him, almost knocking his chair over. Forbish retreated, opening up a view of the sixth player: Constable Irwin Dugald, in civvies, cooling out the situation. "It's only a game, gentlemen. Let's play cards."

"He's a poker fanatic," Makepeace said "He's sent his sidekick off to Starkers, guarding stuff. We're not supposed to tell Zoller about the gambling. He gets uptight."

Felicity Jones, who worked the Brig's tables on weekends, squeezed beside Arthur with an empty tray. "Two more of those gupa slushes, Abraham." She saw the puzzlement on Arthur's face

274

and explained: "One of the fridges they were giving away had two gallons of cold gupa. Works real good with vodka."

Arthur looked around. There were Martie Miller and her husband enjoying Silverson's famous fruit toddy, with its herbs and pinch of Echinacea. As were another couple, weekenders. All of them were acting normal, chatting, smiling.

As Arthur pulled a chair over to Al and Taba's table, Felicity set down his tea, picked up two empty glasses, and replaced them with the vodka-gupa slushes.

"Bring a booze-free one for Arthur, too," Al said, then turned to him. "Terrific pick-me-up, old boy. Good for what ails you."

"I'll stay with my ailments, thanks."

"Are you still missing Jason, poor baby?" Taba said to her daughter, over-sweetly.

"You want to know the truth, Mom? He was a lousy lay."

Al sputtered with laughter.

Arthur said, "You two seem in a celebratory mood."

"Taba and I have our lives back. We've withdrawn our candidacies."

Arthur was taken aback. "But then we're stuck with two extremely marginal characters as Trustees."

"I'm sure Kurt and Ida have the best interests of Garibaldi at heart. They're both too slow on the uptake to do much damage, especially with their guru gone AWOL."

Arthur wasn't sure about that. How would his beloved island survive a three-year reign under the anally retentive Kurt Zoller and his holy-rolling partner? But he couldn't begrudge his friends their restored freedom.

His alcohol-free gupa arrived, and he just stared at it. The fumes found a fast pathway to his nose, pungent, intense. There was no way he was going to drink it.

As Al was looking away, Taba treated Arthur to a short but emphatic wink. He smiled uncertainly. A conspiratorial message? Or one of understanding: all is well, no one will ever know? Arthur decided on the latter and felt a stiffness go out of him.

Emboldened, he took a sip of the gupa. It tasted not bad.

He let his worries lift free — the trial was months away, he was back on his happy little island, at home, enjoying this pleasant Sunday with friends, the carefree bantering around the poker table. The Transformers were gone, the hay was in, his truck re-muffled. And the weather had shifted, the rain had stopped and the clouds were scattering, pursued by mighty Apollo.

He sat back, smiled, and took another sip of gupa. *Carpe diem.*

§

Some time later — fifteen minutes? An hour? — he found himself on Hopeless Bay's public pier, stretched out, leaning over the water, watching it slop and slurp against the pilings, watching the minnows play. Once again, Arthur Beauchamp was at the mercy of an ineffable sense of well-being.

He looked up. A pair of buffleheads bobbed on the waves, occasionally diving, while an osprey patrolled above. The sun was warm, pulling mist from the bay. His worries were forgotten, magically suppressed. Let what comes come; let what goes go.

A shadow fell over him. He turned to see Reverend Al, looking anxious: "Are you all right?"

"I'm at peace with the universe."

"I'm wondering if you should see someone."

THE UNCONSCIOUS MIND

"There's a medical term for it," said Dr. Timothy Dare "Genetic sexual attraction."

Arthur played with that label, rolled the syllables around his tongue. He was pacing about Dare's office, occasionally stopping to watch the small craft plying False Creek below Vancouver's downtown skyscrapers.

"More common than you'd think," said Tim. "But rarely admitted to, and hardly the subject of parlour-room chit-chat." Timothy Jason Dare, MD, Ph.D., was a forensic psychiatrist, tall and bushy-haired, a friend of long standing, much called upon as an expert witness. His office was the upper floor of a houseboat moored off the busy market and expensive boutique shops of Granville Island.

Arthur had spent some time sketching the secret life of Emil Farquist, from birth to paternal defection to inferred incest to bondage and on to bribery. Tim had listened raptly. Though a confessed neurotic himself, with multiple phobias, he was an acute observer of the human condition.

He asked several questions, then sprawled on his patients' divan, and delivered his verdict.

Though Tim was no Freudian, he believed there was much to be learned from the father of modern psychiatry. The theory of the Oedipus complex was not dead, it remained the basis of psychoanalytic theory: every male infant has an overwhelming desire for his mother, every female for her father. Drives so powerful that society demands they be suppressed.

"Normally by the post-Oedipal stage, the incest taboo has become imprinted. In this case, maybe not sufficiently. An innocent adolescent, his father lost to him at the age of eight, he may have succumbed to his lonely mother's needs. She transferred the deep, unanswered love she felt for his father to Emil, thus the genetic attraction. It often begets a sense of repulsion, of shame. One could see how that would translate into a need for punishment. Bondage, pain, humiliation, self-hatred — seeking forgiveness for a sin he could not expunge from memory."

A clean, concise summation. Tim went to a shelf filled haphazardly with books and journals. Several cascaded down as he poked among them. "There's a published paper on GSA. Somewhere."

While Tim rooted through the disarray on his shelves, Arthur took advantage of the break to mention, as casually as he could, his own odd experiences, his occasional ascents into a near-spiritual space of unwarranted peace and bliss.

Tim offered a smile of sympathy. "Have you been under pressure lately?"

"You have no idea."

"Margaret's trial. What could possibly have driven you to represent her?"

It was impossible to keep a secret from this discerning shrink. Tim had an instinct for reading people, their body language. "I did it out of guilt. There was a . . . an episode, a woman."

"You old dog. We're talking intercourse here?"

"I'm afraid so."

"Driven by guilt into a state of emotional frenzy. It's good-old-fashioned stress, Arthur. It's high stress, and, sure, some people snap. But not A.R. Beauchamp, his ego is healthy enough, despite all his self-flagellating, to merely send him to a better place. It's how you preserve your sanity, through escape. Your unconscious mind has found a useful mechanism."

"What do I do if it happens again?"

"Recognize it. Enjoy it."

"It wasn't the gupa?"

"What's gupa?"

"Never mind."

THE SPEAKER

Monday, November 25, was the brief opening day of a runt first session of the new Parliament: three weeks, then a break for the holidays. Margaret fully expected it to be the crappiest Christmas since God set her on this earth. She would have to brace herself for a week of intense prep — her bossy lawyer would fly out to Ottawa for that — then three days cloistered in a room in the Calgary Courts Centre with Emil Farquist, their lawyers, and an official court reporter.

She had just taken her seat in the Opposition backbenches, beside Jennie. MPs were filtering in through the chamber's many orifices, and the galleries were almost full. Today's sole item of business was the election of a Speaker. That promised to be quick because only one name had been put forward: Orvil Legault, a jovial old New Brunswicker. NDP members had been whipped into supporting him, one of the Liberal old guard. That still left the Liberals with a one-vote minority, thanks to Landslide Lloyd, who'd just taken his seat behind Margaret. She had deliberately assigned him that seat, so he'd be out of her view.

"Asshole alert," said Jennie.

Margaret thought at first she meant Chalmers, but Jennie was indicating the heavyweight glad-handing his way along the Opposition front bench. Farquist finally approached his main rival, Clara Gracey — a favourite of the Conservative caucus, which no doubt irritated the shit out of the great man. Yet he had a slight lead in committed delegates, 43 percent to Clara's 38, two outliers far behind.

Farquist made a show of shaking Clara's hand, trading a bit of banter, then lowered his infamous bottom onto his seat on the Opposition front bench. It felt odd to be on his side of the aisle, getting a view of his rock-like skull.

It had been a struggle for Margaret to keep a lid on Glinka's clandestine business with Igor Novotnik. She was seriously tempted to leak it anonymously somehow. No harm in going that far. There was proof, after all! Photographic evidence. It could be the only way to stop Coast Mountains Pipeline. They were already moving machinery into place, preparing to cut a swath through the Rockies.

But her overly cautious counsel would be furious if she even hinted at the Russian connection. Arthur had little appreciation for the art of politics. She was piqued at being held on a short leash.

She perused once again her advance copy of tomorrow's Throne Speech. A lot of brave words, nothing hard, vague blather about tackling climate change. Coast Mountains didn't rate a mention. She would have something to say to Marcus Yates about this. To the House, to the press.

Or she would if she could find the words. She hoped her stress wasn't showing too obviously, her strenuously composed expression, her tight, sappy smile. Her anxiety had been compounded by Arthur's own stress, she'd fed off it. His mood swings, his clipped way of issuing his many cautions during their long-distance calls, then, alarmingly, waxing poetic about the sweetness of life. Jekyll and Hyde. Leave the worrying to me, he would say at those moments, causing her to worry more — about him.

It was her fault for having strong-armed him into taking on this damnable case. She should never have torn him away from his idyllic life on little Garibaldi while she played the distraught victim of an assault by writ and statement of claim. Arthur insisted the plaintiff's claim for fifty million was preposterous, but what was never mentioned between them was the fact that an award of even 15 percent of that would render them penniless. They would have to sell the farm.

This was pitiful: here she was, anticipating the worst, preparing herself for disaster. She must stop being such a weak sister. She told herself to buck up.

Across the way, taking her seat in the government's fourth row, was pretty Francine Lafontaine, Chalmers's current squeeze. She was scanning the Opposition bleachers, beaming a smile in Margaret's direction. She twisted around and saw Chalmers grinning back at Francine, then offering Margaret an apologetic shrug. He'd convinced himself, if not his confidants, that he could woo her over to the Greens. What a generous man, sacrificing his body to recruit for the Party. Francine, a textile designer, wasn't known to have green leanings.

There in the press gallery was Christie Montieth, the author of Margaret's misfortunes while disguised as BDSmother. A charade no doubt enacted with the connivance of her editor and her publisher. Why weren't *they* being sued? But of course Farquist wasn't about to bankrupt his fawning friends in that media group.

Pierette was in the Opposition gallery, and beside her was Francisco Sierra — Margaret wasn't sure why he'd wanted a gallery pass. He was supposed to seek out CSIS agent McGilroy today — Arthur had decided to let him to have a go at the spy.

Sierra had returned yesterday from the Gatineaus with hopeful news, though maybe of dubious value: the groundskeeper at Lac Vert had seen a blue Miata tucked beside Farquist's carport sometime last winter, maybe January. Or at least he thought it might have been a Miata, thought it might have been blue. A drinking man who considered Farquist *un snob*, Sierra said.

282

Pierette nudged him, directed his attention to the public gallery above the Speaker's chair. McGilroy had just taken a seat there. He acknowledged Sierra with a slight nod of his head. Moments later, Sierra rose, departed. After a few beats, so did McGilroy. Their little *pas de deux* meant Sierra's invitation for a quiet rendezvous had been accepted.

Meanwhile, the House was in session. A round of applause as Orvil Legault was acclaimed Speaker. Now to be enacted was the nutty ceremony of wrestling the new Speaker to his station at the front of the chamber. A tradition with roots in antiquity, when English kings might have demanded the head of a luckless Speaker who arrived bearing bad news.

The ritual required the Prime Minister and Opposition leader to drag the Speaker toward his high-backed, ornately carved chair. Orvil, a roly-poly fellow in a black silk robe and a tri-cornered hat, had some experience in amateur theatre and was taking his performance seriously. As he resisted, his robe slipped off, and Marcus Yates had to grab him by his suspenders to prevent a fall. Those suspenders snapped, propelling Orvil forward into the arms of Clara Gracey, who was forced to grasp him around the middle to push him upright, rather like an inflated clown.

Margaret joined in the general laughter. Not smiling, though, was Emil Farquist, who turned to look at Margaret with cold hate.

PART FOUR

A VERY UNMERRY CHRISTMAS

It was the morning before Christmas and not a creature was stirring but Rob O'Brien, who was shovelling a path to his car through nearly four feet of freshly fallen snow. It was half past seven, still dark, the snow still coming down in great gobs. It had been an epic enterprise just getting the front screen door open.

Lou's new home came with a small garage, but he'd left the Cavalier outside, plugged in, so he could get a fast start this morning. He huffed and swore as he whaled away with the snow shovel in the dim glow of his yard light, finally opening a channel to the car.

Listlessly, giving in to the sheer impossibility of going anywhere today, he brushed the snow from the windows and peered inside at the two big canvas bags packed with gift-wrapped boxes: games, books, electronic toys, a massive panda for Lisa, who was not too old for that. She loved her bears. Logan's new bicycle was lying on top. It had come with training wheels, but Lou thought that might be insulting and had taken them off.

Much of this bounty he'd got just across the border in Havre, Montana. No problem there, he whizzed across the border both ways — though it helped that the Canadian customs guy, who lived near Porc Plain, had bought a router from Lou. From a jeweller, Lou had scored a beautiful necklace for Celeste, silver with a diamond pendant. It was still in the house, unwrapped, to be enclosed with a loving note he'd yet to write.

Other stuff, like the handcrafted panda, came from the local Christmas bazaar, in Porcupine Plain's covered rink. He'd spent with abandon, buoyed by the news that the Laurentian branch had agreed to restore his thirty-two K.

His plan had been to make a Christmas Eve run for Calgary, an eight-hour drive, to Upper Mount Royal — a quick check to see that no one was around, drop the bags and the bike by the driveway, and scoot. But that was not going to happen. It would take days for the snowplows to clear the highways.

He trudged back to the house, defeated, trying to convince himself it was the thought that counted. This would be the first Christmas he hadn't shared with his family, and he was haunted by memories of the kids bouncing him and Celeste awake before dragging them off to light the tree and the fire before the attack on their stockings and gifts. Then off to the park to try out the new sled or toboggan, and later back to the warmth of house and hearth and the aroma of a fat bird in the oven.

He sought solace in the comforts of his new home, a solid brick structure, a screened porch and a large attic, well heated and with a handsome fireplace and a full woodshed. The Johnsons had left him most of their furniture.

He had leased it for six months with an option to buy, but remained wary about putting his name on the title — it was a mind-bending effort to avoid a paper trail. He still hadn't got a business licence or opened a credit union account. He hadn't even registered the car in his name, and he'd had a close call talking his way out of a traffic ticket. Everything was cash, he'd stopped using his credit card long ago.

He made coffee, lit his lonely little tree, started a fire, sat down at his desk, opened his laptop.

TWELVE ENTERTAINERS WHO DON'T WANT YOU TO KNOW THEY WEAR TOUPEES. SEVEN SUPER-SENSITIVE EROGENOUS ZONES THAT WILL DRIVE YOUR LOVER WILD. EIGHT CLEVER WAYS TO TALK YOUR WAY OUT OF A TRAFFIC TICKET. THESE TEN ADORABLE ORPHAN PUPPIES FOUND LOVING HOMES.

That last one had paid really well. A collection of kids with puppies. Hits galore for his client, showing up on Facebook pages everywhere. Merry Christmas, everyone.

§

He didn't emerge from the house for the rest of the day, labouring over his love letter to Celeste, studying the entrails of computers and other techno gadgets entrusted to him, then going online, checking the weather sites, cursing them, reading news feeds, wire services, the dailies. Lots of saccharine mush celebrating this allegedly festive season.

On the political pages, he came across an item about the examinations for discovery of Farquist and Blake, set for Calgary between Boxing Day and the thirty-first. Sort of ringing in the new year not with a tinkle but a gong. Lou knew his name was bound to come up. Margaret Blake would have to confess to their meeting, to having been shown Svetlana's video. According to Reuters online, the S&M artiste had gone incommunicado in Russia after a sojourn in the south of France. That left the defence in a tough spot, but surely the legendary Arthur Beauchamp would prevail. Somehow.

It didn't help that Ms. Blake would be in a foul mood. Reports had her being furious at the defection of a prominent Green MP: one of her stars, Dr. Lloyd Chalmers, had gone over to the Liberals, who richly rewarded him with the new ministry of Lands, Forests, and Rivers, created especially for him.

Probably an asshole, Lou figured. That also seemed to be the view of Christie Montieth in her blog, with her gossipy little scoop that Chalmers had been dating a Liberal backbencher — a hot number, as revealed by a photo of the two of them mooning over each other in a bar. The obvious inference being he'd been led by his dick across the floor of the House.

He clicked through to the *Calgary Herald* online. "Whiter Than White Christmas" was the front-page headline, a story about the big dump, businesses shutting early, tangled traffic. The only good news was that the prowling pedophile had not been seen for six weeks. Though that was bad news too, in that he hadn't been nabbed. Police had released a cell-phone photo of a short, bald man driving slowly past a schoolyard, shielding his face with his hand. The car was grey, probably a Saturn Astra. Despite pleas, the driver had not come forward. No one got the licence plate.

As he had often done since arriving here, he Googled *Lou Sabatino*. Lots of old Waterfrontgate stories, the Mafia's attempt to take him down. More recent, an item about the Sûreté looking for him, to serve a subpoena for the trial. There was a photo of Lou looking like a frazzled alley cat after nearly being gunned down in front of his house. Beardless, totally not recognizable as Robert O'Brien.

When he searched *Robert O'Brien*, a million useless hits came up, but when he added *Glinka*, he found a link to a Craigslist inquiry. "Seeking Robert O'Brien," said the heading, under the personals, and it showed up in several major cities. "Urgent," the listing said. "Please call re the Glinka tape. I am a friend. Complete confidence. Text or phone." And a 250 number, British Columbia. Who was looking for him beside the Sûreté?

Lou stared at this scary listing, dazed. It spelled trouble in River City. Any call he made could be traced. So could a text. *I am a friend*. That sounded sincere, but . . . Lou understood urgent. What was urgent was not getting riddled by an AK-47 in his new front yard.

He tried to convince himself he owed no duty to anyone. He had no choice but to keep his head down, and carry on, guiltily, as Rob O'Brien, entrepreneur, of Rural Route 1, Porcupine Plain, Saskatchewan.

§

After dinner — frozen beef stew, microwaved — he added a few logs to the fire and returned to his computer. He was arousing himself with videos on a porn site — disgusting, but he was needy sex-wise — when the doorbell rang.

Sally Rosewell, bundled up, grinning, was holding a bottle of real French champagne. She dusted the snow from her parka, marched in, and kicked off her boots. She looked good, rosy-cheeked. Maybe a little inebriated.

Lou did a hasty Command-Q, closed his laptop, and helped her out of her coat and scarf. He did that with some awkwardness, his stiff joint caught in the leg of his shorts. She was wearing a party dress with optimum cleavage, which didn't help.

"I thought you'd be at the Willards' Christmas Eve thing."

Lou quickly turned away from her and waddled off to get wine glasses from the liquor cabinet. "I would have bummed everyone out. Feeling kind of blah." He dipped into his pants, tried with limited success to adjust his obstinate hard-on.

"Hey, I'm all alone too, and I'm here to bring cheer."

She popped the champagne cork, and, as she cheerfully watched it sail over her head, Lou bolted to the couch and sat, crossing his legs, causing major groin cramp, his pecker trapped, still engorged, still under the influence of the four-way orgy he'd been watching, and now on top of that here was the three-dimensional, touchable, fuckable reality of plump Sally Rosewell.

She poured, then sat next to him, close to the hearth, warming herself, hitching her skirt above her knees, a show of slightly parted thighs. She'd been on offer for lo these many weeks, but Lou had never quite been able to close the gap. They'd almost get past the necking phase, then he'd find excuses — he really liked her but he wasn't ready, vague hints he was recovering from a broken heart. He'd put his wedding ring away, had never mentioned a wife.

She leaned toward him, and as they clinked glasses, her hand brushed the bulge in his pants. Her eyes widened. "Well, I know what I want for Christmas." She downed her champagne, put her tongue in his mouth, and he inhaled her boozy fumes. Meanwhile, her hands worked furiously, unbuckling him, unzipping, freeing his cock, which sprang up like a scared jackrabbit.

Her fingers circled and grasped it, and it looked like she was about to go down on him, and he was about to explode with lust, on the razor's edge of ejaculation, and he hollered, "Wait!"

She released him, startled.

"Sorry," he gasped. "Too fast for me. Got to slow down. I'm only human."

"Okay, got it. Let's hit the sack."

It took him a while to get his temperature down below boiling point. Two refills of chilled champagne helped. Sally's extended visit to the washroom helped. Prepping, putting stuff in her or on her, whatever women did to prepare. He zombied his way to the bedroom, tried to make it look welcoming, straightened the sheets, lit a candle.

There could be no turning back. He was going to do this without a single twinge of guilt about Celeste, who had deserted him. He was owed this, reparation for his forced loneliness.

When he went back out for the champagne, Sally was leaning over his desk, wearing only a towel, and here came the erection again.

And then she said, "Who's Celeste?"

The jewellery box with the silver necklace. His scribbled note.

My darling Celeste . . . He'd completely forgotten it was sitting there, behind a monitor, wide open. He was struck dumb.

"Why aren't you celebrating Christmas with Celeste?"

"She's my wife. She left me. I miss my family."

And that was the end of that. He started to blubber, and Sally began pulling on her clothes.

ARTHUR BEAUCHAMP / THE FULL MONTY

It was December 26, Boxing Day, so called because of the English tradition of the gentry presenting gift boxes to their servants and tradespersons in gratitude for their services and sacrifices. So Arthur had brought his barber such a box, containing a bottle of Hennessy VSOP.

Though it was a bank holiday, Roberto had opened up for him, enduringly faithful to his favourite customer, a regular from decades ago, when he'd started in a storefront with a striped pole on seamy Davie Street. He was then known as Bob the Barber. Now he was Roberto, out of the closet, with a select clientele of, mostly, ladies who lunch, and working out of well-appointed premises in the arcade of a downtown tower.

Arthur saw him on the eve of every major trial, a ritual he wanted to believe brought him luck, so Roberto was confused by this appointment. "But you have no trial tomorrow, Mr. Beauchamp."

"Examinations for discovery. May as well be a trial. If it all comes out in the wash, the trial may be an anticlimax."

"And you will finally be face to face with Satan himself. The battle of the century."

"I'm afraid it will be more decorous than that. One isn't allowed to cross-examine — a habit I have to keep in check."

"We must do something with this ghastly moustache, you're practically eating it. Something clipped, brisk, military. You are a general leading his troops into battle. And the hair! When did the cyclone hit? Over the sink, please."

It was early afternoon. Arthur would comfortably make his flight to snowbound Calgary. Margaret was already there, being rehearsed by Nanisha Banerjee. Arthur had proposed to his companion for life that they take separate hotel rooms. "A brief divorce," was the awkward way he put it, a jest that went flat. He explained that it seemed somehow improper to sleep with a client, that both of them would need undisturbed sleep. She protested, but finally, wearily, agreed.

Margaret had been in such a foul mood for the last week that Arthur had wished he could adjourn the discoveries. But that was out of the question. It would be seen as an admission of weakness and play into the opposition's hands, delay the trial, free up Farquist.

Margaret had exploded when Lloyd Chalmers jumped ship and couldn't be restrained from denouncing him at a press conference as a "self-serving hypocrite" who, only a month ago, had answered a champagne toast with a solemn pledge of loyalty. "Sold his conscience, bought a cabinet job with it." "A slap in the face to the voters in Halifax East." "Thinking with his dink." That one made for ribald, bowdlerized leads in the press.

Chalmers declined to respond in kind, reiterating his view that the green agenda would be better served by his working from a place of influence. He respected the Green Party and its leader, but they were powerless to do what had to be done.

That came near the end of the December sitting, and Arthur had flown to Ottawa to help her through her malaise. Though she'd promised to soldier on, she'd lost some spunk. Arthur could only pray.

He chided himself for not sharing her grief at Chalmers's defection, but he couldn't suppress his glee that the dashing, womanizing bedder of his life companion had proved to be a faithless lout. But, of course, he never said as much.

Arthur wasn't oozing with optimism about the trial. While in Ottawa, he'd met with Agent Fitz McGilroy, who had been forthcoming enough, though he added nothing to what he'd told Margaret. Arthur remained equivocal about using the spy's information — it could backfire. He didn't fully trust McGilroy and worried that this was some kind of setup, with Photoshopped pictures of Svetlana and the Russian spy.

He was also uncertain how to handle the matter of the pregnancy of Farquist's anguished mother. Sierra had found Lee's priest, but he was senescent, in a nursing home.

Roberto whirled him toward the mirror. "I shall call this the Monty, after Field Marshall Montgomery. The *full* Monty."

§

Alone and lonely in a king-sized bed in the Palliser Hotel, Arthur had slept poorly, rolling about and worrying, thinking about his wife next door. But he dragged himself up at eight — Farquist's discovery was to begin at ten — and had a hot shower and combed his Monty and put on his general's uniform: dark suit, white shirt, his lucky blue-striped tie.

He met Margaret in the lobby restaurant, where they both fuelled with coffee and eggs, neither saying much. "Sleep well?" he asked hopefully.

"Like a rock. Joking. You?"

"Okay, I guess. Will Pierette be joining us?"

"She's coming in on a noon flight. Something came up with Agent McGilroy."

"What kind of something?"

"She couldn't say on the phone."

That sounded ominous. Another thing to worry about.

"I am going resign, you know. I mean it."

"Let's do this first."

The day was sunny and they would like to have walked the few blocks to the courthouse, but sidewalks were still treacherous from the snowstorm a few days ago. So Nanisha Banerjee picked them up. She was their shepherd, intimate with her bustling town, and had taken them to a very good curry house last night. Most Calgarians they'd met seemed in good humour, and tension had abated over the wretch who'd been prowling in the summer and fall.

Nanisha let them out at the entrance of the glass monolith that was the Calgary Courts Centre. Most of its work had been suspended for the holidays; an exception had been made for their court-ordered discovery. A small body of reporters and photographers was outside, and Arthur bantered with them as they waited for Nanisha to park.

"No story here, ladies and gentlemen. Just a friendly, private get-together to ask some questions."

"What do you expect to get from Minister Farquist?"

"It's a beautiful, crisp day. Why aren't you all out on your sleds, skates, or skis? Tell your editors I've instructed you to take the day off."

"Fat chance. Will you be discussing settlement, Mr. Beauchamp?"

"Calgary looks lovely all dressed in white, doesn't it?"

"Why all the secrecy, Mr. Beauchamp? Why aren't we allowed in?"

"Because the courthouse is officially closed today. I wish you all the best of the season."

Margaret said nothing, making her best effort to smile. She had begged off sitting in on Farquist's testimony. "I just can't handle being near him. I'd go berserk." She was still bruised by Chalmers's defection.

Nanisha led them in, and they went up to the twentieth floor, where Arthur poked his head into an interview room: a table and several chairs, the court reporter setting up her equipment. She introduced herself as Sarah Blair with a cherubic smile, a Jamaican lilt. "This is exciting," she said.

Margaret and Nanisha sat on a sofa in the waiting room off the corridor, while George Cowper Jr. paced, looking even more lugubrious than usual, impatiently waiting for his client. Finally, twenty minutes after ten, Emil Farquist strolled from the elevator, along with Jonas Hawkes, his chief political operative.

Cowper seemed to want to introduce Arthur, but Farquist merely glanced his way, sizing up the enemy. He studiously avoided looking at Margaret as he followed his lawyer into the discovery room.

Ms. Blair was at one end of the table with her steno machine and backup voice recorder. Arthur and Nanisha sat down across from Farquist and Cowper, whose junior, a thin, prim, grim young man, perched at the end of the table over a thick writing pad. Hawkes remained outside, as did Margaret.

"Very well, we're late starting," Arthur said crisply. "Please swear Mr. Farquist."

Blair administered an oath to tell the truth. "Yes, of course, I so swear," Farquist said. He was in casual dress, a purple turtleneck pullover stretched over his ample front.

"Very well, please state your name."

And so it began.

§

Arthur presumed that Farquist had spent a grim Christmas in training, being grilled by his lawyers in pseudo-cross-examination, but perhaps not in great depth, given the many distractions of the holiday and his political ambitions. Arthur also presumed that he'd been warned the lawyer for the defence was sly and tricky, and to keep his responses short, unembellished, not to argue or indulge in the sarcastic rhetoric he was prone to.

Arthur did not underestimate Farquist's mental agility, but his Achilles heel might be his distended ego, so he played to it, running him through his academic history, achievements as an economist, his electoral successes, his fast climb up the political ranks. Farquist obligingly answered Arthur's soft questions, but often glanced at his shiny Rolex as if to let everyone know he had better things to do.

Arthur found it hard to budge Farquist from his script, and he came off — distressingly — as modest, despite hints of self-importance. (He was "humbled" to have earned two honorary doctorates.) Arthur was cordial and respectful as he waited for Farquist to begin to loosen up, which he finally did, obviously having expected worse.

Cowper watched Arthur alertly, clearly expecting him to accelerate, to stop lobbing his pitches and throw a fastball. That must come soon, Arthur decided — he must unsettle the witness, break him out of his cocoon of safety.

He took Farquist back in time. "I understand your late father, Sandor, was also an economist of no small reputation."

"Without question."

"How would you sum up that reputation?"

"He had an impressive mind and was a powerful influence."

"On you?"

"On me and many others."

"In what way was he a powerful influence on you?"

"As an academic. A father."

An opening. "As a father?"

"Yes."

"A father who disappeared from your life when you were a lad of eight, correct?"

Farquist looked coldly at him for a few seconds, prompting Cowper to butt in. "Mr. Beauchamp, I don't see that this is close to being relevant."

"Surely, Mr. Cowper, it is vital to examine his personal history, given the nature of the alleged slander. It goes to the heart of the case."

"My objection is on record." And there his objection would sit until pre-trial motions, when the judge would decide whether the line of questioning was admissible.

Farquist tersely responded to a series of questions about his provenance: born 1971; sole progeny of Sandor and his youthful wife,
Lee; Sandor's affair; the separation and divorce. During this, he kept
checking his watch, and could not resist a sardonic postscript: "It
happens in the best of families, Mr. Beauchamp."

"The best of families, Mr. Farquist? You'll agree, I hope, that
doesn't include a family that broke apart upon the husband deserting
an unloved wife and their only child?"

Farquist reddened. "Mr. Beauchamp, you will not bait me. There
was a separation. It was on mutual terms. I resent being subjected to
this kind of game, sir."

"Is that how you see this? A game?"

"Can we avoid these exchanges, please?" said Cowper, sending
his client a warning look. "We are delving into matters that are
entirely irrelevant, Mr. Beauchamp."

The tension was palpable in this confined space, Nanisha rigid
beside Arthur, Farquist's junior sitting up like a bear sniffing the air.
Ms. Blair, however, seemed to be suppressing a smile as she recorded
all this.

"How often did you see your father after the divorce?"

"Several times."

"Where?"

"At his office."

"Not in his new home with his new wife?"

"My mother preferred that I not visit there."

In subdued tones, Arthur dealt with her suicide, the barbiturates,
the shocking suddenness of it, the impact on Farquist.

"I trust this questioning will end soon, Mr. Beauchamp. I can't
describe the devastation I felt."

"Is it fair to say that Lee remained deeply in love with Sandor
until her death?"

"There's nothing unusual in that."

"You were living with her all that time, until you were eighteen?"

"Yes."

"And in that time she didn't take up with another partner?"

"She never remarried, if that's what you mean." His tone remained sharp, aggressive. He darted a look at his counsel.

"I am instructing my client not to answer questions along these lines."

"In that case, I shall apply for an order that he answer. That may extend this hearing for several days."

That worked. "Let's get through this," Farquist said.

"I have a standing objection," Cowper said.

"That is on record, Mr. Cowper."

Arthur pushed on. "She had no romantic relationships after he left his home, wife, and child?"

"I refuse to couch the matter in such a way. They separated."

"As you wish, but did she have such a romantic relationship?"

"I believe she was seeing a gentleman, yes."

Arthur wasn't expecting that, and was thrown off balance. "And who might that have been?"

"A widower, I believe. Someone from her church. A gentleman."

Arthur asked for details, but Farquist stayed deliberately vague. A businessman, building management, something to that effect. Edward or Edwin, his surname a blank. Average height, slender. He visited only occasionally.

Arthur assumed a convenient fiction had been concocted. But he had no recourse but to follow through. "Was she sleeping with him?"

"This is outrageous. I am not aware if they slept together. It was none of my business, and it should be none of yours."

Arthur had the sense Farquist had prepared for this peripheral line of attack. He was hostile but not rattled. Arthur's strategy wasn't showing profit.

"In those troubled years, you were very close to your mother?"

"Of course."

"She loved you."

"Is that not what mothers do?"

Arthur let it go at that. He couldn't bring himself to boldly suggest she'd been pregnant with his child. With that mysterious lover on the scene, Arthur would only appear desperate and slimy.

A washroom break for the court reporter allowed Arthur to confer with Nanisha in the corridor. "Keep at it," she said. "He's famous for his temper." Despite her encouraging words, she seemed disappointed at Arthur's meagre results.

Margaret was also famous for her temper, and Arthur worried she would lack Farquist's controlled cool when it came her turn. She was standing by a window, looking at Calgary's snow-thickened rooftops. He wanted to embrace her, offer strength, but his sense of propriety forbade that.

§

"Mr. Farquist, I understand you keep homes in Ottawa and Calgary."

"A residence here and a condominium in Ottawa."

"And, as well, a chalet in the Gatineau Hills near the town of Kazabazua."

"I recently sold that."

"'A stunning, private lakeside chalet on four pristine acres,' to quote your real estate agent. The sale was effective as of December eleventh, two weeks ago?"

"You've done your research." A more relaxed tone. His instructions had been to cool it, to be civil. Cowper would have told him, "Beauchamp is firing blanks. It's all bluster."

"And why did you sell it?"

"Mr. Beauchamp, perhaps your good wife need not be concerned about her legal bills, but I am not so blessed." A gotcha look. A good answer to a bad question. Cowper seemed embarrassed for his opposing counsel.

"And it was then encumbered with a mortgage for $200,000 taken out last May twenty-fifth?"

"As to the date, you have the advantage of me. Close enough."

"And what did you do with *those* proceeds?"

A glance at his watch. A shrug. "The market looked attractive. I turned everything over to an investment advisor. He operates a blind trust, so I have no idea what stocks were bought."

And so the rabbit scampers down another escape hole. Farquist had been prepared well by his counsel. Lugubrious Cowper, his eyes constantly on Arthur, offering nothing, no hint of triumph.

Arthur had abundant experience with lying witnesses, and read them well — the talent was in his bones, almost instinctive. But there was no noticable discomfort here, no perspiration, no shifting in his chair, no clearing of throat, eye contact rarely broken.

He assembled himself, pressed for details. Had Farquist any proof of payment of those proceeds into that blind trust? Yes, there was a record in his personal financial files. He hadn't thought to bring that along. Farquist wasn't reluctant to provide the name of his investment advisor, whose firm was based in Calgary. James Kenniworth, Northern Allied Investments. A trusted friend of long standing.

It would be hard to prove that this trusted friend had funnelled the funds to Svetlana Glinka. He could be subpoenaed, but that might backfire. He may have innocently set up a blind trust that Farquist surreptitiously cleaned out.

"May I suggest that what you really bought was Ms. Svetlana Glinka's silence. After she threatened to go public with your sado-masochistic relationship."

Farquist looked as if he'd been slapped. "That's as ridiculous as it is insulting." He shot an importuning look at his counsel.

"We can be confident none of this is admissible," Cowper said.

Arthur changed tack. "Among the documents your counsel has provided is your day book for the current year." A leather binder, comprising the fifty-two pages marked for each week of the year, crammed with notes and appointments, but nothing politically sensitive. "Please mark that an exhibit, Madam Reporter."

The key date was Sunday, January 6, the date stamped on Glinka's video, but Arthur opened the binder to the first calendar page, the week ending January 5. That Saturday showed Farquist in his Parliamentary office in the morning, the environment ministry in the afternoon, and at his Ottawa home that evening with a few friends over drinks. A reminder: "Rhoda prefers Riesling."

"A busy Saturday for you?"

"We were about to go into session on Monday. We were incredibly busy. We were running the government of Canada, Mr. Beauchamp."

"And that evening you entertained friends at your condo?"

Farquist studied the last entry on the page. "Yes, it would appear I did. I expect it was more of a work party to free up Sunday."

"Let us continue to that Sunday. There is nothing in the morning."

"I would have attended service at the Notre Dame Cathedral. As I do religiously." Finally, a smile.

"You have scribbled 'free afternoon' with an exclamation point."

"I ought to have crossed that out. I worked all afternoon, into the evening. As you see, I have a note halfway down the page, 'all day prep parks bill.' That's the bill I would be introducing, the National Parks Improvement Act."

"And when did you inscribe those words, 'all day prep parks bill'?"

"That day, I suppose, or the previous."

"You will note it was written with a blue-ink pen. All the previous notations were in black ink."

"I imagine I used whatever pen was handy, Mr. Beauchamp. I'm not sure what you are implying. I spent all day at home and slept there that night. I distinctly remember wrestling with the phrasing of my bill — a thorny matter involving fees for roads and infrastructure." He was looking right at Arthur, bold, unwavering. Glinka had spilled the beans to Farquist's investigators, so he knew the importance of this date.

Arthur was certain that the blue-penned task was a recently contrived afterthought, the "free afternoon" having been spent in his log cabin where he was being flogged for his sins.

"Invariably, on your free Sundays you retreated to your chalet in the Gatineaus?"

"On the occasional weekend."

"But mostly on Sundays. I count at least ten visits between January sixth and mid-May."

"Fewer than that, I am sure. We were in session all that time."

"Two Sundays on, you will see another empty page, blank except for the notification; 'Lac Vert!'"

Farquist acceded to that, and affected surprise that Arthur was able to point to several similar notes on succeeding Sundays: "Lac Vert!" "Day off." "Head for the hills!" "Lac Vert all day." Arthur turned to Sunday, April 21. "And here you have, 'Lac Vert, bring NEB file.'"

"Many of those notes were merely hopeful. I was often unable to get away." He cleared his throat, shifted his bulk. "I don't know what the point is of having a holiday home, Mr. Beauchamp, if you don't use it."

"And how did you use it?"

"To relax. Rearm myself for the battle. Build a fire. Read. Go online. Catch up on the world around me. I enjoy the solitude. In the summer, I might go out in my boat. I used to ski. Anything else?"

"Sometimes you took work with you?"

"Rarely."

"You wrote, 'Bring NEB file.' Doesn't that suggest work?"

"National Energy Board. An issue of expediting a hearing."

"That would be with respect to the Coast Mountains Pipeline?"

"I am proud to say that was one of my major initiatives."

Arthur felt relief that Margaret wasn't there to hear this. He imagined the sparks from her silver eyes, the unsuppressed loathing.

"At this sanctuary, you also entertained individuals."

"Again, rarely."

It was time to give him the full Monty. "But in fact one was a regular, wasn't she? Ms. Svetlana Glinka."

"That is simply preposterous."

Arthur tapped the day book, still open in front of him. "On each of these free Sunday afternoons you employed her services as a dominatrix. I put that to you."

"I will say unequivocally that I have never been in the company of any Svetlana Glinka. Never seen her, never talked to her, never even heard of her until I first learned about Ms. Blake's outrageous allegations."

"I'm suggesting you had a relationship with her for four and a half months, commencing last January sixth."

"That is a lie!"

"And that you played sado-masochistic games with her, during which you were whipped with a riding crop while pleading for your mother's forgiveness."

Farquist went silent for a moment, becoming puffy and red-faced, as if he might erupt. But he held it in. "This is intolerable. Mr. Beauchamp, I have been put through hell by your client — your wife! — painted as some kind of depraved idiot. I swear to God Almighty that there isn't an atom of truth in what you say."

Reeking of sincerity, so emphatic it caused Ms. Blair to dart a look of reproof at Arthur, a heartless bully. He was having trouble framing a follow-up, and Cowper took the opportunity of noting it was half past twelve. Lunch break.

BUGGED

Nanisha took Arthur to her favourite lunch spot, an old-fashioned diner festooned with photos of film stars of long ago: Chaplin, Garbo, Barrymore. There they morosely lunched on soup and sandwiches while they waited for Margaret, who'd returned to the hotel to meet Pierette — her flight had arrived late. What was the dire news she was bringing from Agent Fitz McGilroy?

Arthur was in despair. He'd fired his best shots at the plaintiff, and they'd rebounded like rubber balls. He'd rarely encountered such an elusive target — Farquist seemed to have anticipated every line of attack.

Nanisha's gaze was fixed on Charles Laughton. "Either he's an extremely good actor . . ." She hesitated, as if afraid to utter a forbidden thought. "Or, what if . . . I'm just throwing this out, but what if Emil believes what he is saying? What if this is all a hoax, the video was a clever piece of artistry, cut and spliced so seamlessly that, well . . . ?" A helpless, embarrassed shrug.

That was inconceivable. But if Arthur's junior counsel was harbouring doubts, Chief Justice Cohon-Plaskett might also find herself impressed with Farquist's cries of innocence. Her Ladyship might also conclude that Margaret was the gullible and blameworthy victim of a hoax.

He did his best to pooh-pooh Nanisha's speculation. Who would have motive to create such an illusion? Lou Sabatino? That would make no sense. And hadn't Glinka's lawyer in Nice, in couched phrases, practically affirmed that she had filmed the episode, got paid off, suppressed all evidence of it?

"I'm sorry," said Nanisha. "Just a brief escape from reality."

Margaret and Pierette hove into view, both breathless, kicking the snow from their boots at the door before descending on their booth.

"They've tapped our lines," Margaret said, her expression fierce.

"Just mine," Pierette blurted. "My house phone. Fitz told me."

"Sit down, please, and slow down." Arthur called over the server, who took two more orders for sandwiches.

"Just be straightforward, Pierette," Margaret said. "It's okay."

"Well, um, Fitz and I have been getting a little close."

"In bed, close," Margaret added.

"Yeah, my bed. I lost my head a little. It's okay. I trust him, honestly. He couldn't say how he knew, but he has access to all kinds of stuff, and he learned someone put a tap on my landline. He found it, wired to some kind of transmitter outside my apartment. My cell seems to be okay, and all the office lines checked out okay. But they bugged my old house phone. I hardly ever use it, but I'm afraid I did talk to Margaret on it a couple of times." She trailed off, breathless, embarrassed.

Arthur was horrified. Despite all the precautions, all his warnings, she and Margaret had been loose on the phone. Both were looking guilty. He held his temper and began a calm, probing cross-examination.

Pierette's line had been compromised late in October, according to McGilroy, whose insider information he wasn't at liberty to detail. McGilroy's name was not to be mentioned; his career might be at risk. That suggested to Arthur that someone in CSIS had been the tapper. A rogue agent, maybe, a Farquist booster, or one on the take. Late October was when the Conservatives were toiling over their shredders.

Pierette was adamant that only two of her conversations would have been of interest. One was relatively benign, about Chalmers crossing the floor. The other, in late November, was more alarming. Pierette had been laid up at home with the flu, woozy with pills, had rambled on to Margaret about the incest theory, speculating about the Gatineau mortgage, how the funds bought Glinka's silence — areas for which Farquist had so skilfully armed himself — and, infinitely worse, Svetlana Glinka's role as Russian informant. All laid out on a platter for the plaintiff.

"What else?" Arthur demanded.

"Nothing else, I swear to God."

"The video?"

"Absolutely no mention."

"Absolutely," Margaret chimed in, breaking her tense silence.

How could they be sure? Arthur felt sick. He had been played like a fool all morning.

§

As they resumed at two p.m., Arthur was mentally wrung out and weighted by despair. Farquist had calmed down — with the aid of a drink or two. Arthur's nose was well trained to detect the perfume that wafted across the table: rye whisky, he decided, well aged, with an overlay of breath mint. That belied Farquist's show of self-assurance.

Arthur had to bury the urge to accuse him of engineering an illegal wiretap. It would give away too much information, and McGilroy was owed discretion. He refused to believe that George Cowper, reputedly a counsel of honour, was aware of the wiretap or would have countenanced it.

He picked away like a man without appetite. Glinka's blue

Miata? Farquist didn't know anyone with a Miata of any colour. The Lac Vert groundskeeper, Arthur said, had seen such a car parked by his chalet in January. The poor fellow, said Farquist, was of limited intelligence, and just as unreliable when sober as in his accustomed drunken condition.

Arthur wanted to kick himself. Why had he even brought that up? He'd just given them a freebie. Farquist's team would be on the groundskeeper in a flash, buying him off with a case of Crown Royal.

He produced some blown-up glossies taken by Frank Sierra from his triplex across from Glinka's flat. "You have seen these, Mr. Farquist, they were delivered with our affidavit of documents. They were taken on July seventh. Do you know what they depict?"

"I've been instructed that they show the flat of this Glinka woman on Rue de la Visitation in Montreal. I had also seen it on the six o'clock news." The shot of rye had done its job. He seemed on the verge of affability.

"This photo shows a black Lincoln Navigator parked out front."

"I've been instructed that is indeed a Lincoln Navigator."

"Have you ever seen that vehicle yourself?"

"Not that I'm aware."

"The driver is a well-built man, black hair, moustache. With him is a tall young brunette. In this next picture she is ascending the outer staircase to the apartment above Ms. Glinka's."

Farquist examined the photographs, shrugged.

"Do you recognize this woman and man?"

"I have never met them."

"But you know who they are, yes? You've been informed."

Farquist hesitated, then looked at Cowper, who said, "For the record, they are Ulrich Wentz and Jasmine L'Heureux, employees of the Puhl Detective Agency in Ottawa."

"Thank you," said Arthur, hoping he'd found a breach in their defences. He studied a calendar his junior had annotated. June 2, the WWF event, when Margaret blurted out the words taped by

Christie Montieth. Only two days later, Puhl's agents had packed out boxes of electronics from Glinka's flat. That was three weeks before the Freak Out recording went viral.

"And what were Mr. Wentz and Ms. L'Heureux doing there on the seventh of July, Mr. Farquist?"

"I imagine they were making inquiries in the neighbourhood as to the whereabouts of the Glinka woman."

She had bolted for France exactly a month earlier. The likely reason that the private eyes came snooping around that day was they hoped to grill Sabatino, maybe offer him hush money.

"Do you know who occupied that upper suite?"

"Not of my own knowledge."

"But you have been told, have you not, that one Lou Sabatino was living there?"

"Yes, under the guise of Robert O'Brien."

"And who told you that?"

Again Cowper interrupted. "Don't answer that. Solicitor privilege."

"Had you encountered him in his capacity as a journalist?"

"At the occasional press conference. He seemed to have a penchant for asking inane questions. I chewed him out once. I'm not on his favourites list."

"And what role do you see Mr. Sabatino playing in this case?"

"A co-conspirator with Svetlana, I assume."

Cowper spoke sharply. "Please don't speculate, Emil."

Arthur found this exchange interesting. The whisky Farquist downed had finally made its way to the tongue, and his legal team's strategy was as open as a raw wound. They planned to argue that Margaret had maliciously connived with Sabatino to embarrass her sworn enemy, or, alternatively, Lou and Svetlana had set her up with a phony story about a salacious video.

On Monday, at her own discovery, Margaret would testify she'd seen a copy pirated by Lou Sabatino. Cowper would accuse her of lying, but as a backup might argue that the images had been doctored by her techno-savvy co-conspirator, who'd gone on the run under a pseudonym.

"Mr. Farquist, getting back to the Puhl Agency and its two employees, Mr. Wentz and Ms. L'Heureux — July seventh was not their first visit to Ms. Glinka's address. They showed up a month earlier in a white van and proceeded to empty her suite of all electronic apparatus. You know this because I have a statement from one of her clients to such effect — Mr. Harvey Plouffe. You have seen it. It is in our documents."

Cowper interjected again. "He wouldn't know anything about that."

"Please let him answer."

Farquist plowed ahead. "All I can say is that they were probably looking for evidence of Svetlana's . . . Ms. Glinka's extortion plan. A plot to make me look like a sicko."

"They first searched her flat on June fourth. Did they have permission from the tenant?"

"You'll have to ask them, Mr. Beauchamp."

"They had a key, Mr. Farquist."

"Again, I know nothing about it."

So Cowper had shielded him from the Puhl Agency's doings. Arthur had not seen their reports. He had objected to disclosing Francisco Sierra's material, claiming privilege, and Cowper had responded in kind. That now seemed an unwise trade-off.

"Tuesday, June fourth, that was the date."

"If you say so."

"Three weeks before the defendant's words were broadcast across the internet. Why would your detectives have been interested in Svetlana on June fourth? Just two days after the impugned words were picked up by a live microphone?"

Farquist looked at Cowper, as if seeking permission. "He has a right to know," the lawyer said.

"Very well," said Farquist, with an elaborate shrug. "Christie Montieth, who I know well — she's one of my favourite bloggers — played the recording for me in my office on June third. I believe that was a Monday. I declined to comment on record, but I did warn her that it would be dangerous to report or repeat such a calumny. I may have mentioned legal action. I then consulted counsel, and I assume they instructed the Puhl Agency —"

"Don't assume," Cowper admonished him. "Objection. Solicitor privilege."

Arthur was caught short by Farquist's explanation and took a moment to recover his balance. "And you claim not to know how they happened to have a key to Ms. Glinka's premises?"

"I haven't talked to them." Farquist checked his watch again.

"Come now, they clearly had permission to enter Ms. Glinka's home and business and pack up any compromising material. Otherwise they would be guilty of larceny."

"If that's a question, and it seems to be mere rhetoric, I'm at a loss to respond."

"Obviously, your investigators quickly made contact with Svetlana Glinka, and I'm putting it to you that she was paid off to cooperate and remain silent."

Farquist directed a weary look up at the ceiling. "That's an interesting but blatantly false supposition, Mr. Beauchamp."

"In fact, your investigators met with Ms. Glinka in France in a further effort to buy her silence."

"I have not seen their reports."

"Then how did you hear about Mr. Sabatino's alleged role in this?"

Hesitation. "Someone told me. I can't remember."

Arthur spoke quietly to his junior. "Ms. Banerjee, would you kindly attend to the issuing of subpoenas for Mr. Puhl and his two investigators? Thank you."

That might, just possibly, cause his opponents some concern.

Nanisha packed up some papers and headed off to the court registry. Arthur hoped it was still open — he wanted those subpoenas out fast. He wanted Puhl's agents to sweat through the weekend.

He looked at his own watch: nearly four o'clock on this cruel Friday, another half hour to go and he was running out of ammunition. If he could keep Farquist under oath until they resumed on Monday, something might come up. Some miracle.

Should he bring up Glinka's role as a Russian asset? Farquist would be armed for that, thanks to Pierette's telephone tap. But nothing ventured . . .

"Mr. Farquist, you conceded that you occasionally took work to your chalet on weekends."

"Rarely, I said."

"And that work would include confidential government documents?"

"On occasion, yes."

"And any visitor could have chanced upon them?"

"I never entertained visitors at Lac Vert. As I have said, it was my sanctuary." Another peek at his watch.

"You are aware, of course, that Svetlana Glinka, this person you claim not to know, was a paid Russian informer."

"She seems the sort of conniving person who might be."

"Don't speculate," Cowper said sharply. "If you don't know, say so." The normally unflappable barrister was riled. His startled reaction to Arthur's question suggested he wasn't privy to the illegal phone intercept.

"I know nothing about her being a Russian agent. It sounds preposterous." Fiddling with his Rolex.

"Are you in a hurry to go somewhere, Mr. Farquist?"

"I'm late for an important staff meeting, but I'm prepared to endure this to the end."

Arthur affected magnanimity. "Okay, we don't want you

314

distracted by the important matters weighing on you. Let us finish up on Monday."

He began packing away his papers. Cowper clearly would have preferred his client to be off the hook, but gave in to Farquist's eagerness to bolt. And bolt he did, pulling on his coat as he made for the door, joining his aide in a foot race to the elevator. Margaret and Pierette broke off a quiet conversation to watch them. Arthur ventured an encouraging smile, a lie. Margaret rewarded him with an air-kiss.

"Perhaps you and I can have a moment," Cowper said. The court reporter packed up her gear. Cowper's nervous junior checked his phone as he followed her out, leaving the two senior lawyers alone.

There followed an exchange of weary woes about their disrupted holiday season, their absence from home and family in snow-clogged Calgary. They grumbled about the demanding tasks barristers must undertake, the weary hours of preparation, the discomfort of conflict, the waste of it all, the agonizingly delicate handling of clients, with their unerring tendency to stick to fixed positions.

"Especially in emotional issues such as this, wouldn't you agree, Arthur?"

This seemed a lead-up to an offer of settlement — Arthur hadn't expected it so soon. "And what might you suggest, George, that would soften those fixed positions?"

"Let's explore that." But Cowper sidestepped. "By the way, excellent work on your part — as was entirely to be expected — but I hope we can agree that Emil stood up under fire very well indeed. Given his firm denials, you may also want to concede that your defence of justification lacks any evidentiary foundation. And frankly I am loath to put Ms. Blake through the discomfort of a distasteful trial at which, regrettably, she must be accused of a maliciously false accusation."

A pause, then he added, "We probably can't expect judgment for the full amount claimed, and I believe I have persuaded Emil of that. After all, he seeks no personal compensation — he has committed himself to donate the bulk of his winnings, so to speak, to a hospital fund, less his out-of-pockets. He seeks exoneration, but that must come at a cost."

The out-of-pockets doubtless included a substantial legal fee. Maybe a million or more. The Puhl Agency did not come cheap. And Farquist had underlings to pay off, like the wiretapper. Between legal costs, paying off Glinka, and a pricey leadership campaign, he must be almost tapped out, and likely more keen to get this case behind him than Cowper wanted to admit.

"Do I understand, George, you are instructed to make an offer — even before examining Margaret?"

"You're clearly aware, Arthur, that Svetlana Glinka cooperated with our people in Montreal and in France. We have a good sense of what your client will say. She will claim that Lou Sabatino described alleged images of an alleged video recorded — allegedly — by Svetlana Glinka. Once Ms. Blake has put that on record, under oath, there may be no backing down. This is the time to reach an accord."

Arthur found himself impatient with Cowper's fastidious manner. There was little point in making rebuttal, arguing the evidence, the evasions and gaps in Farquist's account. Cowper clearly had those in mind, holes the wily lawyer hoped to plug.

"What's your number, George?"

"Emil insists he won't go below ten million. But I can't believe he won't budge if push comes to shove. Seven and a half might be doable. A full apology, of course."

Arthur rose, found his coat. "Well, it's been a long day."

Cowper stared sadly at him. "If we don't close by Monday, I'm pulling my offer and we go for broke. All the way. Non-stop. Please talk to your client."

DINING WITH THE ENEMY

"Don't you find this weird?" Pierette asked. She had unpacked and was laying out her clothes on one of the twin doubles in Margaret's hotel room. Pierette was referring to the fact that she, not Arthur, was sharing that room. "Like, is he afraid you're going to sap his vital juices?"

"He finds my dual role as wife and client awkward. It's okay. Better this way. He's being awfully moody." And awfully reluctant to talk about the day-long session with the petulant plaintiff. "We'll go over it later," he'd kept repeating.

Day one of the discoveries had ended two hours ago, with Farquist, looking like he badly needed to piss, shit, or throw up, racing to the elevator with his moon-faced flunky. Margaret assumed Arthur had triumphed, but Nanisha, choosing her words carefully, said that discovery, unlike trial, rarely had winners and losers. She'd given Margaret the merest digest of the day's proceedings. Nanisha hadn't seemed upbeat.

As to the chat between Arthur and Cowper, she only said, "I'm not sure what they are talking about. Procedural stuff, I imagine."

There'd been no bantering with the press outside the courts afterwards — Arthur just scythed through them. Nanisha hurried off to her office — something about follow-ups, witness subpoenas — before heading to the airport to pick up Francisco Sierra. They would all meet at the fine French restaurant, Q Haute Cuisine, known to its habitués simply as the Q. Six o'clock, early for dinner, but Nanisha said it had been a "Herculean challenge" to secure a reservation for five.

"Let's just relax this evening," said Pierette. "Enjoy ourselves. We have all weekend to get you ready for act two. You're going to be a star, baby. A shining star."

§

The Q was a former estate home, Margaret had learned: spacious, well staffed, with an open kitchen. By six p.m., its three large dining areas were packed, and customers were waiting for tables.

But they'd got there early enough, and Nanisha had pulled off her Herculean feat, scoring a table with a knockout view of Eau Claire Park and the Bow River shining whitely under a full moon. The river's coverlet of snow was crusting after a daytime melt and reflecting sparkles from street lamps and Christmas lights strung on evergreens.

The maitre d' had recognized the Green leader and awarded her the choice window seat. Pierette sat beside her, Nanisha and Frank Sierra across from her, leaving Arthur the aisle chair. All chose to dine on the tasting menu, a feature offering of the Q.

Margaret's life partner was clearly was not himself, affecting an air of bonhomie that might have fooled the others, but not her. She would have preferred his more familiar self, the cynical grump. He seemed desperate to stave off any mention of the trial or his face-off with Farquist, and held the fort with a treatise on Calgary's constantly reshaping winter: bitter cold, blinding blizzard, the sudden caress of a warm Chinook.

He instructed them in west-wind myths. Zephyrus was the bringer of that wind, a god complimented by Chaucer for his "swete breth." But more apropos was the lovely Aboriginal myth about Chinook-Wind, a princess who, exiled to the prairies from her sea-home, had summoned the winds to warm her.

Sierra, smiling, broke in: "Where the Chinook blows, O'Brien lies low." He reminded them of the loving letter Lou Sabatino wrote to his wife and kids in November. His reference to a warming Chinook had persuaded Sierra to narrow his hunt to the southwest plains. But none of the dozens of clues and hundreds of internet hits had panned out.

Arthur wouldn't be diverted from his diversions, for he'd begun extolling the pan-seared Arctic char. That segued into a lengthy account of his defence of an Inuit char fisher framed for murder in Nunavut. He talked his way through the consommé, the baby shrimp salad with pine nuts, the quail breast, the wild mushroom risotto, and the lamb tenderloin.

Margaret sensed that her lawyer was withholding bad news. *We'll go over it later.* Nonetheless, she was amused, enjoying him, remembering how he'd wooed her with his vivid courtroom stories, his eloquent rambles. Some day, would he have a tale to tell of Farquist v. Blake?

Her thoughts were suddenly interrupted by the sight of someone she recognized climbing from a limousine that had stopped outside. She stiffened in shock then nudged Pierette, who looked out and said, "Oh, shit."

Seconds later, Emil Farquist rolled in, bypassing the waiting line, followed by Hawkes, Cowper, and an elderly man, thin, long-limbed, craggy-faced. Farquist was in full voice, greeting the maitre d' — and for that matter, all in the room — with slurred best wishes for this joy-filled season. More than a little tipsy.

According to Arthur, the wannabe Conservative leader had been in a sweat to get away this afternoon, something about an important staff meeting. Does one normally get drunk at a staff meeting?

The party of four was led to a newly cleared table near the kitchen. Margaret guessed the less-than-prime location annoyed Farquist; his ebullience faded and his voice — his words unclear — took on a complaining tone.

Hawkes, clearly embarrassed, was urging him to sit, but Emil resisted, and turned and scanned the restaurant. He blinked a couple of times, as if in confusion, as he focussed on the table in the cozy window alcove, at his staring enemies.

Abruptly, though with a slight misstep, he turned away and called out: "Michele, champagne, *s'il vous plaît!*" He expelled Hawkes from his chair, subsided into it, so he could sit with his back to his foes. A fifth chair remained empty — Margaret presumed it was for Cowper's nervous junior.

Arthur, who had gone silent mid-anecdote, looked questioningly at Pierette, then Sierra. "Who's the thin man?"

"That would be my old friend Sam Puhl." Sierra waved. Puhl returned a mock salute. They remained for a while in eye-to-eye combat, like gunslingers facing off.

Margaret was aware that Puhl's two investigators were being subpoenaed. He didn't seem very happy; perhaps that was why. Michele, the chef, hung about their table, clucking over them as champagne was poured.

Of those at Margaret's table, only Sierra, a foodie, had taken the kitchen tour the Q offered, and now his counterpart, Puhl, rose to do so. Farquist also stood, but to gesture at someone at the entrance, a tough-looking older dude in a Stetson.

Arthur had to twist around to look. "O'Reilly," he said. "Wouldn't you know."

Jack O'Reilly, the billionaire oilman, proud bankroller of the most right-wing of right-wing causes.

O'Reilly gave Farquist a manly hug. He shook hands with the others before he sat, talking loudly, maybe a few drinks to the worse himself.

The important staff meeting had amounted to two guys sharing a bottle, Margaret decided. Farquist would have been hitting the oilman up for campaign funds.

Everyone fell in line when Margaret declined dessert and coffee — the vibe in here had become strained, edgy. Arthur asked for the bill, Margaret visited the washroom, and Sierra quietly wandered off to the kitchen.

Later, as they enjoyed a moonlit stroll by the park, Sierra explained: "Sam was expecting me, of course. It would have been discourteous to ignore each other." The brief tête-à-tête had involved queries about their mutual well-being, a jest at Sierra's failed vow to retire, and Sierra's own jibe about an illegal wiretap.

"Sam expressed credible surprise and concern. He is a proud professional. He would not want his prestigious agency to be involved in something messy. And he is agitated over his two underlings being subpoenaed."

"What else did you read from him?" Arthur asked.

"A hearty optimism. He hints he has something up his shirtsleeve. But he is an expert bluffer."

Arthur blew out a cloud of breath. Margaret took his arm, slowed him while the others carried on. "Tell me why you're so preoccupied."

"They've made an offer. We'll talk at the hotel. Just you and me."

§

An hour later, Margaret was perched on Arthur's bed in a state of high tension as he paced and talked. A settlement proposal. Seven-and-a-half million, but they would likely go down to six, maybe five. A judgment against them could be much higher. These matters had to be weighed.

He sounded so formal. This was not her gentle, caring Arthur, her lover and husband. This was her lawyer.

"Plus an apology?" She could barely utter that word.

"Carefully worded. Based on incorrect information, that sort of thing."

"But five *million*?"

"A substantial mortgage on the farm can handle some of it. Bully will advance a hefty partnership draw. Lots of trials left in me."

Margaret watched for a sign he was merely having fun with her. "Why are we discussing this, Arthur?"

"I have a duty to inform you."

"You also have a duty to advise me."

"Cowper insists the door to settlement will close on Monday, when you take the oath. That's either a threat or a bluff. "

"Darling, are our chances really so terrible?"

Arthur had already spent half an hour analyzing those for her. The several soft spots in the plaintiff's case, the glaring hole in Margaret's: the missing, possibly non-existent video. The risk of massive damages should Chief Justice Cohon-Plaskett conclude Margaret conspired with a man on the lam to destroy Farquist's reputation.

"They are not good."

"How not good?"

"Less than fifty-fifty. Subject to variables either way."

"Are you afraid I won't love you if we lose?"

Arthur wandered off to the window, looked out into the night at the moon gliding from behind a cloud. "I'm afraid I will fail you, Margaret."

"I will always love you."

He returned his gaze to her. His eyes had moistened, but he was smiling. "Then let's go to trial."

LIONHEART

It was Saturday, four days after the bumper Christmas Eve Lou had planned for his runaway family. But he was finally on the road in his homely Chev, with the two Santa bags, the monster panda, and a kid's bicycle called the Green Flash, with a superhero painted on it.

His plan hadn't changed. He would dip into the city, to Upper Mount Royal, make the drop, and run. Avoid downtown. Calgary would be a beehive of press this weekend, with the ongoing Farquist-Blake discoveries. He wasn't incredibly keen on bumping into one of his old CP cronies. Let alone the combatants and their legal-political teams.

Steam was rising from the wheat fields, the snow melting before his eyes. Still a solid, soggy blanket of it, ditches and sloughs filling with meltwater, streams overflowing. His brave little car had made it like gangbusters across the turbulent water below the Porcupine Creek bridge, and he'd been stalled by snowplows in the Cypress Hills, but otherwise slush was the only hazard.

Though it was sunny, his wipers were on, whacking away the slop thrown at him by overtaking vehicles. Lou had slept poorly, anxiously, and he was taking it slow and easy. He had made it this far in life. A life that still had possibility.

He'd been practically manacled to his computer for the last three days, but was already getting multiple hits on his new website: DR. JOY'S HEALTH TIPS. Arianna Joy, MD, M.Sc., Licensed Nutritionist. PAPAYA, THE HEALTHIEST FRUIT IN THE WORLD. BANANAS ARE GOOD FOR YOU. THESE TEN BEST-SELLING FAST FOODS ARE THE TEN WORST FOR YOUR HEALTH.

Lou's many years on the CP rewrite desk were paying off. The internet was swarming with health sites and blogs, easily cribbed from. All he had to do was to make it look fresh with a jazzy design and easy-to-read prose. And authoritative. Dr. Joy, M.Sc. Holistic Science and Herbal Medicine. Yesterday, his first ad had come in, from a tropical fruit importer.

There was increased bustle on the highway as he neared Calgary, its downtown towers poking above the flatlands. He blinked away the lulling effect of the wiper blades and focussed on the road. He couldn't risk a traffic ticket. Calgary's finest might still be on edge over the pedophile.

At last report, they'd zeroed in on a short, bald driver of a grey Saturn Astra. But surely the perv would have ditched that car by now, its photo in all the papers. A lone dude, in a blue Chevy Cavalier with Saskatchewan plates, registered to Maple Creek Car and Truck Repairs Ltd., who produces a Quebec driver's licence in the name of Robert O'Brien might have some explaining to do.

He'd made an effort to look law-abidingly straight with his professorial beard, trimmed hair neatly combed, preppy sweater-vest, dress jeans, and a green-and-white Roughrider jacket scored at the Porcupine Plain Nu-To-You. Costume designed by Sally Rosewell, who didn't want him looking like a bum.

He had declined her offer to drive him. Sweet Sally. She'd come back on Boxing Day to apologize. She respected him. He had acted honourably in the end, even though he'd kept his wife a secret. She wanted to be his friend. He said he needed a friend, and they had a sex-free hug.

Sally sealed this excellent friendship by arranging for her regular courier to deliver Celeste's necklace. It should have arrived today, a special weekend rate.

He remembered, guiltily, how hot he'd been for Sally, betrayed by his unsolicited, defiant stiffy. However, there'd been a creative side effect. MORINGA LEAF POWDER, THE AMAZING BUT LITTLE-KNOWN NATURAL SUBSTITUTE FOR VIAGRA.

§

It was mid-afternoon when he turned onto Hope, a wide street that the city had cleared by pushing the snow onto boulevards, sidewalks, and front lawns, some of the mounds over five feet high.

No family vehicles at the curb, all of them tucked safely into driveways or garages, just a Shaw Cable truck and a guy up a power pole. A catastrophic emergency for weekend football fans, cable was out on this block. A few dads were using their downtime to shovel walks and driveways. A mom was knocking down icicles from the eaves while her kids repaired a drooping snowman.

No one was outside Celeste's sister's house, but the curtains weren't drawn and the lights were on. The kids had built a snow fort by the in-law suite, and a path had been beaten to the driveway, which had been cleared. The Dodge Caravan was there, and a little Fiat behind it — a visitor?

Lou kept the engine running as he dragged out his canvas bags and heaved them over the snowbank onto the front lawn, making wide snow bursts. Then the bicycle, then the mega-panda, on top of the bank, facing the house, its arms outstretched in greeting.

He stumbled as fast as he could back to his car, and put it in gear. A quick glance back caught a movement in the picture window, a small person, had to be Lisa or Logan.

Though he'd turned a corner by now, he was fighting an intolerable need to go back, to share the belated Dream of a White Christmas now unfolding on Hope Street — or at least unfolding in his mind: Lisa and Logan bursting outside, screaming, "Mom, Mom, Daddy's been here!" Celeste racing behind them with their coats, looking terrific in her diamond pendant silver necklace.

Lou had let paranoia beguile him. No one had been out there on Hope Street sitting in a black van with tinted windows. The Mafia was *not* watching the house. Surely they'd lost interest, the ringleaders having absconded, probably to Colombia. They'd obviously decided to cancel their ridiculous fatwa on an honest, objective journalist who'd reported the facts with no ill intent toward anyone.

He drove on slowly, in the throes of dilemma, worrying about the roads icing over if he didn't get moving — the temperature had already dipped below freezing. He was tired, frazzled. What were the risks of staying in town? He was having trouble weighing them. Don't do anything dumb, he told himself.

He slowed by a park on his right, an outdoor rink where preteen boys were playing hockey, their parents watching, chatting, laughing, drinking from Thermoses. Lou was transfixed by this heartwarming Canadian scene. He parked in a gap between the ubiquitous SUVs, and looked yearningly out the windshield, then turned the engine off and got out for a closer view.

A minor blot on this holiday tableau: a pissed-off eight-year-old girl demanding ice time. Clutching her skates, complaining to her mother, who was urging patience.

He caught her name, Betsy, spunky little Betsy, who showed a definite lack of patience when one of the boys, a smart alec, whizzed by with his stick raised and made a kissy face at her. "Sexist pig!" she shouted.

Lou had to laugh. DR. JOY'S TIPS ON LIVING STRESS-FREE. Add one more: *Sit for an hour each day in front of a playground.* He lingered for a while, watching the game, as the smart alec potted a couple, showing finesse, maybe a future all-star. Lou should be teaching little Logan how to skate. Which would be easier if he knew how.

Suddenly, with a rush of sadness, he realized that this idyll had to end, that he must jettison his daydream of returning to Celeste and family. It took all his resolve to break free, but he pulled out. He was going home. Robert O'Brien had a life there. A house on Main Street. Friends.

The playground gave way to empty parkland on his right. He had not advanced a block before he found himself overtaking the same little girl, Betsy, who was stomping down the roadway with her skates, obviously still in a temper. No sign of her mother, and no way he was going to offer her a lift — that threatened all sorts of awkward scenarios.

Suddenly he went tight. His heart was pounding. He was in cardiac arrest . . . no, something else, a doomy voice in his head, a powerful premonition. *Something bad is about to happen.*

What had probably triggered this (he realized much later) was a niggle of concern about the girl, a subliminal awareness she was in danger. A quick glance at the rear-view caused the niggle to explode into full-blown fright and horror: not a hundred metres behind him, a brown van had pulled up beside Betsy. A man with a Santa beard was leaning through the open passenger door, passing her a gift-wrapped box.

Lou slammed on the brakes, and his tires squealed and threw up ice and slush as his Chevy swerved sideways into a roadside snow pile. He tried to reverse, wheels spinning. Then came utter panic: the pervert had grasped Betsy's arm and was tugging her in through the passenger door. She was screaming. A man and a woman came running from a house across from the park, too late, the passenger door had slammed shut, the van already accelerating up the street.

Lou's car finally, sluggishly, freed itself as the van approached, and he did another wheelie, into its path, forcing it to veer, and Lou got a split-second look at the driver's bug-eyed, gaping face as his van plowed nose first into a five-foot snowbank.

Lou was out of his car in a shot, but slipped and fell, while the pervert struggled to free himself from the airbag, his false beard askew. He was short, bald, and terrified.

Betsy threw the passenger door open, wriggled free of the airbag, and leaped into a snow pile. Neighbours across the street were piling from their homes. Her mom, sprinting from the rink, was screaming. "Betsy! My baby!"

The wannabe child-napper squeezed from the van and scrambled up the dam of snow into the park. Lou pursued him, fuelled by adrenaline: the Green Flash, flying over the snowy field as if with wings. He brought him down with a leap and a leg tackle.

There was exultant hollering behind him: "He's got him! Keep him there, pal, we're coming!"

The bug-eyed scuzzo was already pleading innocence, with hysterical lies: "No, I didn't mean it! I didn't do nothing! She asked for a ride!"

The rest was a haze, later reconstructed, only vaguely absorbed at the time: being lifted to his feet by two men, one in a housecoat, another in a Shaw Cable jacket; being hugged by one woman, then another, then Betsy's mom, sobbing with gratitude. All the while, a cell phone on speaker, the voice of a 911 operator giving quick, firm instructions.

Lou slowly realized that he had either broken his left wrist or sprained it, maybe when he'd braced himself against the dashboard. But he kept repeating, "I'm fine, folks, I'm good. Perfectly fine. Just a little wet."

Meanwhile, Bug Eyes was sitting in the snow feeling sorry for himself, sobbing and burbling. He'd lost his Santa beard and found his glasses, now askew on his nose. Late forties, short, pudgy, prematurely bald.

A wuss, a candy-ass. Lou had finally met someone he could best in combat, but he wasn't going to let that erode his triumph. He was feeling not just perfectly fine but massively, immeasurably jubilant.

He could hear sirens in the distance as he was hustled into a grand, multi-gabled home across the street. "My husband's a doctor, you're in good hands." The woman wrapped him in a towel, offered dry clothes and a shower, then deferred to her husband: "Leave him as is, darling, until the police come and take photos."

He poured Lou a tot of an excellent Scotch before checking his wrist. "Likely a simple sprain. A sling will do for now. You'll need to get it X-rayed though."

There was a knock at the door, and a woman in uniform came in, followed by a man in plain clothes. Geraldson, or something like that. "Major Crimes," he said. "And this is Constable Mickelwump," though Lou wasn't sure if he got that right either. She began taking photos of him once his arm was in a sling.

Geraldson: "Can I shake your hand, sir?"

"My pleasure, Officer."

"I don't think we got your name."

"Uh, Rob, my name is Rob. Rob O'Brien."

"Well, Rob, you are now a national hero."

THE CLIPPINGS FILE

CBC News, SATURDAY, DECEMBER 28, 6:00 P.M.

CALGARY — The mystery man known as Rob O'Brien, hailed as a hero for thwarting a child kidnapping by an alleged pedophile, has disappeared.

Shortly after 3:00 p.m. today, O'Brien was driving through a pleasant, upscale Calgary neighbourhood, when he spotted Betsy Loewen, eight, being pulled into a van.

In what seemed an outtake from a Hollywood thriller, O'Brien did a wheelie on the mushy street, forcing the van into a snowdrift, then pursued the suspect on foot into a park and brought him down. Neighbours rushed from their homes to help O'Brien subdue the suspect, who was then turned over to police.

But O'Brien vanished after he was taken to Calgary General Hospital to be treated for a wrist injury. At last report, his 1993 Chevrolet Cavalier with Saskatchewan plates was still in the hospital's parking area, being watched by two uniformed officers in a cruiser.

Meanwhile, Larry Orvil Jutt, 41, who gave an address in Butte, Montana, remains in custody and will appear in Calgary Provincial Court on Monday, facing charges of assault, kidnapping, and attempted sexual assault. Police sources say he is known to authorities in the U.S. They are seeking to confirm he is the Playground Prowler, as the man was dubbed, whose haunting of Calgary's streets last summer had parents gripped with fear.

After his heroics, O'Brien was invited to the nearby home of Dr. Abram Jerrison, an orthopaedic surgeon, who examined his wrist. Police interviewed him there briefly but were persuaded to delay further questioning until X-rays were taken and any injuries dealt with. Before leaving, O'Brien changed from his wet clothes into dry attire from his host's closet.

The press, along with a growing crowd of onlookers, was held back by police as Dr. Jerrison led O'Brien from the house. Although his left arm was in a sling, O'Brien was permitted to drive his own car. Dr. Jerrison backed his BMW from his garage and signalled O'Brien to follow him to the hospital.

There, X-rays were taken and proved negative for fracture. It is not known how O'Brien disappeared. When last seen, he was wearing a grey pullover and a tan winter jacket.

Police have remained tight-lipped about the missing mystery man, but according to Dr. Jerrison detectives had intended to interview him at the hospital. "I assigned him to a private ward to await them," he said, "but somehow they never connected. I feel dreadful about that."

A search of the Chevrolet revealed it to be empty except for a Saskatchewan Roughriders jacket on the front passenger seat and a toy train engine lodged beneath it. The plates have been traced to an auto mechanic business in Maple Creek, Saskatchewan.

331

Meanwhile, several residents of the small community of Porcupine Plain, south of Maple Creek, have contacted media to advise that O'Brien, whom they identified from TV news footage, is a local computer technician, well known and liked in the community.

Details of his background remain sketchy at this time.

§

CTV Breaking News, SATURDAY, DECEMBER 28, 9:20 P.M.

CALGARY — News of his gutsy rescue of an eight-year-old girl from an alleged sexual predator riveted the nation. Then his sudden disappearance shocked the nation.

Now it has been learned that this hero has been living a double life. Rob O'Brien's real name is Lou Sabatino, a former journalist with a 20-year career at the Canadian Press.

Switchboards were lit up and social media inundated today with messages from Sabatino's colleagues in the media confirming his identity.

"There could be no mistaking him," said Hugh Dexter, CP's Montreal bureau chief, who watched video taken by CTV's mobile unit, showing him about to drive to hospital for an X-ray of his left arm, injured during his sensational rescue of the girl.

Calgary police have continued to stonewall inquiries about his disappearance from the hospital, but it is known that he had been threatened by Mafia mobsters after writing a four-part exposé about their role in the Waterfrontgate bribery scandal.

That was published nationwide in early February. A week later, as he stepped from his Côte-des-Neiges home, gunmen opened fire from a passing sedan, barely missing him as he dove for cover.

He and his family — wife and two children — were then put under witness protection in Quebec. It is not known how or why he moved to Porcupine Plain, SK, where he has been living since June under the pseudonym Robert O'Brien.

Investigators appear to be working under a gag order from the Calgary Police Chief's office, and have adamantly refused to join in speculation that the Mafia have finally caught up to Sabatino. Nor have they offered information about the whereabouts of his family, who are presumed to be still under witness protection.

§

The Canadian Press, SUNDAY, DECEMBER 29
BY Hugh Dexter, CP Bureau Chief, Montreal

He was one of the finest reporters I have ever been privileged to work with. Unassuming and mild — meek might be apt — but quick-witted, a sterling writer, and a formidable digger of buried truths.

The truths he unearthed early this year, published in a shattering exposé of organized crime on the Montreal waterfront, incurred the wrath of the mob. Last winter, they tried to gun him down. They missed.

And now the burning question is whether they have finally succeeded in silencing Lou Sabatino, my colleague and friend during his 20-year career with this venerable wire service.

It is one of the most extraordinary ironies imaginable that within an hour of his daring rescue of a young girl and his citizen's arrest of her alleged assailant, he vanished without a trace.

It is no secret now that he'd been living under the alias Robert O'Brien, so I can disclose that I was one of a handful privy to his double existence. He and his lovely wife and two grade-school children were moved to a secure lodging in the Montreal area. They were a very close family.

Sabatino remained on the Canadian Press payroll until May, when, dispirited that he could no longer work at the job he loved, he asked for and was granted a leave of absence.

Sabatino was the consummate journalist. He began his Canadian Press career in the early nineties with a newly minted journalism degree, worked the rewrite desk in Ottawa, then spent many years covering national politics. On his transfer to the Montreal bureau, he

(See Missing Hero, page 2)

§

THE SIERRA FILE

Monday, December 30, 2:30 a.m.

Dear Arthur,

That you appeared startled and confused by my oral presentation of the events of Saturday was no doubt due to the fact I am less at ease with the spoken word than the written.

But it is important that you have this history clearly in mind for your bout on Monday with Mssrs. Cowper and Farquist, and to that end this weary late-night warrior has begun clacking away at his Olivetti, with a glass of good malt at hand.

So let us back up ten hours to a sunny, snowed-in afternoon, as your correspondent appeared at the door of Celeste Sabatino's sister's home on Hope Street.

You will recall that I was determined to make a last-gasp effort to coax Ms. Sabatino into making a public plea for her husband to come in from the cold. A press release, maybe even a press conference at which she would express her fears for his safety and proclaim her love for him and her desire for reconciliation.

Lucille Wong, the sister, met me at the door and introduced me to her husband, a well-respected geophysical engineer. I had looked him up and versed myself well enough in geophysics to express keen interest in his work, and we chatted pleasantly until he left for his study.

I was led through the bright, airy living room, where Lisa and Logan were playing with toys near a tinselled tree. Lovely, well-mannered children, who both shook my hand.

Ccleste was waiting in a room at the rear of the house, now her studio, with ladies' wear hanging along one wall and a work table covered with large sheets of paper and arrayed with cutting and colouring tools. On a nearby desk was a small, open gift box containing a diamond pendant silver necklace.

I accepted an easy chair beside a naked dummy. The chair was soft and comfortable but the mannequin unsettled me with her lifelike breasts and protruding pelvis. I was afraid I would not be at my best.

Lucille left to fetch coffee, while Celeste seemed anxious and wandered about, making small adjusments to her design wear.

All the while, as I tried to ignore the teasing nude,

I made my pitch. A paean of praise and sympathy for
her beleaguered, hunted, lonely partner, embellished with
quotes from his love letter to her — which I observed
on her desk, near the necklace.

Maybe I am not so ill-adept at the spoken word after
all, because when I told her I believed she truly loved
her husband, she replied with what seemed to be feelings
long pent up, "Yes, I do. I do." And at that point, she
delved into a box of tissues.

Two coffees later, with Lucille's aid, we had worked
out a statement for the press. It concluded with the
simple, ardent line, "I love you, Lou."

Just then there was a commotion at the front of the
house: Lisa and Logan were screaming, but not, I soon
realized, in terror.

The two women bolted from the studio, and I followed.
The children by then had burst from the house, and, as
seen from the wide front windows, were bounding toward a
beribboned child's bicycle and two bulky canvas bags on the
snowy lawn, all guarded by a five-foot-tall panda bear.

The youngsters were yelling, "It's Daddy! Daddy's been
here!"

But there was no sign of Daddy, no vehicle driving
off. Lisa had seen a car, but just its rear as it
disappeared from view. Not a big car, just a "car car,"
maybe blue.

As I hurried to my rented Fiat 500, I called out
to Celeste to keep her phone at hand. I was at a loss
regarding where to go, and was roving aimlessly about
the neighbourhood when I heard the advancing wail
of police sirens. Shortly, I spied two police cruisers
rushing along a nearby street.

I followed them and came upon a scene that has been

well described by news media outlets – understaffed on weekends, their reporters were just pulling in just as I arrived. (My little Fiat made the newscasts, parked beyond the police barricade, but I saw no sign of my portly self.)

But I was busy being invisible, strolling about, listening to the excited chatter of neighbours, putting the pieces together.

Lou Sabatino was inside Dr. Jerrison's home at the time, and when he was led out, his arm in a sling, and then got into his car to follow his host, it seemed likely they were en route to the Calgary General Hospital, only a few minutes away.

Fortunately I was able to wiggle my car out of the logjam of the curious. I rang Celeste as soon as I was underway, briefing her so hurriedly that I feared I was garbling my words.

Luck was with me, for I arrived at the sprawling hospital grounds in time to glimpse Dr. Jerrison walking Lou to the emergency wing.

I hate myself every time I do this, but I nestled into reserved parking, stuck my handicapped decal on the windshield, armed myself with a cane, and limped expeditiously after them, catching up as they arrived at the imaging section.

In the waiting room, I picked up a magazine – Horse and Rider, as I recall, "Stampede Edition" – and sat among several of my fellow injured. Jerrison had no trouble pulling rank and got Lou in immediately.

Several minutes later, the two returned, Dr. Jerrison jovially reassuring Lou the sprain would only take a few days to heal and cautioning that he must avoid punching anyone for at least ten days.

Down the corridor they went, and I hobbled along
behind. Lou was deposited inside a private "Recovery
Room," as it was labelled, and upon leaving him there,
the good doctor paused to say, "They'll be along soon."
I heard only a mumbled response. Then Jerrison: "Not at
all, Rob. It was entirely my pleasure."

Someone must have given Lou a pen and some writing
paper, because as I entered he was sitting on a chair
making notes — not surprisingly, because this experienced
journalist knew he had a highly bankable story to tell.

He may have thought I was a doctor — I have the
manner and the overpriced suit, and I didn't introduce
myself. I merely passed him my phone and told him
to tap the Call button. "That's your wife's cell number.
Celeste is waiting for you."

My hope was to spirit Lou from the hospital before
investigators showed up. But four or five agonizing
minutes passed in fervent conversation between them,
dominated by Celeste. Her husband squeezed in an
occasional gasping declaration of his affection, all the
while shaking with shock or excitement or joy or all of
the above.

I finally took the phone and told Celeste we were
on our way. Lou followed me like an eager puppy as we
quickly went out a side door to a driveway where he took
cover behind a laundry van while I retrieved my car.

In less than the minute it took me to rouse you at
your hotel — and drag you away from the five o'clock
local news — he was in the Fiat, and we were on our way
to the aptly named Hope Street.

The scene inside the Wong house was tumultuous —
they'd been huddled around the TV screen, but all jumped
up, and Lou was buried in enfolding arms.

You showed up in a taxi ten minutes later, and your spent lieutenant was grateful to turn over operations to his field marshal (Monty, as dubbed by your barber?) for a campaign to breach the enemy lines.

Let me reiterate my admiration for the array of weaponry you brought to bear on Lou: your good-natured bantering, your soothing reassurances, your basic kindness. However, he was in such an unusual state of euphoria, besotted with life and love recovered, that he seemed in a hypnotic trance. So please be warned he may not have caught it all. Smiling and nodding one's head like a puppet does not imply comprehension.

Later, if I may say so, you were at your eloquent best in taking on what seemed the entire Calgary Police Department: an exhibition of both charm and firmness as you worked the phone, making your way up the ranks of the hierarchy, finally speaking to the deputy chief and the chief himself.

I was not present at the two-hour tete-a-tete with them at your hotel, but that broad smile as you returned to the war room revealed your triumph even before you spoke of it.

The negotiated terms of surrender seem fair and wise. The national hero, your valued new client (secreted in the suite adjoining mine here at the Fairmont Palliser), is prepared to fully cooperate, but only two days hence. Until then, the cops will keep the lid on and screw it tight.

Altogether, a demonstration of forensic skill that will never garner headlines (though you've had those). But not all great art goes on public display.

I was glad to be of help assembling your team of experts. Professor Deore is reputed to be quite a bright young woman. The voice identifier – that was a coup, the very gentleman Farquist had hired to identify Margaret's voice on the Freak Out recording.

It's nearing three. I shall slide these pages under your door, then enjoy another sip of whisky before heading to bed.

Will you want me at the law courts building today? I'd love to be there.

With best wishes for the new year,

Francisco Sierra

SUCKER PUNCH

It was 10 a.m. on the last day of the year. Tonight, some would celebrate the arrival of the new one. Others would mourn. Arthur aspired to be in the former camp, but now was nagged by doubt and was struggling against the cynical grump within: the doomster whose wife could barely abide his dismal scenarios.

They'd been uncomfortable with each another ever since he proposed they take separate rooms. He couldn't even bring himself to hug his client, except in private, and then awkwardly. Margaret followed his cue, refraining from touching him in public.

But they were allowed smiles, and now she adorned one with a wink before joining her current roommate, Pierette, in the lounge area outside the discovery room. Nanisha was already inside, with the court reporter, setting up.

George Cowper, waiting near the elevators with his junior, seemed impatient, though he preserved his default expression of utter sadness. Emil Farquist finally emerged from the elevator, only ten minutes late, followed by his aide, Hawkes.

In short time, the parties and their counsel were seated in the discovery room. Arthur was sandwiched between Nanisha and

Margaret, who had got up the nerve to share the small, closed room with her arch-enemy. She had confided: "If I feel sick to the stomach, I'll leave."

Farquist, across from Arthur, appeared sober, no hint of a morning libation. Natty suit, modish tie, well combed and deodorized. He looked steadily at his inquisitor, smiling. Maybe he was on a drug. Not a trank — his eyes were too clear and sharp.

"For the record, you are still under oath," said Arthur.

"Of course," said Farquist.

"Then let us resume. Mr. Farquist, certain events of Saturday may have captured your attention."

"Yes, involving this Sabatino fellow. Quite astonishing, wasn't it? I remember him being quite the milquetoast as a journalist." That relaxed manner again. Put on, Arthur decided.

"Lou Sabatino. The man you accused only three days ago of conspiring with Svetlana Glinka. The milquetoast has turned out to be quite the hero."

"I was surprised by that, frankly. But I suppose a man can be brave and corrupt at the same time."

That elicited a gasp from Margaret. Nanisha had her laptop open, her fingers dancing over the keyboard.

Cowper frowned. "Please just answer the questions, Emil."

Farquist waved him off. "I don't remember hearing a question. But if Mr. Beauchamp expects me to join in the general canonization of Mr. Sabatino, I will not. As a newsman he was a cynical smartass. He appears to be an even more unsavoury fellow since he got fired."

Cowper seemed about to cut him off, then for some reason thought better of it. Farquist was clearly set on being his own man. He plowed ahead.

"Stalking about under a false name with a professional sadomasochist who apparently was also a Russian spy. He was related by marriage to that corrupt lawyer the Mafia assassinated. Giusti? Nick

Giusti. I wouldn't be surprised if Mr. Sabatino meets with the same fate."

Maybe he was on speed: cocaine or some manner of amphetamine. "And you wish us to believe that Lou Sabatino, for some reason, and Svetlana Glinka, for some reason, conspired to embarrass you publicly with malicious falsehoods?"

"Of course. Through the agency of Margaret Blake. Sabatino had it in for me. I don't know what Glinka's plan was. Extortion? Well, now she's hiding in Russia, and Sabatino seems to have met a worse fate."

"And your view is that Margaret got set up?"

"Set up and sucked in. They knew how reckless your wife can be. Your wife? Your client? What's the protocol? I'm not quite sure."

Arthur sensed Margaret stiffen — she was about to rise. He stilled her with a hand on her thigh. Time to ratchet it up.

"Mr. Farquist, you are aware — and please be honest — that a video was recorded of you consorting nakedly with Svetlana Glinka?"

"That is preposterous. Utterly impossible."

"Impossible because your detectives' fine-toothed combing failed to find it? Or because you bought Svetlana's video for an exorbitant fee?"

"Because it never existed!"

"I take you back to Sunday, January sixth, exactly one year ago less a week. Your day book had promised a 'free afternoon' — with an exclamation point. You were not at home working on your so-called parks bill. On that day you had your first appointment with Ms. Glinka, in your mountain chalet."

Arthur was leaning toward Farquist, who was not backing up; indeed, he looked like a bull about to charge.

Cowper finally stepped in. "Maybe your dramatics could be saved for a courtroom, Mr. Beauchamp. Emil, I must firmly advise you not to rise to the bait."

Arthur held his ground. "You were filmed by a hidden camera. But you know that, don't you, Mr. Farquist?"

Instead of answering, Farquist took a long drink of water. Arthur nudged Nanisha, who turned her laptop to face the witness. The video was running, and a large bottom glowed from the screen and a voice called out: "I was a bad boy, very bad!" A *thwack* from Glinka's riding crop. "Please, Mother, I beg you!"

Farquist turned white, then scarlet as the blood rushed back, but kept his expression blank, calm, unmoved.

But Cowper lost his cool and accused Arthur of all manner of improprieties: a gross breach of ethics, flouting long-standing rules of disclosure, laying traps, and, in a rare use of idiom, of swinging a sucker punch. As Cowper caught his breath, he seemed dismayed by his own behaviour: his reputation as an even-tempered gentleman had been severely dented.

Nanisha put the tape on pause as Farquist gripped Cowper's shoulder. "Chill out, George, this might be good for a laugh. Let's see what kind of bullshit they've come up with. It's an obvious fake."

The man had balls of steel. Arthur's ploy hadn't worked; he'd gambled on shocking him into blurting an admission of guilt.

Cowper wasn't used to his clients taking over, and seemed to lack the toughness to rein Farquist in. Instead, he sat back, stunned. Arthur felt sorry for him, and apologized. "Please excuse the lack of timely disclosure, George, but this video just came to hand. It might be wise to give Ms. Blair a break while we watch the rest of it." There was no advantage to putting more of this on the official record before they talked settlement.

He turned to Sarah Blair, whose face was glowing with embarrassment, and suggested she spend the next couple of hours preparing transcripts. Cowper lifted a limp hand in assent, and Blair gathered her equipment and hurried off without a look back.

Arthur half-expected Margaret to join her, but she seemed bolted to her chair. Her fingers dug into his thigh.

"Let us resume," Arthur said.

And the video played on. Bondage and humiliation on an Oriental carpet. In background, a blazing fireplace, a wall of rough-hewn logs, an iced-over lake. Action in the foreground, Svetlana trading her quirt for a massive dildo, her client trying to buck her off like a rodeo bronco, all the while pleading for mercy.

Arthur had first viewed this rollick on Sunday morning, and subsequently another half-dozen times, mesmerized. Lou's pirated copy, on a USB drive, remained in a locked drawer in his home in Porcupine Plain, but he had uploaded the file to the cloud, and was able to recall its complex password. In every detail, it matched what Margaret had witnessed early in June. Sabatino's twelve-page affidavit detailed its provenance and history.

On the laptop, seconds passed soundlessly after the dominatrix and her masochist piggybacked off screen. Cowper's junior was showing signs of illness, his face slightly green.

"Is that it?" Farquist demanded.

Then his image reappeared in full frontal view, in lounging pants, pulling on a turtleneck pullover, then ambling out of the frame.

Farquist held a steely silence. His eyes flicked to Arthur, then back to the screen.

Several seconds later, Glinka appeared, still bare-breasted but in skirt and leggings, advancing quickly toward the lens. A close-up of her blue-eyed baby-doll face as she reached up and turned off her camera.

A hoarse laugh from Farquist. "Nice try. Got to give Sabatino credit for balls if not brains. Fabricating that piece of film fiction — the staging was patently amateurish. They used an actor, of course, for their opening scenes, or maybe some tramp off the street. Except at the end, where they spliced me in."

He wasn't even sweating. Arthur couldn't help, in a paradoxical way, admiring the man: his toughness, his control, his straight face, his unshakeable tenacity in bluffing his way through this ordeal. He was one of the staunchest witnesses Arthur had ever encountered, and there'd been thousands. Maybe it wasn't some cocaine-like pharmaceutical. Maybe it was straight-out sociopathy.

"You'll have noted the date stamp," Arthur said. "January sixth, Ms. Glinka's first visit to your chalet. She regularly filmed her initial encounter with a client. In case of hanky-panky, as she explained to our independent witness, Mr. Sabatino." To Nanisha: "The affidavit."

From her briefcase, she drew two copies of Sabatino's sworn statement, one for Cowper, the other for Farquist.

"You'll want to take some time going over this." Arthur rose. "We'll be close at hand." He held the door for Margaret, who was gaping at Farquist and would have walked into the door frame had Nanisha not caught her arm.

"Oh, and here's a copy of the video." Arthur pulled a memory stick from his pocket and passed it to Cowper's junior, who put it down like a hot ember, rose, mumbled something about a bathroom break, then dashed outside.

§

Nanisha led Arthur and Margaret to a nearby courtroom, unlocked, empty. They took padded seats at the back, and Arthur stretched out, feeling the invigorating tingle of apprehension that courtrooms always stirred in him. He imagined scenes of forensic combat at the distant counsel table, the room packed, the prosecutor objecting, the judge sternly reprimanding Arthur for yet another sucker punch. Farquist finally cracking under the onslaught.

Arthur had felt constricted in that cell of a discovery room. With its namby-pamby rules denying old-fashioned, no-holds-barred cross-examination. Here, in a courtroom, was where the real dramas played out. It seemed sad, wrong somehow, not to be confronting Farquist on that witness stand.

He imagined how it could have been. Playing that explosive video in a crowded courtroom. The gasps from the gallery, the howling complaints, the threat of a contempt citation. How he would have enjoyed that.

Nanisha, on her phone, elbowed him out of his reveries. The only words he caught were, "A runner will pick them up." Arthur gathered she was talking about the draft opinions from the experts. Rush jobs, but Cowper mustn't be allowed another complaint about lack of notice.

Margaret slipped her hand into his. She was smiling at him, her silver eyes shining with either relief or excitement, or maybe love. "Fuck propriety," she said, and kissed him on the mouth. He put his arm around her. Held her.

CONFIDENTIALITY CLAUSE

"What I wouldn't do for strong drink right now," Cowper said.

"I know the feeling well."

"Sorry, I forgot, you're . . ."

"An alcoholic. In recovery. Oddly, I've always felt I was a better lawyer in my boozy era. Maybe less inhibited."

They were alone in the discovery room. Summoned by Cowper, Arthur had passed Farquist on the way in: he was stoic and calm, but Arthur caught a heady whiff of malice as their eyes met.

Cowper sighed. "You showed little inhibition this morning. I ought to have expected that, given your reputation in the criminal courts. Sorry for my little outburst."

"It is I who must apologize. Old habits die hard."

"But your impromptu screening didn't elicit, as you intended, any confession. On the contrary, Emil was firm and blunt in his reaction to that tape. We quite honestly suspect it was doctored. If that turns out to be the case — and we'll have it expertly examined — the stakes become very high for Ms. Blake, especially if she is seen as a party to the making of it."

Arthur hadn't expected immediate surrender, but nor had he

expected his opponent to grasp at this flimsy straw. He answered a knock at the door, and Nanisha handed him the three experts' reports, two copies of each. Each comprised several pages of analysis and opinion, and many more of source notes, technical data, and references.

"Full disclosure, George." Arthur handed him the lengthiest one. "Professor Deore is head of film studies at the University of Calgary. Teaches film editing techniques. Former film editor herself. She found no evidence of tampering, splicing, or any manner of editing of the tape."

Cowper scanned through it, looked up. "She concedes this is only a preliminary report and advises further testing."

"And she is doing that. Brilliant young woman. Earned her Ph.D. at twenty-one. And this is the report from Fred Wiggins, formerly Staff Sergeant Wiggins of the Calgary PD. Their lie-detection expert. Hundreds of hours of experience. Testified many times as an accredited expert."

"To little avail, I assume, given the infamous unreliability of the polygraph machine." Still counter-punching, if with grim valour.

"A persuasive opinion, nonetheless. Lou was caught in one falsehood, claiming he harboured no enmity for the plaintiff. I don't know why he would say that, given your client once publicly called him an irresponsible, vacuous twerp."

Unexpectedly, Cowper smiled, and eased back in his chair, as if relaxing in defeat. "What else do you have?"

"Voice analysis. We felt lucky to get Professor Mathews. Your client knows him, of course."

"Let me talk to Emil." Cowper groaned as he rose, expert opinions in hand. He was not looking forward to sharing them with Emil.

He paused at the door. "We will have to insist on a confidentiality clause."

§

Arthur and Margaret found themselves sharing an unusual lunch. Both had sworn they would never set foot in a McDonald's, but little Lisa and littler Logan had been given their choice. One could hardly blame them: the restaurant featured a play area with tubes to climb up and slide down, a ball pit, and rocking zebras with saddles to sit on.

In the end Arthur conceded it had been a wise choice, because the restaurant was so busy that no one paid any attention to the national hero, Calgary's *desaparecido*. He was hardly recognizable from old photos that had cluttered the news; bearded now, he'd dropped thirty pounds. Margaret got a tentative wave from one young woman, but she didn't approach.

It eventually dawned on Arthur that no server was about to attend on them in their booth, and he took orders and lined up, attracting curious glances — the fusty old man in a suit may have seemed vaguely familiar. Margaret and Celeste had asked for salads, but Arthur and Lou were opting for Big Macs with fries, Happy Meals for the kids. The other team members, led by Sierra, had chosen finer dining elsewhere.

Arthur's lunch guests seemed to understand there'd be no talk about the slander action. Lou and Celeste had other things on their minds anyway. Presumably, both hungered for intimacy, and had found it in their hotel suite while the children were asleep in an adjoining room. They were clearly indulging the rush of renewed romance.

Their plans were incomplete. Lou extolled the virtues of Porcupine Plain and of country life: his snug home, his new friends, the lovely little grade school, his expanding internet businesses. He would build "a terrific website" for Celeste and a studio and streetfront dress shop. She could keep a presence in Calgary, for fittings, while doing most of her business online.

Meanwhile, he would write a book, a memoir of his year of trouble and triumph.

Arthur supposed the dark shadow of the Mafia would still lurk, but the danger had lessened since their capos fled the country. The case against the Waterfrontgate conspirators was falling apart anyway, according to Montreal lawyers in the know.

It was nearing two p.m. and another session with Cowper. A driver was waiting outside to take the Sabatino family back to their hotel. Out of habit, Arthur waved for the bill, forgetting he'd paid up front. Should he leave a tip? He dropped a few bills on the table, just in case.

§

On their return to the Courts Centre, a dozen reporters swarmed Arthur and Margaret, then blithely followed them through security to the elevators. A court sheriff caught up to them on the twentieth floor, quickly corralled them, and roped them off near the elevators. They were forbidden to use cameras.

Cowper, Hawkes, and Farquist had stayed in the discovery room, knocking heads together, maybe literally. There were raised voices, then mutters that even Pierette, who had positioned herself close to the door, couldn't make out. She heard a *clunk*, a heavy book being thrown or a chair knocked over.

Arthur paced the corridor, feeling uncomfortable with the media wolf pack over there, salivating for news. There was much stirring when Sam Puhl joined the plaintiff's team. He would be eager for a quick settlement to protect the behinds of his two subpoenaed investigators.

Arthur returned to the nearby empty courtroom, where Margaret was alone, reading Alice Munro, *Too Much Happiness*.

She bookmarked her page. "What do you suppose they're up to?"

"They're wishing they'd brought a straitjacket for Emil."

"Seriously."

"Farquist is desperate to avoid public humiliation, so they're likely struggling over the wording of a confidentiality clause."

She frowned, and he hastened to explain: it was also known as a non-disclosure clause, a consensual gag order, common in litigation. Persons privy to the terms of settlement risked stiff monetary penalties for any breach, however careless.

"Why would I agree to it?"

"You needn't, darling. But there may be profit in doing so." Or not. He dared not remind her of her infamous laxness of tongue.

"All the profit I want is his complete fall from grace. He put me through hell."

The burden of representing his beloved was weighing heavily on him. He must fully take on the role of dispassionate counsel.

"Margaret, you have the power, and maybe the right, to destroy Emil Farquist. That will happen if we deny them confidentiality. But that could mean dragging out these abysmal proceedings for months, maybe to trial and even appeal if they're stubborn, and it will be painful and costly." He spoke the next words with care. "You may be concerned about how the public views you."

She looked at him thoughtfully, then said, "Okay, I hear you — bad optics. I'd be the vindictive, sharp-tongued witch out for revenge. Also, small potatoes in the context of a world facing flood and famine. I have better things to do."

Thinking like the politician she was.

"I'll take your advice, of course, darling . . . Darling — am I allowed to say that?"

Arthur laughed, relieved.

"So what kind of profit is earned by agreeing to non-disclosure?"

He was about to explain, but Cowper entered the courtroom looking exhausted. He beckoned Arthur, and they strolled toward the barristers' lounge, keeping well away from the wolf pack.

"How did they get in here?" Cowper said, annoyed. "The building is closed to the public."

"They talked their way past security. The deputy registrar doesn't want to make a scene." Arthur didn't want to admit they'd followed him in. Or that he had not discouraged them. Cowper would think he'd invited them, a pressure play. Maybe it was.

They shared a few comments about their deplorable lunches; Cowper had suffered through a takeout pizza. Finally, Arthur said, "Where are we, George?"

"Very well, Emil remains convinced, if I may be blunt, that the rear end depicted in the beginning sequence is not his. We don't believe Sabatino is a reliable witness. We will, of course, need to test the tape with our own experts. As you know, for every expert who has an opinion, there will be another who offers the opposite."

Cowper remained deadpan but Arthur could tell his heart wasn't in it — he'd promised Farquist to make this last, desperate pitch.

"I would truly enjoy taking this to trial, George. I can almost promise your client will be arrested for perjury after I have a go at him. What is your offer?"

"Although he is adamant that the tape is bogus, my client wishes to put this matter behind him. Each side to pay its own costs, no admission of liability, non-disclosure of the video recording and all evidence taken on discovery, and we will withdraw the suit."

Non-disclosure was all that was left to salvage. The remains of Farquist's good name.

Cowper added, "Mr. Sabatino will have to be a party to any confidentiality clause, of course."

"Sorry, George, I can't bind him to that. He is already committed to having a long sit-down with police investigators. With the video."

Cowper sagged. "Well, that's . . ." A search for the appropriate word. "Awkward." He pressed his temples, as if to soothe a headache. "That can't be avoided?"

"I gave them my word."

It took Cowper several seconds to recalibrate. "Surely, they would be discreet. Nothing in that tape points to any criminal misbehaviour on Emil's part. Politically damaging, maybe, but that's none of their business."

Cowper had been a fair and honest foe, and he didn't deserve to be forced to his knees. Arthur was prepared to give him the small reward of confidentiality, for what it was worth, given Lou wouldn't be bound. He would not mention Lou's plan to write a tell-all memoir.

"Quite frankly, George, there's zero advantage for us to agree to confidentiality. Emil Farquist's sins deserve to be known: the perjury, entertaining a Russian informer with classified papers lying about, and, not the least of them, laying a false complaint against my wife and creating untold misery for her. Margaret declines to be vindictive, but she deserves recompense."

"What are your terms?" A resigned tone.

"Non-disclosure of the evidence taken on discovery. Its transcripts to be sealed, not to be opened up except by order of a justice of the Queen's Bench. Payment of the defendant's solicitor-client costs on double scale. I'm afraid our investigator's fees are quite handsome. You may be looking at, let us say, six hundred thousand dollars, but let's peg it at half a million."

Cowper had no response. He looked more puzzled than shocked. "How do you imagine my client will come up with that kind of money?"

Arthur had a clear memory from Friday's dinner at the Q: the warm hug between Farquist and his billionaire bankroller.

"Emil's hand is already in Jack O'Reilly's pocket. He just has to dig a little deeper."

SCRUM FLUSTER

Margaret had grabbed a taxi at the Ottawa airport, and it was speeding her to Parliament Hill, where the Speech from the Throne was about to be delivered.

She was travel-weary and disoriented — ten hours ahead of Melbourne or ten hours behind, she wasn't sure, couldn't do the math. Her hair was an unwashed mess; otherwise, she'd done what repairs she could between flights, in the washroom of the VIP lounge in Vancouver, stripping, washing, deodorizing, changing into a too-elegant silky pantsuit that she'd already worn twice — to a ritzy restaurant, then a concert. It looked odd but would have to do.

She had missed the ceremonial opening of Parliament on Monday, thanks to a screw-up on reservations. Then a failed connection in Vancouver. Arthur had left her at the airport there, in an apologetic rush to make the last ferry to Garibaldi.

The trip was inspired by a New Year's call from Arthur's daughter, Deborah, a high-school principal in Melbourne, on summer holidays. The slander action had been settled. Arthur, her hero, had slayed the dragon. What better way to celebrate than enjoying two stolen weeks of summer.

They had stayed four nights in the wooded northeast suburbs, in the home Deborah shared with her husband, an ocean scientist. Arthur and Margaret then rented a car and drove to the heritage town of Port Fairy, where they stayed in a seaside cottage. Reading, wandering, swimming, birding, taking drives to nowhere, cocktails at sunset.

As the pressures of politics and litigation faded away, thoughts of retiring had exerted their pull on Margaret again. For the entire two weeks she'd fought valiantly to break her enslavement to the political life. Aside from a text to Jennie asking her to hold the fort until she got back, Margaret had not touched her BlackBerry. Nor had she brought her iPad or laptop.

But she'd done a whirlwind job of catching up during her long trip back, poring through texts and emails and missed phone calls. The orgy of speculation about the settlement terms had cooled; the confidentiality clause was holding up. It was strict — any disclosure by the defendant or her lawyers would mean forfeiting the $500,000 settlement Arthur had negotiated. The other side had insisted that Pierette, who knew everything, be bound to silence too.

Lou Sabatino had not yet gone public. He was saving the goodies for his book — he'd apparently got a handsome advance from a major publisher. Nor had the Calgary police acted on his revelations. Bondage was not a crime. Bribery was, but the evidence was circumstantial and weak.

It annoyed Margaret that the public had no idea how badly Farquist had been whipped, as it were. In fact, according to Pierette, the right-wing media were being fed hints that Farquist had come out of it unscathed, even with a comfortable settlement.

She had attached a link to a Christie Montieth column about the coming session of Parliament. Several paragraphs down: "Don't expect a lot of electricity to pass between Farquist and Blake when the House sits. They'll be avoiding each other like the plague. Both have been away on vacation — who will return looking rueful and who triumphant?"

Margaret was not going to look her triumphant best. In the taxi, she fussed with her confusion of hair, tied it, pinned it, swore at it. She daubed herself with makeup, applied lipstick. In her chic outfit, she looked like she'd just weathered a wild night on the town.

They were in the city centre now, Wellington Street just ahead, the Peace Tower urgently beckoning her. The Governor General would now be well into the Throne Speech, which, by annoying tradition, was held in the Senate Chamber, that so-called council of sober second thought: unelected, undemocratic, infected with political parasites.

Margaret managed to talk their way into the restricted driveway to the Peace Tower, and tipped her driver generously for helping her with her heavy suitcase. Inside, she was slowed by security personnel, who were in a conundrum over that suitcase. She abandoned it to them, ignoring their protests, and sped to the Rotunda and down the east wing to the Senate Chamber.

The Governor General was holding forth as she cautiously entered, ducking and dodging too obviously as she tried to hide behind a mass of MPs standing at the bar of the Chamber.

But her hopes of going unnoticed were soundly defeated. There was much stirring and nudging, murmured voices, everyone craning to see her: the GG, the Speakers of both houses, the entire Supreme Court bench, everyone except an aged Tory senator snoring in his chair.

The Sergeant-at-Arms called out: "Order in the chamber!"

Beyond, just behind the bar, was Emil Farquist, who twisted around to look at her, then quickly turned his broad backside to her.

Others were slower to disengage — including the minister of Lands, Forests, and Rivers. Chalmers grinned at her, and she felt a swell of anger and shame. She would forever feel mortified by their affair. Her betrayal of a loving and perfectly faithful husband.

As the GG picked up where he'd left off, Jennie whispered from behind her, "Welcome back."

"Do I look awful?"

"Just smile. Look like a winner."

Margaret did her best, and when things settled down, she tried to focus on the speech. She must come up with something to say to the press. No mention so far of the Coast Mountains Pipeline — she could comment on that.

"Let's talk after the scrums," Jennie whispered. She handed Margaret a scarf. "Put that over your head."

§

Out in the foyer, Margaret didn't have to wait her turn — she was top chicken in today's pecking order, Miss Popularity. She smiled hard, but it wasn't easy to look like a winner with her rat's-nest hairdo peeking from the scarf and her slinky pantsuit. *Who will return looking rueful and who triumphant?*

"How was your holiday, Ms. Blake?"

"Blissful."

"Lovely outfit."

"I just grabbed it. I've been on a plane for two nights and a day. Missed connection, I got maybe two hours' sleep."

There were smaller groups around the PM and Clara Gracey, the acting Opposition leader. No sign of Farquist.

A microphone was thrust at her. "Are you satisfied with the settlement, Ms. Blake?"

"You know I can't talk about that. I will talk about an annoying gap in the Throne Speech. The Coast Mountains Pipeline didn't merit a whisper."

"Excuse me, if I heard right they're calling for a full review."

That must have come early in the speech. She hoped she didn't look as flustered as she felt. She bluffed: "We need more action than a review. That has all the earmarks of a rubber stamp."

"Ms. Blake, can you say why you agreed to settle the court action?"

"No, I can't. Ask Mr. Farquist, and I'm sure you'll get the same answer." She looked around. "But I don't see him here." Making a point of it. Jennie was nearby, though, listening in as Margaret continued to deflect questions.

"Can you at least confirm you settled for less than fifty million?" Laughter all around. "Seriously, I understand you were never questioned during discovery. What are we to make of that?"

"What you will. I'd prefer to talk about the government's wimpy approach to the crisis of climate change. Their so-called action plan offers more brave words than action."

"The court case must have been strenuous — any likelihood you'll be stepping down?"

"We have our leadership review in three months." She took a deep breath. "We'll see what the membership has to say."

§

The pleasure of a long hot shower. The bliss of a hair blower on clean, damp hair. Flannel pyjamas and a big fuzzy robe to crawl into. Now all Margaret needed was twenty hours of sleep.

But first she had to contend with Jennie. "We'll talk when we get there," she'd said in the taxi. They had slipped away cleanly after picking up the suitcase and grovelling to security, and were now in Margaret's converted coach house in Rockcliffe Park.

She found Jennie in the study, at the window with its grand overlook of the Rideau River, frozen solid, occasional skaters racing back and forth. Tea brewed in a pot. Jennie poured.

"Sorry about that scrum. A disaster."

"I'm glad you've abandoned the notion of stepping down. Announcing it would have sent the wrong signal. Losers quit. You need to look more like a winner, not the scared rabbit you were in the Foyer."

"Jennie, if you're talking about the settlement, you know my lips are tied." Was that right? "Sealed. I'm a space case, sorry."

"I'm a special case. You can tell me in confidence."

"Did you talk to Pierette?"

"I didn't want to make it awkward for her. She couldn't hide the goofy smile, though."

"It's just as awkward for me. There's a huge penalty for disclosure. Arthur would divorce me."

"Come on. Did Emil cave completely?"

"Jennie . . ."

"Nod or shake your head."

"Honestly, I can't do it. You're my best friend, but . . ."

"Thank you, I'm honoured, but I'm also a lawyer. I'm your lawyer. Give me a loonie, and you have retained me to interpret your confidentiality clause."

"Are you sure that's okay?"

"Of course. Solicitor–client privilege trumps everything."

Margaret found a dollar coin in her purse and handed it over. The fact is she was dying to tell all. "Second left drawer of my desk. It's not locked."

Jennie retrieved the signed agreement, read it quickly, broke into a smile. "Nice. Very nice." Then: "Wow. Five hundred big ones."

"And we could lose it all."

"My lips are tied."

Margaret forgot she was exhausted, and the words spilled out — she unloaded everything: Sierra's interception of Lou Sabatino, the speedy assembling of expert reports, playing the video at discovery, Farquist's dissembling denials.

"Have you got the half-mil yet?"

"Funds are being processed. Farquist was saved by his angel, Jack O'Reilly."

"Man, somehow this has got to get out." She grabbed her phone. "An anonymous tweet should do it."

Margaret nearly spilled her tea.

"Just kidding. Go to bed."

Jennie followed Margaret into the bedroom, tucked her under the covers, pulled the curtains.

"Jennie, I am politically fried. I get it that I have to stay on for a while. A year, two years, then you're it."

"It? Like in blind man's buff?" Jennie's phone rang. "It's Pierette." She listened for a moment. "Say what? Wait, it's okay, she's still up." She turned the speaker on.

Pierette: "I just got back from a quickie press conference with Alice DePaul." The Justice Minister. "This is good."

Margaret struggled up. "I'm all ears."

"The RCMP has issued an arrest warrant for Svetlana Glinka — though good luck with that. The so-called trade officer, Novotnik, is to be sent packing. The surveillance photos of him paying her off will be all over the front pages."

Margaret and Jennie talked over each other, asking if Farquist was mentioned.

"Oh, yeah, his name came up. It was the first question the press asked. DePaul wouldn't bite, just danced around it. She wasn't going to compromise the investigation. But — are you lying down? — her department is seeking a court order to open up your non-disclosure agreement."

Jennie erupted in what Margaret assumed was a Cree victory whoop. Margaret jumped from bed and hugged her. Goodbye, sleep.

PART FIVE

THE AWAKENING

Early spring had been stormy, with tree-bending, limb-splintering winds and deluges of rain: messages from the gods that Garibaldi Island was not to be spared the ravages of climate change. But in May the gods took pity, and the sun burst free. Weary locals staggered from their battened-down homes, shedding their slickers, rubbing their eyes, blinded by the brightness of daffodils flowering along the roadsides, below seas of yellow broom.

And on this halcyon Saturday afternoon, Arthur's fruit trees were thick with blossoms and humming with bees. Barn swallows were swirling, snaring lazy flies for their nestlings. Lambs were cavorting in the field. A Swainson's thrush was serenading its mate with its unbearably beautiful song.

The scene would not be complete without a typical barnyard divertissement: Niko and Yoki were trying to talk down a nimble escapee from the goat pen, Lavinia, who was standing triumphantly on the hood of the Fargo.

"How you get there?" Yoki demanded. "We make you into goat meal."

Arthur waved from the driveway. "Enjoy your day, ladies."

Niko called: "No problem!"

Arthur had just changed into his hiking togs from the formal suit he'd worn this morning at the Annual Spring Flower Show. He had won two blue ribbons, for peonies and begonias, and a few reds and whites, and was off to celebrate at the Brig.

Fortifying Arthur's pleasant mood was the fact that just yesterday the $500,000 in reparations had finally been deposited into the Tragger, Inglis trust account. Jack O'Reilly had had little choice because the credulous fellow had signed on as his hero's guarantor early in January, before Farquist's swift decline and fall.

It ended in a splat at the Conservative convention, where Farquist lost disastrously to Clara Gracey. He'd been deserted by all but the most fanatical of his supporters. No one else was buying his guff, including the media. Including O'Reilly, who was said to be furious at being stuck with the bill.

But so far Emil had escaped prosecution. After a hotly contested hearing in a courtroom closed to the public — Arthur sat on his hands throughout — Chief Justice Cohon-Plaskett had given the RCMP access to the discovery transcripts, but denied it to the public and the clamouring media.

Nonetheless, Margaret was assumed to have triumphed. Whether or not Farquist faced charges, his political doom would be sealed when Lou's book came out. His publisher had slyly leaked word about an explosive videotape.

After deducting the out-of-pockets, the balance of the $500,000 was earmarked for eco-crusaders. Roy Bullingham had balked at enriching such subversive organizations as Greenpeace and the Sea Shepherds, but couldn't deny Margaret's wishes.

She would be returning from Ottawa in a week for the Victoria Day holiday. Don't lay anything on, she warned. "I want it to be just you and me."

Representing his wife had been the right thing to do. He had fully paid his debt to her, and could now forgive himself for his misbehaviour. And to think — he had almost persuaded himself to confess.

§

The bulky bottom of the editor of the *Bleat* was spread out on a bench outside the general store. Forbish was scribbling in a notebook while powering through a bag of corn chips. "These are organic," he said defensively. "Low fat, says right on the package. I'm working on my interview with Mookie about her new movie."

"Mookie Schloss? She's back?"

Forbish pointed up at the Brig patio, where Mookie was presiding at a table of friends and freeloaders. A brunette when last seen, a fluffy blonde this time, surgically fattened lips, forty-two trying to look thirty.

She'd been a year away in Hollywood, resuming a sporadic career in low-budget movies and soaps. Married to well-heeled Herman Schloss. Their history of breakups was epic.

"Mookie's going to do a free showing." Forbish winked. "If you know what I mean."

"I don't."

"Okay, she got a lead role in a romantic comedy, and she's giving a free advance screening at the hall next weekend. She was a little evasive when I asked about adult content but I got the impression it's real risqué, with maybe nudity and worse. I don't want to use the word orgy, but . . ." He shrugged, then added, unnecessarily, "Everyone's going."

He handed Arthur a flyer depicting Mookie sitting in a circle of smiling fellow actors, male and female, joined in a chain of hands, their bare feet gathered in a tangle of toes at the centre. No nudity, but lots of skin. *The Awakening*, it was called.

A few lines of promo: "When her husband confesses he has a gay lover, she seeks solace in group therapy. But as she searches for her inner self things go sideways." A cast list, none of whom Arthur had heard of. Free popcorn and beer. No parental advisory, so Forbish was likely a victim of his own fantasies.

This was an event Arthur would happily miss.

He carried on up to the store and the post office counter. Abraham Makepeace was still sorting the mail.

"Something from your classical book club, it's Greek to me. Hydro bill, your usage is up. Invitation to join the beach cleanup at Starkers Cove. Those Transformers left quite a mess that's just been sitting there all winter. Spooky how they just vanished into the void."

They still held title to the Cove. Reverend Al had gotten nowhere trying to track them down. Google had failed to do its job — just some old references to Silverson's film career. Maybe the gupa made them invisible.

Makepeace dipped into the bag of unsorted mail, brought out a thick envelope. "I can't help you with this one. Return address is a P.O. box in Porcupine Plain, Saskatchewan, if that's a clue."

This would be Lou's miscellany of questions seeking clarifications and the filling in of holes. Arthur had spent many hours with him. He'd wanted Arthur's every thought, conjecture, musing. He had a provisional title: *Whipped*.

"Oh, and this. Normally, you don't like throwaways, but you don't want to miss this one." Mookie's flyer for the screening of *The Awakening*. "I heard she's in a raunchy bedroom scene."

"Heard from whom?"

"Nelson. He got the whole scoop."

Arthur tossed it. "My wife will be here next weekend. We have other plans." *Just you and me.* Nonetheless, he would congratulate Mookie. He crossed the ramp to the patio as she and Herman rose from a table where they'd been entertaining friends. Taba among them, and Cud Brown.

"Get the bill, darling," Mookie said. Herman obeyed like the faithful footman he was — his was a captive heart, despite their quarrels. Tradition required them to maintain the peace for at least a month after each rejoining.

Mookie intercepted Arthur. "Caught you in time." Though they were only casual friends, he got a wrap-around hug.

"Glad to see you, Mookie," he said awkwardly, pasted to her bosom. He untwined and offered appropriate words about her success and her new film. "It sounds . . . interesting."

"I'm doing a special mail-out to special people." She passed him a card, a formal invitation to Arthur and Margaret to attend the showing. Front-row seats reserved. Also a note requesting the pleasure of their company at an after-party at the Schlosses' waterfront estate.

"That's very kind of you, Mookie. I'm really not sure . . ."

"Now don't get all curmudgeonly and silly. It's not *Casablanca*, but it's fun."

"I'll take it up with Margaret." That was his out. She wouldn't want to see this banal and doubtless corny flick, free popcorn or not.

Taba had seen Mookie's big hug and gave him a saucy wink, another of her uncalled-for reminders of their brief entanglement. He wished she would stop teasing him over it.

Mookie offered a farewell salute to her tablemates. "See you on the nineteenth, darlings. Seven o'clock."

With no more free rounds coming, Cud Brown downed his double whisky and rose. He also had a special invitation and flashed it at Arthur. "I got second row centre for this sizzler, man. Forbish says it's got a nudity warning."

Emily LeMay was already pouring Arthur's tea as he hoisted himself onto a stool beside Constable Dugald, who was frowning over the *Awakening* leaflet. His subaltern, Zoller, was behind, hovering — though newly elected as Trustee, he'd stayed on as the island's number two law enforcer. Dugald still treated him as a peon.

"Forbish told me it has an orgy and other scenes of fornication," Zoller said. "Maybe we should have an advance look at it in case we have to cut some scenes."

"Don't be ridiculous," Arthur said. "Mookie isn't about to embarrass herself and her husband in front of the entire island."

"I have to go just in case," Dugald said. "If it gets too specific, I'm gonna have to shut it down."

"Sounds like something I could handle, sir," Zoller said.

"I'll need you outside, Kurt. Crowd control. Make sure no under-agers sneak in."

Zoller took offence. "Excuse me, but yours truly just got elected by acclamation to the highest office on this island. Any idiot could watch the door."

"Exactly."

§

It was May 19, the Saturday of the long weekend. The fine weather had held. Margaret had arrived, and was in a teasing, sprightly mood, having bounced back from the stresses and strains of last year. Arthur noticed more grey hairs, but somehow she seemed younger.

They were watching Dog, their odd-jobs man, split fence railings from a pile of cedar logs. "Going to watch that sexy movie tonight?" Margaret asked.

"No, ma'am. Jesus says put away sinful things." He went back to work. Fully recovered from the Transformers, Dog's spiritual needs were currently being met by the island's Pentecostals.

Margaret has maintained her upbeat humour despite the backtracking of Marcus Yates over the Coast Mountains Pipeline. Faced with the threat of a multi-billion-dollar lawsuit, the Liberal government had reopened negotiations, practically capitulated. "It didn't take long for these gutless mice to drop the mask of being oh-so-environmentally friendly," she'd proclaimed at a crowded press conference. Happily, she'd lost none of her old vigour.

Less chipper was Emil Farquist, who had been notoriously absent from his seat in the House of Commons but apparently not from the barstools of various Ottawa alehouses. Arthur had seen that coming, the descent into alcoholism, and actually felt for him. It was easy to forgive now.

Margaret and Arthur walked to the grassy outlook at Blunder Point to join Niko and Yoki, who had invited them for a picnic lunch of salmon sushi. A welcoming event for Margaret, who hugged them before settling onto their blanket.

Arthur wandered to the shoreline, checking out the postcard view of the islet-spangled Salish Sea and the distant, towering Olympic Mountains. He was enjoying his day, pleased with Margaret's mischievous mood, and — he had to admit — still shamelessly revelling in his role as her Prince Lancelot.

On his return to the picnic, Yoki and Niko were urging Margaret to join them to watch a "most very hot movie tonight." All week the pair had barely been able to contain their excitement over this Hollywood premiere.

"Too sexy for Arthur," said Niko. "He say wild horses can't make him come."

Margaret tried the sushi. "So fresh and tasty. You ladies should open a restaurant." She squinted in thought. "You know what, Arthur? I think we should go."

"Oh, please, darling. Watching things go sideways during group therapy?"

"Maybe they mean grope therapy. It could be funny. Front-row seats, we can't disappoint Mookie."

Don't lay anything on, she'd said. What happened to that plan? "If it stinks, I would be embarrassed for Mookie." Another reason, which he dared not express, was that there could indeed be explicit scenes, and they might incapacitate him in the marital bed tonight. Others might be invigorated, but not Arthur.

"Just for a lark, Arthur. And we really should pop in to her after-party. We'll have two full days to recover."

Arthur felt trapped. Later, he would remind Margaret she had goaded him into this. He imposed a condition: Yoki and Niko would get the reserved seats. He preferred to be at the back for a quick exit.

HAPPY ENDING

Lou was hunkered down over his keyboard in his home office, tapping out the final pages of the first draft of *Whipped*, a memoir by a mild-mannered reporter who, while being stalked by the Mafia, stumbled on an explosive secret about the sex games of a high minister of state, a secret now revealed in these pages . . .

That's what his publisher planned for the jacket copy. Something like that, anyway, maybe with a line about his epic take-down of the pedophile. The opening chapter would be a grabber, his near-death experience when drive-by shooters whacked his snowman. Then slide back in time to set that up, his digging into the Waterfrontgate scandal, the exposé, its repercussions.

Then to the abysmal life of a supposedly protected witness. Being rendered economically redundant by that dipshit Hugh Dexter. Nothing was being withheld. The love of his life regarding him as a twerp, a worm. His family taking off. Bring out the hankies, folks.

Part Two would introduce Svetlana Glinka. "You, the reporter, come." Lou goggling at her recorded whipping of her bare-assed bronco. "I helped him through it, the back-stabbing shit." Part Three: his lonely odyssey in search of his family. Part Four: a happy ending.

The publicist at his house had come up with a piss-cutter of a brainwave: advance review copies of *Whipped* would be parcelled with a small USB drive of the video.

There would be photographs, mostly culled from the press, some from Francisco Sierra: the decapitated snowman; the spiralling staircases of Rue de la Visitation; Svetlana in her sex shop in Nice; Lou waist-deep in Lac Osisko fending off a snarling schnauzer — he'd been too frazzled to see his father-in-law pointing a camera.

Whipped would be dedicated to Celeste, of course. She no longer called him a worm. She was the proud wife of Calgary's Citizen of the Year. All eyes had been on her at the Governor General's reception, in the stunning outfit she'd created.

Lou was relieved that she and the kids had adjusted so easily to life in Porcupine Plain, the only snag being Lisa falling in love with the neighbour's pony. Now she wanted her own. And maybe that could happen — if Lou could swing a deal on the two-acre pasture next door. The Sabatinos now had title to their snug brick house, the advance for his book more than covering the down payment.

Celeste was away too often, in Calgary with her fittings, but always seemed happy to return to her storefront studio and the tranquility of small-town life. She'd never been a city girl — she'd come from rural roots and harsh climes, northern Quebec.

She'd had only bad memories of Montreal, and was totally not interested in returning, despite Lou's former oily boss's endeavour to restore him to the payroll, to his desk at CP Montreal with a bonus and a nice raise.

Apparently he was now Dexter's bosom buddy, his "colleague and friend," who, "dispirited that he couldn't work at the job he loved, sought and was granted leave." Dexter had dashed off that toadying obituary after deciding that Lou, having vanished, was as good as dead. It still rankled. Lou had told him he could stuff the job and the bonus up his ass.

He was doing just fine. His publisher was promising a big run in hardback. He was still making a tidy sum from the internet. The illustrated list of ten secret nudist beaches had somehow made it past Facebook's robotic censors, despite the content warning. A German chain of clothes-less resorts paid ten big ones for a banner ad.

He checked the time. The kids would be getting out of school. He had promised to go biking with Logan and then take Lisa riding up at the Storkovs' hobby ranch. Not his favourite thing. For some reason the idea of mounting a horse creeped him out.

MOVIE NIGHT

Arthur's party of four was stalled at the front of the community hall, where the island had turned out en masse. Kurt Zoller looked besieged, people slipping past him as he tried to block the wide double doors. "Everyone back!" he shouted. "The hall is full! Fire regulations in effect!"

Niko and Yoki looked dismayed, Margaret stoic, but to Arthur this was good news. He would be spared the awfulness of watching ninety minutes of low-budget foolery. He shrugged helplessly. "Well, we gave it a good try."

He was about to usher his flock away when Mookie came out, waving to the crowd, silencing Zoller. "Sorry, everyone. We'll have a repeat showing next week, I totally promise." Some groans, some cheers. "Anyone with passes?" Then, on spotting Arthur's entourage: "Group of four over there. Right inside please."

Arthur was grabbed by both arms and propelled forward.

§

With Niko and Yoki taking the two reserved seats, the hall's two-hundred-and-fifty folding chairs were all occupied. Arthur and Margaret found standing room by the side exit, beside a commercial popper run by Herman Schloss. It was resting now, exhausted, but its droppings crunched underfoot and the smell of buttered corn pervaded the air. Constable Dugald was standing on the other side, arms crossed, trying to look censorious. The front doors were wedged slightly open, Kurt Zoller peeking in.

His fellow Trustee, Ida Shewfelt, was a no-show — she likely feared she would burn in hell for exposing herself to pornography. But Al and Zoë Noggins had been given prime seats, in a group with Taba and her daughter Felicity. At least two dozen more were in the reserved section: several of the island elite — doctor, postmaster, bartender — and an eclectic mix comprising Honk Gilmore, Cud Brown, Wellness, Wholeness, Henrietta Wilks, and, front row centre, Robert Stonewell, master mechanic. Nelson Forbish was next to him, his fold-up wobbling under his weight. All, apparently, had got special invitations, which likely also included the Schlosses' post-film bash.

Mookie's movie would be shown on a drop-down screen and projected from her laptop on a table near the front. But now she was standing on the proscenium, its curtains partly drawn on either side of the screen. She raised a hand microphone. The gabble of conversation ceased.

"Okay folks, here is where I apologize. This is not exactly the romantic comedy you were expecting. I kind of pulled your leg, so please forgive me. You are going to see a movie called *The Awakening*, but it's not the one I advertised. It's a documentary. And I know you're going to enjoy it more than you can imagine. Because it's about you. I love you all."

A mass shifting in seats. Loud murmurs. Arthur and Margaret exchanged puzzled looks.

Mookie scrambled down to her table. The lights dimmed. Images appeared on the screen. An aerial shot of Garibaldi from afar, the island expanding, filling the screen: its coves and hills, its forests and meadows and farms.

A male voice, deep, resonant, amiable, said, "There is a lovely little laid-back island in Canada's Salish Sea on the Pacific Coast, called Garibaldi. We like to think we discovered it, and in a way we did, but of course it was inhabited — by happy folk, wonderful characters, unstressed, uncomplicated, and welcoming to strangers."

Who, Arthur wondered, was "we"? The room was hushed, expectant.

"Their day-to-day needs are met by a variety of small businesses and social venues." A montage of the general store, the Brig, the fire hall, the marina, St. Mary's Church, Evergreen Estates and its commercial centre. And finally, this very community hall, where an outdoor gathering slowly came into focus. In the background was last year's banner: "Wake up! Smell the Roses at the Spring Flower Show!" Doc Dooley was showing off a clutch of ribbons. A sub-title identified him as "family physician and master gardener." Ida Shewfelt, sniffing her prize-winning display of elves peeking from amid the flowers. And here was Margaret flattering her! "Can I take a picture of you with your lovely garland?" The subtitle: "Margaret Blake, Green Party leader, Member of Parliament."

As the opening credits began, Arthur, gobsmacked, realized Garibaldi Island had been hoodwinked with vast panache by Jason Silverson and his camera-toting crew of alleged New Age bohemians.

Then everybody else got it: "Enlightenment Studios presents a Jason Silverson production." The former schlock movie auteur had found a new outlet for his talents. Margaret gasped: "Oh my God!" Similar exclamations from the audience: "No way!" "You gotta be kidding!"

The chorus quieted as more opening credits rolled. Mookie Schloss as co-producer and film editor. The narrator continued:

"Nothing much happened on this sleepy island until we woke them up to a powerful new reality."

The title came on in bright, bold letters: *The Awakening.*

All were stunned into silence. Arthur watched numbly as the blond bombshell himself came on screen ("Jason Silverson, director, playing himself"), charming the simple folk of Garibaldi, inspecting tulips, smelling roses, then turning to whatever camera was filming him and raising his own.

Cut to Arthur ("Retired criminal lawyer") and Margaret watching him, conversing. To Arthur's horror, he heard his own words: "Some folks think he's the second coming of Christ." Amplified by a microphone somewhere nearby. Someone in the hall brayed with laughter, then silence descended again.

Cut to Silverson greeting Margaret. Snatches of conversation about the Personal Transformation Mission and its goal to spread enlightenment with "our little experiment in healthy, cooperative living." Morgan Baumgarten sidling up with his camera and his "Just Do It!" T-shirt and his thousand-mile stare. "They call me Morg." (Subtitle: "Morgan Bromley, actor, narrator.") Arthur turned to see Kurt Zoller with his mouth hanging open. Constable Dugald seemed befuddled too. Reverend Al just stared at Mookie, incredulous.

The opening scenes had adroitly set up the premise of the film, which seemed to involve a lighthearted poke at a community falling sway to a made-up, nonsense cult, but which Arthur took to be an experiment in gulling the innocent. Yet the audience was rapt, silent, no expressions of dismay or indignation. There was some chuckling when Zoller was shown by his Hummer near the store, looking reprovingly at the women dressed as retro-hippies and their flowered VW van. Several bursts of laughter as the beaded, bangled women approached Arthur in the store: "Hey, ask this old-timer."

Arthur found his fellow moviegoers entirely too forgiving — the whole room seemed to relax. There were cheers for the Easy Pieces as they piled into the Transformers' van. Here was Silverson staring at Taba. Cut to her bosom, then to Felicity importuning her mother to visit Starkers Cove: "It's a really radical scene. Just do it, Mom."

Then to Starkers Cove, a panorama of beach and lodge and guest houses; then the camera retreated to the entrance, with its gate, its "Nowhere to Go" sign, its smelly manure pile, a lively sequence of a pig escaping, the fumbling pursuit. All but Arthur laughed.

He bent to Margaret's ear. "How can they get away with this? Did anyone sign a consent? Don't these jokers know they can be sued for breach of privacy?"

"No one's objecting, Arthur."

"*I* am."

"They were very generous."

Yes, they'd gambled on that, the gratitude. Their donations of tools, equipment, utilities, livestock.

Lots of footage of the Transformers' dishevelled farm, its livestock running amok, locals whistling while they worked, echoing the Transformers' mantra: "Just do it." Here again was Arthur, apparently the lead performer of this *comedie bouffe*, upbraiding Zoller: "You don't have a search warrant. You're trespassing." Zoller carrying on about seeing "a lady taking off a brassiere." Loud catcalls at his notions about orgies.

Silverson's office with its security camera filming Martha ("Marian Gillespie, actor, script editor") storming in, attacking Silverson. "I love you. You are my reason for being." Morgan to the rescue. Arthur standing by foolishly with gupa spilled down his pants. More laughter from this easily seduced audience as that comical sequence was punctuated by the splintering sound of Forbish's chair bottoming out. The well-cushioned newsman seemed unhurt, however, and content to remain sprawled on the floor.

Arthur heaved a sigh of relief as the Transformers' cameras finally deserted him. In turn, each of the reserved-seat holders earned their moments of celluloid fame. Reverend Al's scornful salvo from the pulpit about "followers of the fast-food road to enlightenment." Stoney in the Mercedes Cabriolet sharing a joint with the Pasadena hipsters. Cud Brown making a fool of himself trying to hustle them in the bar. Henrietta Wilks: "Sometimes he calls from the forest." Omnipresent Jason Silverson, the charismatic graduate of the Institute for Advanced Hypnosis.

There were scenes from Starkers Cove: therapy sessions on the grass or in tents, Silverson presiding. Yoga exercises, body work, polo in the pool, Frisbee-tossing, table tennis. And many lingering views of scrawny Baba Shree Rameesh in his dhoti ("Ben Bermahdi, actor") teaching glazed-eyed followers how to soothe their troubled minds. "Let what comes come; let what goes go. Find out what remains." His was a consummate performance greeted with applause even by the formerly beguiled. "We are all one!" they cried on screen, and the audience echoed the triumphant call.

But here again was Arthur — he'd had a sense of foreboding this would come: a shot taken from above, from the Brig's patio. Taba pulling Arthur into a full body press, chest to breast, hip to pelvis, then looking up and, caught in the act, quickly disengaging.

Cheers, laughter, loud whistles. Arthur felt his heart thudding. He dared not look at Margaret, though he sensed her suddenly stiffen. He whispered urgently: "Her truck was in the shop. I offered a ride. She'd had a few. It was nothing."

"I'm sure it was, Arthur." Was she smiling? Yes, maybe at his discomfort. He wanted to fall into a hole.

But then came the next sequence: Stoney escaping in the Fargo, Arthur scrambling down the road after it, shouting, waving, surrendering to the inevitable, standing there glowering and panting. This time Arthur joined awkwardly in the laughter, and Margaret couldn't contain herself.

Arthur felt relief — his life companion surely wasn't harbouring dark suspicions. But he also felt shame — he had just lied to her: "It was nothing."

He had a moment of fear that the Transformers had hidden a camera up on East Point Ridge, the site of the steamy romp. But no, the screen was now showing footage of the annual Canada Day parade, Morg piloting a tractor towing the Transformers' float. Under its banner, "JUST DO IT!" there were pots of steaming dry ice, making hazy, ghostly shapes in the air. This elicited light applause, which grew enthusiastic for the funkier local floats, the Sproules and their ghoulish gnomes, the Easy Pieces acting out a baseball game, Cud Brown as guest batsman, striking out. A joke on himself.

Arthur had to admit the movie captured the oddball essence of Garibaldi Island. There were a few more episodes, the political rally for Margaret, people pouring through the gate as the Transformers swelled their ranks, Zoller and Ida Shewfelt campaigning for the Trust, interviews with the newly converted, residents greeting each other with bows and namastes.

Finally, a scene of the November evening when the Transformers' van was loaded, and a score of Californians formed a solemn procession on vehicle, bicycle, and foot to Ferryboat Cove, the locals looking on in shock as cast and crew waved their farewells from the departing boat.

The final credits rolled, listing names of the multitude of islanders who'd played their unwitting roles, all greeted with applause as the happy, unstressed, uncomplicated folk of Garibaldi rose to their feet.

Mookie again mounted the stage, waving everyone back into their seats. "I have another surprise," she shouted.

From behind the curtain emerged a tall, broad-shuldered man in a sports jacket, tie, and tailored shirt, and with a confident, winning smile. He seemed somehow familiar to Arthur. He took the microphone, and in a deep and well-trained voice, delivered a brief, famous line by Virgil. In Latin! He translated: "Fortunate isle, the abode of the blest."

The *Aeneid*, Book VI. The isle of Elysium, where the upright, those chosen by the gods, live in eternal happiness and harmony. Who was this erudite fellow?

"How lovely it is to be back on this blessed island, among my charming, open-hearted friends."

Recognition dawned on Arthur, and on everyone else. Morg. Morgan Baumgarten. Introducing himself by his real name: Morgan Bromley, actor. He was now beardless, in rimless glasses, and his prosthetic scar was gone. His had been the voice-over introducing the "lovely little laid-back island." Obviously, and cleverly, he had sneaked back onto the island.

"I hope no one here is upset by the lighthearted way we have portrayed the island that you love, your homes, your friends, your-selves. If so, our sincere apologies, and we offer amends, as you will see."

"No apology!" a man shouted.

"It was awesome, Morg!" a woman exclaimed.

"Thank you, thank you. Our aim was to honour you, in our way, and we have been honoured too. *The Awakening* is being considered for this fall's Toronto International Film Festival."

Huzzahs, applause.

"Whether it will be accepted may be up to you."

Arthur got it. This pitch was all about getting releases from the cast of Garibaldians.

"And now may I introduce my friend, my gifted friend and cre-ative artist, the portraitist of Garibaldi Island: Mr. Jason Silverson."

There was a roar as Silverson stepped from behind the cur-tain. He stood mutely for half a minute, grinning widely, his eyes sparkling, waving greetings, then ruefully shaking his head as the cheering continued.

Even Margaret was caught up in the moment, laughing and clap-ping. But Arthur felt a tinge of the old cynicism: this hugathon had been too well orchestrated.

"Very kind of you," Silverson said. "Thank you all. What a marvellous audience. You're the best. Good lord, maybe for the first time in my life, I'm lost for words."

"We love you, Jason!"

"Thank you. Wow. And I love you too. I love Garibaldi Island."

Still the master of blarney, the film-flam man. But Arthur could not deny him credit: *The Awakening* was a tour de force of gentle ribbing, however deceptive in its conception.

"Regrettably, I'm on the industry circuit pitching this flick, and I have a water taxi to catch, and a late flight to L.A., but Morgan here is going to hang about for a few days — he has some release forms he'll be asking some of you folks to sign if you're so inclined. But before I leave I'm coming down there to shake hands with every one of my great cast of characters."

Again, he motioned for quiet, then said, "But first, allow me to announce a small gesture of thanks for your kindness and your patience and your forebearing." He pulled some papers from his pocket and held them in the air. "This is a deed of land. It will transfer free title to Starkers Cove to the Garibaldi Land Conservancy. Starkers Cove Park. It will be yours to enjoy for all time to come."

Arthur found himself finally joining in, as everyone stood and applauded the man he'd loathed, Silver Tongue! He felt silly, but . . . what the hell. Even the curmudgeon Reverend Al was on his feet. A brilliant sales job. No one in this room would decline to be memorialized on film.

Watching Silverson work the crowd, touching hands, hugging, signing autographs, Arthur recalled their encounter almost exactly one year ago, at the spring flower show. He'd been seducing them all with his charisma, his flashy smile. "Quite the politician," Arthur had cynically mused.

Euphoric over the fame they were soon to enjoy, locals were crowded about a table stacked with Morgan Bromley's releases, eagerly scribbling signatures as Bromley charmed them with cool

Hollywood panache — a thousand-dollar honorarium was an added enticement.

Herman Schloss had recruited volunteers from the hall committee to stack chairs, sweep up the debris of paper and popcorn. Mookie was outside in the Schlosses' hybrid SUV, waiting to drive the counterfeit guru to the ferry.

Silverson finally made it to the open door, but he made a quick detour when he spotted Margaret and Arthur. "Ms. Blake, I can't tell you how much I admire your commitment to the future of our imperilled planet." He kissed both her cheeks, took her hands in his, and expressed his delight in her election win, her even more smashing victory against that "reptilian reactionary your husband took to the cleaners."

And with that, he pulled Arthur into an embrace. "You sly son of a bitch, you saw through us right from the start. But you didn't blow our cover. That was incredibly gallant of you. The Trials of Arthur Beauchamp — *that* should be my next documentary."

And he was out the door. But Arthur thought he could still hear his voice. "Live in the moment not in the mind." A memory? A voice from the forest? Why was he laughing?

THE AFTER-PARTY

Moonlight glistened on the Salish Sea, and soft jazz poured from speakers positioned on the wide, rolling waterfront lawn. Tables were loaded with smoked oysters and olives and hazelnuts and ham slices and liver sausage and crudités and dips of various hues. There was a tub full of ice and bottles of beer and wine, and hard stuff for those inclined. The night air was filled with the babble of many voices, uncontained laughter, as most of the unwitting stars of *The Awakening* were now in states varying from tiddly to plastered. The air was thick with the pungent essence of cannabis — Stoney had broken out a packet of his powerful homegrown Garibaldi Gold.

These fumes seemed to drift about the encampment like low-lying mist, and Arthur found himself feeling hazy, more than a little high. It was midnight, time to leave, but he was reluctant to coax Margaret away — she was enjoying herself, and she'd earned the gift of a night free of care.

She was chumming it up over there with Taba, no doubt sharing a ribald jest or two, and causing Arthur to feel another bout of anxiety and guilt. Made somehow worse because Margaret had so jauntily laughed off Arthur's filmed encounter with Taba outside the Brig.

Arthur was not used to being stoned, even from second-hand smoke, and strolled off to a distant bench by a gurgling brook still high from the winter rains. He lit his pipe, hoping that somehow nicotine would keep him alert, counteract the effects of the pot.

Morgan Bromley must have seen him wander off, for he soon joined him on the bench with his glass of wine and a clipboard.

"Entrancing spot you've found, Arthur. 'In groves we live, and lie on mossy beds, by crystal streams that murmur through the meads.'"

Virgil again, and again Arthur was startled by this fellow's mastery of the ancient poet. "Excuse my astonishment, but how did you attain your grounding in the classics?"

"I studied ancient history before turning to acting, and fell in love with Latin literature."

Arthur, who regarded himself as an acute judge of character, had been wholly taken in by the role Bromley so expertly played — he turned out to be an urbane man who had written his master's thesis on the glory years of Latin poetry.

They exchanged a few verses, Ovid, Horace, the *Odyssey*, with Arthur feeling more comfortable, puffing away, still quite high but less troubled by it.

"Arthur, I do hope you don't feel bad about the ruse behind the making of *The Awakening*. Prominently featuring you in it was intended as a compliment."

"No problem." Arthur said heartily enough. He had well recovered from his pique — there was no point fighting it. What comes comes. And what was coming was a release form that Bromley detached from his clipboard.

"I can't say I wasn't a little embarrassed," Arthur said. "However ruefully, I admit to having enjoyed your production." He glanced over the consent. Standard stuff. He signed. "Good luck. God bless."

§

When Arthur and Margaret arrived home, he was still feeling stoned, having wandered back to the party, breathing in more of the strong cloud of marijuana. He had felt a little merry earlier, though it was nothing compared to a gupa high. But now came one of his mood swings — a welling of remorse. He watched his life companion contentedly stroll about, humming to herself, checking the thermostat, turning off lights, preparing the house for the night.

"Umm, Margaret . . ."

She paused before mounting the stairs to their bedroom, and turned to him. "Umm, what?"

Arthur was committed, helpless against the demands of guilt, overwhelmed by an irresistible impulse to repent: "I have something to tell you, dear. It wasn't nothing. It was in fact something."

He took a deep breath before continuing, and a great spasm of relief swept over him. Confession would make him free. Let what comes come; let what goes go. He would find out what remains.

Published by ECW Press
665 Gerrard Street East
Toronto, Ontario, Canada, M4M 1Y2
416-694-3348 / info@ecwpress.com

Get the
eBook free!*
*proof of purchase
required

Cover design: Jessica Albert
Cover image © marcobarone / Adobe Stock

Purchase the print edition
and receive the eBook free!
For details, go to ecwpress.com/eBook.

LIBRARY AND ARCHIVES CANADA
CATALOGUING IN PUBLICATION

Deverell, William, 1937–, author
Whipped / William Deverell.

(An Arthur Beauchamp novel)
Issued in print and electronic formats.
ISBN 978-1-77041-390-0 (hardcover)
ALSO ISSUED AS: 978-1-77305-091-1 (PDF),
978-1-77305-092-8 (ePUB)

I. Title. II. Series: Deverell, William, 1937– .
Arthur Beauchamp series.

PS8557.E8775E45 2017   C813'.54
C2017-902415-9   C2017-902994-0

The publication of Whipped has been generously supported by the Canada Council for the Arts, which last year invested
$153 million to bring the arts to Canadians throughout the country, and by the Government of Canada through the
Canada Book Fund. Nous remercions le Conseil des arts du Canada de son soutien. L'an dernier, le Conseil a investi 153 millions
de dollars pour mettre de l'art dans la vie des Canadiennes et des Canadiens de tout le pays. Ce livre est financé en partie par le
gouvernement du Canada. We also acknowledge the support of the Ontario Arts Council (OAC), an agency of the
Government of Ontario, which last year funded 1,737 individual artists and 1,095 organizations in 223 communities across
Ontario for a total of $52.1 million, and the contribution of the Government of Ontario through
the Ontario Book Publishing Tax Credit and the Ontario Media Development Corporation.

Ontario
Ontario Media Development
Corporation

ONTARIO ARTS COUNCIL
CONSEIL DES ARTS DE L'ONTARIO
an Ontario government agency
un organisme du gouvernement de l'Ontario

MIX
Paper from
responsible sources
FSC® C016245
www.fsc.org

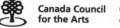

Canada Council
for the Arts

Conseil des Arts
du Canada

Canada

PRINTED AND BOUND IN CANADA

PRINTING: FRIESENS   5   4   3   2   1